Praise for the
"SINFULLY SENSUAL"*
novels of Nina Bangs . . .

"Is there any author who does humor, horror, and romance in one blending better than Nina Bangs does it? The key to Ms. Bangs's clever . . . novels is the cast never does what the reader expects. [She] combines vampires, time travel, and . . . amusing romance that will lead the audience to read it in one enchanting bite." —*Midwest Book Review*

"Bangs puts a . . . darkly brooding hero together with a stubborn heroine; adds an amusing cast of secondary characters . . . and then mixes in several different paranormal elements and equal measures of passion and humor to create . . . [a] wonderfully creative, utterly unique romance."

—**Booklist*

"A witty, charming, sexy read." —Christine Feehan

"Sensuous and funny . . . a true winner." —*Romantic Times*

"A sizzling story . . . With steamy love scenes and touching characters, Ms. Bangs brings readers into her world and sends them away well satisfied with the power of love." —Karen Steele

"I know I can always count on Nina Bangs for an exceptional read! A pure stroke of genius." —*The Best Reviews*

Wicked Nights

Nina Bangs

BERKLEY SENSATION, NEW YORK

THE BERKLEY PUBLISHING GROUP
Published by the Penguin Group
Penguin Group (USA) Inc.
375 Hudson Street, New York, New York 10014, USA
Penguin Group (Canada), 90 Eglinton Avenue East, Suite 700, Toronto, Ontario M4P 2Y3, Canada (a division of Pearson Penguin Canada Inc.)
Penguin Books Ltd., 80 Strand, London WC2R 0RL, England
Penguin Group Ireland, 25 St. Stephen's Green, Dublin 2, Ireland (a division of Penguin Books Ltd.)
Penguin Group (Australia), 250 Camberwell Road, Camberwell, Victoria 3124, Australia
(a division of Pearson Australia Group Pty. Ltd.)
Penguin Books India Pvt. Ltd., 11 Community Centre, Panchsheel Park, New Delhi—110 017, India
Penguin Group (NZ), 67 Apollo Drive, Rosedale, North Shore 0632, New Zealand
(a division of Pearson New Zealand Ltd.)
Penguin Books (South Africa) (Pty.) Ltd., 24 Sturdee Avenue, Rosebank, Johannesburg 2196, South Africa

Penguin Books Ltd., Registered Offices: 80 Strand, London WC2R 0RL, England

WICKED NIGHTS

A Berkley Sensation Book / published by arrangement with the author

PRINTING HISTORY
Berkley Sensation trade edition / April 2005
Berkley Sensation mass-market edition / April 2006
Special Wal-Mart edition / October 2007

ISBN: 978-0-425-22076-4

BERKLEY® SENSATION
Berkley Sensation Books are published by The Berkley Publishing Group,
a division of Penguin Group (USA) Inc.
375 Hudson Street, New York, New York 10014.
BERKLEY SENSATION is a trademark of Penguin Group (USA) Inc.
The "B" design is a trademark belonging to Penguin Group (USA) Inc.

PRINTED IN THE UNITED STATES OF AMERICA

10 9 8 7 6 5 4 3 2 1

To Natasha Kern, agent extraordinaire.
Thanks for guiding my career in the right direction,
encouraging me to stretch my limits,
and always protecting my interests.
You're the best.

Acknowledgment

Thanks to Ken Charles, Regional Vice President of Programming for Clear Channel Houston, who cheerfully answered my radio talk show questions.

Prologue

"You bring the heat, O Evil One." Sparkle Stardust leaned across the candy counter to get a better view of the man entering her store. "And that's bad for business."

She relished the shiver of excitement that always preceded the nightly visits of Eric McNair—who foolishly thought she didn't know that he was really Eric Mackenzie—because something about the centuries-old vampire spoke of dark power that rivaled her own. Secure in her own abilities, Sparkle welcomed a challenge. Winning was so much more satisfying when she pitted her skills against a worthy opponent. And Sparkle was all about winning.

"Deal with it." He acknowledged his amusement with a slight lift of his lips.

Incredible lips. Sparkle was an expert on lips. "You're a hard man." She paused to consider the many nuances of hard. "Every day, as soon as the sun sets, I have to crank up the air at least ten degrees." She shook her head in mock despair. "You steam up my windows so customers can't see the merchandise, and you melt all my chocolate. You should be illegal."

A lie. Yummy vampires should never be illegal. He was everything bad should be—dark, brooding, and cynical. And from their nightly bantering, she knew he didn't think any woman would ever bring him to his knees. *Hah, see me laugh.* Idly Sparkle wondered if he'd run screaming into the night if he knew her store-owner persona was just a front for who she really was—the matchmaker from hell. *Matchmaker from hell.* Had a nice ring to it.

"I'm your best customer, so I guess I'm worth a few melted chocolate creams." Eric shifted his attention to the tough job of choosing his nightly pound of candy.

"A whole pound. That's a lot to eat in one night." She'd had Deimos keeping tabs on him, so she knew her candy was pretty much the only thing sweet in Eric's life. How sad was that? Well, she was about to do what she did best, mess with his emotions. Taking a deep breath, she savored the wicked joy she always felt as she anticipated bringing trouble and turmoil into the life of an unsuspecting victim. The best part? He couldn't stop her. No one ever had.

"Brynn and Conall hit me up for half of it." He bent over the glass case and bit his lip in concentration while he studied the possibilities.

Studying possibilities? Sparkle Stardust was doing the same thing. She'd met seriously hot men before, but Eric blew the top off the heat index. He should have *too tempting to touch* tattooed across his broad chest. With beauty that could suck a woman in with her eyes wide open, along with the coldest blue gaze and the sexiest mouth she'd ever seen, Eric was a primitive call to the wild in every woman. Sparkle heard it loud and clear. Hooked up with the right woman, he could make Texas the heat-lightning center of the universe.

And Sparkle knew exactly what kind of woman was "right" for Eric. No kittens need apply. Eric needed a full-grown tigress to keep him happy.

Sparkle leaned a little closer. *Oh, yessss.* She could feel the dark and dangerous pull of all that powerful sensuality. "Tonight is steamy, so I'd recommend—"

Eric glanced up at her through a thick fringe of dark lashes and actually smiled. *Uh-oh.* Sparkle glanced down to make sure all her precious little mounds of chocolate hadn't melted into one big puddle. She sighed her relief.

"No, I don't want any chocolate-covered cherries. We go through this every night." He splayed his fingers on top of the glass case as he narrowed down his choices.

Great hands. Wide palms to hold and mold a woman's body, along with strong fingers to touch all those secret sensitive spots. Sparkle was a connoisseur of sexy hands.

"You're assuming. Never assume anything about me, because I'm the queen of unpredictable." She knew he was smart enough to take her seriously. "I'm pushing mints tonight, but what's with this thing you have against chocolate-covered cherries? They're so . . . symbolic."

"Symbolic of sex. A little fixated on everything erotic, aren't you?" He moved to the end of the counter to take a look at her selection of filled-center chocolates.

"Forget the milk chocolate, and don't even think about white chocolate. You're a dark chocolate kind of man." He had to know how sexually delish he was. Vampires were carnal creatures by nature, but like any sensual being, he needed direction. And that's where she entered the sexual game. She'd manipulate all that hard-muscled raw sensual attraction for her own purposes. Sparkle loved any game that had sex in the title.

She lifted her hair from her neck, then smoothed her hands down the length of her short black dress. Not a great color for a warm spring in Galveston, but a true expression of her inner being. She loved black. "You've got great hair. All long and black. Makes a woman want to finger-comb it and—"

"You didn't answer my question." He walked back to stand in front of her. "And I'll take a pound of fudge." Again the slight lift of his lips. "Vanilla."

Sparkle made a small moue of disappointment as she put his fudge in a box. "You want to know about me and sex?" She took his money, gave him his change, then met his gaze. "I think it's about time we leveled with each other. Everyone else looks at you and sees Eric the Evil who plays the bad guy in a reality theme park attraction called the Castle of Dark Dreams. Not me. I see a powerful creature of the night."

Sparkle knew her smile was sly triumph. "From the stray thoughts you've neglected to hide, I've also discovered that you and your two brothers aren't really brothers at all. Oh, and your last name isn't McNair. It's Mackenzie. Don't worry, though. I won't tell anyone. I feel a special bond with vampires."

She reached out to touch his lips with the tip of her finger. "I sense your lips guard secrets—dark, fascinating, and very scary secrets. You've shielded most of your thoughts from me, but that makes me even more curious." Sparkle shrugged. "A feline characteristic. I can't stand not knowing everything."

He clasped her finger, holding it captive as he narrowed his gaze in warning. Fear, an emotion she'd rarely felt, slid down her spine, reminding Sparkle that when she chose to play games with powerful beings, she'd better play carefully. But even in anger, his sexual pull was so compelling that she never for a moment doubted he was worth the risk.

"Remember what curiosity did to the cat, Sparkle." His soft murmur was a chilling promise that bad things happened to those stupid enough to mess with any vampire from the Mackenzie clan. "Byrnn, Conall, and I are the McNair brothers to the rest of the world. Don't *ever* call me Mackenzie again." The air around him vibrated with menace and unspoken threats. Still holding her gaze, he released her finger. "Now let's hear about you. I felt your power the first time I walked into the store. You're not human, so what are you?"

"I'm a cosmic troublemaker, and I specialize in sex. The universe is my sensual playground." Sparkle widened her eyes and offered him a smile filled with fake sincerity. "I like to hook up people who're perfect for each other and then help them sail happily into their sexual sunset." *Gag.* The truth? She liked to hook up people who hated each other so she could tow them into rough water. Then she'd watch them flail away at the waves of sensual attraction, suspicion, and mutual dislike washing over them. A fun time would be had by all.

"Right." His expression said he knew a liar when he heard one.

Goody. Cynical men were sexy and challenging. A fascinating combination. Leaning across the counter, she propped herself up on her elbows. "Think of me as your very own fairy godmother." She frowned. "No. Forget the fairy godmother thing. Sounds sort of yesterday. Hmm. Got it. Think of me as your sexual happiness facilitator."

He didn't smile. "Stay out of my life."

Not a chance, my beautiful one. "Too bad. You don't know what you're missing. I've spent over a thousand years preaching the power of *S*—sex and the senses. Now that I own a store where customers can double-dip all things wickedly delicious, I'll add another super *S* word. Sex and *sugar,* the ultimate indulgence." She shrugged. "I won't need you, because I'll have so many others who need my . . . help."

He studied her. "You named the store Sweet Indulgence, but there's nothing sweet about *you,* is there?" His gaze turned suspicious. "I hope you're not thinking of sticking your nose inside the castle."

"The Castle of Dark Dreams interests me. The name evokes such breathtaking sensual images." Sparkle smiled what she knew was a provocative smile. "It's temptingly sinister, and just by looking at it I knew that only seriously dangerous men would play there. I *love* alpha males. All that raging testosterone . . . Mmm. Anyway, I have plans for your castle."

He'd reached the glowering stage. "Don't mess with Brynn, Conall, or me, Sparkle. Just leave us alone." He grabbed his box of candy and strode toward the door.

Sparkle sighed with the pure pleasure of the moment. "I

get off on a glorious display of male temper. It makes me feel all tingly and sexy."

"Everything makes you feel sexy." With that parting shot, Eric slammed from the store.

She allowed herself a smile of anticipation. She'd find the perfect woman and then . . . *Prepare to strip down to bare skin, my hot and gorgeous vampire, because Sparkle Stardust is about to turn up the heat in the Castle of Dark Dreams.*

I

"No." Donna Nolan's word-flavor of the day. She'd been saying it ever since she landed at Bush International. She'd said it all the way to the Houston radio station, and the word hadn't lost its popularity during the drive to Galveston.

"So are you still getting calls from listeners about their fun-filled romps with lust-crazed creatures of the night?" Franco, her technical engineer from the Houston affiliate, took his eyes from the road long enough to grin at her.

"No." At least not since Donna's station decided to screen her calls. She had mixed feelings about that. On the one hand, she wanted to be in control of all aspects of her show, but she sure didn't want to go through another attack of the pod women.

"Hey, let's hear the story. I don't stay up late enough to catch your program." Ken, her show producer for the week, sat behind her in the station's van. He didn't try to hide his amusement.

Donna didn't believe him. He knew the story, but he'd probably get some kind of twisted kick from listening to *her* tell it. She wouldn't bite.

"No." She stared out the van's window as Franco drove across the causeway linking Galveston Island with the mainland.

"What about the Castle of Dark Dreams? Think you'll find any lust-crazed creatures there?" Franco again.

"No." Donna gritted her teeth. They were like a gnat tag team. She'd swat one question away only to find another one whizzing at her.

"You're a real disappointment, sweetheart." Ken tried for sincere, but his chuckle ruined the effect. "You're New York smart and host a program heard by millions. I expected tough gritty insights into the world of lust-crazed things that go chomp in the night."

They drove in silence for a few minutes. Donna closed her eyes, then sighed. Okay, she was tired from the trip and worried about her family, but that didn't mean she had to take it out on Franco and Ken. She'd only be working with them for a week. If she didn't chuck her bad attitude soon, she'd leave Texas with a bitch-from-hell reputation.

She waited until Franco finished pointing out the seawall and beyond it the Gulf of Mexico. "Look, here's the story. I'm only telling it once so you'd better listen up." She continued to stare out the window. "Two weeks ago I got a call from a woman, Linda, who claimed that every night for the past month a pod of nonhuman whatevers had whisked her from her bedroom. Each night a different one seduced her, and she'd have crazy sex with him until dawn. One night it might be a vampire and the next a werewolf. The pod was an equal-opportunity group."

"Pod? Like in killer whales?" Franco drove along Seawall Boulevard with its panoramic view of the Gulf.

"Right. Anyway, some women have no stamina. All that sensual gratification exhausted her, and by the time she got home each morning she was zonked."

Franco looked as though he was giving her story some deep thought. "That's rough. How do you handle someone who calls in with that kind of yarn?"

Good question. Donna could've cut the woman off the

air, but she always respected callers no matter how out there they sounded. "When I first started *Donna till Dawn,* I told my listeners I'd always be open to what they had to say. *All* of them. But this?" She flung her hands into the air. "I mean, hello? Why me? Ms. Night-Creature Magnet should've been out having crazy sex with fang-guy number thirty-two instead of calling my program. I passed on my usual in-depth questions, but the damage was already done."

"Uh, did she mention any lust-crazed female creatures?" Ken sounded serious.

Sheesh. "No."

Undeterred, Ken forged on. "You decided to broadcast your program from the Castle of Dark Dreams for a week because of this woman? Why?"

Night was falling, and Donna paused for a moment to stare at the brilliantly lit entrance to Live the Fantasy Theme Park that dominated the skyline. Like it or not—and she was leaning toward not—she'd be stuck at the Castle of Dark Dreams, one of the park's major attractions, until Friday.

"After that first call, the next few nights were disasters. Each night I fielded dozens of calls about the pod. According to callers, the pod was on a mission to drain the sexual energy from every woman in Texas." She smiled, but it felt strained.

"Think about it. Millions of women sleeping in while hubby and the kids make their own breakfasts and find their own socks. It boggles the mind. And according to all the women who called, the evil pod's headquarters is right here in Galveston, in the Castle of Dark Dreams." Donna had never had proof of the power of mass suggestion. She sure had it now.

"So you caved." Ken sounded a little too satisfied with the thought of her caving.

She shrugged. "Yeah, I guess so. Every morning I went home with a pounding headache, and that last night I knew I couldn't stand another round of pod stories. To stop the calls, I promised my listeners I'd take the show on the road to the Castle of Dark Dreams and do some serious investigating. In return, no one could call to discuss the pod until I was actually here broadcasting."

Ken nodded, finally satisfied. "Makes sense to me."

It was definitely *not* the whole story. Even without the calls from the pod women, she would've had to leave New York to visit some affiliates. But she would've done a better job of planning the trip.

Station heads had been bugging her to take *Donna till Dawn* on the road. Marketing department polls showed a recent ratings slip for her show. Key in *Jaws* music. The heads were right. Ratings were serious business. She needed to meet and greet people to pull in new listeners. *But not this week.* Donna damned the headache that had scrambled her brain cells.

"That's the story, guys. And just so we understand each other, I'll personally kick butt if either one of you mentions the words *lust-crazed* and *creatures* in the same sentence while I'm within hearing distance." Donna tried on a perky smile to assure them she was willing to get along. Perpetual gloom wouldn't win new friends.

"Got it, boss lady." Ken didn't sound intimidated.

Franco made a right turn onto the wide street leading to the park's entrance. Small shops marched on either side of the road, and even at night heavy traffic lined up at the entrance. A high wall with multicolored lights hid most of what was inside, but the arched entrance was a three-dimensional collage of traditional fantasies. She allowed herself a moment of nostalgia. A pirate ship. When she was eight years old, she'd wanted to be a pirate captain, which completely mystified her nine-year-old sister who wanted to be a microbiologist and her ten-year-old brother who'd decided on a career as a corporate lawyer.

As Franco eased into the line of vehicles entering the park, Donna spotted a candy store amid all the other shops vying for business from people entering or leaving. *Sugar.* It always improved her mood, and her mood needed a hell of a lot of improving if she was going to broadcast from here for five nights.

Park attractions didn't all open and close at the same time, making Live the Fantasy a round-the-clock deal. Lucky her that the Castle of Dark Dreams ran their fantasies from dusk till near dawn so she could broadcast live during her usual hours of midnight until four in the morning.

"Stop. Let me out here. I'll get a bag of candy, then meet you inside at the castle." *Castle of Dark Dreams.* Not a very creative name, but then she didn't expect anything too challenging in the scary department, in spite of what listeners reported. It took a lot to scare her. Like falling ratings. Next to her family, her show was the most important thing in Donna's life.

She climbed from the van and walked around the front to the driver's side. Franco lowered his window and grinned at her. "You know, this might not be too bad." He gestured at the surrounding area. "Galveston has some perks. Sun, sand, the Gulf, and a chance to live out a few cool fantasies." His grin turned sly as he started to raise his window. "Maybe even a few sexy ones, like meeting a lust-crazed female creature of the night." He raised his window the rest of the way before she could make good on her butt-kicking threat.

Donna did some mental teeth-baring. No use yelling at him, because he'd already driven away. Besides, she needed to conserve her energy in the South Texas heat and humidity. She supposed it was probably pretty comfortable by Texas standards, but June in Galveston wasn't like June in New York City. She'd feel a lot better once she had a blast of sugar to pep her up. Fine, so the candy wasn't to pep her up. It was a comfort food to assure her that somehow she was still in control of her universe.

She stepped into the Sweet Indulgence candy store and felt the first tingle of anticipation she'd experienced in over a week. If she had to go to battle in the Castle of Dark Dreams, she'd go armed with sugar in her bloodstream. She breathed deeply. Ah, the scent of bliss—sweet, smooth, rich. Exactly the traits she'd like to find in a man. Sure, the few men she'd met who'd fit that description had bored her silly, but she'd find the right one eventually.

"Donna Nolan? This is *so* amazing. You're actually standing in my store." The woman behind the candy counter bounced up and down with enthusiasm. For *her*? Donna glanced over her shoulder. Must be. No one else was in the place.

"Uh, yeah." Donna smiled. People didn't usually recognize radio personalities. This was a real feel-good moment, and boy, did she need one. Come to think of it, how *had* the woman known her?

"I saw your photo on the program's Web site, and I listen to you every night, so I knew you were broadcasting from the Castle of Dark Dreams all week. I'm a huge fan, and I've wanted to meet you forever." The woman stopped bouncing long enough to push her long red hair from her face and smooth her fingers over her black sleeveless top that ended somewhere north of her navel.

"Glad you like the show. I bet with a little sniffing around I'll uncover some paranormal phenomena in the castle." Or not. Candy. She needed lots of candy. "I'd like a—"

"You don't want to be here, and you don't think you'll find squat in the castle. All you want to do is get this week over with so you can fly back to New York." The woman offered her a knowing smile as she watched Donna out of amber eyes that almost compelled Donna to lay out all her problems, eyes that promised she'd understand.

Startled, Donna stared at the woman. "I'm that obvious, huh?" Donna leaned her elbows on the glass counter and sighed her complete unhappiness over the coming week.

The woman's laughter was a light tinkle of amusement, and for the first time Donna *really* looked at her. Flame-colored hair, perfect features, exotic eyes, and a lithe body. She made Donna feel like the before shot on an extreme makeover show. What was the woman doing working in a candy store?

"Don't feel bad. I have a . . . talent for reading what people mean no matter what they're saying." She leaned a little closer to Donna, and her smile widened. "And I work in this store because I own it. I like interacting with people and supplying something that makes them feel good."

For just a moment, Donna had the crazy idea the woman wasn't talking about candy. "You know my name, but I don't know yours." Donna smiled even as she wondered about the woman's ability to answer unspoken questions. Her listeners would call it telepathy, but Donna called it coincidence.

"I'm Sparkle Stardust." She met Donna's gaze with unblinking intensity. "Why don't you tell me what's bothering you? It helps to talk things out." She reached into her display case and pulled out a bonbon. "Have one on the house. Notice how sweet, smooth, and rich it is."

Donna nibbled on the candy. Mmm. Good. Satisfying, but not a wow.

Tell everything? How could she share her problems with someone she'd just met? But against all reason, Donna felt a sudden overwhelming compulsion to blab. She hoped it wasn't the free bonbon talking.

"You'll be sorry you asked." She offered Sparkle a weak grin. "I don't have anything against Galveston or the Castle of Dark Dreams, but the timing stinks. I have some heavy family issues waiting back in New York. I can't afford to spend a week here looking for the weird and unusual."

"What kinds of issues?" Sparkle's gaze never wavered from Donna's.

Keep your mouth shut. This is family business, and Sparkle's a stranger. Her brain sent the message, but her mouth happily deleted it. "My mom and dad are in the middle of a divorce, and it's freaked me out. I mean, they're perfect for each other. They like the same food, the same hobbies, even the same colors, for crying out loud. Why would they want to divorce each other? I need to be home helping them through all the emotional stuff." She finished off the bonbon.

Donna was on a roll now. "Then there's my sister, Trish."

"Here, have some more candy." Sparkle handed her a piece of dark chocolate.

"Thanks. Trish is working on hubby number three. She always picks guys who're works-in-progress, and then thinks she can change them. She never does. She's only known this new one for two weeks. How can you think you love a man after only two weeks? At this very moment I should be sitting in her living room pointing out all of this loser's faults before she marries him."

"Hmm. The whole family thing must be causing you lots of stress." Sparkle looked raptly interested.

Someone who understood. It felt so good to unburden herself. Donna barreled on. "My brother should be on a cruise with his wife this week, but he had to postpone it until I get back to New York. I was supposed to stay with the kids and the dog during the day, then Trish would take over so that I could get some sleep before I went to work. I should be there so they can have a good time. Nate and Carol never go anywhere, and now I'm afraid he won't bother with the cruise at all. Their lives seem so . . . *not there.* I mean, before they got married they went places and did things. Now all they do is work, take care of the kids, and sleep." She paused for thought. "Not that they complain, but how can anyone be happy living like that?"

"What've you learned from this?"

Sparkle looked away, but not before Donna saw the gleam of excitement in her eyes. Nah, it couldn't be excitement. More like her eyes glazing over.

"What've I learned?" Donna bit into the chocolate as she thought about her answer. "Long-term relationships are a crapshoot, so why take a chance? I—" She stared down at the chocolate. "What *is* this?" Someone must've poured the whole bottle of brandy into this piece. Just to check, she put the rest of it into her mouth and savored the deep dark flavor as it slid down her throat. "Mmm. This is—"

"Intoxicating, sinful, and decadent?" Sparkle said each word with slow relish.

Donna stared at her. "Well, yeah. Exactly."

Sparkle looked like a cat about to pounce on a field mouse. "The same words could describe men. Which one would you choose for a sizzling night of sex, Donna? Mr. Sweet-smooth-and-rich, or the intoxicating, sinful, and decadent hottie? I'd take the hottie every time. But then, that's just me." She shrugged. "Want another piece?"

Donna shook her head. "I can feel my arteries clogging even as we speak."

When had the whole candy thing become about sex? And why had she unloaded her truckload of emotions on someone named Sparkle Stardust! "Why did I tell you all that?"

"Because you couldn't help yourself?" Sparkle again met Donna's gaze, but her expression was now open and innocent. "So why'd you pick this week? Couldn't you have done the castle show some other time?"

Donna stared down at the jelly-bean selection. "I made a promise on the air, and I always keep my promises to listeners. It's one of the reasons my show's survived for seven years." She'd told her enough. Sparkle didn't need to know about the ratings.

Sparkle nodded. "Do you believe in the night creatures all those women whined about?" She frowned. "Why would anyone *complain* about having earth-exploding sex?"

Donna thought about Sparkle's question. *Donna till Dawn* was popular from coast to coast exactly because Donna didn't brush off questions like the one Sparkle had just asked. Donna had a few guests and callers who needed to spend some quality time in a mental health facility, but most were incredibly fascinating. Those were the ones who made the whole program experience worth wading through the ridiculous. And whether wacky or fascinating, she treated each caller with the same respect.

"Okay, let's take vampires for example. I think some

people *believe* they're vampires. And I think some people might have medical conditions that could kind of resemble what we think of as vampires. But no, I don't believe vampires or other supernatural creatures exist like the ones we've seen in movies and on TV." The more she stared at the jelly beans, the more she wanted them.

Sparkle smiled as though Donna had said exactly what she'd expected. "I've heard all those people calling about the castle." Sparkle looked thoughtful. "They sound like ordinary women who've had extraordinary experiences. I didn't get any head-case vibes." She shrugged. "Of course, I've never spent a night there, so I can't say if any of the stories are true."

"I'm spending five days and six nights there, so if I meet any creatures of the night, I'll let my listeners know." *As if.*

Definitely the jelly beans. Donna needed a variety of flavors to soothe and smooth each pothole in her road to broadcasting tranquillity. She'd get a whole pound, and she wouldn't share.

Once again Sparkle fixed her with an unblinking stare that made Donna want to swallow hard and back away. "Have you thought about all the possibilities for Live the Fantasy? What secret fantasies burn in you, hmm?"

Donna shrugged. "Oh, I don't know. . . ."

The corners of Sparkle's lips turned up in a small sly smile. "Sure you do. For example, think about pirate possibilities. You could be the evil captain of a pirate ship who captures hot men and then demands that they give you long pleasure-filled nights filled with exotic sex acts. You'd only release them when they completely satisfied your . . . appetite. That could be a very, very long time." She slid her tongue across her lower lip in a strangely feline gesture.

Pirates? Was it just a coincidence that Sparkle had zeroed in on her childhood fantasy? Just a coincidence that Sparkle had deftly manipulated it into a very tempting adult fantasy? She didn't know. "Park commercials don't say anything about sexual fantasies."

Sparkle frowned. "Well, they should. If I'm going to pay big bucks to play in that park, there'd better be a sexy man attached to my fantasy."

Donna *needed* those jelly beans. "I'll take two pounds of the jelly beans. Mixed."

"Two pounds?" Sparkle bent down to scoop up the candy, but not before Donna saw her grin. "You have something in common with Eric the Evil."

"Eric the Evil?" Donna didn't care about Eric the Evil. She wanted her jelly beans.

"He's the McNair brother who plays all the bad guys in the castle." Sparkle handed her the bag of jelly beans.

"Oh, yeah. I have a file on my laptop about all the brothers." A very small file. Her Web search had turned up no trace of the McNair brothers before they took over the running of the castle. Donna paid Sparkle, then opened the bag. Life as she knew it would end if she didn't have one right now.

"You both love candy. That's good. I think everyone should feed their senses whenever they have the chance. And taste is so sensual, so fulfilling." Sparkle gave a small shiver to emphasize her point.

Sensual? Fulfilling? Donna had never thought of taste in quite that way, but she supposed everyone had his or her own vision of taste. And right now, taste was a lime jelly bean.

Donna bit down on the candy, and as she savored it she considered Sparkle's take on her pirate fantasy and admitted it had possibilities.

Donna was walking toward the door when she heard Sparkle's final words of advice.

"Be open to new experiences, Donna. You might find more than you expected in the Castle of Dark Dreams."

No problem. She was *always* open to new experiences. Except with lust-crazed creatures of the night. She drew the line there.

Donna had finished the lime jelly bean and was peering into the bag to choose her next victim. Cherry? Sounded good to her. Cherry was a cheerful flavor, and she needed tons of cheeriness to get her through this week.

She was so fixated on picking out her cherry jelly bean that she didn't see the person who passed her on his way into the store. But she knew he was male because she *felt* him.

Surprised, she forgot about the jelly bean. He hadn't touched her, so how could she feel him? She paused, riveted. No, that was wrong. It had been more than just touch. All of her senses were clamoring to report their impressions when they couldn't possibly have anything to report. But they wouldn't be denied.

Touch insisted his passing had been a slow sensual slide of fingers across her body. Scent promised his essence was erotically stimulating and all that was heated male. Hearing was convinced he'd whispered carnal promises in passing. And taste stated emphatically that his kiss would reveal the flavors of hot male and dark chocolate. *Chocolate?*

This was so dumb. Explanation? It had to be all that sinful, intoxicating, and decadent stuff Sparkle had been hawking.

Sight would prove that all of her other senses needed a black jelly bean to ground them in reality. She'd just turn around and there'd be a little old lady standing at the candy counter.

She turned.

He was tall, with long black hair that lay across his broad shoulders and skimmed his back. A black sleeveless T-shirt showcased muscular arms to go along with the rest of his well-defined torso. And would you look at that butt. Incredible. She always enjoyed watching a buff male bod in walk-away mode. Faded jeans didn't hide his strong thighs and legs.

Sight had betrayed her. On the other hand, if he was an example of the Texas male, maybe this week might have an up side.

Donna started to turn away. She wanted out of there.

Fast. The whole candy-store experience was too weird, and while she was an expert on weird, she only wanted to deal with it during working hours.

Just before stepping outside, Donna's gaze met Sparkle's. There was something so cunning, so . . . expectant in the woman's amber gaze that Donna felt a chill ripple through her even in the warm Texas night.

Okay, enough. She was outta here. Donna left the store and headed for her fun week at the Castle of Dark Dreams.

2

Before ordering his candy, Eric went to the door to watch Donna Nolan walk away. So she liked his butt. He smiled. Not a nice smile. She *wouldn't* like that he could read every one of her sexy thoughts. And New York's queen of late-night radio would pretty much hate all of him by the time he finished with her.

He narrowed his gaze on the rhythmic swing of her shoulder-length blond hair that matched the sway of her hips in those white shorts. Sort of hypnotic, and her round little behind just led naturally down those long tanned legs. Probably an artificial New York tan. He wondered how much of a fake the rest of her was.

When she got inside the park, she'd probably stop for a minute to stare at the dramatically lit castle with its impressive moat and drawbridge. Everyone did. Too bad he hadn't stocked the moat with gators.

"I'm sensing all kinds of negativity here." Behind Eric, Sparkle sounded amused.

He turned and strode back to the counter. "I wish I knew

who the jerks were that called in about the castle so I could rip their throats out one at a time."

"Don't you think you're overreacting a little?" She fiddled with the chain at her neck as she studied him. "I think you need some caramels tonight. All that chewing will work off some of your aggression."

"Do you know what caramels do to a vampire's fangs?" His demon radio hostess had carried a scent of lavender with her that was sensually arousing, or would've been on any other woman. He'd barely noticed it on her.

"Hopefully, they gum up your dental works enough so you can't tear out any throats. I don't think you want that kind of exposure."

Sparkle plucked at her clingy black top, and if Eric didn't know better, he'd think she was nervous. But he did know better. The only thing that would shake Sparkle Stardust was someone declaring sex extinct.

He exhaled sharply and let some of his fury go. Sparkle was right. A frontal attack would accomplish nothing except make Ms. Media Shark suspicious.

"You're right. Losing my temper won't help." Eric frowned. "But I have to make sure she doesn't find out the truth." He didn't want her reporting to her listeners that a vampire, sexual demon, and immortal warrior ran the Castle of Dark Dreams. She had the kind of audience that would actually believe her. He glanced down at the candy, but his heart wasn't in his choice tonight. Of course, he didn't have a heart, so it could never be involved in anything. He ran on pure instinct and intellect. His only true enjoyment came from his companionship with Brynn and Conall plus the gratification of his senses. And with his enhanced senses, Eric was talking gratification on a mythic scale.

"Why're you so worried? You're an immortal. You have superhuman strength, superhuman eyesight, superhuman everything. She barely comes up to your shoulders, for crying out loud." Sparkle paused to reload. "And I'd strongly suggest the chocolate-covered cherries tonight."

"Yeah, give me the cherries." He hardly noticed Sparkle's shocked expression as he thought out his plan of attack. "And I'm worried because if she gets the truth out there, I'll have to find somewhere else to live. I won't let that happen. I can't kick her out, though. The owner told Holgarth we had to welcome her. She'll be great for business." To hell with business. "But I have to protect Brynn and Conall. We still have enemies who'd love to take us down. I'll have to keep her busy doing other things besides snooping around and then broadcasting her discoveries to the world."

"So you'll distract her?" Sparkle's eyes glittered with rapt interest as she handed him his box of cherries.

"In a major way." Eric met Sparkle's gaze and for the first time let her into his mind to catch a glimpse of who he really was. He watched her eyes flair in alarm as she took a step back. She understood now—what lived in his dark places, and what he was capable of. And no one, not even a cosmic troublemaker, had better mess with him. "Fear and confusion are powerful distracters."

"You could always sidetrack her with a week of sizzling sex and depravity." Hope lived in Sparkle's amber eyes.

Eric knew his smile was cold and emotionless. "Whatever it takes." He speared her with a hard stare. "And I know you've forgotten all about Eric Mackenzie. Only McNairs live in the Castle of Dark Dreams."

"Of course. I'm very good at keeping secrets." The wicked gleam in her eyes said that she was no stranger to secrets.

"Got to go. It's almost time for my part in the next fantasy." Dropping his money onto the counter, he left the store. But just before he closed the door behind him, he heard Sparkle's excited, "Yes!"

Donna walked across the drawbridge, then stopped at the massive castle gates. The guys had already taken care of the equipment and gone into the castle, but she'd wanted a few minutes to glance around the park. She hadn't gone far, just far enough to get a glimpse of the pirate ship as it sailed around the lighted man-made lake. For a mini-second Sparkle's pirate fantasy flashed across her mind trailing the memory of black hair, broad shoulders, and spectacular buns.

Put it away, Nolan. She'd procrastinated too long. No more excuses for not facing the three brothers and her quest for all things dark and evil. Fine, so she'd do the facing and questing tomorrow. Tonight she'd sleep the sleep of the dead.

Donna frowned. Maybe that hadn't been the greatest metaphor.

All thoughts of dark and evil vanished as the massive gates slowly swung open accompanied by a crack of thunder and jagged streaks of lightning. Hey, pretty impressive special effects. A thin gray-haired man with matching long pointed beard waited for her inside the gates. He wore a gold-trimmed blue robe, and his tall conical hat was decorated with gold suns, moons, and stars. Clichéd, clichéd. But he was still a pretty imposing wizard until you realized the hat added almost a foot to his not so imposing height.

Her gaze shifted to his face. Narrowed gray eyes and pursed lips assured her she was lacking in all ways that were important. Donna decided he was ten feet tall if you factored in his power to skewer victims with just a gimlet stare.

"I am Holgarth, and you are late, madam. Everyone has grown impatient waiting for you. Customers are scheduled at twenty-minute intervals. You have set back our schedule exactly"—he paused to glance at his very nonwizardy watch—"fifteen minutes. That is *not* acceptable."

"What?" That's about all she could muster in the face of his disapproval.

"Please hurry." He stepped forward, clasped her arm, and propelled her into the courtyard. The gates closed behind her with an ominous thud. "The castle's owner insisted that you be introduced to the Castle of Dark Dreams by taking part in one of our fantasies. I haven't the foggiest idea why. Now, what type of fantasy did you have in mind?"

"Fantasy?" In her mind's eye a hard-muscled pirate captain beckoned to her from the deck of his ship. "Uh, what're your choices? Give me a minute to—"

"We don't have time for indecision. Schedules must be maintained." He paused at the keep's intricately carved doors and raised his arm.

For the first time she noticed the wand he held. Of course. What was a wizard without his wand? He waved the wand with a dramatic flourish and the doors creaked slowly open.

"So I see I must choose a fantasy for you." He sighed as though her indecisiveness was a burden almost too great to bear. "You will be the beautiful peasant serving girl attacked by the deadly vampire Eric the Evil, who craves your blood and wishes to turn you into a wicked creature of the night like himself. Are you paying attention?"

"Right. Peasant girl. You know, you guys should have your fantasy choices posted—"

"Good. Upon attack you will make some appropriate noises of distress which will alert the Immortal Warrior."

"Who?"

"Please refrain from interrupting. We are now"—he looked at his watch again—"eighteen minutes behind schedule."

He hurried her into the great hall. It was empty except for a small gallery at the end of the room filled with people who Donna assumed were watching the action while they waited for their turn at a fantasy. In the distance Donna could hear voices raised in anger. She glanced around. High vaulted ceiling. Stone fireplace big enough to warm the toes of a whole army. Long table set on a raised platform. Colorful tapestries hanging on the walls. The assorted armor and weapons looked authentic. Impressive room.

"The Immortal Warrior will engage the vampire in

battle. And while the warrior is defeating the forces of evil, the handsome prince will carry you away in his arms." Holgarth slid his gaze down his long nose in an obviously contemptuous assessment of her body. "I do hope the prince has been working out."

Donna opened her mouth to voice her outrage, and then . . . she laughed. She couldn't help it. This whole thing was ridiculous.

The wizard arched one brow at her. "I am amusing you, madam?"

Donna's laughter faded to chuckles. "Look, I'm tired and all I want to do is go to bed. I don't want to play games. I have to be ready to do some preliminary investigating tomorrow so I have something to report to my listeners."

If Donna hadn't shifted her gaze to his eyes at that exact moment, she would've missed the flash of triumph there.

"If you insist. I'll tell the owner you chose not to participate."

Donna narrowed her gaze. He'd manipulated her. He didn't want her to take part in the fantasy and thought if he was obnoxious enough she'd refuse. Which she had.

"Why the hell does she have to be part of a fantasy *tonight*? It's bad enough she's going to be here for a week poking her nose into everything." The unidentified male voice echoed from somewhere in the castle.

The wizard glanced toward a doorway. "It's unfortunate you heard that, but I'm sure once everyone is exposed to your sweet nature they'll change their attitudes. I'll just go and tell them you chose not to participate in the fantasy." He offered a smile rife with insincerity.

"Wait. I've changed my mind. I want to do the fantasy." She *hated* being manipulated, and she'd poke her nose anywhere she wanted this week. Donna didn't know what the problem was with these people, but she intended to find out. The castle's owner had assured the station she'd be welcomed.

Some welcome.

"Very well, madam. I wouldn't worry overmuch about the angry glares of those in the gallery who see you cutting in front of them. Although when you're finished, you might want to leave by another exit." Holgarth was chipped ice over stone. And as he turned toward the hallway, he muttered a word Donna easily identified as having four letters.

She smiled. Everyone here would learn quickly her loyalty was to her listeners, and she definitely did *not* have a sweet nature.

Minutes later the actors drifted into the great hall. The king and queen took their places along with all of the other costumed extras needed to reenact a medieval feast.

A woman wrapped a large apron around Donna and tied it in the back. "Sorry. Usually we'd give you time to change into period dress, but Holgarth's all bent out of shape because we're running late." She came to stand in front of Donna and studied the effect. "Afraid you don't look too medieval."

"What should I do?" *I should take off this dumb apron and go to bed.* Too late now.

The woman smiled at her, and Donna felt a little better. "Just do what they tell you to do. They'll guide you through the fantasy." She hurried away.

Marooned in the middle of the great hall while everyone bustled around her, Donna did some silent whining. Where were Ken and Franco when she needed support? And why hadn't the three brothers, maybe even the mysterious owner, welcomed her instead of a grumpy wizard? She'd be giving this place tons of free publicity during the next week. Where was the respect?

"It grows warm in here. I have need of my fan." The queen beckoned imperiously to Donna. "Bring me my fan at once."

Show time. If she was going to be here for a week, she may as well get over her mad and make the best of it by showing a little enthusiasm for her fantasy. Hey, she might even meet a lust-filled creature of the night. *I should be so lucky.* "Uh, where *is* your fan, Your Majesty?"

"Where it always is, stupid girl." The queen pointed to one of the many darkened doorways.

Okay, Donna would play the game. She didn't have to know where the fan was. The fan was just an excuse to lure her into the dark where the evil vampire would jump her. At least she'd get a look at the three brothers in action.

While Donna went in search of the fan, the players continued acting out their feast. Once in the hallway she found it led to a spiral stone stairway that disappeared into the darkness. She started to climb. Only a few dimly lit sconces broke the suffocating blackness. At the top of the stairs the darkness was complete. How creepy was this?

Suddenly Donna froze. She wasn't alone. Primal senses whispered that something waited for her. Something so scary that fear clogged her throat. Its presence touched her with malevolent fingers. And every one of her survival instincts inherited from very smart ancestors shouted for her to race down the stairs and never climb them again. Okay, cancel her wish for a creature-of-the-night encounter.

"You canna escape me. 'Tis useless to try." The voice emerged from the darkness, a low husky promise of impending doom. Male. *Very* male.

Reality check. This was just an actor, and no one threatened her. Yeah, tell that to her primal instincts.

Time to take control. She was letting the voice and the darkness get to her. *Lights.* Whatever was about to happen couldn't happen in complete darkness because then she wouldn't be able to see the show. And it *was* only a show. She had to remember that.

Donna stood still while her imagination filled the silent darkness with menace, and whoever stalked her drew slowly closer.

She could feel a cold shiver beginning between her shoulder blades and creeping down her spine. Donna wouldn't let the shiver turn her spine to mush. It was the complete silence that fed her fear, so she'd break the silence.

"I need the queen's fan, evil vampire. So why don't you

turn on a light, jump me, I'll scream, and we can keep Holgarth's schedule moving right along?" There, she'd addressed the situation, and now she felt more in control. Sort of.

One candle flickered to life in a wall sconce, and in its dim glow Donna saw the dark shape of a man.

"Come to me, woman." His voice was a husky temptation, making carnal promises of unspeakable pleasure if she obeyed him. Sure sounded like one of the lust-filled pod members to her.

Donna to brain, this . . . is . . . not . . . real.

Panic started in her throat, cutting off any "appropriate noises of distress." Her panic spread in overlapping waves. His voice was a compulsion, and strictly without her permission her feet started moving toward him.

No! She wouldn't let this—whatever "this" was—happen. Donna pictured herself, always the queen of calm and cool, admitting to her audience that a silly role-playing fantasy had scared her witless. She stopped walking.

"You resisted my call. That intrigues me. But you willna escape." His soft laughter mocked her foolish attempt to defy him. "Give yourself to me, and share with me the life flowing through you."

She did *not* want to intrigue this man, and no way would she share *anything* with him. "What happens to women who resist your call?" Stupid, stupid question. *Please don't tell me.*

She sensed his shrug. "It matters not. Few have tried, but those who did couldna escape their fate."

What fate? All kinds of biting and sarcastic replies piled up at the back of her throat, but she couldn't get them past the huge boulder lodged there.

Donna controlled her need to swallow hard. No use in calling more attention to her throat than necessary. She tried to think logically, because logic was the only thing that might defeat his all-enveloping sexual compulsion. And the vampire's call *was* sexual. She recognized it on a primitive level that needed no explanation.

She had to make him human like any other man. *Talk to him.* "You must be Eric McNair. Or should I call you Eric the Evil? You're good, you know. And that Scottish burr is perfect. A vampire Highlander—symbolic of all things sexual, sinister, and über alpha male. Talk about great premises. I can understand why some of my listeners think this whole thing is real."

"You speak so you may push back the darkness. But if you surrender to its heat, its *need,* you'll know what joy it may bring." He moved closer, but he was still in shadows.

"Right. Joy. I don't think so." She opened her mouth to scream.

Suddenly he loomed over her, blocking out the flickering candle's meager light. When had he moved? She hadn't *seen* him move. The darkness distorted her perceptions of time and space. Fear washed over her. Her scream froze in her throat. What good was a scream if you couldn't use it when you really needed it?

"Dinna scream yet, or you'll miss all the pleasure." He leaned toward her, his long cloak a dark symbol of ancient evil and folded bat wings.

She'd pass on the pleasure. Now if she could just make her vocal cords work and her feet obey her command to run like hell, things would be okay.

Then she did something incredibly stupid. What a humbling experience to know that in a time of crisis, you didn't always do what was brave or smart. Donna closed her eyes. If she didn't see anything, maybe it wouldn't happen. Was that logical, or what?

Now that she couldn't see, her sense of touch scurried to take up the slack. Rough cloth scraped against her arm while smooth strands of his hair touched the side of her face. His breath heated her neck, and then his lips touched her throat where her pulse pounded so hard it might as well be shouting, "Bite me!"

The warm glide of his tongue across her skin sizzled and sparked to nerve endings unused to any kind of sizzling or sparking. The chain reaction was cataclysmic.

Fear was no longer part of the equation. Her nipples were sensitive points of pleasure-pain as they rubbed against her blouse, and nothing less than the pressure of his lips, the heat of his mouth on her breasts, would be enough. Need pooled low in her belly, and a sense of heaviness, a belief that *something* had to happen, that she couldn't stand it unless he . . .

Then she felt the slide of his fangs against her throat.

She stilled as fear made a return appearance. Teetering between unreasoning lust and numbing fear, she balanced on the thin edge of reason. *This isn't real. What I'm feeling isn't real. He's just a terrific actor.* But it sure felt real to her.

The decision was taken from her. He raised his head and stepped away just as she opened her eyes. Now that he wasn't blocking the candle glow, she could see his face.

Horror warred with fascination. Long black hair was a dark curtain around his face. Overlarge elongated eyes with pupils so dilated she couldn't tell what color his irises were seemed almost hypnotic. And the slight slant of those eyes gave him an exotic look.

His mouth. She drew in her breath on the savage beauty of that mouth. Sensual lips made fuller by the fangs they hid, lips that made her slide the tip of her tongue across her own bottom lip as she remembered the feel of them touching her neck. Lips that tempted her to stand on her toes so she could press her mouth to his and test their firmness. *Lips made to bring pleasure to a woman's body.*

He smiled. A smile filled with wicked knowledge. Mesmerized, Donna stared at his bared fangs and finally understood. She'd never believed women who claimed the lure of a vampire could be a sexual turn-on, but she did now. It was the uncertainty. He could use his mouth, his body, to give incredible pleasure, or use that same mouth to end a lover's life. The power, the choice, was his. A vampire was the ultimate alpha male.

The thing that bothered her the most? He'd made her hot for him by merely putting his mouth on her neck, while at the same time making her feel more vulnerable than she ever had in her life. For a woman who liked to be in control of herself and the things that touched her, Eric the Evil was a very scary creature.

He leaned forward once again, but Donna didn't feel threatened this time. Her senses had their doubts, though, and they were taking lots of notes so they could positively ID him in the future. His scent was of wild untamed places, dark steamy nights, and . . . chocolate. *Chocolate?*

"You may scream now. Holgarth will be sorely fashed that you've spent so much time with me and upset his schedule." He didn't try to hide the laughter in his voice.

She screamed. Loudly and with lots of enthusiasm.

Then made plans to buy more candy tomorrow. Chocolate.

Dark chocolate.

3

Turning her back to Eric the Evil, Donna riveted her gaze on the darkened steps as the sounds of pounding footsteps grew louder and louder.

"The prince and his faithful warrior rush to your rescue." His soft voice mocked her. "But mayhap you dinna wish to be rescued."

Faster, faster. Silently, she urged her rescuers on. They had to get here before . . . Before what? She wasn't sure.

"Mayhap you wish to lay with me this night while I slide my fingers across your body and learn the many places that give you pleasure." He was close. Very close.

His nearness touched her with heated awareness, and she couldn't remember the last time a man had connected with her on such a primal level. Sex with him would be hot and intense, but she could forget about any warm emotional afterglow. Uh-uh, she liked a little more thought to go into her loving. Mindless sex had never been her thing. And sex with a fake vampire? She'd laugh at herself in the morning. Well, maybe not laugh.

Until her champion reached her, she'd have to hold back

the night with words. "Wow, what an intro to the Castle of Dark Dreams. Whoever does your makeup should get a raise. Very creepy. And what can I say about your acting? Impressive. You pulled all the right emotional strings. I was scared, confused, and intrigued at the same time. Maybe you could spend a little time with me on the air." She frowned. "But do you offer to slide your fingers over all the customers? I sort of thought the park was G-rated."

His quiet laughter prickled the back of her neck. "Each person's experience in the Castle of Dark Dreams differs. I know what crouches in the darkened corners of people's minds, and I give them what they crave." He brushed his fingers over her hair. "I know *you,* Donna Nolan. You believe you must control everything in your life."

If he moved any closer, his body would be pressed against her back. Amazed, she realized the little frisson she felt wasn't fear but excitement.

"If we were to mate, you would know what it is to lose all control." He twirled one strand of her hair around his finger and pulled gently. "And you would gain great pleasure in the discovery."

Hah, she knew it. A primitive domineering jerk. Probably always had to be on top. *Come on, Prince.* "Uh-huh. Well, I got a peek at your next customer. I'd rethink your lines. He's about six five, two eighty, and looks like he wrestles alligators for fun and relaxation. I wouldn't offer to slide your fingers over any part of him." Donna breathed a sigh of relief. "Oh, goody. Here's my rescue party." She edged away from Eric's sensual circle of influence.

The first man to reach the top of the stairs rattled her almost as much as Eric the Evil. Cripes. He should be rowing a boat across the River Styx. Big, muscular, ferocious. With shaggy dark hair, a hard face, and intense angry eyes, he looked like he'd rather eat her than rescue her. Great, just great. But hey, at least Mr. Congeniality looked kind of medieval: tight-fitting hose encasing strong legs, leather ankle boots, and a knee-length tunic.

Without even glancing her way, he rushed past waving

a very big and very real-looking sword. "You'll not get a chance to sink your wicked fangs into another fair maiden, vampire. I, Sir Conall, will slay you in the name of my prince."

Donna curled her lips. Eww. Somehow "sink your wicked fangs into" didn't have the same sensual ring as Eric's phrasing. She assumed Eric had also produced a sword because she could hear the ring of metal on metal as they fought behind her. She refused to look.

"You dinna think to defeat me with such a puny weapon, do you, warrior?" Eric produced a satisfactorily evil laugh.

"You'll pay for eating the last piece of candy, Dark One." Sir Conall's whisper was fraught with angry promise.

Last piece of candy? Donna blinked. She guessed Sir Conall hadn't meant her to hear his comment. Kind of took her out of the fantasy.

But she was flung right back into it as the final player joined their little group. He paused at the top of the stairs, and Donna could only gape.

He was simply the most spectacular man she'd ever seen. He'd pulled his hair back from his face and secured it at the nape of his neck. Loose, it would probably fall a little past his broad shoulders. Color? When was blond more than blond? It was old gold shading to warm honey, softened in the candle's dim glow. Yet the whole effect wasn't soft, as in weak. It was sensual. There was no other word for that color. But it was his face that drew her unblinking stare—firm jaw, full lower lip, and wide-spaced eyes that even from where she stood promised breathtaking. *Can we say perfect?*

Then why wasn't she dissolving into an embarrassing puddle of want? Why was she tempted instead to turn around to get a last glimpse of her dark tormentor? Everything about Eric the Evil was intense light-absorbing black.

Prince Perfect, wearing a white flowing robe edged in

gold, would carry her back to the safety of the light. Then why did a part of her she didn't recognize wonder what it would be like to remain in the shadows with the darkly erotic vampire?

She shook her head to rid it of all random stupid thoughts, and then waited for the prince to stride over to her. "Prince Brynn, I presume?"

He smiled at her, and she resisted the urge to shield her eyes from the glory of that perfect mouth and those perfect teeth. It would take a supremely confident woman to date a guy who looked like the prince. Who wanted to be invisible?

"Ah, the beauteous Maid Donna." The prince bowed slightly.

Donna narrowed her eyes at the hint of mockery in his deep voice. "Doesn't roll off the tongue quite like Maid Marian, does it? Wait, that was Robin Hood. Sorry, wrong legend." Sheesh, couldn't the powers that be have cut the rest of humanity a break and given him a high reedy voice?

At least his laughter sounded sincere. "While the battle rages between the forces of good and evil, let us be gone."

She didn't have time to ponder how they would "be gone." He leaned over, scooped her up in his arms, and carried her down the steps. Donna squeaked her alarm and then clung to his shoulders.

For the first time she got a good look at his eyes. Whiskey-colored with a dash of gold, his eyes should've been a perfect fit for the rest of Prince Brynn. They weren't. She sensed darkness behind those beautiful eyes. A remembered line drifted through her mind: "Something wicked this way comes."

Donna hoped he didn't notice her involuntary shiver as he carried her into the great hall and set her on her feet. She needed a good night's sleep to get rid of all her weird feelings about this fantasy. Maybe she wouldn't do any eye-rolling the next time one of the pod women called her show.

She turned away from Prince Brynn in search of Holgarth and a key to her room, but the prince clasped her hand to stop her. "Wait. I must make the announcement so all can celebrate."

Oh, for heaven's . . . All she wanted to do was crash and forget about everything for about eight hours. Fine, so the truth was that since Eric had probably been dispatched by Conall the Vampire Slayer by now, the fantasy had lost its zing.

Prince Brynn held up his hand and everyone grew silent. The king and queen, assorted lords and ladies, and an army of loyal servants waited expectantly. "Let us raise our glasses in celebration. I have rescued Maid Donna." Cheers filled the hall.

Yeah, yeah. Donna finally spotted Holgarth. He was staring at his watch. Ken and Franco were still nowhere in sight.

"And I have slain the Dark One who has plagued the kingdom." Sir Conall strode to the side of the prince. "Let us raise our glasses to the freeing of our kingdom from Eric the Evil."

She understood the meaning of the "Dark Ages" now. Because with all the drinking to celebrate rescues of fair maidens and slayings of dragons, vampires, and other scary whatevers, the local folk must've spent most of their time facedown on the great hall floor.

"Your beauty is only exceeded by your ability to destroy my schedule, Maid Donna." Holgarth had found her. "Of course, I have too much breeding to ask what could have possibly made you linger with Eric the Evil. The only acceptable explanation would be that you found him so loathsome you fainted."

"I don't faint, and actually he was pretty hot." Who would've guessed? She had a mean streak. She felt absolutely gleeful at the thought of irritating Holgarth.

He raised one narrow brow that expressed without words his contempt for her. Very cool. Maybe he'd show her how to do that.

"Admirable." Translation: Slut. "I'm confident you

could have ripped the vampire's heart out with no help from Sir Conall. You would never need a hero to rescue you." Translation: Amazon.

Holgarth's talent awed Donna. He could insult her with a carefully crafted phrase or a meaningful tic of his eyelid. "Why don't you show me to my room. I'm tired of trading barbs with you."

After casting a worried glance to where the next fantasy was being set up, he hurried her toward a closed door in the back of the great hall. The door led to a large lobby. A quick glance assured her there were the usual array of gift shops, a restaurant, and a bookstore. All made to look like castle chambers. The hotel's check-in counter had a few people in line. There was an elevator at each end of the gallery along with two staircases. People still streamed in from the night through the massive authentic-looking doors. Ancient and modern lived in uneasy coexistence in this part of the castle.

"You'll find a complete list in your room of when things open and close. Our fantasies begin at eight each night and the restaurant opens at noon. The castle has four elevators, one at each corner. They lead to the guests' rooms on the second and third floors and the towers. If you feel the need for exercise, the stairs are available." He seemed in a hurry to get rid of her as he pushed the Up button for the nearest elevator.

She didn't want to talk with him anymore tonight, either, but curiosity was an important aspect of her job. "Where do you end up if you press the down button?"

Holgarth looked at her with what could only be relish. "In the dark, dank dungeon where curious maidens have been known to perish."

"Why am I not surprised?" What was it with this guy? Question: Could she survive the week without flattening his pointed hat or breaking his wand in half? "I want the answers to two questions. If I don't get them, I might just tag around after you for the rest of the night interfering with your schedule."

He pressed his thin lips together before nodding.

"First, who's the owner's attorney? My boss said all communication with the park's owner has to go through his mouthpiece." Donna hoped she wouldn't have any problems that Eric, Brynn, or Conall couldn't solve, but you never knew. If this whole trip hadn't been so rushed, she would've remembered to get the lawyer's name from her boss. "Second, why don't you like me?"

Holgarth offered her a wintry smile. "*I* am the owner's lawyer, and I assure you I am no one's *mouthpiece,* madam. And I don't dislike you. I find you a bit of a nuisance, like a gnat, but perhaps you'll provide a few entertaining moments." He glanced toward the door leading to the great hall as a shout went up.

Talk about being damned by faint praise. "*You're* the lawyer? And you moonlight as a wizard? Hey, makes perfect sense to me." She must've fallen through the rabbit hole when she wasn't looking.

"The owner compensates me well for my efforts, and I have a warm and fuzzy proprietary feeling toward the old place. How better to make sure problems are addressed immediately than by being here when they arrive?" He stared down his long nose at her, assuring her that, yes, he was speaking about her.

Old fart. She exhaled wearily. Okay, that was mean. "Look, give me my key, and I'll find my room by myself. I bet they need you in the great hall. Maybe one of the extras celebrated the vampire slaying a little too heartily, fell off his chair, and bumped his head. Sounds like a lawsuit waiting to happen to me. Better check into it."

For a nanosecond Donna almost imagined she saw a gleam of real amusement in Holgarth's sharp eyes.

"They're holding your key at the check-in counter. This elevator will take you to the top of the tower. We've put you in the Wicked Nights room. You should be very comfortable there. I had someone take your bags up. If you wish anything else, please let the staff know." He started to turn away, then paused. "I noticed you referred to the owner as he. Since the owner has chosen to remain anonymous, one doesn't really know, does one?" A chuckle trailed after him as he returned to the great hall.

Donna picked up her key and returned to the elevator. She was trying to judge the exact degree of malevolence in Holgarth's chuckle as she stepped into the elevator and pushed the button for the top floor of the tower. By the time she got off the elevator, she'd decided she really needed that night's sleep before passing judgment on the Castle of Dark Dreams. Things wouldn't seem so weird in the cheery light of day.

She glanced around, but there wasn't much to see. Only two rooms on the floor. A metal nameplate beside the door identified her room: Wicked Nights. Too bad it wouldn't live up to its name. The ever-present wall sconces lit the hall area, and opposite the elevator was the stairs. Authentically medieval-looking, of course.

Donna slipped the old-fashioned key into the lock and then paused. Were those footsteps coming up the stairs? She resisted the urge to fling open her door, rush inside, slam the door shut on whatever horror was coming up the steps, and then bury her head under the bedcovers. This damned castle brought out the five-year-old in her.

Instead, she waited. It was probably the person staying in the room across from hers. Notafraidnotafraid. A large silhouette emerged from the stairwell gloom. *Afraid.* Her fingers felt like they had frozen to the key, and she couldn't have turned it if her life depended on it. *Poor phrasing, Nolan.*

The silhouette resolved itself into a flesh-and-blood man as he stepped out of the shadows. "You can relax. I've put my fangs away until the next fantasy."

That voice. That deep, husky, have-sex-with-me-if-you-dare voice. "What happened to your Scottish burr?" She turned the key in the lock and nudged the door open just in case she needed to put a solid barrier between herself and Eric McNair. Relax? Her instincts thought not.

"I only use it when I become vampire. It's a nod to my

Highland roots." He moved closer. "I hunted you down because Ken and Franco wanted me to tell you they were looking the park over and would see you tomorrow."

Hunted you down. As she stared up at his shadowed face, she knew the phrase fit him, in human or vampire form. "Predator" was a soft hiss of truth in her mind. She accepted the truth without questioning, when she rarely accepted anything without solid proof.

"Thanks for taking the time to pass on the message. Maybe tomorrow we can get together over lunch. I'd love to hear some inside stories about the castle to share with my listeners." She was babbling. Men never made her babble, and yet he seemed able to do it at will. And he did it by just *being.* An interesting phenomenon she'd love to explore if she could get past the babbling stage. Offering him the universally understood huge yawn of dismissal, she pushed the door open and stepped into her room.

He stepped in behind her and switched on the nearest light. "I won't be around for lunch tomorrow. We can talk now. It won't take long." He walked past her and turned on the other lamps in the room.

"Gee, and here I thought vampires couldn't enter a room without an invitation." Donna's sarcastic-bitch voice usually did the trick, but she wasn't sure it would work on him.

"This used to be my room before I decided to move . . . elsewhere. It remembers me." Instead of choosing one of several chairs, he sat on the massive bed that dominated the room. Or maybe it just seemed to dominate the room because he was sitting on it. He turned his head to meet her gaze directly, and for the first time the lamp's glow revealed his face. "The same way *you'll* remember me, Donna Nolan."

If Donna could've formed the words, she would've peppered him with them, and they all would've been synonyms for arrogant. But no matter what words she might have thrown at him, they wouldn't have changed the fact that he was right. No woman would ever forget this man.

In the radio industry, where words painted the picture, she'd describe Eric McNair as ruthless beauty. A strong jaw, well-defined cheekbones, a sensual mouth that promised soft seduction, and deep blue eyes that should warm with passion. A dark slash of brows and long dark lashes to frame those eyes completed a face that would live in every woman's memory.

But Donna was good at what she did because she sensed what was going on beneath the surface noise. She listened not only to what a caller said, but also to what he didn't say. The unspoken was often the truth, and she asked her questions accordingly.

Eric's face was a lie. She'd guess his sinful mouth was more likely to whisper calculated lies than seductive words. He looked like a whatever-it-takes kind of guy.

And his eyes would only warm with passion if it suited his purpose. But even recognizing the coldness in those eyes, she couldn't control the sneaky slide of awareness that wondered what those eyes would look like during the heat of sex. They were the beauty of an ice storm that turned the world into a glittering wonderland at the same time it snapped branches and brought down power lines.

His face was a weapon, and she wondered how many women had fallen for it. She also wondered where that analysis had come from and why it was important.

Now that she could drag her gaze from his face, she realized he had other weapons. During the fantasy, the darkness and her fear had kept her impressions to a minimum. But now . . . He was tall and hard-muscled, his arms and chest showcased by his sleeveless black T-shirt. Worn jeans hugged strong thighs, long legs, and a spectacular ass. She knew he had something on his feet, but her vertical adjustment was stuck and she couldn't move her gaze from his hot bod. As weapons went, his were pretty potent.

"What're you thinking?" A meaningless question since Eric was in her head and knew exactly what she thought of him. Her intuitive distrust of him wasn't important, but it did intrigue him. No woman had ever seen him this clearly until it was too late. She could be a danger if she looked too closely at Brynn, Conall, or himself. He'd try to keep her focus on him so she wouldn't think too much about his two friends. And, oh yeah, he thought she had a few weapons in her arsenal, too.

"I'm thinking that I want you out of here so I can get some sleep." She ignored him in favor of unpacking her garment bag that hung from the top of the closet door. "But if you're determined to talk tonight, I have a few questions."

"Go ahead." Fascinated, he watched her pull a short red dress from the bag. Red, the color of passion and heat. Interesting. She'd chosen that color just as she'd chosen the pale gold color of her hair. He smiled. The hair color looked natural, looked like it fit her, but he sensed a darker shade beneath it. She liked to control the image she showed the world. Her pale hair said cool and contained, but the red dress said something else entirely.

She paused in the act of hanging a black suit in the closet. Black, a powerful color. If he didn't see her as a threat, he might enjoy discovering what the black suit said about her.

"What do you know about the owner of this place?" She glanced back at him. Brown eyes, the color of warm sweet chocolate. Right now, though, they had a calculating gleam.

"Holgarth is the only one who knows the owner's identity." Holgarth, a sharp-eyed old snoop who insisted on living in the castle and greeting customers. "All we know is that, according to Holgarth, the owner is a he, she, or possibly it."

He caught her smile as she hung up a couple of blouses. "So does Holgarth have an office somewhere?" She smoothed her fingers over the last top she'd hung up.

His enhanced senses reacted immediately with an image of her sliding her fingers across his naked body, lingering between his thighs, and skimming his arousal. "I doubt it. The owner has him on retainer, and the castle is his total responsibility. He's here every night. I don't think Holgarth comes cheap, so the owner must have deep pockets."

She finished with the garment bag and moved on to her suitcase. Eric caught a glimpse of panties and bras. Another chance to get a handle on who Donna Nolan was.

"He sure throws himself into the wizard thing." She laughed as she transferred the panties to the drawer of the antique dresser.

He's had almost four hundred years of practice. Holgarth had let that slip during one of their last poker games. They'd stopped inviting him to play when they caught him using his magic to cheat. "Wizards and lawyers. Sleight of hand and the creation of new realities. I guess they have a lot in common." Black and white panties. Hmm. He wondered if she saw life that way. If she did, then the Castle of Dark Dreams would blow her mind. He frowned. Wrong. He couldn't allow her to see beyond what any customer might see.

On a more positive note, she didn't seem to mind him watching her put her underwear away. That said a lot about her self-confidence. He liked strong women.

"Okay, I understand Holgarth. What I don't understand is the hostility I'm feeling from all of you. I asked Holgarth, and he danced around the truth." She put her bras into the drawer beside her panties.

His cock had started to take a real interest in this unpacking thing. Once again, her bras were mostly black or white. There was hope though, because she'd thrown in a red one. Size? They looked like they could cup a woman with full tempting breasts.

"You're problematic. I've listened to your program, and your audience seems to be open to all possibilities." Too open. "Everything people think they see here is just high-tech and great makeup. But some of the people who listen to your show might think it's something more. Those women who called in about having wild sex here are cases in point. You don't want to know how many women have shown up here wanting to get it on with our 'creatures of the night.' "

She abandoned her unpacking to sit down on one of the room's ornately carved chairs. He had her interest. "I'd think you'd be happy with all the free publicity."

He tried to control his sudden spurt of anger. She didn't know what he was, so she couldn't know the danger she brought with her. "You don't think that you broadcasting from here each night, trying to play up how spooky it is so you'll up your ratings, won't attract every weirdo who listens to your show? We don't need people running around trying to drive a stake into a vampire's heart or kill a werewolf." Okay, he was diving off the extreme end of his emotions, and she had no idea why he was steamed. He wanted to stay here. He didn't want anyone chasing him away with a media blitz.

She was mad. He didn't need to touch her mind to know that. Narrowing her gaze, she proved that warm sweet chocolate could change instantly to permafrost. "I have some of the most intelligent listeners in the world. Guests on my show are recognized experts in their fields of interest. And no, I've never had a vampire hunter as a guest. Every talk show has a few callers who're over the top, but I guarantee hordes of my listeners aren't going to descend on your precious castle." Standing, she flung the last of her things into the drawer and slammed it shut.

Time to back off and change the topic. If he made her too mad, she might purposely say things to energize the fringe elements of her audience. He glanced around the room.

"I see you inherited Sweetie Pie and Jessica." He knew his smile didn't reach his eyes.

"Who?" She followed his gaze, and then stared, puzzled.

"The plants. Holgarth says the owner's into plant research, and the two you'll be sharing your room with are favorites. You should feel honored the owner is entrusting them to your gentle care." The enjoyment he felt at the thought of telling her Sweetie Pie and Jessica's secret worried him. Eric didn't want anything about her to bring him joy. Except sex. He thought he'd like sex with her just fine.

She walked over to take a closer look at the plants that rested on the floor beneath the arrow slit that passed for a window. "They look kind of limp and wilted."

He lay back on the bed and clasped his hands behind his head. "That's because they were in the Wilsons' room all last week."

Her narrowed gaze told him how she felt about him making himself comfortable on her bed. In a perverse way, the angrier she grew, the more he wanted her.

"What did the Wilsons do to them? And I'll have to tell Holgarth I don't water plants." She walked over to the bed. "Get off my bed. Go sit in a chair. Better yet, leave."

Eric had thought he'd just stay long enough to give her a brief warning. But he was dragging it out too long and having too much fun. Warning flags were popping up everywhere. So instead of arguing, he rose and walked toward the door.

"Tell me about the plants before you leave." She sounded surprised that he'd obeyed her.

He paused and looked back at her. "The owner's research has shown that plants respond to external stimulus, especially from humans. They pick up on emotions and things like that. The Wilsons did nothing but fight the whole week. I guess it depressed the plants." He offered her his most sensual smile, and half meant it. "The owner claims the plants get all green and bushy in a room where the humans have sex a lot. I guess you'd better figure out something to keep those plants happy. You don't want to tick the owner off."

He'd finally succeeded in shocking her. She stared at him with wide eyes.

"You're kidding." She glanced back at the plants.

"No." He pulled the door open and stepped into the hall.

She firmed her lips. "I guess they'll have to make do with a really big box of plant food."

4

“So did they talk about sex?” Sparkle leaned over the counter to stare at Deimos. She’d closed the store an hour ago, and then waited impatiently for him to report.

“Don’t think so. Couldn’t hear too much. They left the door open, and I had to stand back far enough so they wouldn’t see me.” Deimos ran his hand across his shiny scalp and then flexed his impressive biceps. “Whatta you think of my new form?”

“I don’t think it’s age appropriate. And if you’d kept your cat form, you would’ve heard everything. Cats can hear someone opening a tuna can a block away. Now tell me what Eric and Donna talked about.” Next time she chose an apprentice, she’d do a better background check on him. She didn’t know if Deimos was going to work out. He already had a major strike against him. Deimos was a virgin. The concept of a male virgin was obscene.

“I hated being a cat. Every time I tried to jump, I landed on my face. I want to be an action hero.” He stuck his bottom lip out in a sulky pout.

“Hate to break it to you, babe, but action heroes do a lot

of jumping. And I think you should rethink your new form. You were created four years ago. Four-year-olds don't look and sound like Vin Diesel." How the hell had she saddled herself with a *virgin,* for crying out loud? It was probably too late to give him back, and besides, she couldn't take the total embarrassment. After all, she was the maven of all things sexual. She had to uphold her reputation among the lesser cosmic troublemakers. How would she look if she kicked Deimos back into the newbie pile? A failure, that's what.

"They didn't say much. Sounded like they were mad at each other." His expression had turned mulish. "And I'll be an action hero if I want to be. You can't stop me."

"Knock yourself out. Now tell me what you *did* hear." She was talking through gritted teeth.

He shrugged and turned to stare out the store window into the night. "Eric told her about the plants needing sex to grow right."

Deimos actually blushed when he said the word *sex.* Sheesh. Sparkle had sent him home with a pile of sex manuals, sort of a Remedial Sex 101, but she didn't think it'd done him much good. Bad enough that he'd never had sex, but even watching or talking about it embarrassed him. Fat lot of help he'd be in her quest for the perfect sexual setup.

He paced back to the counter. "Donna said the plants would have to be happy with plant food."

He scuffed his toe back and forth nervously. Sparkle could tell him that action heroes didn't scuff their toes. As for Donna Nolan, by the time Sparkle finished with her she wouldn't need plant food to make Sweetie Pie and Jessica bushy and bright.

"Do I have to sneak around again tonight checking which guests are getting it on with each other? I hide my eyes so I won't see, but I can still hear them. Can't I do something important?" He looked hopeful she might order him to lay waste to all of Galveston.

Important? The little snot didn't think what she did was important? Sparkle allowed herself a resigned sigh. "It looks like if you want something done, you have to do it yourself. From now on, you watch the store while I take care of business in the castle." Yes, Donna and Eric would be better off in her expert hands. They deserved the best, and that would be her. She hoped Sweet Indulgence wouldn't lose money with Vin Diesel behind the counter. The best she could hope for was that he wouldn't throw anyone through the store window. "I'll need a disguise. Hmm. Got it. I'll be the ghost of Lola L'amour, infamous madam of Texas's most notorious bordello, the Cock Crows at Dawn."

Deimos's expression said he didn't care if she turned into a bowl of pudding. "Watch the store? Jeez, action heroes don't sell candy. I want—"

"Shut. Up." Sparkle narrowed her eyes to pinpoints of amber menace. "You'll do what I say or I'll stuff you in a box with a Return to Sender sign on it." Kids. Sometimes you just had to put your foot down.

Deimos swallowed hard and backed up a step.

Sparkle softened a little. "Look, I'll keep my eyes open for a girl you'll like. I know you were created full-grown, but you have a lot of maturing to do. Once you have some sexual experience, maybe you can help me more." She watched him perk up a little. "There is one other thing you can do for me. Asima is here."

"Asima?" He walked around the end of the counter and stole a handful of jelly beans.

Sparkle frowned. Thoughts of Asima always made her frown. "She's the messenger of Bast. Bast is the Egyptian goddess of cats, the moon, sexuality, physical pleasure, and on and on. Asima always takes the form of a Siamese cat. I don't know why she decided to stick her snooty nose into my game. Probably just to piss me off. She thinks she knows more about sex than I do just because she has goddess connections. Ha! See me laugh. Anyway, I want you to keep an eye on her when you're not busy in the store."

"Wow, think I'll see any action?" His eyes glittered with excitement.

"Mess with her, and the only action you'll see is Asima's foot as she kicks your butt into the Gulf." Sparkle allowed herself a grim smile at the mental image. "Don't engage her, just watch what she does."

Ignoring her disgruntled assistant, Sparkle prepared to launch her first offensive. Could a late-night talk-show host find sexual ecstasy with an eight hundred-year-old vampire? Definitely a yes when Sparkle Stardust was in charge.

Okay, what was her problem? She'd tossed and turned for hours. Lifting her head, Donna glanced at the clock. With a disgusted groan, she lowered her head and tried to punch her pillows into more comfortable lumps. Almost four in the morning. Even though she didn't usually get to sleep until about six, she would've sworn nothing could keep her awake tonight. Wrong.

Finally giving up, she turned onto her back and stuffed her two pillows under her head. The only thing that would usually keep her awake when she was this tired was worry. Had she taken care of everything on her to-do list? Her brain didn't think so. It hummed happily along.

She'd made her ritual call to her parents listing her newest reasons for them to stay together. Then she'd called her brother and threatened him with a slow and painful death if he canceled the cruise in favor of a family trip to a Yankees game. Last, she'd called her sister to pass on a rumor she'd heard about Trish's hubby-number-three hopeful. Basically, everyone told her to mind her own business, but maybe they'd at least think about what she'd said. There, she'd taken care of the home front.

Her job? She'd ask Brynn to be her first guest, and then Phil Hughes, a ghost debunker, would talk to her listeners by phone. Donna didn't have a chance to run any more plans for tonight's show through her mind, because without warning her door slowly swung open. Her heart and lungs took a coffee break while her ears registered the soft swish of the door scraping over the carpet, and every hair on the back of her neck stood straight up and shouted, "Serial killer!"

The quiet click of the closing door signaled she was no longer alone. Donna's heart and lungs got back to work with a vengeance. Her heart pounded at jackhammer speed while she sucked all the oxygen from the room with a few horrified gasps.

Say something. Her radio mission statement had always revolved around the belief that talk freed the truth. Okay, talk followed closely by screaming and running.

"Who are you, and why are you in this room?" Throwing back the sheet, she swung her feet to the floor at the same time she reached for the lamp.

There was no sound of footsteps, no heavy breathing, but suddenly a large male shape materialized out of the darkness. The bed and her heart sank as he sat down beside her.

Donna knew. She didn't need to hear his voice or turn on the light. It was as though in the unrelieved darkness her senses grew more acute. His heat and scent were familiar. They bypassed her civilized veneer and spoke directly to the primitive in her. And what they said was pretty scary. Hot sensual male looking for like-minded female. Desires to have sex in interesting locations using creative positions.

She shook her head. Panic was making her stupid. "What're you doing here, Eric?" Donna had ruled out the serial-killer angle. More likely he was here for an after-midnight snack. Chomp, suck, aah. Another talk-show host drained dry. She mentally slapped her own face. Even if she believed in vampires, that would be a sick thought.

"You sent me a note." His voice was smoke and darkness. "I came."

"I didn't send you a note." Once again she reached for the light and fumbled around for the switch. "I locked the door before I climbed into bed. How'd you open it?"

He tensed beside her. "The note said you had important

information to pass on, and you'd leave the door unlocked. It was unlocked."

Donna paused in her fumbling attempt to find the lamp's switch to think about what he'd said. Without warning, a shape shimmered into view at the foot of the bed.

Glowing, transparent, and floating a foot above the floor, it slowly took a recognizable form. A woman. It was the Pillsbury Doughboy in female form. Old, gray-haired, with chubby cheeks and an apple shape, she was the quintessential grandmother prototype. "Hello, dearies. I'm so happy my note worked." She smiled at them, a cozy sweet smile that made Donna think of hot apple pie and Norman Rockwell paintings.

"What's your game?" Eric sounded cold, unmoved, and dangerous. The apparition evidently didn't trigger any warm fuzzy memories of Granny for him.

Donna was in awe of his ability to articulate a logical question. She could only manage a startled squeak. Not from fear. Eric scared her a lot more than this grandmotherly ghost, if indeed it was a ghost and not another of the castle's special effects. But if it really was a ghost, the possibilities for her show boggled her mind.

Grandma Ghost chuckled and shook her finger at him. "Just like a vampire. Always cynical and distrustful. How sad. Although all that negative energy is quite invigorating. Don't you agree, Donna?"

"Sure. Invigorating." Vampire? Maybe Grandma had lived too long in the castle and had bought into the fantasies. "So tell us who you are . . . were. And what's with the note?" Was she actually talking to a ghost? She'd never had any paranormal experiences before, but her callers kept her mind open to what might be out there.

"Forgive me my little trick, but I just had to get you two together in an intimate setting. And what could be more intimate than both of you sitting on Donna's bed? So cozy, so . . . tempting." She floated over to the night table and glanced at the clock. "Oh, dear. I'll have to make sure I'm finished before dawn. I know how sensitive your skin is to the sun, Eric. Have you tried a good sunscreen?"

"Talk. Now." The fewer words Eric said, the more dangerous he sounded.

Grandma didn't seem intimidated. "You're such lucky duckies. Did you know the Castle of Dark Dreams was built on the very same spot where the most famous bordello in Texas once stood?" She didn't give them a chance to answer. "No, of course you didn't. But it's very fortunate for you, because it allows me to come into your lives. I'm Lola L'amour, madam of the Cock Crows at Dawn. On this very spot thousands of horny men found sexual fulfillment." She paused as though waiting for applause.

"That is so cool." Donna meant it. It was one thing to listen to callers talk about ghost sightings, but to meet one herself was beyond amazing. And Lola talked. A lot. Callers always reported that spirits never had much to say. "Tell me about your bordello. You don't look like a madam. What was it like—"

Donna stopped in midsentence. She felt Eric's stare burning into her. *Felt* it. How strange was that? And he didn't feel happy.

He rose from the bed in one lithe motion and stalked around Lola. "Get to the point."

Even Lola seemed a little flustered. Donna understood. Eric did scary well.

"Back off, vampire." Lola delivered her demand with a sweet smile, but she'd sort of tarnished her grandma image. "Now, I'm sure you'd expect an old madam to be skinny, wrinkled, with bright red dyed hair, and a cigarette hanging from her mouth. But I'm so much more than a tawdry cliché."

Eric was giving off waves of male impatience. "Just tell us why you're here."

"You are such a bloodsucker." When flustered, Lola didn't sound as old as she looked. "I'm here because I'm still on the job trying to bring sexual bliss to worthy couples." She cast Eric a pointed stare that indicated her doubt about his worthiness. "For some the path to sexual ecstasy is longer and more difficult."

Donna had a sneaking suspicion Eric's path to sexual fulfillment was very short and well traveled. He probably had ruts worn in his path. "I hate to break this to you, Lola, but Eric and I aren't even friends. So maybe you need to move on to someone else in the castle." And maybe her imagination needed to forget about scenarios that involved her stalling in the middle of Eric's sexual ecstasy path. He'd probably just call a tow truck.

"No." Eric seemed pretty definite about that. "I won't have her harassing my guests."

Lola blinked her faded blue eyes, but Donna sensed something sly behind her expression of gentle hurt. "I certainly won't bother your guests"—she smiled gently—"if you allow me to drop by now and then to pass on the wealth of sexual knowledge I've accumulated over the years."

This was so bizarre. They were being conned by the ghost of a long-dead madam who looked like everyone's favorite grandmother. Added to that, Donna still didn't understand Eric's reluctance to capitalize on the free publicity he'd get from any hint of paranormal activity in the castle. It didn't make sense. And what didn't make sense needed to be investigated . . . as soon as she got over the shock of maybe talking to a real ghost.

"Drop by all you want, as long as you stay out of guests' rooms." Eric's tone said he hated caving to blackmail.

"Whoa. Stop right there. Let's do some tinkering with the wording here." Donna was great at negotiating. "I don't need a ten-step program to incredible sex. But I wouldn't mind some insights into the spirit world."

Lola shook her head, making her short gray curls bounce. "I'm sorry, dearie, but your sex life sucks." She smiled. "I like to use contemporary slang now and then when it's really descriptive."

"Let's get on with it, Lola. Say what you want to say,

and then leave." Eric didn't seem awed to be talking with a ghost. He just sounded mad.

Well, Donna was awed. And she intended to squeeze every last drop of ghostly information she could out of Lola. "Didn't your grandmotherly image hurt business? I mean, wouldn't customers feel sort of guilty talking about sex to someone who looked like their granny?"

Lola's light tinkle of laughter sounded strangely young. "I looked as good as my girls when I first opened for business, although age has its uses, too." She glanced toward the window. "Oh dear, it's really getting light outside. Enough chatter for now. But just so you don't miss me, I'm leaving a little gift on your night table and giving both of you a homework assignment."

Donna glanced at the table beside her. She blinked. "A white cat cookie jar?"

"The white cat brought back memories. Some of them quite exciting." Her expression turned expectant. "Look inside, dearie."

Donna lifted the lid, peeked inside, and then slammed the lid firmly down again. "I was hoping for chocolate chip cookies."

"Oh, but condoms can lead to much more fun than a cookie." Lola shrugged. "Of course, I'll admit I've met a few men who made a chocolate chip cookie look like the perfect date." She pointed at the cookie jar. "I was going to fill it with glow-in-the-dark and flavored condoms, but I thought we'd work up to that gradually. We'll start out with plain and ordinary."

"Uh, well, thanks." Donna now had a lifetime supply of condoms. At the rate her love life was going, when she died she'd still have half a jar left. She'd leave the half-filled cookie jar to Trish in her will. It would last Trish maybe two weeks.

Lola rubbed her hands together. "Now for your homework assignment. As soon as I leave, I want you to imagine each other naked." And then she was gone.

The silence and darkness closed around Donna. "Did that just happen?"

"Yeah, it did." Eric reached over and switched on the light. "And no, it wasn't any high-tech effect dreamed up for the castle." In the lamp's pale glow he towered above her, his eyes hooded, his expression guarded. "You're not going to mention this on your show, are you?"

Donna thought about lying. She wanted to lie. She didn't want to be sitting in the path of his gale-force anger when she told him the truth. But this was all about her listeners' rights to know. "I'm going to tell them every little detail." She thought about that. "Well, maybe not the homework and cookie jar part."

His fury was a living, breathing presence in the room. "What else are you going to tell them?" The savagery in his voice was out of all proportion to the situation.

Eric saw the exact moment anger flared in her eyes.

"Whatever I damned well please. If I see a real ghost, hey, the world will know. That's my job. The owner, who's *your* boss, wants me here. And as far as I know, no one said I couldn't report on ghosts, vampires, werewolves, or the tooth fairy if that's what I wanted to do." The anger faded from her eyes, replaced with curiosity. "Lola acted like she thought you were a real vampire. I wonder why?"

Control it. If he didn't get a handle on his temper soon, Donna would see proof that ghosts weren't the only things that went bump in the night. Strong emotion could trigger the change, and he was starting to get the feeling it wouldn't send her screaming into the night. It would send her running for her mike so she could blab to the world that yes, vampires do exist.

"You don't believe in vampires?" He knew the answer, but making her talk would give him time to cool down.

"I didn't before, but now that I've seen a real ghost, maybe I'll take the castle more seriously." She narrowed her gaze on him. "You don't want me to investigate, and I wonder why. I don't buy the reason you gave me. Your boss evidently wants the publicity. Tomorrow I'll make sure there's no wiring or anything that could've created Lola, and then I start asking questions. And if that ticks you off, too bad."

He felt his rage building again. *Think of something else.* Homework time. Picturing Donna naked would've been a lot easier if she were still wearing her shorts instead of the long shirt that came to mid-thigh. Smooth sleek thighs leading down to those long slim legs. He could imagine those legs wrapped around him as he rose above her and—

"My info on the castle says you, Brynn, and Conall have Mondays and Tuesdays off. I think I'll ask Brynn to give me a few minutes tomorrow night. Listeners would love to hear him." She shifted restlessly on the bed. "Do you think he'll go for it?"

He made her nervous. Good. "Not if he's smart." If he took one stride and then slipped that shirt over her head, would she believe he was just doing his homework? It might be worth the punishment to find out. He could almost picture the soft flare of her hips and her round bare behind. She'd kneel on all fours and wiggle that behind to tempt—

"I'll probably get buried by calls from women wanting to know about the lust-filled creatures of the night. Actually, Lola couldn't have shown up at a better time." She stared fixedly at the buttons on his jeans. "Phil Hughes will be my main guest. He'll discuss ghosts from a skeptic's point of view. He isn't into opposing viewpoints, but he's a reliable guest and after I report on Lola, tons of calls will pour in."

"Hey, love those calls." He hoped she didn't miss his sarcasm. And if she didn't move her gaze from between his legs soon, she was going to see button failure on an epic scale. He didn't dare finish his homework, because visualizing her full soft breasts and the curve of her neck . . .

Her *neck*. Even thinking the word began the change. He could feel the slide of his fangs and fought it. He had to get out now before the change and morning light caught him.

"Look, I'm tired, but we still need to talk. I'll catch you tomorrow before your show."

She widened her eyes in surprise as he abruptly turned and strode to the door. Pulling the door open, he paused to look back at her.

"Just out of curiosity, what're you thinking?" He needed to leave. He didn't *need* to know what she was thinking. He didn't want to *care* what she was thinking.

Her smile was a slow slide of wicked enticement. "I'm doing my homework."

5

Eric woke to a sense of urgency, and that urgency had a name—Donna Nolan. He had to talk to Brynn and Conall before Donna did her first show tonight. They had to understand the danger of letting her interview them on air.

Luckily, he found them both together in Brynn's room on the second floor of the keep. Eric's room was next to the dungeon, a windowless escape from the sun. Even though living in the castle cost him nothing, Eric still would've liked his own home where he could put some stronger security in place. But the owner had insisted all three of them live in the castle. And Eric liked working here enough to go along with the owner's strange requests.

One room and a bath were okay with him. He rarely formed attachments to people or things. People died too soon, and he didn't go all emotional over things. He moved a lot, and it would be a real hassle to drag a bunch of possessions along. Except for his dragon. He stubbornly refused to leave his dragon behind.

As he lowered himself to the couch beside Conall, he noted Brynn's frown. "More woman problems?"

Shirtless, Brynn was stretched out on his bed. "The only kind I have. The same woman's come back for a fantasy three nights in a row. Each night she's made an excuse to stay with me a little longer. Maybe she'll hook up with someone else during my two nights off." He raked his fingers through his hair and exhaled sharply. "If she stays with me for more than an hour, I'm screwed. I'll have to offer her my body. Slavery might come all sexed up, but it's still slavery."

Conall shook his head. "Tough. A demon doesn't have choices. A man should always have choices." His hard gray eyes promised that Brynn was a man first and his friend. Eric knew if Conall ever found the entity responsible for Brynn's enslavement, he'd tear it apart and stomp on the pieces. You didn't mess with an immortal warrior.

Eric hated not being able to help Brynn, but you couldn't fight what you didn't understand. "You don't have a clue where this compulsion came from? No memories of your past or who created you?" At least Eric had a clan, an extended family who cared about him. He knew what he was and his clan's history.

Brynn shrugged. "My first memory was rising from a bed, looking in a mirror, and seeing a man who looked to be in his late twenties. I knew two things—I was a demon of sensual desire, and my job in life was to have sex." His smile was bitter. "Nice, huh? If I try to resist the compulsion, the pain starts. It feels like lust is burning me up from the inside out. It's an agonizing sexual hunger that doesn't let up until I have sex. I can't take it, so I give in. And every time I give in, I hate myself a little more. I've lived for five hundred years, and I don't have much of me left to hate."

Eric winced. He'd heard Brynn's story before, but each time he hoped he'd think of something to free his friend. It didn't look like it was going to happen, and he knew Brynn wouldn't last another five hundred years this way. But Eric doubted whatever controlled Brynn would let one of its demons destroy himself.

"Look, guys. I dropped by to make sure you don't give

Donna Nolan any interviews. We don't know what kind of crazies she'll bring down on our heads. Look at all those women who've come searching for the pod of lust-filled night creatures. Those women are harmless, except maybe to Brynn. But we don't know who else is out there." Eric relaxed against the couch, confident they'd agree with him.

Conall rose and paced to the arrow slit. "I know how you feel about our safety, but don't you think you're overreacting a little?" He turned to grin at Eric. "We're immortals. We've lived almost two thousand years among the three of us. Who's going to take us on? Together, we can kick anyone's butt. Besides, everyone thinks we're just three ordinary brothers who've teamed up to run a theme park attraction."

Eric stared at Conall in disbelief. "You're kidding. Kick *anyone's* butt? We all know there's a whole world of powerful entities outside these walls that humans don't know exist. Even if they can't destroy us, they can sure as hell mess with what we have here."

Conall's grin faded. "We're about the same age, Eric, but you're a lot more paranoid. Hate to say it, but I want lots of people to visit the castle. It's the only chance I have of ending Morrigan's curse. She said I had to protect every last stinking lousy descendant of Sean Kavanagh. Well, there's only one left, and he's living in Galveston somewhere. I'll know the bastard's a Kavanagh when I see him. And the more people who walk through this place, the greater the chance Kavanagh will be one of them."

Brynn pulled himself from his funk long enough to ask, "How do you know it's a man?"

Conall's anger rolled off him in waves. "Down through the centuries, all of Sean's rotten descendants have been men. I don't have much information on this one, but I do know he doesn't have any kids yet." A smile of pure evil slid across his face. "And when I find him, I'll make sure there won't be any procreating going on even if I have to cut off his—"

"Yeah, yeah. I get the idea." Irritated, Eric stood.

"Maybe I *am* paranoid, but my gut feeling is that Donna is more dangerous than we think." His body thought that in certain situations dangerous could be a lot of fun. But his body's thought center was housed a little lower than his brain.

Brynn looked defiant. "I promised to go on the air with her tonight." He smiled without humor. "Maybe I'll tell her listeners the truth. Who'd believe me? And even if they did, what could they do about it? Galveston doesn't have a town ordinance against demons."

Horrified, Eric stared at him. "Why would you do that?"

Brynn shrugged. "Just for the hell of it. Maybe a mob of crazed exorcists would believe it and storm the castle." His expression said he'd be cheering on their attempts to exorcise him, but he didn't think they'd make it happen. "Don't worry, you guys are safe. I'll make it clear that I'm the only strange and unusual thing in the castle."

Conall scowled. "You're not a 'thing.' That's part of your problem. You need to stop putting yourself down. You're as human as we are."

Brynn smiled, but it didn't reach his eyes. "Hey, I feel a lot better now."

Conall muttered a curse in Gaelic and turned his back on Brynn.

Eric was too steamed to think of a retort. Demons could be real butt-heads. Without another word, he slammed from the room. Once he cooled down, he'd think of a way to avert tonight's catastrophe.

Donna glanced at her notes. She was ready for Brynn. She'd finished her opening comments about the castle and was waiting for the station break to be over. Ken and Franco had everything running smoothly. They'd set her up in front of the castle bookstore. A small crowd had gathered, but they were all friendly and human. No glowing eyes that she could see.

A quick scan told her Eric wasn't in the crowd. He'd promised to talk to her before the show, but he'd probably forgotten. Hey, that was fine with her. She'd not only done Lola's homework but had thrown in a little extra credit as well. She didn't know if she could face him without cringing.

Okay, show time. Someone sat down in the seat next to her, and assuming it was Brynn, she didn't glance over before launching into her intro. "I'm really excited about our first guest. He's one of the three brothers who run the Castle of Dark Dreams. He plays . . ."

Uh-oh. Her senses were signaling that the person beside her was hot, hot, hot, and was *not* Brynn. They were pretty sure it was Eric. She recognized his scent of dark excitement and sinful purposes. A quick peek verified that the yummy heat spreading from where his bare arm touched hers was indeed Eric's. She could hear the ocean in her head, a sure sign of impending panic.

Rats. Donna turned to meet his intense stare. She mouthed, "Where's Brynn?"

Instead of mouthing his answer back, he leaned close to her ear. "He couldn't come. I'm it, talk-show lady." His warm breath fanned the side of her neck, refreshing memories of last night and her duty to Sweetie Pie and Jessica. She wondered if banging her head on the table a few times would jog her brain back into place.

Talk. She had to say something before her listeners got suspicious. "He plays Eric the Evil, the castle's resident bad guy. Eric McNair has agreed to give us an inside look at the Castle of Dark Dreams. How about telling us something about the characters you play, Eric?" *Please don't destroy my show.*

"I play a vampire most of the time." His tight smile said she wouldn't get anything else out of him without a few instruments of torture.

Twenty minutes later Donna was growing desperate, and the instruments of torture were looking like viable options. Eric the Jerk refused to elaborate on anything. One-word answers did not a talk show make. Throwing caution to the wind, she abandoned the questions on her notes. "I've never met a vampire, but if I did, what do you think he'd have to say to all the listeners out there?" Let him answer that in one word.

For just a moment emotion flooded his gaze. Well, that was a first. He'd spent the whole interview up till now staring at her with those cold beautiful eyes.

"What do I think he'd say?" Eric looked like he was actually thinking about a meaningful answer.

Be still my heart. If she was lucky, she might even get a whole paragraph out of him.

"I'm not a vampire, so I really don't have a clue what the real deal would say. But common sense says the vampire life, or maybe death, wouldn't be all midnight orgies and blood cocktails." His smile was tight and mirthless. "Everyone thinks vampires have it all—sex, power, and infinity to build a lights-out stock portfolio. Nothing much would matter, though, if someone took your head. And hunters are using technology to help them now. Progress isn't vampire-friendly. So you'd keep everyone at a distance because who're you going to trust?" He shrugged. "What good would the power or the stock portfolio be when you'd had, done, and seen it all, but didn't have anyone to share it with?"

She blinked at him. "Wow. That was really insightful." Where had *that* come from? Sounded pretty personal to her.

Eric looked as though he was thinking the same thing. She watched the coldness return to his eyes. Maybe she should get to the calls before he bolted. She was just about to take her first caller when someone in the audience spoke.

"What do you think a vampire should do if a member of another clan destroys his brother?" The man's voice was low, compelling, and completely scary.

Eric stilled. A stillness so complete Donna could almost believe he wasn't breathing. He looked into the audience and Donna followed his gaze.

All this stillness translated to dead air. She needed to fill the silence, but she couldn't get her lips to work. The audience shifted away from the speaker, and Donna got her first look at him. *Lethal* was the first word that came to mind. She didn't have time for a leisurely analysis, but he was tall, strong-looking, and not smiling. Come to think of it, no one was smiling. Ken and Franco were definitely not smiling. Ken was making frantic motions for her to start talking.

"Sorry. I have to leave." Without another word, Eric rose and moved away from the table. His gaze never wavered from the man who'd asked the question.

Fine, so her night was shot. She'd had bad nights before, but she'd kept on talking. She'd always been able to talk. Donna refused to watch where Eric went, and when she glanced up, the other man had disappeared.

As she swept her gaze across the audience, a hand waving madly in the back caught her attention. She paused to acknowledge the question, and then heaved a huge mental sigh as Sparkle Stardust stood. Donna's gut told her that whatever Sparkle had to say would not improve her night.

"Legend says that vampires are incredibly sensual and make awesome lovers. That's because their sexual equipment is, well, so *there,* and they've had centuries to practice. What do you think, sister?" Looking smugly satisfied with the uneasy stir around her, Sparkle sat down.

Okay, now would be a good time for a station break. She glanced over at Ken. Guess it wasn't going to happen, because Ken was busy staring open-mouthed at Sparkle. As well he should. If vampire equipment was so there, then Sparkle's little black dress was so *not* there. If she bent over, anyone in front or back of her could go home knowing they'd experienced a Sparkle happening. Adult entertainment at its best.

She'd better say something. This was why the station paid her the big bucks. "I think that, just like humans, vampire sexual performance would be an individual thing." She'd dated some guys who'd need a thousand years to rate an awesome.

The rest of the night passed in a blur. Like most of her guests, Phil spoke with her by phone. A reliable if uninspired guest, he was just as delightfully close-minded as ever, spouting scientific speculation about what apparitions were, and rejecting the idea that they could possibly be interacting with humans.

She told him about Lola with unashamed glee and then opened the lines so her listeners could heap their ghost stories on his pompous head. And throughout it all, she refused to think about Eric. It was only as she wearily left the table that she realized no one had called about the pod. Strange.

She'd already decided to hit the restaurant for something to eat before heading up to her room when she changed her mind. Luckily, the restaurant stayed open until five. So if she moved fast, she could find Eric, vent about what he'd done tonight, and still have time to grab a sandwich. By tomorrow she would've calmed down, and she wanted to hit him with the full force of her anger. She also wanted to know why Brynn hadn't showed.

Glancing around, the only person she saw was the bookstore owner. She'd kept her bookstore open during Donna's show and it'd paid off. A lot of people had drifted in to browse and had come out with a bag of books.

"Hi. Do you know where Eric's room is?"

The woman paused from her locking up and smiled at Donna. "Take the elevator or stairs down to the dungeon. His room is right next to it."

"Thanks." What a weird place to live. She didn't remember seeing any windows from the outside. But at least it wasn't underground. Ken had told her that the main part of the castle was built above ground level because of hurricanes. So the dungeon actually was at ground level.

Busy thinking about how she'd verbally slice and dice him, Donna stepped into the elevator, punched the button for the dungeon, and watched the doors slide shut. It took exactly three heartbeats for her to realize she wasn't alone. She looked down to meet the stare of a Siamese cat. A blue point if she remembered her Siamese colors. Elegant and aloof, it sat watching her from unblinking almond-shaped blue eyes.

"Well, hello, kitty." Donna bent down to slide her fingers over its chiseled aristocratic head and sleek back. She liked cats. "Where did you come from?"

"London, actually. It was a terribly rough flight, and I do so hate that queasy feeling. I don't think I'd live through the humiliation of having to use a barf bag. Where did you *come from?"* The cat's gaze never wavered from Donna's face.

"New York." Donna's automatic response came even as her brain registered an it-ain't-happening moment. She absolutely had *not* heard a woman's voice in her head. Glancing up at the numbers showing the floors, she noticed they hadn't reached the dungeon yet. Why not? They'd been moving long enough to drop one floor, for crying out loud. She pressed the back of her hand to her forehead. Nope, no fever. Could she hallucinate without drugs or a fever?

"Of course you're hearing me. I chose to speak to you because I could tell you were a woman of taste and refinement. Like me. And finding out that you came from New York, one of the world's cultural centers, makes it even better. Have you been to the opera or ballet lately?" The cat rose and rubbed its head against her leg. *"I feel myself bonding with you already."*

Ack! She was trapped with a telepathic cat that wanted to go to the opera, in an elevator that had passed dungeon in favor of a lower floor—hell. Maybe the elevator was a portal to an alternate universe. Maybe—

The cat sat down again and yawned. *"Americans are endearingly emotional. When you've finished being hysterical, I'll pass on some need-to-know info."*

Donna focused on ignoring her urge to pound on the elevator doors and scream like a banshee. "Okay, I'm listening. But this better be good."

"I'm Asima. You don't need to know my real purpose here, just that you intrigued me." Asima managed to con-

vey sly without moving a muscle. *"You had a visit from this Lola person last night. I just happened to have my ear pressed to your door while she was there. Her sexual advice was, how should I say this, tasteless. Lola is the type who'll suggest a glow-in-the-dark condom, while I would offer a bottle of champagne in front of a roaring fire. Eric is unique and an incredibly sensual male animal. Only someone who has my talent and sensitivity can guide you to a glorious sexual experience with him."*

"Umm. Wow. Thanks." She had to get out of here. A ghost and a cat wanted to mess with her sex life, and maybe she should check herself into the nearest mental health facility.

The cat laughed at Donna. In her head, of course. The laughter was low, seductive, and female. *"Such an innocent mind. I'll enjoy filling it with wonderful sexual possibilities. And I'll do a much better job than Lola. Now when you get off the elevator, go directly to Eric's room. Make sure you get inside. Pay particular attention to his bed. It's a wonderful bed to have sex on. Lola would tell you it's only about the action, but a sensational setting adds so much satisfaction to the total experience. Oh, and ignore the dragon."*

Dragon? Huh? Donna backed against the elevator door in an attempt to put as much space as possible between them, and almost fell on her behind when the door unexpectedly opened. Once she caught her balance, she glanced around. Asima was gone.

It must've been the Mexican food she'd eaten for dinner. Great Mexican food. Very hot. It must've boiled her brain. Because she would not believe she'd just had a conversation with a cat. The whole thing had freaked her out, and Donna didn't even think she wanted to talk with Eric anymore. She'd walk up the stairs to her room. Her legs would be rubber by the time she reached the top floor. But nothing, absolutely *nothing,* would get her into the elevator again tonight. She had her foot on the first step when she heard the shouting.

Donna identified one of the shouters as Eric. Hey, it was his room and he could shout if it made him happy. It wasn't her business. She hesitated. Fine, so she was nosy. She wanted to know what he was so ticked off about.

Without her complete consent, her feet took her past the dungeon to the room where the three male voices were trying to outshout each other. The door was slightly ajar, and she stood far enough back so she could escape if someone came out.

"Who the hell gave you the right to put a shield over your door so I couldn't get out? I spent the whole night locked in your freakin' room. I should knock you on your ass." Sounds of furniture being kicked.

Hmm. Brynn. Well, at least she knew why he hadn't shown up for her show. But what was a shield?

"I couldn't trust you not to blurt out the truth. Five centuries and you're still impulsive. And you couldn't kick my butt on your best day." Sounds of derisive laughter.

Eric. Five centuries? She must've heard that wrong. What was he so afraid Brynn might say? Donna assumed the owner did a background check before hiring the brothers, so they couldn't be hiding something criminal. Still . . .

"Cut the crap, both of you. Eric, what's so important that you dragged me out of bed to tell me?"

Conall. Donna held her breath waiting for Eric's answer.

"Taurin's here. He was in the crowd watching Donna's show tonight." His voice was a mixture of weariness and anger.

There was a long silence, then a single word. "Hell." That would be Brynn.

Okay, she'd heard enough. Didn't want to know any more about this Taurin. He must've been the guy who asked Eric the question. So Eric had a problem. She had a problem, too. Ghosts and cats talked to her. Time for beddy-bye.

She'd started to turn away when Eric's voice reached her.

"Don't run away without saying hello, Donna." His

hard voice intimated bad things would happen if she turned down his invite.

How had he known she was in the hall? Didn't matter, she'd deal with it. She had a few things to say to him, so she may as well get it over with. Shoring up her courage with the memory of how he'd tried to sabotage her program, she strode into his lair. Refusing to look at anything except his face, she scowled and let him have it.

"I don't know who died and made you king of the castle. Last time I looked the owner had the final say on what did and didn't happen here." She gained momentum with every word. "Don't you dare try to ruin my show again. Because maybe Brynn and Conall won't kick your butt, but I'm mad enough to get the job done." Had she been a little too aggressive? Perhaps somewhat belligerent? From his narrowed eyes and thinned lips, she'd guess now might be a good time to start running.

Brynn and Conall's barks of laughter deepened Eric's glare to murderous. "You two, out." He hooked his thumb to indicate the door. Still laughing, they left, closing the door behind them. "You, stay."

Donna glanced around. Yep, she was the only one in the room. Guess he meant her. Holy cow! For the first time she got a look at Asima's dragon. "Wow, where'd you get *that*? It's incredible."

Eric tried to hold on to his righteous anger at her spying, but he couldn't. He knew his scowl was easing into a smile. He couldn't stay mad at anyone who admired his longboat's figurehead. It was his past, the one memory of his Viking days that he could reach out and touch, the only "thing" that he treasured. His brother, Var, had carved the figurehead when he was twenty-five and still human. He hadn't lived long enough to become vampire. He'd died somewhere along the Scottish coast during a raid. Eric had kept the dragon, dragging it along with him when the clan settled in the Scottish Highlands, and later to all the places in the world he'd lived during his eight hundred years of existence.

She tipped her head back to take in the whole of it, exposing her smooth beautiful throat. "It's huge. You're lucky to have such high ceilings. I can't imagine how you got it into this room. Look at the detail. Whoever carved it is really gifted. Tell me the story."

She'd forgotten her anger for the moment, and he wanted to keep it that way. Eric tore his thoughts away from what it would feel like to place his lips on her neck and taste all that was essential warm female in her. "My brother was really into Viking history. Most of the Viking longboats had a carved dragon's head on the prow to protect them from the perils of the sea and to warn the villagers they were raiding that their visit wasn't friendly." He couldn't remember the last time he'd had the joy of talking about the dragon to someone who showed interest. But then, the only ones who'd ever seen it were Brynn, Conall, and a few of the women he'd had sex with through the centuries. Brynn and Conall didn't care about his dragon, and the women were more interested in his bed than his figurehead.

She wandered over to where the dragon rested in the corner nearest his door—forever frozen in the act of scaring the crap out of all Viking enemies—and slid her fingers over the long sinuous neck. The instant impact on his body, the sensation that she'd smoothed her fingers over his cock, widened his eyes. This wasn't good. Arousal took his mind off important things, like surviving.

"Your brother did a great job of making him look authentically ancient." She abandoned the dragon to take a look at his bed. "Now this is a for-real alpha male's bed. Made from rough-hewn logs. It has a primitive splendor. I like it."

She liked his bed. That opened up all kinds of possibilities. And then he noticed her frown had returned.

"Now, about what you did to my show tonight."

Uh-oh. He'd let his excitement over her interest in his dragon distract him. He had to find out what she'd heard and keep her from asking any questions. Eric resorted to his favorite diversion.

He moved behind her and leaned down to whisper in her ear. "I did my homework last night." And then he touched his tongue to the sensitive skin beneath her ear.

"What?" She spun to face him, her eyes wide and startled. But something moved in her gaze that had nothing to do with surprise.

Before he had a chance to slip into her mind and identify the unknown emotion, she grabbed his arms with both hands to steady herself. When she started to teeter backward, he simply went with her. She ended up laying half across his bed with him leaning over her.

"You were supposed to stand there like a pillar of strength and hold me up, not fall over with me." She sounded like she couldn't decide whether to maintain her anger or laugh.

"I think ahead. This position is a lot better for discussing homework assignments." *Find out what she heard.* His brain was fully activated and on the job. Unfortunately, so were his super-sized senses. And his senses were directly attached to a few instinctive vampire behaviors.

She looked a little worried now. "Let me up. That was a dumb assignment."

"Oh, I don't know." Leaning down, he slid his tongue across her lush lower lip, then tugged at it with his teeth. "It had its moments. Want to know what I imagined?"

"No." Her eyes said maybe.

"I visualized a small bare foot—"

"I have big feet." She shoved at him, but not too enthusiastically. "All the better to kick you with."

"That's the wolf's line, and that would be me. Anyway, I love a small bare foot with a sexy arch. No bigger turn-on than kissing the smooth curve of that arch." This wasn't turning out to be a great interrogation technique, but his senses didn't care.

"If that's your biggest turn-on, you need a few sessions

with Lola. *I* did better than that." Contemptuous, she looked down her small straight nose at him.

That might've hurt more if he hadn't noticed where her gaze landed once it slid down that perfect nose. His sex didn't miss a thing and swelled with pride. "I doubt it. Next I pictured long slim legs and strong sleek thighs. You needed the strong thighs so you could wrap your legs around me."

"In your dreams." She shifted beneath him, and his body leaped directly to the excited stage without passing go. "I didn't piddle around with any little stuff. I went for the whole torso. Wide hard-muscled shoulders, great pecs with sexy male nipples, six-pack abs, and . . . Well, you never could live up to the length and width I had in mind. But that's what's great about the imagination. It doesn't have to be realistic."

How long? How wide? He'd try to live up to her ideal. Something dark and hungry inside him began to growl. "Here I thought women always wanted hours of anticipation. You finished before you had time to enjoy it. I took my time picturing a sweet round behind, full breasts with nipples I could tease with my tongue, and the sexiest mouth . . ." He paused to think about her mouth. "Of course, I could see your mouth even with your clothes on, so technically it wasn't part of my homework."

The growl had grown to a roar. Eric didn't care if she'd heard him trying to decide between type A and type O blood. He just knew he had to taste her. And he'd start with her lips. Lowering his head, he took her mouth.

Nothing gentle or tentative, he was in full berserker mode. As her lips parted, probably to tell him this wasn't part of the homework assignment, he took complete advantage. His tongue explored the taste and texture of her. She was smooth and moist, sweet and tempting. She was a . . . chocolate-covered cherry. Sparkle had a lot to answer for.

And when she suddenly wrapped her arms around him and returned his kiss, the powerful need to change shook him. He broke the kiss and buried his face against her neck while she slid her fingers though his hair.

Reflex actions retained from a time when he was human kicked in. He could almost feel his heart pounding, hear the labored rasp of his breathing. But other physical reactions were not quite so human. He felt the slide of his fangs and the sudden onrush of uncontrolled hunger fueled by his enhanced senses, a hunger he'd damn better resist.

Say something. The siren call of her life force flowing strongly just beneath her skin was driving him crazy in a way he couldn't remember ever feeling before. The suddenness and strength of his need was a red flag. He hadn't survived for so many centuries without learning that an out-of-control vampire didn't last long. Especially in his clan. Too much human blood led to madness and ultimate destruction.

Through the rising chaos within him, he felt her hands on his chest, pushing him away. *Thank you.* Calling on all the discipline that had enabled him to survive when so many others hadn't, he lifted himself off her and strode away from the bed. He kept his face turned from her until all signs of the change were gone.

Eric heard her stand up and slid into her mind to experience her emotions—shock and confusion overlaid with receding waves of sexual arousal. He felt her effort to organize her thoughts and make sense of what had just happened. He allowed himself a mocking smile. *Good luck, talk-show lady.*

"Take-charge kind of guy, aren't you?" Her smile said she'd decided to play it light, but her mind wanted to know exactly when she'd lost control of the situation.

If Eric hadn't cared whether she knew he was in her mind or not, he could've told her he thought control was going be an issue between them—who had it and who was losing it. "I'd rather think of it as a moment of intense sexual attraction. Better not tell your listeners about this, or they'll think you found one of the lust-filled creatures of the night."

Her lips tipped up and her expression said she knew how to play the sexual banter game. "Why would I tell them when I can keep you all to myself?" She gripped her full bottom lip with her teeth.

A totally sexual invitation Donna was unaware she'd extended. Surprised, he realized he'd already decided to accept. Not now, but soon. On his bed. And it could very well be one of the stupidest decisions of his long existence.

"I don't want to pry. . . . Okay, I'm prying. What could Brynn have said on air that would've been so awful you felt the need to lock him up? And what's a shield? Oh, and who's Taurin?" She paused, and her gaze turned uncertain. "Do you know anyone in the castle who has a Siamese cat?"

Great. How was he going to explain his way out of this? "Brynn has an overactive imagination. When we were kids, we'd pretend aliens were attacking us. A mind shield was a make-believe way the aliens had of imprisoning us. I guess a mind shield would be fun, but all I used was a plain old lock. Sure, locking him in was overkill, but he's too impulsive. He'd think it was a hoot to tell your listeners some crazy story that would bring them running to the castle just like the pod story did." *Weak, really weak.* "Taurin? His brother and I were good friends once. Taurin and I had a . . . disagreement a lot of years ago. He carries a grudge a long time." He shrugged. "The cat? Conall is always feeding strays. Maybe one got into the castle."

"Uh-huh. I haven't forgotten what you did to my show, either. Why?" Her narrowed gaze never wavered.

Eric flashed what he hoped was a boyish grin. Probably wasn't very good. He'd been many things in his life, but boyish wasn't one of them. "I froze up. There I was, getting ready to answer your first question, and I suddenly realized there were millions of people listening to me. I've always been a private person."

Donna nodded but didn't look convinced. "I guess that explains everything."

Eric tuned into her mind. She thought his explanations were a little inadequate. So did he.

He watched her leave his room, her hair still tousled, her cute behind still working its magic on his body. Eric turned back to his bed. He hadn't anticipated having a woman in it this much for a long time.

He smiled. "That doesn't explain one damn thing."

6

Donna awoke to the sounds of passion. Small whimpers of pleasure from the woman, sex words grunted out between thrusts from the man, and the squeak of bedsprings in rhythm with the surge to completion.

In the moment right after waking, Donna lay there just listening. Then her mind kicked in. What? How? She forced her lids open to find Lola sitting at the end of her bed. A quick glance at her clock told her it was three in the afternoon. A quick glance around the room told her they were alone. Wow, yesterday must've exhausted her. And what was going on?

Wait. She stared at Lola, all shimmery and real in the middle of the day. "Ghosts are supposed to show up at night."

"Myths, dearie. All myths." She smiled her sweet apple-cheeked smile. "I was going to bring you some yummy treats for Eric until I realized food wouldn't work on him. Did you know that hot cinnamon buns cause blood to engorge a man's penis to make him hard?"

"Uh, no." *Cinnamon buns?* "Why're you here, and what were those sounds I heard?"

"I'm here to continue your training for glorious sex competition. You get an A on your homework. Your visuals of Eric were quite inspiring." Lola kept smiling as though she was doing nothing more than passing on a cherished recipe for cherry pie.

"How do you know what my visuals were?" Suspicion gave way to certainty. "You read my mind." It amazed Donna that she could accept so easily something so fantastic. But all things seemed possible when she was around Lola.

"Only a few discreet peeks. And those sounds of sexual play were meant to put you in the mood." Lola didn't seem to have a CD player anywhere in sight. "The sensual enjoyment of hot sex revolves around your senses. I've left you a little something to entice Eric." She pointed to a small bottle on the bureau. "The scent of pumpkin pie will turn a man into a sexually ravenous beast."

"A beast." Donna might be the queen of late-night talk radio, but even she had no words to deal with this olfactory fact. "Question. If the taste of food won't work on Eric, what makes you think the smell of food will? And you've been hinting that he's somehow different. Why?"

"Hmm. You might be right about the food smell. I'll get something else to you if the pumpkin pie doesn't work. And Eric is so much more than a man. He's more powerful, more sensual, more . . . everything." She waved her hand in the air to demonstrate how much more than a man Eric was.

"Why?" Donna tried to ignore her prickle of unease at Eric's more-than-a-man status.

Lola chose to ignore Donna's question. "My real purpose for today's visit is to sex up your wardrobe. And we'll start with your nightwear. Can I be honest?" Lola didn't give Donna the chance to decide if she could survive her honesty. "That shirt thing you wear is hideous. Throw it away. Please. I'm leaving a few little things to liven up your bedtime." She pointed to the desk chair where Donna could see a pile of clothing.

Curious, Donna climbed out of bed and padded over to the chair. Ohmigod. Black fishnet stockings, calf-high leather boots with stiletto heels, a black leather bustier with cups pointy enough to drill holes in wood, a black mask and gloves, and the ever-popular whip. What to say? When in doubt, resort to sarcasm. "You're too traditional, too timid in your nightie choices, Lola. Sometimes you have to experiment, let it all hang out." Hah. The bustier would let more than she had and some of what she didn't have hang out. She would *never* wear this in front of Eric.

"Oh, you will, Donna. Trust me." Lola's smile never wavered, but her eyes had the feline intensity of a night hunter. "You're after big game, not Mr. Mouse. A powerful sexual animal like Eric won't be intrigued by the ordinary. He'll want a woman as powerful as himself, a sexual challenge. A woman with the capability to tame him will intrigue Eric." Lola's eyes lost their intensity and once again became happy granny eyes. "A woman with a big whip is really sexy."

"Right. I'll morph into Donna the Dominatrix next time I trap him in my room." She put on a thoughtful face. "I probably should carry my gear around with me just in case I corner him in the dungeon."

Lola didn't see the humor. "No, you have to do it here. Sweetie Pie and Jessica need you."

"How did you know . . ." Her mind. Lola could access her mental files anytime she wanted, so of course she knew about the plants. How scary was that? All this interacting with a ghost was giving her a pre-caffeine headache. "You've done your good deed for the day, Lola. And as much as I treasure your input on my sexual life, I have to get some coffee and make sure everything is set up for my show tonight."

"I'll pop in again soon. Oh, and don't pay any attention to Asima. She's such a tight-ass." Lola's shimmery shape started to fade.

"Whoa." Donna had sort of pushed Asima to the back burner, assuming she was a consequence of that hot Mexican food, until a better explanation came along. "Asima is real?"

Lola chuckled. "You thought Asima was last night's jalapeño peppers? I should be so lucky." She sighed her regret over Asima's realness. "Asima thinks you can finesse sex. She knows *nothing*. Sex is hot and sweaty and *real*. By the way, don't go to the opera with her. She tries to sing along. Ever heard cats on a back fence? You've been warned."

"Wait. Who or what is Asima?" She hoped Lola would forgive her for the sounds of rising panic in her voice.

Lola didn't answer. The Cock Crows at Dawn's late great madam faded away leaving Donna with a bottle of Eau de Pumpkin Pie and a Bitch Woman costume. She needed coffee. Perhaps her daily shot of caffeine would make sense out of the senseless—a cat who sang along at the opera and a ghost who often sounded a lot more now than yesterday.

Dumping the complimentary packet of coffee into the coffeemaker, she picked up the phone and started her daily calls to her family.

By the time she'd finished drinking two cups, she'd managed to once again make everyone mad at her. Modern technology was so cool. She could reach out and irritate the world long distance. Her sister, Trish, bothered her the most. Trish's newest obsession wouldn't tell her where he worked. Donna had only suggested that a man who kept secrets wasn't someone to trust your future to. Trish had countered with the I-love-him-so-I'll-trust-him garbage. Donna would always steer clear of men with secrets.

Secrets. That reminded her of the strange conversation she'd overheard last night and Eric's even stranger attempt to explain it. And his kiss. She couldn't forget that toe-curling, hormone-exploding, totally awesome kiss. Note to self. Stay far away from Eric McNair. Unfortunately, self thought he was really hot.

Finished, she dressed and headed toward the door. Time to find out more about the castle to pass on to listeners, and then talk to Ken and Franco.

* * *

Donna was cursed. This castle was cursed. And if she got out of Galveston with her career intact, she'd kiss the ground that New York stood on. "What do you mean the vampire canceled? He was a live guest, or maybe dead, who knows. Anyway, I didn't want to talk to him on the phone. I wanted to make an impact by having him here in the castle. I don't have a damn guest now." *Breathe in, breathe out, breathe in—*

Ken grinned. "You're turning red. Hey, you have me, and I'm good. Bill, the guy-who-would-be-vampire, has a friend who also thinks he's a vampire and offered to fill in. Bill said his friend lives in Houston, and he left a half hour ago. Not much traffic this time of night, so he should be here within fifteen minutes."

Donna was *not* mollified. "What's this new guy's name? How do we know he's not a crazy?" She thought about that. Okay, so someone who thought he was a vampire already had a wire shorted out somewhere. She might now be open to ghosts and telepathic cats, but she absolutely did *not* believe in the supernatural type of vampires, only cheap imitations. "How do we even know he'll talk? Remember Eric? I always check out and interview guests before putting them on the air." She paused to suck in air so she could continue her rant. "Bill really lives his life as a vampire and could discuss the whole vampire culture intelligently. Who knows what this new guy will say?"

Ken shrugged. "Take him or leave him. It's almost airtime and we're out of options. If you don't want to take a chance, you can go to open lines for the whole night."

Donna made her decision. She didn't want to take listeners' calls for four straight hours. Somehow she'd escaped any pod calls last night, but she wouldn't stretch her luck two nights in a row. "We'll go with him. You didn't tell me his name."

"Bill forgot to tell me, and I forgot to ask. So sue me." Ken grinned, his good humor restored. "I'll get his name and make sure he's sitting next to you when he's supposed to be. Trust me."

She sat down at her table and forced herself to relax. Everything would be great. The new vampire would show, dazzle her listeners, and inspire tons of admiring calls. Donna was just beginning to believe herself when she looked into the small audience gathered in front of her and spotted Eric. She remembered that he had the night off. He'd pulled up a chair and was evidently settling in for the long haul.

Arrgh! He made her nervous. Almost nothing other than missing guests or those of few words made her nervous. Maybe it was the sensual smile he offered her that promised he not only remembered every detail of his homework assignment but also *The Kiss.*

Forget about him. Right now she had to concentrate on her show. "Welcome to the night and *Donna till Dawn.* Once again we're broadcasting from the Castle of Dark Dreams." She filled the next few minutes with some facts about the history of Galveston and then zeroed in on her bombshell for the night. "I can hardly wait to tell you about another fascinating and strange experience I had in the castle last night. I'll fill you in on all the details right after the station break." She loved that quick break after her intro monologue. It whetted her listeners' curiosity.

She dared a quick peek at Eric and wished she hadn't. His expression was thunderous. But then the humor of it struck her, and she smiled at him. He didn't smile back. He had no idea what she was going to blab to her millions of listeners, and Eric didn't strike her as a man who wanted to be out of the loop. Too bad. She upped the wattage on her smile. Eric the Evil might've controlled their kiss, but she controlled the airwaves.

The break over, she launched into her tale. She told them about Asima. Not too much, only the parts about the barf bag and the opera. But she knew it was enough to motivate all the listeners who had an opinion on, had seen, or thought they *were* telepathic animals to call the show.

Donna took calls for about twenty minutes, and then she was ready for the main attraction.

Out of the corner of her eye, she saw Ken hurrying toward her with a man following behind him. She didn't get a look at her vampire, but it was enough to know she had a warm body to talk to, or maybe a cold one. If it could talk, she'd interview it. "Tonight I'll be talking to a vampire. Our guest was kind enough to fill in on short notice for Bill Sykes. I've never met him before, so we'll be meeting him together for the first time." She turned to smile at her guest.

And froze as the man Eric had identified as Taurin lowered himself to the chair beside her. He smiled at her. A beautiful smile filled with warmth, charm, and deception. She lifted her gaze to his eyes. A mistake. They were cold, dark, and utterly ruthless. He didn't attempt to mask them behind a false layer of friendliness. Donna rubbed her arms to dispel her sudden rash of goose bumps. She didn't dare look at Eric.

Say something. Ken poked her in the side and whispered in her ear. "All of America probably thinks you took a bathroom break. His name's Taurin Veris. Do your thing."

She nodded and put on her professional face. "Taurin Veris is a practicing vampire and has been kind enough to stop by to tell us something about his life." Or death. Donna tried on a bright smile and hoped the corners didn't sag. "Welcome to *Donna till Dawn,* Taurin. Why don't you tell us a little about yourself first." While he was talking, she'd scope out Eric's reaction.

"A practicing vampire? You make it sound like a religion." His voice was smooth and compelling, his laughter sincere. "First of all, you have no idea how much I wanted to be on your show. You're very special."

Taurin sounded as though he was delivering a coded message. But it wasn't meant for her, because she didn't have the key. He looked into the audience, and Donna followed his gaze. Eric's chair lay on its side where he'd evidently knocked it when he rose. Taurin and Eric locked gazes, and the air almost crackled from the tension. Eric stood with hands clenched. His hands said furious, but his expression said nothing. No anger, no fear, just . . . stillness. It scared her into speech.

"Thank you. But this is about you now. Tell us where you're from and how you became a vampire." She chanced a glance at Eric. He'd taken a step toward the table.

"I was born in Italy six hundred years ago, but in the last five hundred years I've lived in many parts of the world." He paused to allow the audience its collective gasp. "I became vampire when I was twenty-eight years old."

Donna recognized a possible great guest when she heard one. Her talk show host persona kicked in. "Wow, that's fascinating. Who turned you, and how did you feel about it?" She slid her gaze over to Eric. He'd moved forward a few more steps. It was a slow deliberate stalk. Uh-oh.

"My older brother turned me. And no, I didn't think it was too cool." He shrugged. "I guess in his own mind he didn't think he had a choice. I'd been wounded in battle, and it was either turn me or let me die. It took me a few hundred years to get over my mad."

Okay, so far so good. "Tell me a little about your lifestyle. Do you live alone or belong to a group? What're your goals?"

Eric had shifted his approach and was working his way around to the back of the table. He must know he wasn't going to be able to sneak up on Taurin. Then what? That's when she saw Brynn, Conall, and Holgarth. They were unobtrusively placing themselves at different spots around the table. This was not good. Taurin might be trapped in the middle of their circle, but so was she. Donna didn't know what was going down, but she didn't want to be part of it.

Taurin was also assessing the situation and acknowledged it with a slight smile. "I belong to a loosely knit group of vampires called night feeders. Most of the night feeders aren't very powerful, so three or four hunt together."

"I see. Does that mean you have other night feeders here with you tonight?" Please, no. She didn't intend to sit here talking to her listeners while the three McNair brothers did battle above her unprotected head with a bunch of phony vampires. She had her standards.

Taurin smiled at her, and for the first time she realized what a spectacular-looking man he was. Dark hair that had been a little tousled by the wind softened his hard face, and he'd probably have a great mouth and eyes if he weren't so scary. Of course, he wasn't any scarier than Eric, and she thought Eric was fine indeed.

"No, I hunt alone. Two hundred years ago my brother was destroyed. Another vampire clan caught him alone, and he wasn't powerful enough to protect himself. That was a wake-up call for me. I focused on making myself strong enough to bring closure to my brother's destruction. The time has come."

He speared Eric with a glare that even Donna understood. We were talking bad blood on a mythic scale. *Keep him talking.* "Describe how you get . . . nourishment." Fine, so she was a weeny. She didn't want to say blood for fear it might be a trigger word.

Taurin turned his attention back to her, but Donna could see he was distracted. "Since I'm so old, I don't have to feed very often, once every week or so. And it doesn't take much blood to satisfy me." He smiled. "You don't have to worry about me leaving a trail of drained bodies as I drink my way through Galveston."

"All of Galveston just sighed its collective relief." She'd roll right into the calls. She didn't think even Eric would pounce on her guest while all of America and a live audience listened. Talk about unwanted publicity.

Thank heavens there were tons of calls that ate up the rest of the night. Donna learned more than she'd ever wanted to know about vampires. The weird part? Taurin made it all seem real and logical. He was a wonderful guest, and she'd love to have him back on the show if the McNair brothers didn't tear him apart as soon as the program ended. During one of the commercial breaks, she pulled her cell phone from her pocket so she could call 911 if hostilities escalated.

Just when Donna thought she was home free, someone in the back of the audience put up her hand. Donna's early-warning system said it was Sparkle-the-sensual-pissant-Stardust. *Don't answer that hand.* But with a sense of inevitability, she pointed toward the waving hand. "You have a question?" Her whole show was built on a foundation of always acknowledging questions from listeners. She might not know the answer, but she was always willing to give the caller a voice.

Her early-warning system was right on target. Sparkle stood up and offered a finger wave to Taurin. "Reports say that vampires are so much more sensually satisfying than humans because they can manipulate the human mind. I mean, they're supposed to be able to create all kinds of erotic images and sensations in our brains. Personally, I find that incredibly sexy. What do both of you think?"

Taurin's smile glazed the eyes of all the women in the front row of the audience. "A vampire has more sensual tools than you could possibly imagine, and mental seduction is only one." He turned his smile on Donna. "What's your take on it, Donna?"

I think Sparkle should stay in her damn candy store. Donna smiled sweetly at Sparkle. "I agree." She'd taken a page out of Eric's "How to Answer Questions in Two Words or Less" handbook and found it immensely satisfying. Especially when Sparkle glared at her and sat down. But the satisfaction was fleeting. What was it with Sparkle and vampires? And would she pop up during every show to ask a vampires-and-their-sex-lives question?

Four seemed like it would never roll around, but finally she was able to sign off with "Thanks for giving us some fascinating insights into vampires, Taurin. And thanks to all the listeners who've joined us. Stop by tomorrow night, everyone, as we once again broadcast from the Castle of Dark Dreams in Galveston, Texas."

Donna felt completely drained as she did her limp noodle imitation and watched people slowly drift away. No one spoke while the drifting took place. Personally, Donna was too scared to talk. Finally only the McNair brothers, Holgarth, Taurin, and Chicken Little remained.

Taurin leaned back in his chair and smiled. "Well, Eric, it's been a few years."

"How did you find me?" His voice was soft, deadly. Suggesting that finding him was not a good thing.

Taurin shrugged. "I paid a lot of people a lot of money to find you. Someone finally reported they'd seen you in Galveston, and the castle seemed a logical place to start. Last night Donna mentioned her guest for tonight. I paid Bill a visit. It wasn't hard to remind Bill of that important meeting he had at midnight and how happy his old pal Taurin would be to take his place. Bill's mind is open to all kinds of suggestions." He glanced at Donna. "By the way, Bill's a fake."

Eric nodded as if Taurin's mad rambling made perfect sense. He was into his still mode again. "It ends tonight, Taurin."

"I don't think so. I really only stopped by tonight to let you know I'd be hanging in the neighborhood. Don't want to mess up your *brothers'* nice castle, so we'll take this somewhere else on another night." He glanced at her. "And I sure wanted to meet Donna." Again, a look passed between the two men that only they understood.

"I don't think so." Eric moved closer, a cold pitiless predator stalking his prey.

Donna might not know what history lay between the two men, but her gut instinct told her Eric was the more dangerous of the two. His silence spoke of deadly intent, and suddenly Donna knew she had to stop whatever was about to happen. She was a talk-show host, for crying out loud. She hadn't come to Galveston to referee a brawl. *You know it's more than that.* No, she wouldn't think about it being more than a brawl.

"You're making me really nervous, guys." She stood and pushed her chair away from the table. "I pass out at the sight of even the teeniest drop of blood, so that's why I'm going to walk Taurin out to his car. He was my guest, and I'm sort of responsible for him." She glanced down at Taurin, who was looking at her with a bemused expression on his face. "To avoid murder and mayhem, I'd advise you to come with me now."

"No." Eric's voice was a soft hiss of menace.

"No?" Donna raised one brow. "No, as in I may *not* walk my guest to his car?" Okay, Eric was scary. She pumped up her deflating courage with false bravado. "Sorry, but unless there's a minefield between here and the parking lot, I'm walking." She cast Taurin a withering glance. He'd come here looking for trouble, but she'd save his butt this one time. "Let's go."

Only when they were finally in the almost empty parking lot did Donna dare breathe. Every second she'd expected to feel Eric's hand on her shoulder, but surprisingly, no one had followed them. Taurin stopped beside a silver Honda Accord, kind of a tame car for someone who claimed to be a vampire. Where was the rush, where was the Batmobile?

"Thanks for trying to keep me safe." He leaned against the car. "But you only postponed the inevitable."

"And that would be?" She wanted to shake the truth from him.

He shrugged. "One of us will be destroyed."

Donna wrapped her arms around herself as a sudden cold breeze whirled past her. Could Galveston even produce a cold breeze at this time of the year? Obviously, yes. "Destroyed? Don't you mean killed? I can guess that whatever is between you and Eric has to do with your brother, but resorting to savagery isn't the answer." This guy had some heavy issues, and she didn't know what to do to keep him away from Eric. Donna knew Eric-the-publicity-shy would be furious for what she was about to do, but it only made sense. She eased her hand toward her pocket. She'd already memorized Taurin's license number. As soon as he started to drive away, she'd call the police.

Reaching out, he pulled the phone from her pocket. "Sorry, I can't let you do that. You think I'm crazy." His smile said he wouldn't hold it against her. "But I really am a vampire, and that breeze you just felt was Eric warning me off."

"Vampires don't exist, and give me back my phone." Maybe saying he didn't exist wasn't the smartest thing to tell someone who needed to check into the nearest mental health facility, but it was almost dawn and she was tired.

Some emotion moved in his eyes. "Oh, we exist. We certainly do exist. Look at me, Donna."

For the first time, she felt a little afraid of him. Wide-eyed, she stared at his face and watched in horror as it changed. His eyes elongated and grew almost black as his pupils swallowed the irises. His mouth seemed to grow fuller, and she had a sickening suspicion of what was causing that fullness. He smiled at her, exposing long, sharp canines. "Next time I appear on your show, we'll share this memory with your listeners."

Every breath seemed to be instantly sucked out of her lungs. She couldn't even muster a terrified squeak. But there was nothing wrong with her feet. Turning, she raced toward the relative safety of the castle. Scaredscaredscared. Her heart pounded, her breath came in gasps, and Taurin had *not* turned into a vampire right in front of her eyes.

"But he did, talk-show lady."

She heard Eric's voice a split second before she slammed into the rock-hard wall of his chest. And as she looked up at his unsmiling face, she realized he had just read her mind. But that seemed relatively minor compared to what she'd left in the parking lot. Fearfully she looked over her shoulder. The Accord was still there, but Taurin was gone.

"Where?" Where were her bags? She was going home.

His soft laughter seemed out of place in the horror this night had become. "Where did Taurin go? That's not his car, so you wasted your time memorizing the license plate. And you won't need your bags. Taurin is no danger to you. I'm the one he wants. After a good sleep you'll see the advantage of staying the whole week."

Surprised, Donna glanced at him. From the moment she'd stepped into the Castle of Dark Dreams, she'd felt that everyone would sacrifice to the gods of late-night radio if they thought it would send her back to New York. "You want me to stay?"

For a moment she read confusion in his eyes. "Yeah, I guess I do."

Too bad. It wasn't going to happen. "He's a *vampire.*" What else was there to say? Once a vampire moved into the neighborhood, there went the property values, and she was gone.

"Hmm. I think that's what he was trying to tell you all night." He put his arm across her shoulders and pulled her to his side. They walked to the castle together. "I'll take you to your room and stay with you until you calm down."

She simply nodded. Amazing how relative fear was. Just a few short hours ago, she would've pegged Eric as the scariest of the scariest. Now Taurin had leap-frogged right over Eric.

"Will you go hunting for him?" *Please say no.* The intensity of the fear she felt for Eric shocked her. Sure, she'd be concerned for anyone in danger from a . . . vampire. But not this concerned.

As he pulled the great hall door open, she could sense his frustration. "No, it's almost dawn and he's gone to ground until the sun sets. After I leave you all snug in your bed, I'll take some precautions."

She didn't ask what kind of precautions, because he probably wouldn't tell her. No one wanted to tell her anything. Except for Lola and Asima. They wanted to tell her everything.

"I'm definitely going home. Since Sunday I've met a

ghost, a telepathic cat, and a vampire. Things like this don't happen in New York." She followed him into the great hall, where everyone sat around the banquet table waiting for them.

"Yeah, you're right. New York is normal America. And you didn't tell me you'd met a telepathic cat. It'd be nice to know things like that before you dropped the bombshell on the air." He waved to his friends, indicating he had everything under control.

He didn't have everything under control. There was a real vampire somewhere outside the castle. That didn't sound like under control to her. And why didn't Eric seem more afraid of Taurin? Donna was sure afraid.

She made Eric take a detour to the restaurant. It closed at five, so she just got in under the wire. She ordered a sandwich and chips to go. Donna also bought a piece of chocolate cake. Chocolate cured almost everything. She didn't know about vampiraphobia, though. Eric ordered nothing. She was almost to her room when she realized she'd forgotten to order lemonade. Oh well, too late now.

Once inside her room, Donna sat on the side of her bed while Eric stared at Sweetie Pie and Jessica. They were looking a little puny. If vampires really existed, then maybe plants *did* thrive where hot sex happened. What did she know?

Leaving him to contemplate the plants and what lies he should tell her about tonight, Donna went into the bathroom and changed into her "hideous" shirt. She'd save the bustier and whip for another night.

When she came out, he hadn't moved. "I'll be okay." *Please say you'll stay for a while.* She probably should've squeezed out a few hysterical tears to convince him not to leave, but she didn't manipulate people that way. She believed in a direct frontal attack, which was why her family spent most of their time being mad at her.

Eric shifted his gaze to the arrow slit where the first light of dawn showed. "I can't stay, Donna. Hysterical tears would've made it tougher, but I'd still have to go."

He could read her mind. So what? Everything paled in comparison to Taurin. Later she'd want to know how he did it. Right now she didn't care. "Sure. I understand." No, she didn't understand, and yes, he'd hurt her.

She propped herself up in her bed with her food. She'd eat the cake first. Chocolate cured hurt feelings.

And she wasn't kidding herself about him staying. If he'd stayed, it wouldn't have been to merely hold her for a few hours. If she ever climbed into bed with Eric McNair, it would be heat, light, and magic. She'd been ready to have sex for all the wrong reasons, but it would've been right for her tonight.

"Donna . . ." He stared at her, and for the first time she felt he was at a loss for words.

This was so not comfortable. "Hey, no problem. You have to go and take care of those precautions you talked about. Wouldn't want Taurin to slither in through a crack in the wall." *Get out. Now.*

His gaze darkened. He'd gotten the message. "I'll send Brynn up with your lemonade."

She shrugged. Whatever. Leave it to a man to think a drink could make everything okay. He wasn't going to even offer her a hug. Insensitive jerk.

A smile tipped up the corners of that expressive mouth. "If I touch you now, I'll probably stay. That wouldn't be a good idea for lots of reasons." He opened the door and then paused. "What else do you know about this telepathic cat that you didn't tell your listeners?"

Donna shrugged. "Asima likes opera. She'd probably appreciate a CD next to her cat food bowl. That's it." She deliberately turned her back on him. Two could have secrets.

She heard his soft laughter as he closed the door behind him.

7

As dawn approached, Eric fought his body's demand for rest. The vampire's deep rejuvenating sleep might call to his body, but his brain thought he had too many things to worry about to waste his time sleeping.

He'd asked Brynn to take lemonade up to Donna. Brynn had agreed to stay with her a short while to make sure she was okay. A very short while, because Brynn knew the consequences of staying with Donna for more than an hour.

He'd like to think his choice of Brynn was random, but his ploy was pitifully obvious. He'd chosen Brynn instead of Conall because Brynn would have less time to get to know Donna. *He* wanted to be the only one getting to know her. Eric couldn't even begin to figure out the implications of that. Besides, he should be concentrating on defeating Taurin, not thinking about Donna.

He reached his room and removed the shield from his door. Donna would be safe until sunset, when Taurin rose from sleep. Eric had the advantage over Taurin there. Even powerful night feeders couldn't rise before sunset. But Eric could function in the late afternoon as long as he didn't expose himself to daylight. He'd be sluggish, but able to protect Donna if he had to.

She hadn't been in danger tonight because Eric had been with her every step of the way on her short walk out to the parking lot. And Taurin knew it. No, Taurin would choose a time when he could lure Donna away from the castle without Eric knowing it. Then he'd use her as bait the same way he figured Eric had used him to lure his brother to his destruction.

Taurin thought he was as powerful as Eric, that all he had to do was to get Eric away from Brynn, Conall, and Holgarth in order to destroy him.

He smiled grimly. Taurin had no idea what Eric could do when he was mad, and the rogue vampire was really ticking him off. He pushed his door open and then grew still. The lights were on. Someone had bypassed his powerful mind shield to enter his apartment. Eric only knew of one person with that kind of power.

"Okay, Holgarth, where are you?" Walking into the room, he glanced around and groaned. "I'll kill you for this."

"Idle threats. Of course you won't." Holgarth emerged from the bathroom still dressed in his wizard's outfit. Eric suspected he slept in it. "I just finished bringing some order and ambience to that horror you call a bathroom. I've seen more attractive outhouses."

Eric drew in a deep breath of patience. He didn't need Holgarth messing with him right now, not when he had Taurin as well as the mysterious invasion of Lola and Asima to think about. "Bathrooms don't need ambience. And you've painted my walls, changed my furniture, and organized the hell out of the whole place. You've done enough damage for one night. Don't you need some sleep to renew your creative genius?"

Holgarth waved his hand to indicate how exhausted he was and dropped into a strange-looking yellow chair. "I tried to replace that archaic figurehead of yours, but the protection you put around it was too strong even for me. It'll just have to squat there, a bull elephant in a room full of gazelles."

"Don't. Ever. Touch. My. Dragon." For a moment Eric was tempted to vent his anger on Holgarth, but the resulting battle would destroy the castle and the contented life he'd built here.

Holgarth got the message. He waved Eric to the chair opposite him. While Eric was sitting, Holgarth touched the glass table resting between them and replaced Eric's longboat sculpture with a floral display and a scattering of books. "I put the boat in your closet. The flowers say sensitive, and the books say intellectual. The longboat said Viking barbarian. Women prefer sensitive and intellectual."

"You didn't just come here to destroy my place. Let's hear it." He looked at the flowers with distaste.

Holgarth eyed Eric's jeans, T-shirt, and boots critically. Eric gave him a warning glare.

"Fine. If you want to look like biker-dude, who am I to stop you?" He finally met Eric's gaze. "The owner is worried about Taurin. You can't fight him anywhere near the castle. It might put guests in danger. Do you want me to destroy him?"

Maybe Eric was as archaic as his dragon, because the warrior in him rejected Holgarth's offer loudly and vehemently. "Taurin is my problem. I'll take care of him."

Holgarth knew better than to argue this point with Eric. "Taurin sensed your interest in Donna. He'll try to use her to get to you."

What was going on? How could Taurin and Holgarth sense something that wasn't there? *Want to run that lie past me again, pal?* All right, so he wanted to have sex with her. That didn't mean he'd let his body rule his brain.

Eric nodded. "I've figured that out. She'll be safe until sunset. And tonight I'll make sure one of us is always with her." Which might be tough. "She'll be doing her show from midnight until four, so whichever one of us isn't taking part in a fantasy at the moment can slip out to watch her."

From sunset to midnight would be the dangerous time. She could be wandering anywhere. He'd have to get one of the subs to play his part in the fantasies until midnight, and then he'd need an excuse to stay with her. And if he couldn't think of an excuse, he'd have to cloak his presence and sneak around after her. He didn't do sneaking well. In the parking lot, he hadn't been able to resist the impulse to announce his presence with the cold wind.

"The owner has decided on a way to keep her safe from sunset until midnight, at least for tonight. The owner will be contacting Donna's boss today insisting she play a part in tonight's fantasies so she can tell her listeners what it's like. The owner felt Donna would be less resistant if the order came from her boss." Holgarth seemed fascinated with Eric's boots. "You and the others need to get together to plan how to fit her into your fantasies. After tonight we'll only need to come up with a plan for two more nights. But I think Taurin will make his move before she leaves. Once she's gone, he's lost his bait."

Eric nodded. Sounded good to him. He refused to admit he liked the plan because it would allow him to spend more time with Donna. He watched as Holgarth stood, and he didn't even blink when the wizard disappeared in a puff of smoke. Holgarth loved the drama of being a wizard as much as he liked the power.

And Eric wasn't surprised when he glanced down to find he was wearing a pair of sandals. He hoped Holgarth hadn't hidden his boots.

Stripping, he showered and then climbed into bed. But not before returning his longboat to the table. He left the flowers there, too. Just in case Donna liked that kind of stuff.

He assumed his body's need for rest would do its normal thing. Wrong. As he tried to sink into the dreamless sleep his body craved, his mind stubbornly kept on pulling up nightmare scenarios. Taurin fooling everyone and coming for Donna as dawn broke or before sunset. Taurin hiring someone to kidnap Donna from her room. Conall thinking that someone should stay with Donna after Brynn left. Conall staying and staying and staying.

An hour and a half later Eric dragged his resentful body from the comfort of his bed to check on Donna. He was almost out the door when his phone rang. Who would call him now? Donna? Worried, he hurried back to answer it. He didn't know whether to be angry or relieved when he recognized Holgarth's voice.

"I was almost asleep when I remembered that Brynn hadn't given me the plans for this week's Vampire Ball. I thought I'd give him a quick call while I was thinking about it. No one answered. Do you have any idea where he might be?"

Damn. Eric dropped the receiver without answering Holgarth and put his preternatural speed into high gear.

Donna owed Brynn big time. He'd stuck around to talk to her without being asked. Not that talk would make her forget the night's horror, but at least it gave her something else to think about for a while.

Brynn was funny, understanding, and all things wonderful. That on top of being the most beautiful man in the world. He was simply perfect.

Then why did her thoughts keep drifting to Mr. Not-So-Perfect? Eric the Deserter. He was probably sound asleep, sprawled across that magnificent bed. Sprawled *naked* across that bed? Hmm.

"Wow, I didn't realize how late it was." Brynn glanced at his watch and then stood. "It was so great to find someone who liked talking about sci-fi movies, I lost track of the time. If you think you'll be okay, I'll let you get some sleep." He looked nervous as he strode to the door.

Donna frowned. What was this all about? She watched him reach for the doorknob and pull. Nothing. He yanked again, this time harder. Still nothing. He turned desperate eyes toward Donna.

"Help me get the freakin' door open." All of his surface

charm had disappeared, and panic seemed to be his emotion of choice.

The door wasn't locked, so it must just be stuck. Even as she added her weight to the effort, reason told her if the door was stuck, Brynn could've jerked it open with one pull. They both yanked together. The door stayed shut.

Donna turned toward the phone. "I'll call the switchboard and have someone come up to get this door open."

"Never mind. It's too late." His voice had changed, become deeper, more sensual.

"Huh?" Surprised, she looked at him.

Ohmigod, what was happening? Right in front of her he was changing. Not like Taurin, but just as scary. He'd pulled the leather strip loose that held his hair back, and it flowed around his face, a shining temptation for some woman to thread her fingers through its silky strands. His face was the same yet different. The gold in his eyes seemed almost to glow, but that had to be her imagination. They were heavy-lidded with sexual invitation, and she *wasn't* imagining that. His lips looked fuller, eager to taste a woman's body. He caught his lower lip between his teeth and then released it. Instinctively she knew she was watching a sexual animal being born. And she was locked in the room with him. *Eric!*

Even as he ripped his shirt off, he stalked her. Hard muscle rippled beneath golden skin. She backed against the door and prepared to scream her lungs out.

"Take my body. Use it any way you want. Tell me what makes you scream with pleasure, and I'll do it." Lips slightly parted, he enticed, promised.

Even scared and wishing for Eric, she felt Brynn's erotic pull. And rejected it. Since he hadn't leaped on her and dragged her onto the bed, she decided against the scream. She was about to make a dash for her phone when she looked directly into his eyes.

And saw pain and self-disgust there. She mentally shook her head to clear it, but when she looked again she saw the same emotions. What was going on? She drew in a deep calming breath. "I don't want your body, Brynn."

That quickly, the sexual creature was gone. Brynn picked up the leather tie for his hair, stuck it in his pocket, and then pulled on his shirt with shaking fingers. He didn't meet her gaze. Without a word he turned toward the door.

"Oh no you don't." Donna put her hand on his shoulder, and he actually flinched. Something was awfully wrong here. "Sit down and tell me what just happened."

Brynn hesitated and then sat on the chair next to the plants. "Are you going to add this to your tales of the bizarre you'll use to entertain your listeners tonight?" He sounded like he might choke on his bitterness.

Donna slumped onto the floor next to his chair. She rubbed eyes burning from exhaustion. "No. I don't barter in people's pain. But I'd like to understand."

He nodded. "Eric wouldn't want me to tell you, but I figure since you already saw a vampire change in the parking lot, my story won't send you screaming from the castle any faster."

She remained silent, giving him space to tell her in his own time.

"Specifics? I'm a five-hundred-year-old demon of sensual desire." He paused, probably waiting for her to race for the door and do some more tugging and yanking. "I don't know who created me, but I do know my purpose. If I stay more than one hour with the same woman, I have to offer her my body. If I try to resist the compulsion, I suffer excruciating pain. And yes, through the centuries I've tried every way I can think to escape." He shrugged. "There is no escape."

Demon? Five hundred years old? Maybe this was a little more specific than she wanted to get. Okay, she'd survived a ticked-off vampire, so she could deal with a demon of sensual desire. She drew in a deep, calming breath.

"No offense, but your delivery's a little abrupt. Most women would have the same reaction I did." Even as she said it, she wasn't sure she believed it.

His glance ridiculed her naïveté. "I can't resist the compulsion, but nothing can force me to turn my 'delivery' into a seduction. I purposely make the whole thing as sleazy as I can. But you'd be surprised how many women accept." He looked away. "I hate it."

Donna believed him. What she'd seen in his eyes was real, and the agony she heard in his voice was just as sincere. She placed her hand on his knee in compassion. "Your brothers, are they all—"

He shook his head and smiled weakly. "We're not brothers, Donna. We're—"

Brynn got no further, because suddenly the door crashed open and Eric stood there, feet and chest bare, his eyes blazing as they shifted from Brynn to Donna's hand which still rested on Brynn's knee.

"What the hell? When was the last time you looked at your watch, Brynn?" He stepped into the room and then paused. "I mean, Donna needs her sleep and . . ." He stared at Brynn. "Did you ask her?" His voice bristled with barely contained violence.

Brynn stood. "Yeah, I did."

Eric looked torn. His expression said he wanted to rip Brynn apart verbally and physically but was afraid to say too much in front of Donna. "Did she take you up on it?"

"No." Brynn walked past Eric and paused in the doorway. "The door wouldn't open. Both of us tried. How did you get it open?"

Donna watched the tension drain from Eric. He shrugged. "It was unlocked and I just walked in. Wait. The Siamese cat was sitting beside the door when I got off the elevator. She didn't say anything, just walked away. You don't think . . . ?"

"I think she purposely locked us in here." Donna would cheerfully end one of Asima's nine lives, but something good had come from the experience. She'd found out the truth about Brynn, and indirectly, more about Eric.

"I told Donna what I am, Eric. She promised not to tell her listeners, and I trust her." He stepped into the hallway and closed the door behind him.

Eric stood in the middle of her room—big, beautiful,

and still glowering. "Don't let me stop you from packing. I thought I could convince you to stay by pointing out that this was a once-in-a-lifetime opportunity to interact with nonhuman entities. But I have to admit you've had a few too many interactions. I don't blame you."

Eric felt bad about her leaving. Bad? Just a few days ago he would've hired a band to celebrate the event. Just a few days ago all he would've worried about was what she intended to say on her show. Now? He was interested. But he couldn't deny she might be in danger. If she went back to New York, she'd be safe. A lot safer than if she stayed here, because even with all their precautions in place, you could never predict what a vampire like Taurin would do.

Donna padded to her bed on bare feet. Sitting on the edge, she rubbed the back of her neck. "No packing now. I need sleep. When I get up I'll think about it. And I'll have lots and lots of questions, Eric whoever-you-are." She frowned. "Brynn said something about you guys not really being brothers. Good thing, because if you *were* his brother, that would make you very old and very . . . different, too. I've had all the *different* I can take for one week." She made a shooing motion toward the door. "Now go away so I can crash."

"I don't shoo, Donna." Moving over to the other side of her bed, he unbuttoned his jeans and slid them off. He hadn't put briefs on before coming up here.

Her gasp was gratifying, but he was too groggy to enjoy it. Now that his adrenaline rush had worn off, his natural need to sleep was asserting itself. "I've decided you're the castle's weak link."

"Weak link? And why are you naked?" She sounded a little breathless.

"Brynn, Conall, Holgarth, and I can all take care of ourselves. You're high profile." *And Taurin knows I'm interested.* "Taurin might decide it would be easy to snatch you, and use you as bait." He turned to face her.

"You still haven't told me why you're naked."

She surprised him. He'd expected her to turn red and

keep her gaze fixed on his face. She didn't. Sliding her gaze over his chest and stomach, she bypassed the body part that was really interested in her, to study his thighs and legs.

"If you're talking to me, my face is up here." Even through the familiar lethargy, with his arms and legs lead weights, and his eyelids drooping lower and lower, she stirred him.

Then she raised her gaze to his sex and focused. "Mmm. I figured if you got naked, you wanted me to look. I looked. Very nice. Now you can leave." She climbed beneath the covers and reached for the switch on her lamp. "Please lock the door on your way out."

"Sorry. Can't do." He pulled the heavy drapes across the arrow slit. "I'm staying here to make sure nothing happens to you before you leave." *And I'm placing a mind shield over your door.* "If you wake up before me, get me up, too. It won't be easy, but keep trying until I wake up." If he was lucky, she'd sleep until at least three. She'd probably get all panicky when she couldn't wake him right away, but there was nothing he could do to change that. He just hoped she didn't try to leave the room and realize she couldn't. Eric returned to the bed and slid under the covers.

He felt her stiffen beside him. "Get out of my bed."

"No." Eric could feel himself drifting.

"I'm in control now. I don't need you." Instead of edging away from him, she moved closer.

"How do you need me? Let me count the ways." He could feel her heat, smell her warm woman scent, and if deep sleep weren't beckoning, he'd show her the many meanings of need.

"Paraphrasing Browning? I'm impressed. You're not just a body and a pretty face." Closer, and still closer.

"Oh, I'm much, much more." She had no idea.

Donna was so close that her breath whispered across the back of his neck. "I snore. I walk in my sleep. I talk in my sleep. And I'm very territorial about my bed. I could kick you out in the middle of the night. You never know what sensitive body part my tootsies might connect with, either."

"Dangerous woman. Sexy."

An irritated huff, and then silence.

"Sleep tight. And make sure you wake me gently. I'm easily aroused when I first wake up. Any sudden move by you could be . . . dangerous." This would be a rarity. He tried never to wake beside a lover. Either he or she left right after sex. No time for either one to form a connection. Of course, Donna wasn't a lover. Yet. If she was smart, she'd get out of Dodge by sundown.

"Right. I bet you're a real animal in bed." She sounded half serious.

"Who knows. You've met every other damn thing in this castle." As sleep slid over him, he decided that maybe it wasn't wise to put ideas in her head.

"Don't you dare fall asleep in my bed."

He slept.

8

Donna sat cross-legged on her bed watching Eric sleep. She glanced at her clock. Three-thirty. Talk about sleeping like the dead. He hadn't even twitched since she'd woken an hour ago.

He hadn't turned over once as she talked to her brother, who'd patiently tried to convince her that he didn't need a cruise to renew his love for Carol, that happiness with the one he loved wasn't contingent on being in a certain place. Donna didn't get it. Hypothetically speaking, if she cared for Eric, wouldn't her caring bloom more easily under the warming rays on some exotic beach than in the Castle of Dark Screams? Well, yeah. Made sense. Didn't it?

Eric hadn't even moved restlessly as she talked to Trish. Amazing since she didn't seem able to have a simple conversation with her sister anymore without raising her voice. Trish had announced she was marrying her latest loser no matter what Donna said. Her sister's last accusation had really hurt. Trish had said that at least she had the courage to keep searching for love, while Donna didn't have the guts to even try. Low blow. Donna didn't think it made sense to take chances on something as important as love.

Look at Mom. Donna didn't remember her parents ever arguing about anything. Every day of her childhood had been serene, unchanging. *Boring?*

What to do? Should she pick a man who shared all her interests, someone calm and reliable like Dad? Or should she go with Trish's theory on love—choose a hottie who turns you into a lust-bunny, and to hell with things like character and stability? How could she ever allow herself to love a man when she didn't know the *right* answer? Neither path had worked for Mom or Trish.

"So what do you think?" she asked Sleeping Gorgeous next to her.

Lust was looking pretty good right now. Eric had kicked the sheet off him while he slept, and that, more than a need to call her family, had kept her from waking him. Scenery this good only came by a few times in a lifetime.

"I agree. And the love thing? Personally, I've never been in love, but I've had centuries to observe. You don't analyze love, you just accept it." As usual, Asima sounded like she had the defining opinion, and all other opinions were nonsense.

"Where?" Donna tore her gaze from Eric to look around the room. She spotted Asima sitting on the floor beside Sweetie Pie. Or was it Jessica? "How'd you get in here?"

Asima did the equivalent of a cat shrug. "How *isn't important.* Why *is the essential. I'm here to wrest you from Lola's crass clutches."* She padded over to the bed and leaped onto the foot, where she crouched staring at Eric. *"He's enough to turn even you into a sensual dynamo."*

Donna frowned. Sounded like an insult to her. "Sensual dynamo isn't at the top of my priority list right now. Living till the end of the week has edged it out."

"Don't worry, you'll survive just fine. Eric has layers of power Taurin couldn't begin to equal. Let's get back to what we can do to wow Body Beautiful here when he wakes up." She sidled closer to Eric.

"Layers of power? What's that supposed to mean? No, don't tell me." She needed time to let all the weirdness she'd experienced this week soak in before making any new discoveries. Fine, so that was a lie. She wanted *Eric* to reveal what needed revealing. "And I can take care of my own sex life." Sort of.

"Don't be shy about admitting your sexual inadequacies. That's why I'm here. To help. Now, let's look at the prize, shall we?" She moved even closer to Eric. *"I love those silky strands of black hair spread all over his pillow, and that hard but sensual male face. Can't you imagine tangling your fingers in his hair and pressing your mouth to his? Think how that mouth will feel, still soft from sleep. And did you ever see such thick dark lashes on a man? He'll lift his lids and look at you out of those hot blue eyes. He'll murmur your name as he stretches his arms above his head and arches his back like some lithe jungle cat—"*

"Whoa. Cease and desist." Donna could see where Asima was going. "I want a brief explanation of why you're here, and then I want you to leave. Oh, and please stay out of my mind."

Asima widened her cat eyes. *"How can I help you if I can't look into your mind? Your mind is a treasure to me. But I know you're anxious to kiss your sleeping prince awake, so I'll make it short."*

Sleeping prince? Donna did some mental eye rolls.

"I saw the fright-mistress sleepwear that Lola gave you. Her bad taste never ceases to, well, scare me, actually. Don't wear it. I've left the perfect nightie hanging in your closet. Go take a look." Asima waited while Donna slid off the bed and looked in the closet.

What could she say? White. The nightgown was long, flowing, and made her want to run barefoot in the night away from some dark and tortured hero who lived in his dark and decrepit ruin. "It's . . . white."

"It's virginal. Men are crazy about virgins. It's the whole 'to go where no man has gone before' syndrome." If Asima got any closer to Eric, she could sit on the body part

of her choosing. And Donna had no doubt which body part that would be. *"I hope you appreciate what you have lying here all unwrapped. If not, I wouldn't mind changing into my human form for a night. I've accumulated lots of vacation time."*

Human form? Asima was a shape-shifter? Donna felt like stuffing her fist into her mouth to hold back the hysterical screams. She forced herself to breathe in and out, in and out. Hyperventilating would solve nothing. Okay, she was semicalm again. Trying to hold logic at bay for the moment, she looked at the bottom line. A ghost and a shape-shifter were manipulating her sex life. To make both of them happy, she'd have to become the Virgin Dominatrix Donna. Hey, no problem. "It's not all about sex, Asima."

"Sure it is." She put one exploratory paw on Eric's bare thigh. *"Of course, I have my day job, but this is my hobby. Lola? She's made a career out of it. Sex drives the world. Never doubt it. Do you think Eric would mind if I walked on his body, sort of got a feel for him? Hmm?"*

Sheesh. "I think it'd upset him."

Asima made a moue of disappointment. *"I'm leaving you some lavender. It's over on your bureau. Consider it a safeguard against evil. Oh, and your cell phone is on the bureau, too. I found it in the parking lot."*

Donna swallowed hard. Why had Asima been out in the parking lot, and what did she know about what had happened there? Up till this moment, Donna had tried not to think about why Eric was sleeping in her bed. She couldn't ignore it any longer. Taurin. "Thanks. I won't keep you from whatever else it is you do here." Secrets. Was there anyone in this castle besides her who didn't have them? Okay, maybe Brynn didn't. He'd laid everything out last night.

Asima leaped from the bed and padded to the door. She stared at the door and it swung open. *"Oh, I want you to hear something before I leave. No one else in the castle shares my love of opera."*

The sound of some operatic aria filled the room. Asima must have the same invisible CD player as Lola.

"It always brings tears to my eyes, and I feel the urge to break into song." So she did. Of course, since Asima was a cat with a cat's lungs, she sounded like a cat. A cat who was being murdered slowly and painfully.

Asima was right. The music was bringing tears to Donna's eyes, too. Would it be rude to stick her fingers in her ears?

"What the hell is that god-awful screeching?" Eric almost fell out of bed. And as he rubbed his eyes in an attempt to wake up completely, he looked wildly around the room. When he spotted Asima, he narrowed his gaze on her.

Asima's song ended in mid-screech. *"He's beautiful, but has absolutely no musical taste."* With an offended twitch of her whiskers, she padded out the door.

"She walked out the door." He seemed puzzled by that.

"Uh, yeah. That's how people usually leave a room." Donna was getting a rear view at the moment. Strong muscular back tapering down to lean hips and an incredible ass. Not a behind or buns. Those were weak, ineffectual descriptions. What she was looking at were tight and tantalizing, symbolizing strength but with something substantial enough for a woman to grab as she guided him . . . Anyway, *incredibleass,* two words said as one, was the only description that did them justice.

Eric walked over to the open door, stared at it in the same way Asima had, and then closed it.

"Why'd you stare at the door before you closed it? Asima did the same thing before she left." For a moment, Asima's comment about Eric's layers of power slid across her mind.

He shrugged. "It doesn't look like it, but the castle has lots of high-tech stuff. I was just deactivating a protective power grid I put across the door last night. I wonder how Asima got through it."

Yeah, like she was buying that. "So where's the remote

control? You didn't flip any switch that I could see." Let him wiggle out of that.

"In my pocket?" His smile was warm and self-deprecating, meant to call her attention to his bare body sans pockets. And once her gaze was focused on his naked splendor, she was supposed to forget her original question. "Why don't you call down for something to eat while I take a cold shower to wake me up. And the castle supplies an extra toothbrush for emergencies. I guess I qualify as an emergency." He walked into the bathroom, leaving her alone with Sweetie Pie and Jessica.

She sighed. She'd let him get away with the power-grid lie for the moment because Asima had worn her out. "Well, girls, there's no better pick-me-up in the morning than a naked hunk. Do you think?" Evidently, they thought it was all good, because Donna could swear their leaves looked perkier. "Shame on you. You're nothing but dirty old viney voyeurs." She grinned at them. Her leafy friends and she had something in common.

To distract her mind from creating a shower scene in living color and Dolby Surround sound, she called down for a late, late breakfast. By the time Eric finished his shower and emerged from the bathroom with his jeans on, she'd finished her orange juice and was starting on her cereal. Donna paused in the act of lifting her spoon to her mouth. She remembered. No underwear. Woo-hoo.

"I was going to order something for you, but I decided you'd probably want to order for yourself." She sipped her coffee and looked at him over the edge of her cup. "It's pretty dark in here. Why don't you pull back the drapes?

"That's okay. I'll pick up something after I leave. And I like the dark." His voice was a low and delicious suggestion of things that flourished in darkness. He returned to the bed and propped himself up beside her. "Do you always eat in bed?"

"When I want to feel decadent." She grinned at him. "And what's more decadent than sharing a bed with a man who doesn't wear underwear. It might just be the highlight of my whole week." Donna frowned. "Other than Lola, Asima, Brynn, and Taurin."

"We need to talk." He leaned over to slide a strand of hair away from her face and then smoothed his fingers lightly along her jawline. "Brynn, Conall, and I can protect you during your show, but until then you need to stay close to me."

"Why? Vampires don't rise until sunset, do they?" She took a bite of her toast that turned her lips into buttery temptation.

This one has risen way before sunset. Eric tried to convince his cock that life would go on even if his impressive erection found no admirers. His cock didn't think so.

"Not usually, but that wouldn't keep Taurin from hiring someone to do his dirty work." Eric hoped he wasn't reading the other vampire wrong. But Donna seemed the most logical target. If Taurin wanted to attack Eric while he was away from the castle, he'd have plenty of opportunities. Eric didn't intend to hide from Taurin. But Taurin would want to recreate the same scenario that ended in his brother's supposed death. It would appeal to Taurin's twisted sense of justice.

Donna took a peach from her tray and then set the tray on her bedside table. She studied the peach. "How long ago did his brother die?"

He didn't need to slip into her mind to sense the beginnings of suspicion. Eric didn't blame her. He could tell her the truth, but then what? She'd either curl her lip in disgust, or terror would fill her eyes. He wasn't ready to see either reaction, and so he lied. "Ten years ago."

Donna nodded as she met his gaze. "How did it happen?"

Eric wouldn't chance another lie, because each lie he told might trip him up later. "Look, can we talk about something else? That was one of the more upsetting episodes in my life."

Her eyes warmed with sympathy. "Sure." Her gaze slid over his chest and stomach. "If Brynn is really a demon of sensual desire, and you guys aren't brothers, then what does that make you and Conall?"

There it was, the direct question. "Nothing you need to worry about right now, Donna." He rubbed his palm across his chest to dispel the warmth of her gaze where it touched his pecs and nipples. If just her glance was lethal, he might go up in flames if she touched him there with her fingers.

She speared him with an intent stare, and he was afraid she might push it. Then she nodded. But her expression said she'd demand an answer later. "I've decided to stay for the week. Now that I've calmed down, I realize this whole castle experience is too amazing to miss. And my boss wouldn't be understanding if I abandoned the show and ran back to New York claiming I was chased out of town by a vampire." Her gaze slid away from him again. "Besides, I trust you to keep me safe."

Yes. He didn't understand why her decision and her trust made him so happy. Maybe it was only certain body parts that felt the joy. No, the joy seemed pretty widespread. "We'll keep you safe." *I'll keep you safe.*

Her expression turned musing. "I've asked myself why I'm not having a screaming fit of hysterics." She smiled. "Maybe I expect someone to stand up at the end of the week and yell, 'Gotcha!' I don't think the reality has really sunk in yet, and when it does I don't know what I'll do or how I'll feel."

Eric didn't know, either. He just hoped the sinking-in thing didn't happen right after she found out he was a vampire. *Okay, back up.* From the moment he heard she was bringing her program to the castle, he'd been sure of only one thing—Donna couldn't find out he was a vampire. It would spell the end of what Brynn, Conall, and he had together here. Well, she knew about Brynn, and life as they knew it hadn't ended.

"Maybe I'll take a week off to get my head together." She bit into the peach she'd ordered, and he watched, mesmerized, as a drop of juice clung to her bottom lip.

God, he was only human—or not—and there were

some temptations no man could resist. He leaned over and slid his finger across that full luscious lip and then slowly licked the juice from his finger. Peach juice wasn't his beverage of choice, but it was the symbolism of the act that counted.

"Why'd you wipe my lip with your finger? I had my napkin. . . ." Her gazed darkened with sensual awareness as she watched him lick the juice from his finger. Yeah, she got the symbolism.

"Because I figured if I slid my tongue across your lip, you might bite it. Hey, I'm not a morning person, so I know how vicious morning-haters can get. Not that it's morning, but for me"—he shrugged—"it's morning." No doubt about it, his focus was shifting where Donna was concerned. He wasn't worrying as much as he should about Brynn and Conall. He was becoming an all-about-me kind of guy.

Her lips tipped up in the beginnings of a smile. Amazing how any movement of her lips fascinated him.

"Okay, what you're saying is that if I stroked your lips with my tongue right now, you'd bite me." She was openly laughing at him now.

"Absolutely." She had no idea.

"Oh." She had that cute line between her eyes, the one she got when she didn't know what to say.

Cute line? Give me a break. This was getting serious. Not only was he allowing for the possibility that she might find out how much he really enjoyed biting, but he was also worried if she could bond with a bloodsucking fiend. For someone who'd worked hard to keep from getting involved with humans and their emotions, he was caring about Donna's feelings way too much.

Enough soul-searching, though. Right now he wanted to touch her again. His sexual need, like his other craving, was a surging compulsion that couldn't be allowed to run loose. But he had no problem with taking it out on a leash.

"You know, Asima mentioned that you had layers of power. What did she mean?" Donna took another bite from her peach, but this time she quickly licked her lips free of juice.

Too bad. He could get used to her peach-flavored lips. "It depends on what kind of powers Asima had in mind." He deliberately let her see the flare of sexual hunger in his eyes.

The truth? Members of his clan accumulated power as they aged. Eric had chosen to make himself invulnerable to attack. He had superhuman strength, preternatural speed, the ability to become invisible, power to call the elements to himself, and if pressed, he could shape-shift. And he could mess with human minds with the best of them.

Eric shrugged. "Sorry to disappoint you, but I won't be giving Spiderman competition anytime soon." Oh, and his power to lie straight-faced was legendary.

"Okay, what about weaknesses? Come on, tell." She smiled as she dropped the peach stone onto her tray and wiped her sticky fingers on her napkin.

Great. A question he could answer. "Candy. I love sweets." When he'd grown powerful enough to feel safe from enemies—human or otherwise—he'd decided to indulge himself. He'd used his accumulated power to change his system enough to allow him to enjoy candy. No other food, just candy. From the first time he'd smelled the rich sweet scent of chocolate, he'd known that candy would be his one human weakness.

"That's it? Candy?" Donna made a face at him. "What a disappointment. You don't look like a man who only has one weakness. You look like a man who has lots of weaknesses for the dark and dangerous side of life." She cocked her head to get a better perspective on him. "But then, maybe you're lying. Who knows?"

"Maybe." He was lying. Eric had just realized he had a second weakness—Donna Nolan. Over the centuries he'd had sex with lots of women and enjoyed all of them. But he'd never spent the night with a woman twice, because it made him vulnerable.

He could defeat challenges by other powerful entities as

long he remained focused, without distractions. Once he began thinking more about the woman in his bed than the dangers that lurked without, he opened himself to destruction. His body might be able to regenerate and repair mortal wounds, but it was pretty tough to regenerate a head.

And yet, Eric sensed he could be in danger of losing his head over Donna, figuratively and literally. No, he was smarter than that. He'd enjoy her, give her pleasure, and wave goodbye when she left on Saturday.

He watched as Donna climbed from the bed. She went into the bathroom and came out a few seconds later with a glass of water that she poured into Sweetie Pie's pot. She repeated the process for Jessica.

She knelt down to study the plants. "Do you think they need plant food? When they saw you naked they perked up a little, but I don't see any new leaf growth. And the bottom leaves are starting to droop again. I don't think the water I gave them has many nutrients. Should I get them bottled water?"

Eric grinned. She was making it way too easy for him. He rose from the bed and knelt down beside her. "You *know* what they need." From force of habit, he started to touch her mind with an image of what they would share together, and then stopped. No image. No compulsion. When it happened, he wanted to know it came completely from her. "I want to make love with you, Donna."

Eric winced. He sounded like Brynn, a lot blunter than his normal approach. Usually he crept up on what he wanted with slow seduction and light sexy banter to convince the object of his interest that he wasn't dangerous. He smiled. A lie, but all in a good cause. Today, slow seduction would take too much time, and he was too eager.

There was a little self-disgust mixed into his wince. The phrase *make love* wasn't what he meant at all. He wanted to have sex with her. Love wasn't part of the equation. Throughout the centuries he'd always told women he wanted to make love with them because that's what they wanted to hear, but the lie had never bothered him until now.

She turned her attention from Sweetie Pie to him. Her expression gave nothing away, but he expected the usual reaction. First shock, then an admission that maybe she could be interested, followed closely by an unspoken challenge to convince her.

"I want that, too." Her smile was self-deprecating. "My sister, Trish, could tell you that instant lust is way out of character for me, but she'd be applauding wildly."

Her answer surprised Eric, and his response amazed him even more. His senses engulfed him, washing away the control that had allowed him to survive for eight hundred years. The scent of peach clung to her body, and he could imagine the smooth slide of her skin beneath his fingers, his mouth. His enhanced hearing noted the soft sound of her breathing, the subtle flow of her life force, and he fought back his need to change.

The sexual beast that lived in all vampires howled its demands. His desire hit him, hot and insistent, along with his dark hunger. A hunger he'd better control if he didn't want her on the first plane out of Hobby Airport.

Tell her the truth. Maybe she'll accept you. Nope, it wasn't happening. Even if she was okay with him as vampire, she wouldn't want his body or his teeth. Been there, done that.

So much for inner discourse. If he didn't touch her right now, his fingers would fall off along with a very important body part. Still kneeling in front of the plants, he pulled her into his embrace.

"I can't make it to the bed, so don't even suggest it." Lowering his head, he traced her lower lip with his tongue. "You taste of buttered toast and peach juice." He'd never had buttered toast in his life, but maybe when he'd accumulated enough power, he'd add it to his short list of human weaknesses.

Leaning into him, she tangled her fingers in his hair and pulled him closer. "Someone I know suggested I do this. It works for me."

The first time he'd taken her mouth, he'd surprised her.

This time she was armed and dangerous. Donna met his kiss with all the fervor she'd been storing up for this moment. The mind-blowing part? She hadn't realized until now that she'd been storing up anything.

Parting her lips, she invited him in. But as his tongue touched hers, she gleefully sprang her trap. She stroked and teased his tongue, tasting her toothpaste and his passion.

"You're a wicked woman, talk-show lady." His soft laughter did shivery things to her as he broke their kiss and trailed a path of pleasure with his lips over her jaw and down her neck.

"I try. I really try." She knew she sounded breathless.

He'd paused at her throat to trace a circular pattern of yummy heat with his tongue right where her pulse pounded out her excitement.

A shudder rippled through him as he leaned away from her. He looked . . . different. His eyes had darkened, his mouth looked fuller, more tempting. If she had to describe him, she'd say he looked untamed and barely under control. She clenched her thighs around the visual of what would happen if his control snapped.

She'd just bet that her own eyes were darkening, too, as she reached out to stroke the warm skin of his chest. "You have a beautiful chest. I've lusted after it since last night." She ran her fingertip across each of his nipples. "Smooth warm skin over hard muscle. Very erotic." She glided her hand across his sculpted pecs and then over his ridged stomach. "With so many interesting topographical features."

"And you haven't even reached the mountain region." Some of his intensity of a few moments ago seemed to have eased. "And I know *your* chest intimately even though I haven't seen it yet. I do great creative imaging." His banter sounded light and careless, but his gaze said he was working hard to control his growl-and-pounce instinct.

Which gave her an immediate shot of adrenaline. She was teasing the beast, and one wrong word would loose it.

Donna searched her database of wrong words. Once she found it, she'd use it, because her body's mob mentality was clamoring for a sexual experience short on foreplay and long on orgasmic ecstasy. You didn't mess with a mob.

She reached for his jeans. Surprised, she realized her hand was shaking as she fumbled with the buttons. "Clothes just ruin the artistic flow of the body's symmetry for me." And they made it a lot harder for her to jump his bones. She managed to work his jeans partway down his hips before shortness of breath due to a sudden hormonal surge forced her to hand the rest of the job over to him.

His smile was hot and needy. "I guess my reasoning is a lot more basic. Clothes get in the way when I want to touch all the spots that'll make you scream with pleasure." Clasping the edges of her nightshirt, he slid it over her head. And then he stared at her, his gaze sliding the length of her body, leaving a path of molten possession. "You're beautiful and you're mine until our pleasure ends." His smile was more a baring of teeth to reinforce the word *mine*.

Usually, she'd verbally carve out the heart of any alpha male foolish enough to claim possession, but right now, with this man, it felt kind of right. "I don't scream." The truth. She wasn't a screamer. Donna enjoyed sex, but she enjoyed it quietly, with a few murmurs of appreciation for her partner. Funny thing was, she felt a strange need to whimper. Whimper? How stupid was that?

"Maybe you never had anything to scream about." He was all arrogant male.

She sort of liked that about him. Her New York lovers had all been sensitive caring men. They'd let her lead. Maybe it was time for someone who challenged her. Donna smiled at the possibilities. Maybe she'd make *him* scream.

While she was busy considering the power structure of their sexual play, Eric took action. In one smooth powerful motion, he rocked back until he lay flat on the floor and at the same time grasped her hips to lift her on top of him. It took her a moment to shift her thoughts from amazement at his strength to a realization that her knees straddled his hips, and her bare bottom was planted firmly on his power center.

"A lesson on tops and bottoms. And who's *really* in control." His smile was a wicked promise that his lesson would be accompanied by plenty of hands-on opportunities.

"I wasn't thinking about control." She *was* thinking about control. And she was honest enough to admit those thoughts shouldn't have any part in her enjoyment of sex with Eric. But how did she shut down the habit of a lifetime, get rid of thoughts that were second nature to her?

"I'll get rid of the thoughts for you." He reached up to touch her nipples with the tips of his fingers and then rolled them between his thumbs and index fingers.

Ignoring her gasp at the shock of sensation, he lifted his hips to press his erection hard between her legs. "Being on top doesn't automatically mean you're in charge, talk-show lady. Right now the pleasure starts on the bottom." His voice was cool certainty. "And I'll be in charge of the pleasure-giving today. Screaming is encouraged."

Widening her eyes, Donna revved up her vocal cords to let him have it. Of all the arrogant . . . "First off, stay out of my mind." As soon as she could think straight, she'd have to find out how he did that. "And second, don't tell me . . ."

His smile was superior, smug, and beautiful. He didn't say anything, but simply put his finger over her lips. She tried on her own superior smile as she parted her lips and closed them over his finger. His gaze darkened.

She bit his finger.

"Well, well." His eyes turned predatory. Something dangerous moved in the dark blue depths.

She released his finger. There. She'd stated her opinion. Donna could see the imprint of her teeth on his finger. She hoped she hadn't overstated it.

"No woman has ever bitten me." His soft laughter suggested it had been a brave though foolish gesture. "It excites me."

Suddenly he sat up and lifted her off his lap. Damn, she wished he didn't make all this lifting and moving seem so effortless. Before she could voice her objection, he placed her flat on her stomach. "Hey, what're you doing?" The rug tickling her nose didn't have an answer.

"Relax." His voice mesmerized her and promised that relaxing would be a good thing. Had she ever heard a voice like his? Deep, reaching inside her and soothing her from the inside out. "Let your senses live." He nudged her legs apart and knelt between them. Then he began a slow deep massage starting at her shoulders. "Open yourself to my touch and to the touch of all that surrounds you." His voice was a seductive whisper, a brush of warmth next to her ear.

His magic fingers moved lower on her back, kneading the tightness from her muscles even as her lower body parts anticipated his arrival with drunken revelry.

Touch. Suddenly she was aware on a level she'd never experienced before. She could feel every strand of fiber in the rug beneath her cheek, every nuance of his fingers as they touched her body, even the slide of air over her bare body.

"Close your eyes. Listen, smell, taste." He smoothed his fingers over the base of her spine and she felt the message in her brain as an instant flash of pure hot red. "Open yourself to what I offer, to the seduction of your senses." His voice seemed merely a murmur in her mind, but she couldn't focus her attention long enough to think about that possibility.

Normally, Donna would've analyzed each of his directions for motive and do-ability. But she was into the moment. She closed her eyes.

The window of Donna's mind looked out on a land she'd never seen, and the clarity and brilliance of what she saw drew a gasp from her—hills, a lake, and an ancient castle that crouched on a small island in the lake. Only a stone footbridge connected the island to the mainland. The shades of green, purple, and blue almost hurt her eyes. Where was she?

She forgot to worry about her location as all her other senses came alive. The scents of damp earth, green growing things, water, and the essence of life itself. Sounds of ripples flowing onto the shore, the wind sighing through branches, the scurry of small animals, and someone talking deep within the castle. And taste was a part of the whole. She wrinkled her nose at the brown bitterness of the argument taking place in the castle. How could anger have a color and taste? She felt as though she'd experienced her whole life through a fogged-up window, and now she'd rubbed a clear spot to look through. What she saw was a reality no longer fuzzy but sharply focused. Donna wanted to keep rubbing more and more of the window clear until there was nothing between her and what *was*.

"Very good." Eric had moved down to her buttocks. He kneaded and stroked them.

With her enhanced senses she could hear the slide of his fingers over her skin, taste his sexual arousal, and feel the sensual energy surrounding them spreading out in waves.

And when he kissed a path down her spine and then traced a heart on one cheek with his tongue, her senses celebrated the event as a never-ending river of deep, smooth, rich chocolate. Her eyes popped open. *Chocolate?*

His husky laughter was pure Godiva. "We have something in common. There are few things on earth as erotically symbolic as chocolate. That's why I chose . . ." He'd evidently thought better of what he'd been about to say.

She didn't have time to think about things left unsaid, because Eric suddenly eased her onto her back. Whoa. She was *not* a lump of bread dough to be rolled and kneaded to just the right consistency. She'd discuss this arbitrary repositioning of her body without her prior consent later. Right now he still knelt between her open thighs and demanded all her attention.

"Look at me, Donna." His dark tangle of hair framed his face and lay across his bare shoulders. His strong muscular body blocked out what had been and what might be, leaving only *him*. His sex rose thick and hard. While he'd been encouraging her to relax, he'd been going in the opposite direction.

She lifted her gaze to his face and saw things she hadn't noticed before. The gleaming intensity in his eyes with their layers of thoughts and emotions she imagined led back to his very soul. An old soul, her instinct whispered. The smooth perfection of his face. No age lines, no laugh lines, nothing. His face was a contradiction.

"Don't look *that* closely." His smile focused her attention on his mouth, his lips, his teeth.

His teeth. There was something different about his teeth. But before she had a chance to investigate that thought, he covered her mouth with his.

It was a long drugging kiss, so powerful because of her enhanced senses that she almost wanted to cry. The rich erotic taste of him added to the moist heat of his mouth awakened something primitive in her.

As he kissed her neck, her breasts, and then closed his lips around each nipple and teased it to a hard nub with his tongue, she raked her fingers through his hair and gripped his shoulders with clawed fingers.

Arching her back, she moaned her pleasure as he gripped her bottom and slid his tongue over her stomach. She lifted her hips and spread her legs wider, inviting him in even as something important tried to make itself heard over the drumroll of spiraling sexual excitement.

Eric had evidently reached his own threshold of endurance, because with a muttered oath he lifted her hips, and she felt the nudge of his sex between her legs. She was open, moist, and her body was clenching in delicious anticipation.

Protection. The important word had fought its way into shouting distance. Nooooo! "You don't have—"

"Where's the damn cookie jar?"

"Closet." If he didn't get it fast, she'd implode.

Donna blinked. She must be hallucinating, because no man could've gotten to the closet and back that fast. In fact, she didn't even remember seeing him move. But he must've, because he was rolling the condom over his erection.

Finished, he once again lifted her to meet his thrust. He entered her in one smooth motion that drew a cry of pleasure from her. Eric gave her no time to recover. As she wrapped her legs around him, he withdrew and plunged deeper, filling her, and triggering something else. . . .

Even as she moaned her aroused delight at the increasing speed and force of his hot possession, another sensation was intruding. Like a split screen, she experienced both. She felt Eric touch her *there* with his tongue, when she knew his tongue was nowhere near *there.* She opened her eyes to make sure. Nope, he'd thrown back his head and closed his eyes tightly just as she had.

But when she felt him flick the tip of his tongue back and forth across the most sensitive spot in her personal universe, she lost it. Who cared how he was doing it? Her cries at the multiple sensations were suspiciously close to screams.

She was close, so *close,* that she had to anchor herself to the rug with fisted hands so she wouldn't bounce off the ceiling when she came. She was breathing in harsh gasps, and she recognized the sounds she made as throaty growls. He could truthfully claim that he brought out the beast in her.

And then he plunged one more time, so deeply that she knew they'd merged forever. Everything became a blur of pleasure. She reached desperately for that moment of perfect stillness followed by cascading spasms of "Oh. My. God!" Just as she teetered on the knife-edge of her orgasm, Donna thought she felt the slide of teeth over the excruciatingly sensitive flesh between her thighs that was her personal sex-fuse. Her mind didn't pursue the thought because the countdown had begun.

Her orgasm was a spectacular fusion of her senses. As her body clenched around him, color exploded behind her closed lids, wind swirled and roared, and taste and smell melted into all that was sexual.

When she finally became aware of her surroundings again, she was flat on the floor and Eric was sitting back on his heels watching her. Donna lifted a shaking hand to brush a damp strand of hair from her forehead. "What train rolled through here and caught me standing on the tracks?" She tried to quiet her breathing and ignore her still pounding heart. It took her liquefied body a few minutes to harden into human form again.

His smile was filled with sensual triumph. "You screamed."

"No kidding." She narrowed her gaze on him. "Where was that place you put into my mind, and how'd you mess with my head to make me feel your mouth on me? And what about those powers you said you didn't have, huh?" Now that she'd settled back into the real world, the things he'd done would qualify as scary.

"It was my clan's ancestral home in Scotland." His expression said he didn't intend to answer anything else.

"Ah, a man with secrets." Her gaze drifted over his body. "You did what you promised. You gave me spectacular pleasure, and I suspect I screamed loud enough to wake any of Lola's girls from the Cock Crows at Dawn who might still be hanging around." She drew in a deep breath of courage. "*How* did you do it?" *Can I accept your answer when you finally give it?* Because he *would* eventually tell her even if she had to nag him to the gates of Hell.

"Maybe you're already there, talk-show lady." He didn't smile when he said it. "I have to go change. Conall will be waiting outside your door when you get ready to go down to the great hall. I'll meet you there." Without another word, he pulled on his jeans and left.

No postorgasmic chitchat. No assurances that he'd never had better sex. *Insecurity alert!* Maybe he'd had lots of better sex. And why did she even care?

A few minutes later in the shower, she had lots to think about. Eric had promised he'd do it all for her, and he'd delivered. Donna hadn't contributed much of anything to their sexual feast other than a few moans, screams, and wiggles. Next time would be different. She'd be a major contributor.

And as the warm water flowed over her body, she thought about the all-important question: Would there be a next time with a man who could not only read her thoughts, but also generate pictures and physical sensations with his mind? A man who refused to explain himself even though he had to know his secrets might send her scurrying back to New York with enough conjectures to keep her show energized for months?

Her body thought it was a definite yes for a next time. Her heart sort of agreed. Her mind? Her mind thought everyone was nuts. And somewhere Trish was laughing her ass off.

Dressed and ready to venture down to the great hall for another fun-filled night of the bizarre, Donna paused to look at Sweetie Pie and Jessica. Both plants were bursting with newly invigorated vines creeping over the sides of their pots and exploring the floor and wall. They looked . . . happy.

"Me, too, girls. Me, too." She closed the door quietly behind her.

9

He'd screwed up. The danger had smiled at him, and he'd embraced it. Literally. Eric had survived for eight hundred years because he'd never let interest in a woman override his caution. So what had he done a few hours ago? He'd shot Donna a mental picture of his clan's ancestral castle complete with all sensory details. Then he'd compounded his stupidity by giving her the physical sensations of his tongue doing things it couldn't possibly be doing if his cock was already deep inside her. He'd been so hot for her that when she paused for a protection break he'd almost shouted that, damn it, he was a vampire so he couldn't get her pregnant and he couldn't carry a disease. He'd stopped just short of that idiocy.

Did she notice that all this was kind of weird? You bet. And she was going to nail him for an explanation. *Smart. Freakin' brilliant.*

Why after eight centuries had he suddenly suffered a major brain cell meltdown? Ego. He wanted Donna to see him as special. And since he couldn't reveal his more spectacular powers, he'd wanted her to remember him as the guy who gave her the Super O—the orgasm able to leap tall buildings at a single bound.

What about the other reason, hotshot? Yeah, yeah, so he'd wanted to share his own intense sexual sensations with her. Unfortunately, he'd abandoned the lessons learned over his long existence to make it happen. He refused to analyze his sudden interest in sharing.

As he climbed the stairs to the great hall, he thought about damage control. He'd opened Pandora's box and there was no way to stuff everything back into it again. But maybe all wasn't lost. Donna might suspect his mental talents went beyond just reading her mind, but that's all. She didn't suspect he was a vampire.

He paused in the doorway to the great hall and scowled as he realized he was eagerly scanning the room for her. Who was he kidding? Donna didn't have to know he was a vampire to make a juicy meal of the castle and everyone in it. She'd seen enough to whet her appetite for more sensational disclosures, and she'd probably be lobbing questions at Conall and Holgarth next.

Finally Eric spotted her. She was deep in conversation with Holgarth. And judging by her body language, it wasn't a friendly chat.

Eric smiled as she flung her arms in the air. It looked like Holgarth was annoying the hell out of her. He understood the feeling. But he was also smiling because when she lifted her arms, her short pink top rode higher, exposing a strip of smooth skin that triggered recent memories. She'd opted for jeans this afternoon instead of shorts. Too bad. He liked looking at her long bare legs.

"Your tongue is dragging on the floor. You might want to fling it over your shoulder so you don't trip on it." Conall's amused comment startled Eric. How had Conall walked up beside him without Eric noticing?

"You'd better get over there before they start swinging at each other. If I were a betting man, I'd put my money on

Donna." Conall grinned. "She goes for the jugular when she smells blood." He widened his eyes in mock surprise. "Hey, you guys have something in common."

Eric clenched his fists. Conall's teasing shouldn't bother him, but it did. Maybe because it hit too close to home. If she managed to drain the castle of all its secrets, everyone who mattered to him here would have to leave. And he had absolutely *nothing* in common with Donna. "I'm only interested in how we can minimize the damage she'll cause." Okay, so her body interested him, too. So what? He could handle it. He exhaled sharply. No, he couldn't handle it. He hadn't handled much of anything since meeting her. His smile slipped back. Well, maybe he'd handled a few things.

Conall nodded. "She's on the hunt. I think she hauled off and hit me with a hundred questions in the few minutes it took to get from her room to the great hall. Most of them circled back to you. She didn't come right out and ask what you were, but I got the feeling she wanted to." His grin widened. "She asked what my special power was. I told her I had the power to resist questions from nosy talk-show hosts. She sort of humphed and then shut up. But I could hear her brain still whirring."

As Eric started toward Donna and Holgarth, Conall nodded and moved away. Eric knew he could depend on Conall to protect the castle. He'd had centuries of practice in the protection business.

"I don't know where you get off telling everyone what to do. Did I miss the part where you were crowned top turd? I don't *want* to play the wicked consort of Eric the Evil. Last time I looked, there wasn't a wicked consort clause in my contract." Donna turned to Eric as he stopped by her side. "I can't believe he thinks he can harass me like he does the rest of the poor wretches who work here." She glared at Holgarth. "Why not rent a wig and *you* can be the wicked consort?"

As one of the castle's poor wretches, Eric didn't offer anything to the conversation because he was too busy picturing Holgarth in a wig. And from there, he went on to imagine Donna in her wicked consort costume—short on cloth with lots of bare skin showing. Things were looking up.

Holgarth looked down his long nose at Donna, an action known to reduce grown men to five-year-olds caught with their fingers in the cookie jar. "Of course I can't *make* you do it, but I believe your employer can. He called to say the owner insisted you play this part so you could observe customers' reactions firsthand. Personally, I doubt your ability to convince anyone that you're a wicked consort." He dismissed her acting talent with a disdainful sniff. "A pity the owner didn't seek my opinion. It would have saved embarrassment for all interested parties." His thin-lipped scowl indicated his disapproval of any decision that didn't go through him.

Donna's mood seemed to lighten in direct proportion to Holgarth's displeasure. "Well hey, I think we finally agree on something. Personally, I think you'd make an incredible wicked consort—fiendish but totally sexy. Besides, it would give you something useful to do, because so far I haven't figured out what your job description is."

A faint tic at the corner of Holgarth's mouth was his version of unrestrained guffaws. "I harass the help. It's what I do. And very well, I might add." He smoothed an imaginary wrinkle from his wizard robe. "Oh, and never think for a moment, Ms. Nolan, that you are my equal when it comes to biting sarcasm. Next to me, you are a marshmallow waiting to be toasted."

Donna grinned and glanced at Eric. "I want to hate this guy, but he's just too funny." She returned her attention to Holgarth. "I'll call my boss and get this whole thing straightened out. I don't do wicked consorts. Ever."

Holgarth chose to ignore her. "Eric, would you show your consort where the costumes are? Ms. Nolan will want to practice her part—a futile effort, I might add. Be sure to explain how our wicked consort stalks her prey, then pounces and sucks them dry." He blinked as though just realizing something. "But of course she won't have to practice. She can simply be her own delightful self."

Donna growled low in her throat as Holgarth turned away to oversee several castle employees readying the great hall for the night's fantasies. "Maybe I'll practice on him. Bring on the fake fangs."

"Let's go to the restaurant. You can make your call and order something to get you through the night." Eric guided her out of the great hall and toward the restaurant. Sharing meals with her made him uneasy. How many times could he make excuses for not eating anything? Meals were usually a nonfactor in his relationships with women because said relationships didn't extend beyond his bed. Things were different with Donna, but now wasn't the time to analyze what that meant. At least the restaurant gave him an excuse to guard her without being too obvious.

Once seated in the dimly lit restaurant, Donna ordered a burger, fries, and iced tea. Then she pulled her cell phone from her purse and called her boss. Eric settled in for the one-way conversation.

A few minutes later she glared down at her sandwich as though it were personally responsible for all of life's injustices. Hers in particular. "Do you think if I shook Holgarth until his teeth rattled he'd tell me how to reach the owner? I have to convince Mr. or Ms. Mysterious that I'll make a pathetic wicked consort. For once Holgarth is right. I'm a lousy actress." She sighed her defeat. "I guarantee I'll be bad for business. Besides, I have stuff to do."

"There's exactly zero chance of you making direct contact with the owner. I've tried. Guess I'll have to show you those costumes." The plan was perfect. She'd have to stay close to him until it was time for her show. Eric was honest enough to admit his glee wasn't just because the plan had worked. He'd get to tell her the responsibilities of being a consort. He was making them up even as he paid for her meal, such as it was.

Donna frowned. "You didn't eat anything."

"I grabbed something to eat right before I met you in

the great hall." He waited impatiently as she finished her fries. "While I'm showing you the costumes, I'll explain your part in tonight's fantasies." The weather was bad, so they probably wouldn't have many customers. But Eric was determined to make the most of the few fantasies he'd have with Donna.

She looked mutinous as he guided her out of the restaurant. "Candy first, then costumes. I'll need chocolate to recover from my reign of fanged wickedness. Walk over to Sweet Indulgence with me."

Uh-oh. Eric did some quick calculations. It was a little after seven. Still some light, but overcast and raining. If he put on his Astros cap and used the rain as an excuse to drive instead of walk, he could probably make it to the candy store and back with only a nagging headache to show for his exposure to daylight.

As he guided his car into a parking space in front of Sweet Indulgence, Donna smiled at him. "You know, we could've walked. I wouldn't have melted."

No, but I might have. "You don't need to start your acting career looking like a wet cat." Maybe reminding her of tonight wasn't a good idea.

Donna raced for the door of the candy store on a renewed surge of irritation. She hated being manipulated, and the castle owner had gone over her head to talk to her boss. It would serve the owner right if she drove every last paying customer from the castle tonight. Hmm. She narrowed her gaze on the many possibilities for payback.

Eric held the door open, and she hurried inside to escape the downpour. Sparkle Stardust perched on her tall stool behind the counter. Legs crossed and black dress riding high on her bare thighs, she was the black widow of sex looking for a man to devour.

Sparkle smiled a predatory smile as Eric followed Donna into the store. "Two of my favorite people. Donna, you've saved me from death by boredom. A little rain and no one buys candy. Do I understand how the human mind works?" She uncrossed her legs and leaned forward as she answered her own question. "I don't." Sparkle waved a hand in the air to indicate the vagaries of human reasoning. Her nails were long and a deep rich red. Hunting nails. "On a night like this all women should curl up with a good man. . . ." She paused for thought. "Or bad. Whichever tickles your tush. And they should eat lots of chocolate."

Donna opened her mouth to comment, but Sparkle wasn't finished. Her gaze slid past Donna to where Eric stood wearing an amused expression. "Personally, I'll take bad every time. Bad men are unpredictable. I find that very sexy in the male animal."

"Yes, well . . ." Donna wasn't quite sure how to respond to Sparkle.

She needn't have worried, because Sparkle was still focused on Eric. "How's my big bad beautiful—"

"I think I'll try something different tonight." Eric walked down to the end of the counter, effectively cutting off Sparkle's comment.

Donna frowned. What had Sparkle been about to say?

Sparkle returned her attention to Donna. She wore her secret smile, the one that said she knew exactly why Eric had cut her off. "If you're looking for something to heat up a damp rainy night, try my chocolate-covered cherries. Have you ever licked a melted chocolate-covered cherry from a man's navel?"

"Not in the last week." Donna wanted to get her candy and leave, but not before she found out where Sparkle was headed. Her first encounter had taught her that Sparkle was always headed somewhere. She glanced over to make sure Eric was still studying the candy selections. "So what's the best technique?"

Sparkle practically glowed with the joy of explaining. "You place the chocolate in his navel, and then you pass a lighted candle back and forth over the chocolate until it melts. Once the chocolate is warm and smooth, you slowly scoop it out with the tip of your tongue. Leave the cherry for last. Make sure when you scoop it out you wiggle your tongue around. Finish off by giving him a long sensual kiss with lots of tongue so he can taste the chocolate. Very erotic." She stopped to stare at Donna as though something had just occurred to her. "You do turn off the lights and just use candlelight to set the mood during sex, don't you?"

"Sure. All the time." Never. But the chocolate navel thing sounded like fun. Maybe she'd try it on . . . "Give me a pound of the chocolate-covered cherries." *Impulse buy, impulse buy.* She ignored her inner voice that warned this would probably end up on her hips, not in Eric's navel.

"Great choice. Did you know that sex is biochemically no different from eating large quantities of chocolate? So sex and chocolate together have to deliver a meteor-impact orgasm, right?" She happily changed subjects without giving Donna a chance to respond. "How's your family doing?" Sparkle placed the chocolate in a box.

Donna shrugged. "Nothing's changed. No, that's not true. My sister, Trish, has decided to marry the guy she met two weeks ago. What do they have in common? Zip. *Nada.* Nothing. I give it a month."

"You know, having things in common isn't all it's cracked up to be." Sparkle slid her gaze to Eric, who had returned to stand beside Donna. "You rub two stones in the same direction, you don't get any sparks. And life is all about sparks, girlfriend."

That was deep in a twisted kind of way. "Did you sit in the audience for all four hours of my shows?" Eric's heat and scent surrounded her, distracting her in the most basic way. Donna's wet clothes would begin steaming any minute now.

"Would I miss a minute?" Sparkle widened her eyes to indicate the unlikelihood. "Lola and Asima really interested me. I get that you didn't tell all on your show, but here's some advice." She recrossed her legs and then stared at her knee. "Jeez. I missed three hairs."

"Your advice?" Eric refocused Sparkle.

"Oh, sure. If both Lola and Asima try to give you sex advice—not that they will, but just in case they do—ask yourself which has more street cred: the madam of a famous bordello or a nobody hiding behind a cat form. Absolutely a no-brainer." She glanced down at her knee again. "As soon as Deimos gets here to take over, I've got to get rid of these hairs. Knee hair is so not sexy."

Donna narrowed her gaze as Sparkle continued to obsess over the three hairs on her knee. Sparkle knew more about Lola and Asima than Donna had told her audience. How? She didn't get a chance to ask.

"Look, we've got to get back for the first fantasy. How about giving me a half pound each of the chocolate-covered raisins and nuts." Eric turned to glance toward the door as someone entered the store.

Donna followed his gaze. Yikes! Scary-person alert. Huge, hulking, and not happy. She looked at Eric to see his reaction.

"Hey, Deimos." Eric casually greeted the man and turned back to watch Sparkle scoop his candy into a bag.

Deimos? This was the person who was going to "take over" the store? The man was massive. Complete with shaved head, tattoos, and many many body piercings, he didn't look ready to dish out jelly beans.

"What's up, Eric?" Deimos's expression said, *"Don't mess with me because I'm one mean dude,"* but his eyes shone with hero worship when he looked at Eric.

"Not much." Eric paid Sparkle for both Donna's and his own candy.

"This candy-store gig sucks. I want to do some action-hero stuff. Maybe I can go with you some time when you—"

"No problem." Eric scooped up all their candy and strode toward the door.

Donna's suspicion antennae were waving wildly. When you *what*? She wanted to know. But Eric was not about to stop while she asked.

"Wait, Eric." Sparkle's command stopped them.

Eric had already started to open the door. He paused to look back at her. "We have to hurry."

Donna glanced at her watch. They weren't that late. For some reason, Eric wanted to get away from Sparkle and

Deimos. She'd have to come back to talk to Sparkle when Eric wasn't with her.

For a moment she felt something subtle move in her mind. She widened her eyes. "Are you in my mind, Eric?"

"No." He sounded irritated as he waited for Sparkle to speak. He also sounded like he was telling the truth.

Donna frowned. If *he* wasn't in her mind, then what was that—

Sparkle beamed at Eric. "Your candy has inspired me, hot bod." She was obviously so excited she even forgot about her knee hair. "Don't worry, I'm not going to compare you to a raisin."

She shifted her attention to Donna. "Just think about this, sister. *Chocolate* covered *nuts*. Give you any ideas for really fresh sex play?" Turning to the shelf behind her, she picked up a container and then hurried around the counter to give it to Donna. "Dipping chocolate. Do with it what you will. If you must do homage to me, write my name in the chocolate."

Donna thought about turning red, but Deimos actually did it. His head looked like a super-heated bowling ball. "Jeez, can you talk about something else already? I don't want to listen to this crap."

Sparkle offered Donna and Eric an apologetic smile. "Ignore him. He's working through virginity issues. It's hard to get good sexual minions nowadays." She stopped smiling as she turned to glare at Deimos. "Action hero, hah! See me laugh. You're going to have to toughen up before you walk the mean streets."

Donna tried to return the dipping chocolate that Sparkle had forced into her hands. "I don't think—"

With an impatient grunt, Eric took the container from her. "Let's go. We need to get you a costume."

Donna offered Sparkle an insincere smile and a finger wave as she fled the store.

Eric didn't say anything as he drove the short distance back to the castle or as he guided her to the costume room. That was fine with her. She needed some recovery time.

He put their candy and dipping chocolate on a shelf, rooted through the many costumes hanging in the room, and finally handed her one. "Here's the wicked consort's costume."

Donna blinked. "Where's the rest of it?" It had a top. Sort of. And a skirt. Kind of. "It's all black and looks like a harem outfit. Let me guess. The sheik died, and I'm going to his funeral. I could've sworn this was a medieval fantasy. Doesn't look too medieval to me."

"Sure it is." He smiled at her. A smile that said he was lying like crazy, but he'd dazzle her with his sexy grin so she wouldn't care.

It worked.

"Look, we're playing vampires, and people expect us to look sinister and sexy. That outfit says sexy, and you can add the sinister as you go along. Change behind the curtain. I'll change out here." He locked the door so no one would walk in on them before he waved her toward a curtained-off area.

Sheesh, he was bossy. She didn't like bossy men. Usually. Okay, so maybe his take-charge attitude was a little sexy. She thought about complaining, but he had a crease between his eyes that hinted at a headache. She'd save it till later.

Her inner bitch said ugly things as she changed. Once she got her clothes off, it didn't take long to get into her costume. Because, well, there wasn't much of it to get into. The skirt was deceiving. It was long enough to keep her sandals from showing, but that didn't mean there was a lot to it. The whole outfit was made from some light clingy material. When she finally had both top and bottom on, she sucked in her breath at the wide-open spaces between them. *Bare* spaces. Someone would pay for this.

Donna stomped out from behind the curtain. "I'm a vampire sex object. Cheap, cheap, cheap. I bet you didn't make yourself into a sex . . ." She looked up. She swallowed hard. He had.

He was the Highlander from hell. Black shirt, black

plaid, and black heart. Because only evil could tempt women to dark and dangerous fantasies by just looking at him. His kilt wasn't the neat modern-day version, but the more primitive one where the extra material was flung across his shoulder. That's what she'd mistaken for a cape that first night in the dim light. He must have run his fingers through his hair, because it lay in a tangled glory across his shoulders. But it wasn't what he wore or his hair that sucked all the air from her lungs.

It was the feeling that this was who Eric really was. And she liked it. His hard sensual face and muscular body spoke of a contained savagery that touched something darkly violent in her. Violent? Not a word she'd ever associate with herself. She put the *C* in *civilized.* But Eric was the primal growl that made her want to mount a horse and ride beside him as he besieged castles, and afterward make fierce uninhibited love beside a cold mountain burn. How weird was that?

Donna put her hands on her hips as she slowly slid her gaze over his total awesome package. "You're going out in public like that?"

His smile said he dressed for effect, and the effect he wanted was dark, dangerous, and sexy. "Here're your fangs."

She took the fake teeth but didn't slip them into her mouth. "You had some kind of makeup on when I met you."

He was silent for a moment before answering. "Yeah, well, tonight I don't have time to put on any makeup. I'll just use the fake fangs like you."

Opening the door, he guided her toward the steps leading down to the floor where his room was. "We're doing tonight's fantasies in the dungeon." Once there, he pushed open the dungeon's heavy wooden door. It made a satisfying groan of despair. Flicking a switch, he turned on several lights in wall sconces that mimicked candle flames along with a fake fire in the hearth. The artificial flames cast shadows that crept and danced along the realistic-looking cold stone walls. Chains and various instruments of torture made the whole thing pretty scary. Donna shivered.

"So what do I do?" Clumsily she shoved the fake teeth into her mouth.

He flipped on another switch, and faint moans and shrieks echoed in the distance. "You're my consort and a slave to my slightest wish."

Donna raised one brow. "Really?" She had to enunciate carefully around the huge fangs.

"A virginal maiden will be flung into the dungeon as punishment for resisting the lecherous advances of the dastardly Prince Timothy. We'll be waiting to sink our teeth into her. She'll probably appeal to you as a woman to help her. But you'll explain that I'm your lord and master, and you'd never think of disobeying me, because I'm the head vamp and an all-around great guy." He paused to think and then smiled. "Make sure you look sexy while you're saying all this. My consort is sexy as hell even if she isn't the brightest bulb in the lamp."

Donna narrowed her eyes to annoyed slits. "Got it. Sexy, dumb, and a slave to your slightest wish. Wow, I can hardly wait." She decided Mr. Evil Vampire might not like the improvisations she had in mind. Donna Nolan led, she didn't follow.

"That's the general plot. The rest we play by ear. Eventually the maiden will scream, bringing Conall and Brynn to her rescue." He reached into the sporran at his waist and pulled out a pocket watch. "Time to get this show on the road." Sliding the fangs into his mouth, he pushed the door shut, moved into the shadows, and pulled her with him.

He tucked her close to him as they waited, and her senses acknowledged that this was pretty cool. "Will you use your Scottish accent?"

"Aye." He slid his hand up and down her mostly bare back.

Her body translated it as pure erotic sensation. Her senses shook off their ho-hum attitude and leaped into the enhanced mode she was coming to expect when Eric was touching her, or even in close orbit to her.

Goose bumps trailed behind the smooth glide of his fingers. And the scent of him tightened her stomach and loosened her inhibitions. If she could identify it, she'd bottle it and keep it to sniff on cold New York nights when she was feeling alone. Whoa. She widened her eyes. What was that all about? He was a great-looking guy and they'd made awesome love together. End of story.

Someone pushed the dungeon door open, ending her exploration of her senses. "Get in there and pray that Prince Timothy doesn't demand your sorry head." There was the sound of someone being shoved into the room and then the door slammed shut.

They got their first glimpse of the virginal maiden.

He was about five feet ten of overweight male, most of it stockpiled in his belly. A receding hairline and scraggly red mustache didn't improve the image. Dressed in baggy shorts and a Hawaiian shirt, he bent his knobby knees, spread his skinny legs, and glared belligerently around the room.

Donna met Eric's startled glance. "You didn't tell me Prince Timothy was as blind as a bat."

IO

"My old lady has the runs. She's still in the john, but the old fart in the wizard getup wouldn't wait for her because it'd upset his frickin' schedule." When the man spotted Donna and Eric, his eyes lit with undisguised glee. "So I'm holdin' her spot. But I'm not the sucker—get it, *sucker*—that she is. Bring it to me, bloodsuckers." He beckoned.

Eric mentally scanned fantasy scenarios to find one that would satisfy this guy. He'd want one where he got to defeat the vampire and play the hero, a part he probably never played in real life.

"Just wing it," Eric murmured to Donna as he began a slow stalk of the man standing in the middle of the dungeon.

Uncertainty touched the man's eyes as Eric emerged into the light and he got a look at how big the "bloodsucker" was. He swallowed hard and backed up a step.

Eric would have to guide him. "My wicked consort and I will drain your body of all blood. You canna defeat me unless you sprinkle the holy water from yon bottle on me. 'Twould make me weak, and you'd be able to chain me to the wall."

The man's eyes widened in understanding as he grabbed the bottle from a small table and flung its contents on Eric. "Take that, you evil bastard."

Eric scowled as the water hit him full in the face. They'd have to find different props. Maybe the customer could just hold up a cross or a clove of garlic. Remembering his part, Eric made loud noises of distress and staggered toward the wall. The man hurried over to secure him with the fake cuffs and then turned toward Donna.

"Hey, little lady. Your vampire dude is out of commission. Maybe I can take his place." Wink, wink. "I don't think we traded names. I'm Dwayne."

Donna walked toward Dwayne, her hips doing amazing things inside that wicked consort costume. Eric growled low in his throat to express his appreciation.

"Well, hi, Dwayne. I'm . . . Nightshade, and you've chained the wrong vamp to the wall." She smiled at him, exposing her fake fangs. "You are so in trouble, sweetie."

"I am?" Dwayne looked uncertain again.

"Uh-huh." She leaned toward Dwayne.

Eric growled for a completely different reason this time. He knew exactly how much of his wicked consort good old Dwayne could see when she leaned forward like that. Jealousy? No way. He'd never cared about any woman enough to be jealous, and he wasn't about to start now. He kept on growling.

"I'm the more dangerous of this deadly duo." She skimmed her fingers along Dwayne's jaw. His mouth fell open, and his eyes glazed over. "Eric the Evil is a slave to my slightest wish. I'm his mistress, and he'd never think of disobeying me because I'm the head vamp and an all-around great gal." Donna cast a dismissive glance Eric's way. "He's as sexy as hell even if he isn't the brightest bulb in the lamp." She returned her attention to Dwayne, who watched her with an unblinking stare. "Still want to take his place?"

"Oh, yeah." Dwayne's enthusiasm hinted at a long suppressed obsession. He dropped to the floor and looked up at Donna with puppy dog adoration. "Walk on me, mistress. Use me like a worn-out old rug."

Now it was Donna's turn to look uncertain. She glanced at Eric. He shrugged and tried to look fierce. "You canna be her rug. 'Tis my joy and honor to be such. When I free myself you will be a verra frayed rug." Lord, he'd kill to have a tape of this to play for Brynn and Conall.

"Shut up, bloodsucker." Dwayne snarled at Eric and returned to begging Donna to walk on him. "Leave your tread on my chest, your imprint on my heart. Jeez, this is better than *Monday Night Football*."

Eric was torn. The fantasy had spiraled out of control, but he hated to end it by yanking his wrists from the cuffs, hauling Dwayne off his ass, and then telling him his time was up. That kind of finish to a fantasy didn't make for good customer relations. For the first time, he wished he carried some kind of beeper to alert Brynn and Conall so they could launch their rescue act before things got any weirder.

"Well, maybe I'll just take a few steps to see if you're as good as Eric the Evil." Donna threw Eric a desperate glance.

"Dinna walk on him, Nightshade. He'll disappoint you sorely. He willna be soft where I am soft, nor hard . . . where I am hard." What else could he say? Where was Dwayne's wife, and why wasn't she here to slap him upside his head?

Donna evidently decided she may as well get the walking over with and stepped onto Dwayne's chest. He moaned his bliss. She tiptoed onto his stomach, and he murmured words of ecstasy. This was sick, and Eric was putting an end to it. Jerking his arms from the wall, he started toward Donna. When she saw him coming, she lost her balance on the mountain slope of Dwayne's stomach and stomped on his groin. All Dwayne could manage was a high-pitched squeak.

"Hell." Eric rushed to where Donna had leaped off Dwayne's body. "I'll get him up to the great hall." Lifting Dwayne to his feet, he half carried him up the steps.

Dwayne cast Donna one last pain-filled adoring glance. "What a woman."

Donna watched them disappear up the steps. "Oops." She figured she could safely count herself out of all future fantasies. But it hadn't been half bad. A little kinky, but not bad. She'd particularly liked seeing Eric chained to the wall. All kinds of erotic possibilities came to mind. First she'd strip him naked, and then—

The sound of slow deliberate clapping spun her around.

"Don't mess up a perfect show with sexy thoughts about Eric. Too bad those chains weren't real." Taurin stepped out of the shadows.

Donna's breathing stopped at the same time her heartbeat accelerated to warp speed. He hadn't lost any of his dark menace since the last time she'd seen him. How had he suddenly appeared, and why was he here?

"How did I get here? Eric isn't the only one with extraordinary talents. And I'm not here to snatch you away, so relax." He smiled as he moved closer, but that in no way dispelled the deadly aura surrounding him. It didn't help that he was in his vampire form, and there was no way he could smile without scaring her witless.

Donna drew in a deep breath of courage and picked up her breathing where she'd left off. She prepared to scream for help.

"I wouldn't scream if I were you." He offered the suggestion casually, but his gaze was wary. "If you scream, Eric will run to the rescue. There'll be one hell of a fight that every customer will see and hear. I'll make sure of that. Even if I lose, I'll win. Because Eric will have to leave the Castle of Dark Dreams. And he likes it here." Taurin shrugged. "Of course, I don't intend to lose, so he'll be dead."

"Why're you here?" She wouldn't scream for the moment, but if he made a move toward her . . .

"I want to talk to you. Besides, I have to prove to Eric that I can reach you whenever I choose. Make him sweat a little." He didn't come any closer, but his expression grew calculating. "Guess I can't do that, though, because Eric doesn't sweat. Ever."

He strolled over to study the fake instruments of torture. "I remember seeing the real things a few centuries back." Turning, he speared her with an intense stare. "Maybe I'm all wrong here, but I get the feeling you don't know that Eric's a vampire just like me."

"No." That's all Donna could manage, because her breath had taken a hike again. Sure, she'd known that Eric had some unusual mental powers, but not this . . . this . . .

"Yes." Satisfaction filled Taurin's vampire eyes. "Okay, so maybe not exactly like me. He belongs to a clan of vampires with powers that are off the charts. But I've worked hard to up my skill level. Now I'm ready for him."

"No." The word was starting to sound weak even to her. But she couldn't wrap her mind and emotions around what Taurin was telling her. She would've known, would've sensed . . . Good grief, she'd made love with Eric.

"When you finally decide to accept what I'm telling you, think about this." Taurin's eyes filled with hate. "Two hundred years ago Eric and a few others from his clan captured me. They didn't really want me, they wanted Dacian, my brother. They kept me in an abandoned warehouse and used me as bait. When Dacian came for me, they set the warehouse on fire." Despair joined the hate in his gaze. "Dacian got me out safely, but didn't have the strength to save himself. I never saw him again."

Donna just stared at him. What could she say to his story when she was still trying to deal with the concept of Eric as vampire, and if Taurin's tale was true, Eric's savagery? The silence stretched between them as the sound of someone coming down the steps reached her.

Eric appeared in the dungeon doorway, and Donna saw the exact moment he realized that Taurin was with her. As she watched in horror, Eric changed from the man she'd made love to into the vampire of her first fantasy. He hadn't been wearing a mask or clever makeup. He was the real deal. His eyes grew larger and elongated, with black pupils that dilated until no blue remained. His lips became fuller with the promise of deadly fangs beneath them.

Eric began a slow deliberate stalking of his enemy. Donna was beyond terrified. She didn't know him now, didn't understand how she'd made love with him and not realized. Every tacky grade B vampire film played in her memory as a frightening background to her real-life horror happening.

Eric's anger radiated in waves of power that pushed her against the wall. With his change to vampire, he seemed to have grown bigger and a lot scarier. His eyes almost glowed with his fury, and he'd drawn his lips back from his fangs in a vicious snarl. If she could crawl through a crack in the floor, she would. She did *not* want to be a witness to what would happen next.

Even Taurin looked a little intimidated. "This isn't the time or place, Eric. I just stopped by to pass on a little info to Donna." And then he was gone.

"He vanished." She stared at the spot where Taurin had stood. Donna didn't understand the how, but she was eternally grateful that he had. She was on shock overload and her emotions were teetering on the edge. No way did she want to end up babbling to some shrink about the time she stood in a dungeon and watched two vampires fight to the death. A definite shortcut to a cozy padded room and many many meds.

Okay, look at Eric. How bad can it be? Scraping her last bit of courage off the floor, she lifted her gaze. Donna almost collapsed with relief. He'd returned to human form. She should ask questions, demand explanations. But first she'd race to her room and hide her head under her pillow until her shivering stopped.

"Donna." He took a step toward her, his gaze filled with regret and his eyes swimming with an emotion she was too shattered to interpret.

"No. Don't come near me." She held up a shaking hand to ward off whatever he was, because he was certainly not what she'd believed. And the sadness of that thought almost pushed aside her fear. Almost. Without meeting his gaze again, she ran for the stairs. He didn't try to stop her.

By the time she'd locked her door behind her and flung herself onto her bed, Donna was in control enough to pass on hiding her head under her pillow. *A vampire.* She'd made love with a vampire, an immortal bloodsucking fiend. Fine, so maybe she was piling it on a little too thick. *Calm down. Think clearly.* Ack, she'd made love to a real live—or not—vampire.

Her listeners would be disappointed in her. How many times had she encouraged them to approach their paranormal experiences without fear and with an open mind? Arrogant. Smug. Stupid. It was easy to hand out advice when she wasn't the one nose to nose with a vamp. She'd probably left scorch marks on the stairs as she'd trucked out of the dungeon.

And she could never tell this story to Trish. She'd lectured Trish her whole adult life about choosing the wrong men. At least Trish had never gotten it on with a creature of the night. Donna felt herself bonding with the pod women.

"Are you finished with your hysterics, dear? Because if you are, we can talk about all the wonderful sensual gifts a vampire brings to the love table." Lola's voice sounded matter of fact. The scent of oatmeal cookies hung in the air.

Donna was tempted to keep her eyes closed. She didn't want to deal with Lola now. "Could you come back later, Lola?"

"No. We have to talk now before you do something foolish like telling Eric never to come near you again or running back to New York. So open your eyes and look at me." Lola's voice sounded eerily like Grandma Lily's when she'd caught a five-year-old Donna drawing horse pictures on the dining room wall.

Donna rolled onto her back and opened her eyes. A steely-eyed Lola hovered next to her bed.

"I've left some of my home-baked oatmeal cookies

along with your candy on your night table. Oatmeal cookies are always good for a warm fuzzy feel, and heaven knows you look like you need all the warm fuzzies you can get." Lola wore a long flowered dress, and her white hair formed a halo around her chubby-cheeked face. She placed her hands on her hips. "I thought you were a woman in control. But look at you, cowering behind a locked door—which won't keep Eric out, by the way—and letting life's little taps on your shoulder scare the hell out of you." Lola offered her a motherly smile. "I love the power a good curse word brings to a discussion."

"Taps on my shoulder?" For the first time since seeing Eric change, outrage pushed fear aside. "How about a knockout punch? Hey, this is a big deal."

"Only if you make it one. You're talking to a ghost, dear. And you've talked to a cat—time wasted if you ask me—so why is it such a big stretch to accept that the man you had sex with is dentally challenged?" She flung her hands into the air to emphasize her frustration. "Vampires have feelings, too, you know. I bet Eric is crushed that you ran away from him. Why don't you have a cookie and then have a nice long talk with him, hmm?"

Lola made everything seem so reasonable when it was anything but. She had one thing right, though. Donna had to pull herself together and get ready for her show. And Eric could relax, because no way would she share this experience with her listeners. In fact, she wouldn't be revealing any of the phony brothers' secrets. Why? She wasn't sure. Curiosity made a brief appearance. What was Conall? She'd find out eventually.

Eventually? Did that mean she was staying? Donna surprised even herself, because her answer was a resounding yes. Maybe she was developing immunity to weird and scary experiences. Maybe her willingness to take the chance of being kidnapped by a vengeance-obsessed vampire proved how far she'd go to up her ratings. *Maybe your interest in Eric transcends abject terror.* Maybe she'd have an oatmeal cookie.

"See what you've done? You've upset Sweetie Pie and Jessica." Lola had floated over to get a look at the two plants.

"What?" Donna took a bite from her cookie and tried to shove everything from her mind except happy memories of Mom baking cookies on Christmas Eve. Didn't work. All she could see was the moment Eric changed into someone she didn't know.

"The girls have bonded with you. They sense you're upset, and they're sad. See how sad they are?" With an accusing glance, Lola pointed out the droopy leaves on both plants.

Jeez, plant guilt. "Look, my guest tonight is an expert on UFO cover-ups, and I have to do a little research on the Web before the show." A lie. She'd done all her research before leaving New York. But she needed everyone to give her some space.

Lola turned away from the plants. "Get over your hissy fit because Eric is a little different, and get on with keeping the girls happy. Once you've had your little chat with Eric, why don't you use up all your chocolate-covered cherries in his navel?" She pursed her lips as she thought. "Or perhaps he'd like to melt a few in your navel." Lola cast Donna a piercing stare. "You do have an innie, not an outie belly button, don't you?" Her expression said she might not survive if Donna had an unacceptable navel, one not able to hold a melted chocolate-covered cherry.

Lola had a bad case of belly-button bias, and Donna was tempted to lie just to watch her expression. But then Lola would hang around trying to convince her that there were many many places on a woman's body where a man could melt chocolate. "My navel's fine."

Lola smiled her comfortable granny smile as she drifted toward the door.

Donna frowned. "Wait. How did you know about the navel thing?" Suspicion reared its head. "You weren't hanging around when Sparkle suggested it, were you?"

Lola widened her eyes to demonstrate her shock that

Donna would suggest she was spying. "Of course not. But doesn't everyone melt their chocolate-covered cherries that way? As soon as I saw the bag, I simply assumed . . ." She blinked. "You weren't just going to *eat* them?" She managed to imbue her voice with the horror she felt at someone so misusing the chocolates.

"I, umm . . ." Somehow Lola had put her on the defensive. How did she do that?

"Well, dear, I'll leave you to work out your own destiny." She paused before disappearing. "But please make sure it's the correct one or else I'll be forced to haunt you until your dying day. Toodle-oo." And she was gone.

At last. Alone. Donna had a little while before going down for her show. She'd take a shower and try to absorb what she'd seen. Maybe then she could face—

A sharp rap on her door shattered her belief that she'd achieved some semblance of calm. *Please don't let it be Eric.* She couldn't deal with him yet. Her gaze skittered around the room. Did adults hide under beds? Okay, how about closets? *Get a grip, Nolan.*

"Hey, Donna. It's Conall. Could I talk to you for a minute?" He sounded like a normal human.

What were the chances? Not good. If she opened the door, would he morph into a werewolf? But she wanted to know more about Eric without talking directly to the resident vampire lord. Conall gave her the chance to do just that. Taking a deep breath, she opened the door.

Conall strode in, glanced around the room, and settled his large body in one of the room's two chairs. "Feeling any better?" He looked worried. "When you passed me on the dungeon steps, you were nothing more than a blur and a stiff breeze." He smiled.

She appreciated his attempt to put her at ease. "If you mean, have I been up here carving a chair leg into a wooden stake, then you can relax. No stake, but not much calm, either. And before we talk about anything, tell me what you are, because I know you have to be something."

His smile widened. "Something, huh? I guess you could

call it that." Conall's smile faded. "I don't turn into anyone else. What you see is what you get."

"And . . ." She waited for the other shoe to drop.

"My real name is Conall O'Rourke, and I'm an immortal warrior. A pissed-off goddess cursed me a long time ago." He watched her warily.

He probably expected her to lose it if he told her everything. Conall didn't understand. She'd just seen her lover turn into a *vampire.* Nothing he pulled off his shock shelf could make her blink.

"How old? And don't worry. I couldn't fling myself out the window even if I wanted to. It's too narrow, and I'm too wide."

His smile returned. "Eight hundred years. I'm the same age as Eric."

Oh. My. God. She'd lied. She blinked. "And you're here, why?"

"Here at the Castle of Dark Dreams or here in Galveston?" He held up his hand. "Never mind. You probably want to know both."

She nodded.

"Hand me one of those bags of candy."

Donna picked up Eric's bag of chocolate-covered raisins and took it to him. She didn't even consider giving him her cherries. Then she sat down across from him. "Let's hear it."

"I'm giving you the short version. I killed one of the favorite warriors of Morrigan, the Irish goddess of war and death." He popped some chocolate into his mouth to fortify himself.

"Goddess? Gods and goddesses are real?" Like that should surprise her?

"More things than you could ever imagine are real." His smile was probably meant to reassure her. It didn't. "Anyway, Morrigan's vengeance was a real bitch. She cursed me to act as protector for all my dead enemy's descendants until no one was left. I'm down to one, and he's living in Galveston. I've never seen him, but he's bound to walk through the castle's gates one of these days and I'll know him. All of the damn Kavanaghs look alike. He doesn't have any kids yet, so if I can stop the descendant thing right here, I'll be free of the curse."

Donna could feel her eyes crossing even as she stared. "Okay, I get it. The three of you made up the name McNair so you could pose as brothers. Then what's Eric's last name, and why is *he* here?" Her heart had stopped pounding in her ears, and she was almost sure she wouldn't have to breathe into a bag to keep from hyperventilating.

"Eric is a Mackenzie, and I think you need to ask him the rest of what you want to know." Conall stood. "I'll walk you down to your table. Eric's sub will take over for the rest of the night, so Eric'll be free to watch you during your show." His gaze turned serious. "You can't be alone at any time until Eric takes care of Taurin." His grim expression said exactly how permanent the taking care of would be.

Eric sat right behind Donna for the entire show. He alternated between anger and hurt. She'd *run* from him. Hurt? Human females didn't have the power to hurt him. But whatever the emotion was, it bothered him. He tried to pull his sense of self-worth around him—the knowledge that he wielded immense power, that he'd lived for centuries before Donna was born and would live centuries more after she died. Right. Now he was depressed.

She didn't turn around to look at him once, but he could feel her emotions—a mix of unease, curiosity, and . . . yes, desire. He smiled for the first time since he'd entered the dungeon to find Taurin there. If she still desired him, then he had something to work with.

He'd spoken to her once. Right before she went on the air, he'd leaned close and then frowned when she flinched away from him. Trying to ignore the twinge he was positive couldn't be hurt, he'd asked if she was going to tell her listeners about what had happened. She hadn't answered, just shook her head. He'd been slow to draw away from her. Her scent of lavender and warm vital woman was a giant sensual suction cup.

Finally. Her show was over. Now he'd ask her—

Donna turned to look at him. "I want something to eat. Keep me company. We have to talk." Nothing she said sounded negotiable. Nothing in her expression said friendly.

"Great." Eric wasn't complaining. Things could've gotten ugly if she'd given her audience a blow by blow account of her evening. Worse yet, she could be on a plane back to New York. Now, that thought scared him on a whole other level.

Once seated in the restaurant, she stared across the table at him, her expression unreadable. She'd dressed starkly professional for the show in a black skirt and jacket. Probably going all civilized to give her the courage to face the unspeakable evil. He scowled.

Calmly she ordered a steak and baked potato, but he noticed her hand had a slight tremor as she picked up her knife. Score one for the unspeakable evil. If you were going to scare the crap out of humans, make sure you did it right. Did that thought make him feel better? No. He pulled a slightly flattened Snickers bar from his jeans pocket.

She paused in the process of cutting her steak to stare at the Snickers bar. Then she laughed. Sure, the laugh sounded a little hysterical, but he was pathetically happy to hear any kind of laugh.

"What?" He took a bite from the candy bar and tried to shove away thoughts of what he'd rather be doing with his mouth.

"You're eating a Snickers bar?" The laughter had faded to a few chuckles.

"Yeah. I was going to ask the chef to send out the blood from your steak in a wineglass, but I didn't want to gross you out." He was lying, but a dark need he didn't understand wanted to see if she'd turn from him in disgust, *expected* her to turn from him in disgust.

"You drink cow's blood?" She really looked interested in his answer.

"Is this off the record?" He'd play her game as she tip-toed around what she really wanted to know.

She propped her elbow on the table and rubbed her forehead with her hand. "I'm not going to tell anyone about you, Brynn, or Conall. So yes, this is off the record."

"I never drink cow's blood." Eric paused for effect. "Only human blood." He'd give her credit. Other than growing a little paler, she didn't react.

"Instead of feeding negative stereotypes, tell me about the real you." She sipped her coffee. Her hand was steady on her cup. He applauded her courage.

"What if the real me lives down to all your stereo-types?" Eric watched her eyes narrow and knew he was pushing her. Why? It didn't make sense.

If he really scared her, she'd raise holy hell when he told her he'd be staying with her until Taurin was located. And if Brynn and Conall scoured Galveston without find-ing out where Taurin had gone to ground, then he'd help them search. But he'd take her with him, because she wasn't leaving his side.

She took a sip of her coffee and then raised her gaze to his. "Then I'll know what to do. Tell me, Eric."

Know what to do? What did that mean? Suddenly it hit him. She could go home. *No.* His instant denial resonated in places that had nothing to do with great sex. A surprise, because he'd thought it was all about mind-blowing sex.

He leaned back and stared at his water glass. "Look, this place is about to close. Let's go to your room to talk." No way would he take her to his room, because they'd have to pass the dungeon to get there. She didn't need any reminders of tonight's disaster. Question was, would she go anywhere alone with him?

She studied her napkin. Finally she sighed. "Sure. Let's keep a positive flow going, though. Sweetie Pie and Jessica are sad. I guess I loaded them down with tons of negative energy tonight." She looked up and offered him a weak smile. "That means no changing into vampire form or nuzzling my neck. Absolutely no neck encounters of the bloodsucking kind."

Now she'd ticked him off. "I only feed once every few weeks." He offered her his most seductive smile, the one he knew from centuries of experience few women could resist. Then he met her gaze and let her see every sexual act he wanted to visit on her body. "And the encounter is always of the erotic kind."

II

As Donna opened her door, she tried to organize scattered thoughts that were like pop-up ads on her computer screen. They kept getting in the way of what she should really be thinking about. *Why . . .* POP—sexy male lips guaranteed to make any female wet and wanting. *Was she . . .* POP—eyes hot with promises of what he'd do after he stripped her naked. *Bringing a . . .* POP—strong muscular thighs showcased in soft worn denim. *Vampire . . .* POP—cut torso looking fine in snug black T-shirt. *Into her room?* POP—a sexual package that could deliver pleasure on a mythic scale. No use. Every time she closed one window, another opened up.

Vampires were supposed to be able to spin sensual webs around humans, making said vampires irresistible, weren't they? Would that work on her? Nope. Wouldn't happen. Her survival instinct was too strong. Okay, so it might work a little. Very little.

She watched as he closed the door and then stood in front of it for a moment.

"What're you doing? And please don't give me that

high-tech power-grid garbage again, because I don't believe it." Kicking her shoes off, she settled into a chair and motioned Eric to the one Conall had sat in. Maybe all her sexual thoughts were getting in the way of her important revelation because there *was* no important revelation. No matter how much her mind tried to whip up a sense of impending danger to her neck, she couldn't maintain it. She might be horrified by the concept of vampire, but she couldn't believe he'd just walk over and sink his teeth into her. If he'd wanted to bite her, he would've done it while they were making love and she was at her most vulnerable.

"I put a protective shield across your door. I don't think Taurin's powerful enough to get past it." Before joining her, he picked up his bag of chocolate-covered nuts. Sitting, he glanced around the room. "What happened to the rest of my candy?"

"Conall took it." When all the important stuff was out of the way, she'd ask him about the candy. "Talk to me, Eric."

He stared down at the bag in his lap, and for a moment she thought he wouldn't answer. "I was born human but became vampire when I was twenty-nine. Until I became vampire I could be killed as easily as any human, and I ate what all humans ate." A shadow of sadness touched his eyes. "I could father children."

Which probably meant he couldn't father children now. The realization sort of made her sad, too. She frowned. Donna had absolutely no interest in his daddy status. Besides, it was none of her business. She'd ignore the comment and go on to more important stuff. "Umm, do you have any children?" This was scary. The more she was around Eric, the more her impulsive self overruled her sensible self.

His smile was self-deprecating. "No. I was too busy raiding, pillaging, and being a pain-in-the-butt to the rest of the civilized world."

Time to get back on track. "I assume someone turned you." Startled, she realized her interest in every detail of his life didn't feel like objective scientific curiosity. It felt personal. A dangerous trend.

Eric continued to study the candy bag as though it held the secrets of the universe. “No. I belong to a vampire clan where everyone is born human and becomes vampire as they mature.”

“You were born in Scotland?” Eight hundred years ago. No wonder his raw primal sexuality drew her. Men born in modern times were too civilized, had too much of the basic male leeched from them.

He finally looked up at her. “I was born in Norway. I was a Viking, Donna. I raided the coast of Scotland. My clan eventually settled in the Highlands and took the name Mackenzie to blend in.” His smile was slow and wicked. “I have the best and worst of Viking and Highlander in me. The worst would intrigue you more.”

She wouldn’t ask what he meant, wouldn’t even think about what he meant. Until later. “Tell me about your clan.”

Donna could sense him sifting through information, trying to decide what to tell her first and what not to tell her at all.

“First of all, we’re not dead, just changed. We need human blood to survive, but not much. I feed about once every two weeks, and I don’t take enough to endanger anyone’s life. In fact, if I took too much it would destroy me.”

“How?” The thought of him being destroyed clogged her throat and made her feel sick, a reaction she didn’t expect. Good grief, she’d only known him a few days.

“Too much human blood taken at one time dilutes our vampire blood and heightens the blood lust. It becomes a death spiral. The vampire needs more and more human blood. He kills because the blood lust demands all his victim’s blood. Eventually he becomes a mindless killing machine.” Eric shrugged. “At that point the clan destroys him.”

Okay, didn’t want to hear any more of this. “Tell me about your powers.”

“We don’t start out with any real powers other than our immortality. We don’t get sick and minor wounds heal quickly. But someone can kill us without too much effort. If we're wounded badly enough and don't have a source of new blood to replace what we've lost, we can bleed to death."

Donna thought about that. "It must be a catch-22 situation. If you take too much human blood to replace what you've lost, you go crazy and the clan offs you."

He nodded. "And if someone takes our head, well, that's it. Can't generate a new head." He opened his candy bag but didn't reach inside. "As we grow older, we gradually accumulate powers. We choose which powers are important to us, and concentrate our energy on gaining those first. I've concentrated on powers that'll assure my survival. Some clansmen choose to gain back human qualities they lost when they changed."

"Like being able to eat candy?" The first smile-worthy piece of vampire info he'd tossed her way.

He almost looked embarrassed. "I like what I am. Once I changed, I never went all sentimental about the good old days when I was human. But the first time I smelled chocolate . . ." He lowered his lids and a hungry smile touched his lips. "It involved all my senses. I wanted to feel it melt in my mouth, the smooth slide of it on my tongue. I wanted to experience the dark rich taste of it. The scent of it was almost erotic." He raised his lids, and his gaze was soft with the remembered joy of chocolate.

Hmm. "So if a woman, say, dipped herself in chocolate, she'd drive you crazy with lust?" This question had no personal ramifications. This was absolutely a question asked in the interest of scientific discovery.

Before answering, he dug into his candy bag and put one chocolate-covered nut into his mouth. Riveted, she stared at his lips. The heat of his mouth would be melting the chocolate as he slid his warm wet tongue across the nut, slowly laying the nut bare while he let the chocolate linger on his taste buds. Then he'd grind the nut into delicious submission before swallowing it. Donna's gaze dropped to his throat to witness the swallowing process.

"Here I thought I was the only one who liked throats." He sounded hungry, in an arousing way. "If a woman I desired dipped herself in chocolate, it would drive me into a sexual frenzy. Nothing could stop me from licking the chocolate from every inch of her naked body. Should I elaborate?"

Donna didn't need to go any further down this path. Too many dangerous potholes. And when she got involved with thoughts of the sensual animal that was Eric Mackenzie, she tended to forget the point of the whole conversation. He was a *vampire.* Somehow the word didn't send cold shivers of dread down her spine this time.

"What about Taurin's brother? I'd like to hear your side of the story." Back to the serious stuff.

Eric frowned. "A lot of what Taurin said was true. Dacian was one of the most powerful night feeders, and he hated us. He'd killed some of our clansmen, and we had to stop him. Yes, we used Taurin as bait, because he was Dacian's only weakness."

He paused to rake his fingers through his hair. "But we didn't set that warehouse on fire. We don't work that way. Dacian would've been given a sword so he could fight for his existence." He set his candy aside. "We assumed he was destroyed in the fire because no one ever saw him again. But I've never been sure. Dacian was too powerful, and I can't see him . . ."

Emotion touched his eyes. "The night feeders have always been our enemies, but once a long time ago, Dacian and I were close friends. I don't know what turned him to hatred, but no matter what he became, I never would've destroyed him that way." His expression hardened. "I don't have any friendship bonds with Taurin. He's threatened to take you, so he's finished."

Donna believed him. Not because she had any proof that he was telling the truth, but because her intuition gave him the thumbs-up. Good thing she hadn't decided to be a lawyer. A jury wouldn't be impressed with a my-gut-tells-me-this-guy-is-innocent defense.

Eric watched her eyes. She didn't have a clue how to mask her emotions. So he knew the exact moment she decided in his favor, and he struck. "I have to stay with you, Donna. Here. And once you leave this room, Brynn, Conall, or I have to be near you at all times."

She widened her eyes as she rushed into speech. "Why can't—"

"No. Brynn can't stay with you. You saw what happened when he's with a woman for more than an hour. Conall's immortal, but he doesn't have the powers to match Taurin. It has to be me." There. He'd taken away all her options. Except one. The one she *should* take to insure her safety.

The primitive part of him, the part that for centuries ruled his actions, shouted a resounding, "No! Mine." Mine? When had he decided that? But his primitive self always seemed to be a step ahead when it came to possessing women. His more civilized self grimaced at having to deprive himself of what he wanted, but said what he knew he had to say. "You know, if you fly back to New York, you'll be safe."

"Not necessarily. If Taurin came to New York and took me, what would you do?" She watched him, her unblinking stare hinting that his answer was important.

He forced back the rage he felt whenever he thought of Taurin taking Donna. "I'd fly to New York, hunt him down, and free you."

Her radiant smile told him he'd given the right answer. "There you go. Taurin could follow me anywhere I went, so I may as well stay here." Her smile faded. "Besides, I want to stay. And that decision has nothing to do with my job. I need to know you're safe."

Something warm touched the spot where his heart used to be. Who was the last person to worry about his safety? He couldn't remember. His parents, probably. Both had died before becoming vampire—his mother in childbirth and his father in battle. That was so long ago he couldn't recall, though. He knew that Brynn, Conall, and Holgarth wanted him to stay safe, but they assumed he was so powerful that no one was a danger to him.

Celebrating her decision was selfish, but he couldn't help it. And Eric vowed that Taurin wouldn't catch her alone again. They'd find him and make a preemptive strike before he launched his attack. Eric clenched his teeth to hold back his anger. Every time Taurin threatened Donna, the thought of destroying him got easier and easier.

"Well, now that you guys have the vampire disclosure followed immediately by the horrified reaction over with, we can talk about a night on the town. Not that Galveston could compare with Paris or Rome, but we make do with what we have."

"Thor's bloody hammer!" Eric leaped to his feet and spun to find Asima sitting in regal splendor next to Sweetie Pie and Jessica. "That's the second time you've gotten past my protective shield." He fought for calm.

"So make a better shield. I go where I choose to go." Asima looked down her patrician cat nose at him and then shifted her gaze to Donna. *"Excitable, isn't he?"*

This must be his night to be caught off guard. The thought worried him, and so he used anger to push it from his mind. "Who are you, and why're you popping into rooms where you don't belong?" Eric frowned. "You aren't going into other guests' rooms, are you?" He sat down again.

"I'm Asima, and that's all you need to know. I've only visited Donna's room. I've thought about visiting Conall. He likes cats. Have you noticed how he feeds strays at the service entrance to the restaurant after lunch each day? No, of course you haven't. Noon is still vampire nap time." She padded over to where they sat and leaped onto the small table between them.

"This isn't a good time, Asima." Donna got up to draw the drapes over the window where the first light of morning could be seen.

"Whatever you want, make it quick." Eric could feel the heavy lethargic pull of sleep.

Asima narrowed her blue cat eyes at him. *"Don't you dare go to sleep on me."* She turned her attention to Donna. *"We're going to the Grand 1894 Opera House tonight.* La Traviata *is being performed, and tonight's the last night."*

"No." Eric had to stop this before it gathered steam.

"I can talk for myself." Donna cast him an irritated glance before shifting her attention to Asima. "I'd love to go, but—"

"I know, I know. The great protector has to go with you." Asima wrapped her tail around her. *"And before you ask, yes, I know because I listened in on your conversation. If I didn't spy, how would I know things?"*

Couldn't argue with that. Eric almost felt like smiling. Almost. "Right. I go where Donna goes. And I have to work tonight." When he wasn't so sleepy, he'd have to find out why Asima had chosen his castle to bless with her snooty self. Lucky him.

"No problem." She raised one aristocratic paw and licked it. *"I planted a suggestion in the mind of a woman at the registration desk. She called your sub and said you wanted him to work tonight. We'll be back before midnight so Donna can do her show."*

"You what?" Eric didn't usually thunder. Soft menace was more effective. But this called for thundering. "Who died and made you queen? I don't want to—"

Asima put down her paw, padded to the edge of the table, and leaped into his lap. She stared up at him from gleaming blue eyes. *"You have to go. Donna is the only one I know here who appreciates opera."*

Donna's grimace behind Asima's back said she didn't appreciate it as much as she should.

"Donna deserves a night out before she goes back to New York. Here's your chance. You can take her to dinner—I'll eat yours—and then on to the opera. I already have two tickets. Please, please, please." Asima rubbed her head against his stomach.

Uh-oh. He could resist Asima, but Donna was starting to look sympathetic.

"Let's go, Eric. It'll be nice to get away from the castle for a few hours. I'll be safe with you and Asima." She stopped short of lying about how much she wanted to experience *La Traviata.*

Opera. Why would he want to sit through a couple of hours listening to people singing to each other in a language he didn't understand? If Asima had already called his sub—and that had to stop—then he was free to spend the hours until Donna's show exploring her uncharted wilderness areas.

Whoa, a disturbing thought. What if she was afraid to have sex with him now that she knew he was vampire? The thought upset him, and the fact that it upset him, well, that upset him even more. He'd spent his whole existence enjoying one-night stands. Sex was a lot safer that way. No messy emotional disconnects and no betrayals. A desire for multiple nights with one woman was cause for concern.

"You've locked me out of your mind, vampire, but I know you're not thinking about my trip to the opera." Asima dug her claws into his thigh to remind him who was important in this room.

Eric grabbed at one more escape line. "I guess you'll be changing into human form, because you sure can't go anywhere the way you are now."

Asima actually purred. *"I have to stay in this form as long as I'm on the job, but I've already figured out how to get around the problem."* She leaped from Eric's lap, padded to the door, and waited as it swung open. *"I'll meet you guys here at seven."*

Eric glared at Asima. Nothing had been decided yet. "Wait just a minute, I—"

"She's gone." Donna sounded amused. "I wish I had her talent for getting her own way."

"But you do, talk-show lady. You most certainly do." He knew his gaze was heat and sexual need, but he didn't care. "We'll talk about it." He yawned. "When I wake up. I can't keep my eyes open. Don't worry about sleeping beside me, because I won't be dangerous until late afternoon."

"Comforting. I'll set my alarm on that promise." Her gaze followed him as he reached her bed, stripped off his clothes, and collapsed onto his side of the bed.

His last memory before sleep claimed him was of Donna retrieving her bag of candy and popping a chocolate-covered cherry into her mouth.

Once again, Donna sat cross-legged on her side of the bed watching Eric sleep. Naked. Very naked. She'd had to leave him that way because he'd fallen asleep on top of the covers, and she wasn't strong enough to pull them from underneath him.

Why didn't knowing he was a vampire blow an icy blast of reason across her sexual hot spots? The ones that continued to register burning whenever Eric was near. Was someone not clear on the concept? Hello? There was no such thing as safe sex with a vampire.

The sad truth? Reason came in a distant second to her attraction for Eric. All that black hair spread across his pillow, those sinfully long dark lashes, his sensual lips relaxed in sleep, and that unbroken expanse of smooth warm skin over hard-muscled maleness left her heavy-lidded and breathing hard from her multitude of sexual fantasies.

Just sex? Was feeling more alive than she ever had in her life just about sex? Was worrying about him, wanting to be with him, and rethinking lifetime beliefs just about sex? She didn't have the definitive answer on that, but she was getting close.

And about those lifetime beliefs. Before Eric, she'd been certain she knew what was best for her family. But a few minutes ago she'd found herself saying things like, "Go for it, Trish. If he makes you feel so good you can't think straight, then take the chance. So what if you don't have much in common. *Viva la difference*." Trish had offered to let Donna stay at her place while she was on her medication.

Donna had called Mom next. There'd been extended silence on the line after Donna said, "You know, Mom, I hate to see you and Dad go your separate ways, but I respect your decision. Maybe it's time for both of you to spread your wings." Mom had offered to take her temperature and then make her some chicken soup.

Nate? Well, her brother had never been much for long speeches. When Donna had agreed that "Not going on the cruise is no big deal. Take the kids to Disney World, and then Trish and I can baby-sit while you guys lock yourselves in your bedroom for a weekend of hot loving. Oh, and I have something really sexy you can do with chocolate-covered cherries." Nate had just chuckled.

Donna glanced at the clock. Time to wake her vampire protector so he could remove his shield from her door. She was starved. Hmm. How to wake him? Asima had done it by singing. But then, Asima's singing could reach alien civilizations on far distant planets.

Reaching over, she shook him. Nothing. She whispered in his ear. Nothing. She shouted, "Priest with cross and chef with garlic cloves at door!" at the top of her lungs. Nothing. Finally she gave up. She still had a few of Lola's cookies and his candy left. No way was she eating any more of her cherries.

Climbing from the bed, she grabbed her robe and headed for the bathroom. "Fine. You sleep while I take a shower. Jeez, what a slug." Her muttered protest died away as she tried to close the bathroom door only to have it pulled from her grasp.

"Sorry. No closed doors between us until Taurin is taken care of." He stood in the doorway, his naked male glory almost blinding her.

Would he think it strange if she got her sunglasses from her purse? Yeah, he would. "So what woke you, O Mighty Prince of the Night? Oh, and I shower alone."

His smile was a white slash of sexy male amusement. "The word *shower.* Make sure you leave the bathroom door open enough for me to hear and see if Taurin decides to do a shower snatch." He walked away from the door before she could comment.

Donna frowned. Hadn't Eric told her that Taurin wouldn't rise until sunset? Then what were the chances he'd materialize in her shower while the sun was still shining its little heart out? She narrowed her gaze on the door. If she were the suspicious sort, she might suspect ulterior motives here.

Donna made sure she was standing out of Eric's line of vision if he was still near the partly opened door and then yanked her nightshirt over her head. Sure he'd seen her naked before, but it was the principle of the thing. Slipping into the roomy shower stall, she slid the door closed. He still might see her outline through the frosted glass, but not the important details.

She adjusted the water temperature to comfortably warm and then reached for the soap. Turning her back to the spray, she started to soap her washcloth . . . and uttered a startled squeak.

Eric lounged on the shower's small seat. He watched her from hot predatory eyes. His large bare body seemed to fill the stall, his wicked intentions evident in the hard length of a body part that spoke its mind. "You're a beautiful woman." The deep huskiness of his voice was liquid sex, sliding over her body and coating her with desire.

"Uh-uh. Isn't going to happen, vampire." She purposely invoked his official status to remind them both of how much things had changed since last night. Had she gotten over her panic? Yes. Did he still terrify her? No. Was she ready to make love to him in the shower? Not yet. She'd leave the possibility open for future consideration. "My shower is a sex-free zone today."

"Understood." He lifted his arms above his head and stretched, tightening and delineating everything that could be tightened and delineated in his muscular body. "No sex in your shower."

Did that make her feel all safe and secure? No. He'd agreed too easily. "You can leave now. And while you're waiting for your turn in the shower, why don't you get rid of the door shield and order me something to eat?" *And put some damn clothes on.* Not ready to make love with a vampire? Who was she kidding? When she looked at Eric Mackenzie, she didn't see a deadly creature of the night. She saw the sexiest man she'd ever known and someone she wanted to spend more time with. Maybe if she saw him doing a few authentically evil or disgusting vampirish things, like biting Holgarth's neck—a service to all mankind, actually—or turning into a bat, eew, she might do some attitude adjusting.

"Why don't we leave together?" He reached out and took her hand.

Donna didn't have a chance to mount a verbal assault because suddenly everything blurred. Sheesh, he made her so mad she really couldn't see straight. She put her free hand over her eyes to try to clear her vision.

"You can look now." His voice was a murmur of amused anticipation.

"When I take my hand from my eyes, you'd better be gone from this shower." She was almost afraid to take her hand away, because the blurred vision could only mean two things. Either anger had driven her blood pressure sky high and she was in danger of a medical crisis, or Eric the Evil was messing with her puny mortal mind again.

Slowly, as though if she looked in small increments everything would be okay, she took her hand from her eyes. She sucked in her breath so she'd have enough oxygen left until her heart started beating again. "Tell me we're not floating in the clouds? Naked?"

"You don't like it?" He rolled over onto his back and stared up at the bright blue sky above the clouds. "You said the shower was a no-sex zone, so I took you someplace else." His lips turned up in a small self-satisfied smile.

"Are we really in the clouds or is this just happening in my mind? And shouldn't it be colder up here?" It was a testament to the week's weirdness that she could discuss this with some degree of calmness.

Looking around, she felt like all her senses would explode with the pure exhilaration of experiencing total beauty and freedom. A sky so blue it hurt her eyes, white fluffy clouds shading to light gray, air so cold and clean that she couldn't stop breathing it in huge gulps, and best of all, no clothes to filter out all the sensations.

He turned his head and raised one expressive brow. "Cold? You've talked to people who floated naked in the clouds, and they told you this?" He waved away her concern. "I guarantee you'll never be cold when you're with me."

She believed him.

He sat up, reached out, and pulled her to his side. "Relax, enjoy the view, and play with me."

Donna cast him a suspicious glance. "Define *play.*"

Kneeling, he scooped up a fluffy section of cloud and dropped it on her. She gasped. It felt like tiny ice crystals touching her body, shocking yet . . . stimulating.

And then he leaned forward and touched his tongue to one of the crystals on her shoulder. It was more than a momentary sensation of heat against her skin. The warmth slid into her, reaching spots far removed from her shoulder.

Before she had a chance to recover from his first touch, he moved on to other crystals melting in more strategic spots. Eric flicked the tip of his tongue over an icy crystal on her nipple, and she waited expectantly for steam to rise.

Between gasps of pleasure, she fought to get in a few coherent words. "Not fair. Let's alternate. Me, then you." Not giving him a chance to object, she grabbed a large handful of cloud and flung it at him. She licked her lips at the thought of all that warm male skin exposed for exploration before touching her tongue to a crystal low on his stomach.

He sucked in his stomach and murmured his appreciation. Then he found a crystal on her stomach to lick into submission. Hey, this was great. Body parts that had a vested interest in his mouth waited impatiently.

Laughing, she wrapped her arms around his waist and

rolled, taking him with her. Then, as soon as she released him, she scooted down to find the perfect crystal glistening on his sex. Her laughter died and she swallowed hard as she realized how serious Eric took his play. The length, breadth, and hardness of him triggered a heavy rush of warmth low in her belly. Before she could ruin the play by straddling his hips and lowering herself until she felt the head of his cock stretching and sliding into her, she smoothed her tongue over the crystal and retreated.

His soft laughter mocked her. "Coward." He rolled onto her, driving her into the soft cloud. As she fought to the surface, he took advantage of her distraction by pushing her legs apart, and lifting her bottom so he could reach the icy drop that had conveniently nestled on her body's most sensitive hot button.

What were the chances that a single crystal would score a bull's-eye? "You planted—" But as he glided the tip of his tongue over that tiny but amazing center of her sexuality, she completely forgot what he'd planted. She moaned. Had he planted turnips? She lifted her hips and spasmed as he slid his tongue smoothly into her. Sweet peas? Oh, who cared? He could plant a Kansas wheat field for all she cared.

It took her a minute to realize he'd moved away. His eyes were heavy-lidded with desire, and his mouth . . . Well, his mouth definitely qualified him for the Sexual Hall of Fame.

"This was play, Donna. You're not ready for what comes next." He sat cross-legged watching her. "Now that you know I'm a vampire, the playing field has shifted. Next time we make love, I hope you can accept that part of me."

She met his gaze. He wanted to bite her. Wasn't going to happen. There was nothing sexy about someone biting her neck.

"Wrong. It's one of life's most sensual experiences." He gazed past her into the distance. "But it also demands that you give up complete control and trust me in every way."

Give him complete control? She didn't think so. "Uh-huh. And you're in my mind again." What was he staring at? She turned to follow his gaze. Nothing but an endless sea of clouds.

"I've been in your mind from the moment we left the shower." He sounded distracted. "There's a plane coming."

"A plane?" Her voice was a horrified squeak. "Do you mean a big old jumbo jet is going to fly past us?" Desperately she looked around for somewhere to hide. "Hundreds of people will be glued to their windows watching the naked chick and her vampire hottie?"

Eric smiled what he probably thought was a calming smile. "I can see it now. It isn't a jumbo jet. In fact, I think . . ."

She saw it, winging its way toward them. Ohmigod!

"Yeah, I'm sure of it." He looked pumped. "That's Air Force One."

"Air Force One?" Horror clogged her throat. "The president's plane?"

He didn't have to answer, because the plane had reached them. It seemed to fly past in slow motion. "Hey, look. There's the president. He's waving at you. Wave back."

Donna gaped. The president smiled at her and waved. Weakly, she waved back. "Hope he doesn't find out I voted for the other guy last year." This was absolutely the most embarrassing moment of her life. Did he recognize her? Please, God, no.

As the plane disappeared into the clouds, Donna turned to Eric. "The president saw us naked."

Eric shrugged, and then smiled at her. It was his bad-boy smile, guaranteed to make mush of any female foolish enough to try to resist him. "You're cute when you blush all over."

"I want to go home." Home as in the cozy crazy Castle of Dark Dreams where no public officials would see her naked.

He simply nodded. And as her vision blurred again, she

thought deep thoughts about sex, control, and playing naked in the clouds.

When her vision cleared, she was standing in the shower with warm water flowing over her, and Eric was still lounging on the seat. She closed her eyes for a moment to center herself and then opened them. "How'd you do it?"

He uncoiled from the seat, all gleaming flesh and lithe animal grace. Gazing down at her, he smiled, but it didn't quite reach his eyes. "From here"— he touched the side of his head—"to here." He placed his finger against her head. "I can take you anywhere. You can experience anything you choose, no matter how improbable. And in this case, without ever leaving the shower."

"Why?" Why had he done it, and more to the point, why did she care? He'd probably just shrug her question off with a for-the-hell-of-it.

Eric quit all pretenses of smiling. His intense gaze seared her, exposing all her uncertainties, all her conflicted emotions where he was concerned.

"I needed to balance things. You have all these preconceived notions of what a vampire should be—dark, brooding, definitely not a fun guy to have around." He traced her jaw with the tip of one finger. "I want to be around you, so I needed to show you that hanging with a creature of the night has some pretty spectacular perks."

Since Donna couldn't think of anything witty or meaningful to add to that, she silently watched him leave the shower. Then she grinned. He was right. What a rush. All past and possibly future boyfriends faded into the sepia tones of boring.

"Maybe we can try Mars next." She hummed as she washed her hair.

12

"Tell me how Taurin became invisible. Can you become invisible? And what about Asima? How'd she get through the shield you put up?" Donna rattled on, hopefully keeping Eric busy answering her questions while she stared at him and occasionally remembered to wipe the drool from her chin.

"Taurin is visible. *You* just can't see him." Eric paced the room, his impatience making Sweetie Pie and Jessica nervous. They folded some of their leaves.

"Uh, yeah. Sooo, why can't *I* see him?" She'd had Eric pegged for a jeans and T-shirt kinda guy, but wow, what a transformation. Black suit, white shirt, red tie, and hair tied back from that hard masculine face with its hot blue eyes and full sensual lower lip. Would he look like all the other men in suits tonight? Never. Suits would tame other men, label them as civilized and willing to bend to convention. Any woman who looked at Eric would sense that on this man, a suit was meant simply as an outer shell, a shiny veneer that didn't hide the dark, dangerous, and completely fascinating man who wore it.

"Taurin has mastered some mental powers that other night feeders haven't. The power to cloak his presence is one. Your brain processes only some of the images around you. Taurin has the ability to manipulate minds so that your brain doesn't include him in the things it chooses to 'see.' I saw him, but I decided not to follow him out of the castle because I was . . . distracted by your reaction to my vampire form." He glanced at his watch. "Where's the cat? She's late. Maybe she won't show." He looked hopeful.

Donna wasn't going to let him sidetrack her with a discussion of Asima's lateness. "My reaction bothered you?"

He speared her with an angry glance. "We'd made incredible love, and then you were looking at me like I was a monster who'd just risen from the primordial ooze. Yeah, it bothered me." He exhaled sharply. "Look, that's the reaction I always get, so don't blame yourself. Logically, I expected you to be freaked out." His tight smile said he'd hoped she'd be different.

She watched him rub his hand over his face and sensed he was attempting to close the door on any more unexpected emotional discharges. Donna wasn't quite sure what it meant, but she was glad her response to his vampire form had upset him. Why? Hadn't a clue.

"You asked about Asima." He continued to pace. "I don't know what she is, but—"

"She's here and she's ready to rumble."

Eric stopped pacing to stare at the bed where Asima sat in regal splendor with her tail wrapped around her. She wore a jeweled collar in honor of the night's festivities.

Donna rose from her chair and walked over to the bed. "Your collar is stunning. Real diamonds, I presume?"

Asima offered her an offended cat sniff. *"Of course. And since Eric didn't have a chance to explain his theory of why I can bypass his puny shield, let me do it."* She used a paw to smooth down a hair that had the temerity to stick up on her smoothly elegant Siamese face. *"I've existed for thousands of years, and I get my power from one who has existed for even longer. So don't mess with me."* She tried to look fierce, but the effect was ruined by the almost childlike excitement gleaming in her blue eyes. *"And I absolutely love your dress, Donna. Short, black, and sexy. Works for any occasion."*

Eric joined Donna at the bed. "I've borrowed the castle van for the night. It doesn't have windows, so if Donna drives I can get to the restaurant with minimum damage from the daylight. I made reservations at a restaurant where I know the owner. He's set aside a table in a corner away from any windows and hopefully not too close to other diners." He glanced at his watch again. "I've done my part, Asima. Now tell me how you intend to get yourself into the restaurant and opera house."

"I'd say this is the most bizarre thing I've ever done in my life, but hey, I just came back from romping naked on a cloud, so I guess it's a toss-up." Donna made slitty-eyes at Eric. He sat across the restaurant table from her trying not to laugh, because even one snicker would end his immortal life. "Is anyone staring? Tell me no one is staring."

Eric glanced around the restaurant. "Not now. But a few minutes ago—"

"Give me a piece of Eric's fish." Asima's hissed demand probably interrupted something Donna didn't want to know.

Donna reached over and stabbed a piece of the fish on Eric's plate with satisfying viciousness. She lifted it toward her mouth but changed directions at the last moment. Without taking her death glare from Eric—just in case he thought he'd laugh when she wasn't looking—she rerouted the fork to a spot beside her right ear. "I can't believe I'm wearing a cat as an accessory."

Asima delicately removed the fish from the fork, chewed, and swallowed before answering. *"Stop complaining and admit it's a brilliant idea. I drape myself around your neck like those unfortunate little animals I've seen some women wearing. Truly gruesome and never at-*

tractive, I might add. And then I just make sure I cover my face with my paws so no one knows I'm a cat. Voilà, I don't get a second glance."

A smile escaped Eric's iron control. "Our waitress gave you three or four glances." He aimed his smile at Donna. "And congrats on the quick thinking, talk-show lady. When she asked what 'it' was, your creativity blew me away. Imagine. You have one of the first fake corimanki furs, and New York women are fighting each other for them. The corimanki, as in a small just-been-discovered mammal from an uninhabited region of Scandinavia, is the latest trend in neck decoration. Your mind is a scary thing."

Donna scowled as she glanced around and then fed her furry necklace more fish. "I bet she goes online and Googles corimanki as soon as she hits her front door. At least she didn't recognize me, so she can't track the lie back to my doorstep."

"We'd better get going if you want to catch the beginning of the opera." His grim expression said he'd rather roll around naked in a pile of garlic cloves than sit through *La Traviata.*

After Eric paid for their meal, she followed him while loud whispers of "corimanki" trailed her to the door. It was growing dark out, but Eric still had to run for the van. Once inside, Donna followed his directions as she drove to the Grand 1894 Opera House. The drive didn't take long, but she filled the silence with not so subtle threats of what would happen if Asima even twitched during the performance.

"I won't move." Purr. *"I'll simply soak in the wonder of the music."* Purr. *"It's a tragic story, and I always cry at the end, but not tonight."* Purr. *"Tonight I'll be as quiet as a mouse."* Purr. *"Although, come to think of it, mice aren't all that quiet. Especially when you catch them by their tails."* Purrrr.

Jeez, she'd had enough. "For crying out loud, stop purring in my ear." Donna let Eric off at the front of the building, so he wouldn't have far to walk in the fading light, and then parked the van. "Now, from this moment on, no sounds. A noisy accessory will attract attention."

Asima covered her face with her paws. *"Cross my heart. Of course, I haven't had any contact with my heart lately, so I don't know how much of an impact that will have on—"*

"Just shut up." Oops. Think before putting mouth in motion. Nearby people turned to look at her, and then fixed their gazes on her most obvious fashion statement. She smiled weakly. "Corimanki."

Once she joined Eric in the lobby, they made their way to their seats. Asima had bought tickets for the first level in the middle section. At least they were at ground level and on an aisle in case they had to make a fast getaway. "This is a beautiful place."

"It's the Official Opera House of Texas. It survived the 1900 hurricane that just about leveled everything on Galveston Island." Asima moved one paw away from her eye to peer at Donna. *"I'm so happy that I can share this with you."*

Surprised, Donna admitted her unconventional semi-friendship with Asima kind of made her feel good, too. She glanced around at the many tiers of boxes and the two higher balcony levels. The opera house had a warm Old-World charm.

"Maybe you'd like to visit a few opera houses in Italy." Eric placed his hand on her knee and slid his fingers smoothly up the exposed length of her outer thigh.

She thought about her most recent field trip above the clouds. "Sounds cool. But dressed. Definitely dressed."

He leaned toward her, and his wicked smile had her thinking that maybe *La Traviata* would be a great experience after all.

"Oh, I don't know. Naked in Italy isn't a bad place to be. You'd be a goddess there."

"Goddess? Someone mentioned me?" The whisper came from behind them.

Donna turned her head to meet the interested stare of Sparkle Stardust. "You like opera?"

"I like many things, sister." She leaned closer. "Tell me you're not wearing a cat around your neck. We have to do lunch tomorrow and talk fashion, because you so need my help." Sparkle paused to narrow her gaze on Asima as the music began. "Is this the telepathic cat you talked about on your show? An opera lover. How . . . improbable. Who would've thought." She didn't try to hide her amusement.

Beside Donna's ear, Asima's angry hiss sounded like escaping steam. *"And who would've thought sex-obsessed one-dimensional candy-store owners would have an interest in anything cultural. Especially one with such pitiful taste. Trying to look sexy by wearing a sleazy top that plunges to your navel is so . . . so . . ."* Asima struggled for exactly the right word. *"Insecure. Someone truly comfortable with their sexuality wouldn't need to expose their bodies to feel sensual."*

Whoa. Donna widened her eyes as she glanced at Eric. He returned her look, his expression uneasy. So that meant he was hearing Asima, too. Panicked, she glanced around and then sighed her relief. No one else seemed to be picking up on Asima's chatter.

The music swelled as Donna waited fearfully for Sparkle's wrath to fall on Asima. Luckily, they'd turned the lights down and the audience was into the performance, because Asima had removed her paws from her face and turned to glare at Sparkle from gleaming blue eyes.

Donna could feel Sparkle's sharp exhalation on her neck as she went nose to nose with the cat.

"How many sensual techniques to bring people together have *you* racked up over the years? Oh, wait, I know the answer to that one. None. You might be able to name every freakin' opera in the world, but you don't know squat about sexual attraction. My minion, Deimos, is a virgin, but he could probably teach you a few things." Sparkle dug her fingers into the back of Donna's seat. "Damn, now look what you've done. I broke a nail. How can I enjoy the rest of the show with a broken nail?" Sparkle had kept most of her rant to a furious whisper, but the discovery of her broken nail raised her volume to a stricken wail.

Donna winced, but she put her growing panic on pause for a moment to wonder where Asima and Sparkle had met before. Two strangers wouldn't go at each other like that.

Asima was vibrating with fury. *"Slut queen!"* Evidently she'd decided to abandon cultured behavior in favor of rolling around in the mud with Sparkle.

"Goddess gofer!" Obviously Sparkle's ultimate put-down.

A chorus of shushes from the surrounding audience put a halt to Sparkle's insults that were rapidly rising in volume to compete with the tenor on stage. The shushes also subdued Asima, because she quickly put her paws over her face again.

What was a goddess gofer, and what did it have to do with Asima? Donna continued to watch the show, but she couldn't get rid of the feeling that she needed to know a lot more about Asima and Sparkle.

Donna didn't worry about Asima and Sparkle long, though, because Eric continued to do arousing things with his amazingly talented fingers. It was a good thing the opera house was darkened or else the audience might wonder at her glazed eyes and dazed expression. Then again, they'd probably chalk it up to her reaction to the emotional tragedy being played out on the stage.

Emotions were running pretty high in seat L12, too. Eric had transferred his attention to her inner thigh, walking his fingers under her dress and applying pressure to her go-spot through her panties. She'd worn black panties when she should've worn no panties. Donna made a mental note—no panties—for the next time she attended an event with Eric that included wearing a dress.

Her sexual pressure built along with the escalating drama of the opera. Any minute now she'd pop her cork, leap to her feet, and scream her own personal climax, which in no way coincided with the opera's climax. This would *not* be a good thing and would alienate opera fans everywhere. To distract her need to do any popping, she concentrated on returning Eric's caresses by sliding her fingers up his thigh and drawing circles on his growing interest. Anything he could do, she could do better. Sometimes.

Donna had forgotten about Asima. A mistake. The opera's dying Violetta was singing her tragic last song when Asima took her paws from her face. Tears filled her huge expressive eyes and . . .

Oh. My. God. No! Donna attempted to clap her hand over the cat's open mouth, but she was too late. Asima broke into song. She probably knew every word and note, but unfortunately she was in Siamese form. Someone had told Donna once that a Siamese's voice was distinct and never-to-be-forgotten. No kidding. She pressed her hands over her ears, but nothing could drown it out. It was the sound of a baby crying at full volume magnified ten times.

People turned to glare. Donna grinned weakly. Now would be a good time for the floor to open so she could disappear. She only had the presence of mind to pull the shoulder of her dress over Asima's head. Asima didn't miss a note.

Uh-oh. Eric winced. Damn cat. Two objectives. Think of an excuse for the people gaping at them and get the hell out of there. He reached into his pocket, pulled out his cell phone, and tried to look sheepish. Which was tough, because he'd never been a sheepish kind of man or vampire.

"Sorry. Our first kid. Thought it'd be cute to hear little Elise crying instead of a regular ring." From the looks he was getting, no one else thought little Elise's crying was cute. He grabbed Donna's hand and hauled her up the aisle. By the time they burst from the opera house, Asima had wound down.

"I'm so sorry, guys. I just lost control. The passion and beauty of the music washed over me and carried me to another place. It was a wonderful night." She paused to con-

sider how wonderful it had been. *"Except for Sparkle. But she was only a blip on my happiness screen."*

Eric was winding up to deliver another blip to her happiness screen when his cell phone rang, for real this time. He dug it from his jacket pocket.

A few minutes later he stood staring numbly into the darkness.

"What's wrong?" Donna touched his arm.

Even in this moment filled with fury and guilt, he realized her touch comforted him in a way he'd never expected. "I underestimated Taurin. Foolish of me. He never meant to take you. He made us think you were his target, when it was Conall all along."

"Conall? What's happened to Conall?" Asima's voice held a note of fear he hadn't heard before.

He raced for the van while Donna tried to keep pace. Asima clung to Donna's shoulder, for once silenced. "That was Holgarth on the phone. They'd begun a new fantasy, but when it was time for Brynn and Conall to do their thing, Brynn realized that Conall wasn't in the hall. They'd just plugged someone in to take Conall's place when Holgarth got a call from Taurin."

Eric climbed into the driver's seat and waited while Donna climbed in beside him. Heedless of speed limits, he burned rubber leaving the parking lot and sped toward Seawall Boulevard.

"Where's Conall?" The fear was gone from Asima's voice, and in its place was a strange ferocity.

Eric didn't have time to puzzle over Asima's unusual interest in Conall. "Taurin said he'd taken Conall, just as I'd taken him. I don't know how he caught Conall off guard, but that's not important now. He said Conall would stay alive until I came for him."

"Conall represents your brother, so Taurin's setting up the same scenario you guys played out before, only he thinks he's in control this time." Donna sounded worried. "Where does Taurin have him, and how're we going to free Conall?"

"He's holed up in a beach house on the west side of the island." *We.* Donna had only known them a few days, and yet she was willing to put her safety on the line to help rescue Conall. Even with fear for Conall clogging his throat, he silently applauded his talk-show lady. Eric had been a Viking warrior and a Highlander. He admired courage and loyalty. Donna would be a fitting mate for a warrior to ride into battle beside.

"If Taurin told Holgarth where he was holding Conall, why don't you fly there instead of driving? What about the police? Maybe they could help." She lifted Asima from her shoulder and set her between the seats. "And what about you, Asima? Can't you just sort of, I don't know, beam yourself there?"

"Can't do." Eric prayed to whatever deities might have him tuned in right now that no cops tried to stop him for speeding. He turned onto Seawall Boulevard and floored it. "I can't fly in my human form. I'd have to shape-shift into my great gray owl form. That would take time, and around here it might attract some attention. The cops? They'd try to handle it like a normal hostage situation, but they wouldn't have a clue how to handle a vampire with Taurin's power."

"I don't 'beam' places. I can break down my molecular structure and transfer it to another place, but that won't do much good if I don't know where I'm going." Asima had calmed down enough to wash her face. *"Besides, Conall will be safe until Eric reaches him."*

She didn't say it, but Eric got the feeling Asima wouldn't be standing on the sidelines. He frowned. He didn't need anyone trying to help and instead putting Conall in more danger. But he'd deal with Asima when the time came.

"Conall's really like a brother to you, isn't he?" She reached over and stroked his arm.

"Yeah." Funny how her touch assured him that she completely understood the bond he had with Conall. "I've lived among humans for most of my life, so I didn't dare form many long-term friendships. People notice when you stay twenty-nine for thirty years. Brynn, Conall, and I are all immortal, so we share a lot of the same experiences. In the time we've worked at the castle, we've become good friends. I don't have so many friends that I can afford to lose one." He'd left the seawall behind and was now driving toward the less populated west end of the island.

They completed the rest of the trip in silence. When he finally found the address Holgarth had given him and parked in front of the small boarded-up beach house, Eric's anger was running high. He'd stripped away his civilized face. He'd wear his Viking face tonight, and Taurin wouldn't live to threaten anyone else Eric cared for.

Eric had barely stopped the van before Donna got out and Asima leaped to the ground beside her. He joined them. "Look, don't you think everyone would be better off if both of you stayed in the van?" He knew better than to tell Donna he was trying to keep her safe. He sensed *safe* would be a trigger word for her.

"No." Their answers were simultaneous.

That settled that. He didn't have time to argue with them. Besides, he had a feeling he couldn't keep Asima from doing whatever she damn well pleased. Brynn's car was parked in front of the van. They walked together up the driveway and around to the back of the house. Brynn and Holgarth waited there for them.

"Holgarth?" Somehow Eric had expected the wizard to stay at the castle to keep things running.

Holgarth allowed himself a long-suffering sigh. "I closed the fantasies for the rest of the night. What else could I do? Someone with good sense and a military background should be here to organize the rescue."

Eric raised one brow. "A military background?"

Holgarth cast him a withering stare. "I advised Napoleon during some of his more spectacular victories. I was pre-Waterloo, of course. Wizards have a variety of talents."

"Napoleon?" Donna looked at Holgarth, her eyes wide with shock. "How old are you?"

Holgarth offered her a superior smile. "Very, very old, child. I would expect you to show the proper respect for one of my age and wisdom."

"Yeah, sure." She turned to Eric. "Let's get this rescue going."

"No. I'll take care of Taurin." Eric moved to Brynn's side. "Anything I should know?"

Brynn turned to look at Eric, and for the first time since meeting him, Eric saw the demon that was Brynn. His eyes glowed golden in the darkness, but Eric sensed no warmth. Brynn's eyes were so cold Eric had to suppress an involuntary shudder. The demon's eyes promised that if anything happened to Conall or him, Brynn would hunt Taurin down and destroy him.

Brynn turned his attention back to the house. "I haven't seen anyone on the beach since we got here, and the nearby houses probably belong to weekenders. Anyway, no one's home. So maybe we can pull this off without an audience." He raked his fingers through his hair as he glanced at Donna and Asima. "We already have too many here." He returned his attention to Eric and grinned, but the demon still shown from his eyes. "Maybe that's good, though, because no way will Taurin get past all of us."

Eric nodded as he swung to include everyone in his next statement. "I'm going in. Just me." He raised a hand to forestall an argument. "If I need backup, I'll call for it. But Taurin wants *me,* not Conall. Once Conall is safe, Taurin and I will settle things permanently. If all of you rush in with me, Taurin might panic and hurt Conall." He wouldn't need backup.

Holgarth scowled. "I believe your plan is militarily unsound, but Taurin is your enemy, so the decision is yours. For the moment. I'll deploy the rest of our forces around the perimeter of the property so that Taurin can't escape. If at any time I feel that you or Conall is in imminent danger, I'll take offensive action."

Eric nodded. "Whatever." Holgarth was a bossy pain-in-the-butt, but he wanted to help. That touched Eric. He'd never tell the old wizard, though, because Holgarth would just add it to his arsenal of weapons.

Before leaving, Eric turned to Donna. For the first time tonight he saw fear flood her eyes, but not for herself, for *him.* She really cared what happened to him. The emotional hit rocked his world. "Everyone here will keep you safe. Trust them." *Trust me.*

She reached up and smoothed her fingers over his tense jaw. "Come back in one piece, vampire, and bring Conall with you."

He forced a smile to his lips. "Will do, talk-show lady." Eric wanted to pull her into his embrace and kiss her hard, but instead he turned away and strode toward the back door.

Such a small, white, ordinary-looking house to hold so much evil inside it. Eric could feel Taurin's hatred and fury beating at him. He sensed nothing from Conall. That worried him. He tried the back door, and as he'd expected, it opened. Stepping into the kitchen, he paused to let the darkness settle around him. The total blackness didn't bother him. As he clothed himself in vampire form, objects in the room became clear.

"In here, Eric." Taurin's voice came from what Eric assumed was the living room.

Eric moved silently across the kitchen, but he didn't really expect Taurin to strike as soon as he entered the room. This was all about revenge for Taurin, so he'd want to talk about his brother, taunt Eric with threats to Conall, and brag about his power that he thought equaled Eric's. It didn't. Never would. And once Eric made sure Conall was out of Taurin's reach, he'd end Taurin's vengeful existence.

Eric paused before moving into the living room. Taurin wasn't taking any chances with Conall's incredible strength. Chains secured the warrior to an upright steel pole that Taurin had driven into the floor and ceiling. Conall would have to bring down the ceiling to release himself. Not beyond Conall's ability in a conscious state. But Conall hung inert from his chains.

"What did you do to him?" If Conall was dead, Taurin wouldn't live beyond the next minute.

Taurin ignored Eric's question. He leaned against the front door, his posture relaxed, but his eyes wary. He smiled at Eric, a smile that was open and boyish, a smile that could lure the unwary to their deaths. To show his contempt for Eric, he hadn't changed to vampire form yet. He did so as Eric stepped nearer. "I put a shield around the house earlier. I opened it enough for you to get inside, but I've closed it again."

Eric wasn't surprised that Taurin had the power to produce a shield, but it made things harder. Even though Taurin's shield was probably weak, Eric would still need a few minutes to dissolve it. And he might not have a few minutes. He'd take his chances if he just had to worry about himself. But if Taurin didn't release Conall, he'd have his friend's safety to think about.

"Conall is a sucker for a hard-luck story, particularly if it involves a cat." Taurin pushed away from the wall and moved closer to Conall. The threat was implicit. If Eric tried to take him out, he'd kill Conall. "I paid someone to tell Conall there was an injured cat under a car that was parked outside the restaurant's service entrance. I cloaked my presence, and as soon as he stepped outside I hit him with a spray guaranteed to seriously mess with his eyes. While he was trying to see, I shot him with a tranquilizer. He's been out since then."

Eric watched Taurin with unblinking intensity as he tried to probe the other vampire's thoughts. No luck. Taurin's mind was in lockdown mode. "Since we're playing out that other time, let me call someone in to take Conall out of here. Conall represents you, and you escaped."

He allowed himself a smile, one that mocked Taurin. "Does it bother you that your brother helped you escape, but you were too weak to help him? Do you ever think about how things would've ended if you hadn't been stupid enough to walk into a trap? Am I the only one you're mad at?" Eric watched the fury build in Taurin's eyes.

Good. If he lost all that smooth control he was holding on to by a thread, he'd make a mistake.

Eric didn't find out what Taurin would do next, because suddenly Asima materialized beside Conall.

"What the . . . ?" Taurin widened his eyes.

Eric narrowed his. Couldn't anyone follow directions?

"How'd that cat get through my shield?" Taurin took a threatening step toward Asima.

"I wouldn't do that if I were you." Eric might not know much about Asima, but he knew enough to suspect she was a little more than a mere opera lover. And even though she could probably reduce Taurin to a pile of smoking ashes, something from his Viking past demanded that *he* be the one to take Taurin down.

Asima crouched, her ears flat against her head and her tail whipping angrily. She lifted her lips from her teeth and growled at Taurin.

Eric figured it was the demonic glow in her eyes that made Taurin pause. Smart move. She had the same expression in her eyes that Brynn had a few minutes ago. He wouldn't want to mess with this kitty.

Taurin turned a frustrated gaze on Eric. "What is it?"

Eric shrugged and then watched as a brilliant white glow formed around Asima and Conall. With no one touching him, Conall's chains fell away. Then the light disappeared and with it, Asima and Conall.

Wow. Impressive. *Very* impressive. Asima had meddled where she shouldn't, but Eric was thankful she'd solved his biggest worry. Conall was safe. Now he could concentrate on Taurin.

"Looks like Asima solved our problem. Now you can get on with your revenge thing." Eric moved a little closer to Taurin. The vampire couldn't use Conall as a threat any longer. "You know, I've been thinking about Dacian and that night. First off, none of the Mackenzies started that fire. We don't destroy that way. Dacian would've been given a chance to defend himself."

"You were his friend once." Taurin's fury was bubbling just below the surface.

Was Taurin even listening to him? "We. Didn't. Kill. Him." Eric forced himself to relax. He couldn't let his own anger make him careless. "I'm not even sure Dacian died in that fire. He was the most powerful night feeder I've ever met, and I can't believe he couldn't escape. And afterward, nothing of him was ever found. No metal from buckles or weapons. Not a trace. Don't you think that's a little strange?"

Taurin's face paled, his eyes black and stricken. "If Dacian escaped, he wouldn't have let me think he was dead. He was my brother. I would've died for him. He wouldn't walk away from me." He lifted his lips from his fangs in a feral snarl. "You're lying."

Eric recognized the moment before Taurin's anger exploded. He projected enough power toward the other vampire to knock him on his ass. Too late. Taurin had a lighter hidden in his palm. Even as Eric's wave of power knocked him backward, he flicked it on and dropped it to the floor. Flames leaped between them and then ran across the floor and circled the room. Taurin must've used some kind of accelerant. They were trapped.

Taurin grinned at him across the flames. "You thought you had more time, didn't you, Eric? You didn't think I'd be willing to keep you company on your trip to hell. But I know your friends are outside. No way could I escape. And from the instant I knew Dacian was dead, I've planned for this moment. There's nothing much left for me to do in this existence."

The heat of the flames beat at Eric, the smell of burning wood and choking smoke reminding him of that other time. But he didn't let the memory distract him. His Viking and Highlander warrior past served him well. He felt no fear, only an icy determination to survive while Taurin died.

Whatever Eric was going to do, he'd better do it fast. But first he needed to keep Taurin busy talking so he wouldn't realize what Eric had in mind until it was too late. "Why'd you center your revenge on me? I wasn't the only one there that night."

"You were the only one there who'd been his friend." Taurin's anger sounded like it was almost strangling him. "You betrayed him."

Eric doubted Taurin was thinking beyond his hate, and that lack of thought would doom him. While Taurin answered, Eric projected his power outward, beyond the room, beyond his waiting friends, and called the elements to him. Or at least the two he had power over. Too bad fire wasn't one of them.

Thunder crashed and lightning flickered around the cracks of the boarded-up windows. Wind shook the small house and then the rain came. It beat against the house, pounding on the roof with a fury that drowned out even the crackling flames.

"That rain won't do much to put out the fire in here." Taurin sounded triumphant.

Eric allowed him his small joy. It wouldn't last long. Death by fire for a vampire was a particularly painful way to go. For a moment Eric considered strengthening the wind to hurricane force so it would tear the house apart, but abandoned the idea. That kind of wind would harm people and destroy property. Besides, the wind was only a distraction.

As Eric prepared to abandon Taurin to the fire he'd created, he paused as his mind was suddenly filled with a rush of voices.

"I detect the presence of fire within the house. Identify your location so we can mount a rescue. And do forget about that warrior nonsense and accept our help. Even Napoleon needed me to get him out of a tight spot occasionally." Holgarth.

"I give you one minute to get your ass out of there, Eric, before I come in. By the time I'm finished with Taurin, there won't be enough pieces for even the devil to claim." Brynn.

But it was the third voice that took his breath away, that flooded him with emotion, and filled him with a joy he had no right to feel in the middle of the inferno the living room had become.

"Eric! Get out of there. Now." The hint of tears lurked within the voice. *"Dammit. I've been saving those chocolate-covered cherries, and you're not going to cheat me out of the chance to use them."*

Donna. For the first time she'd reached out to him with her mind. Tonight was a good time to live.

13

Eric stared across the roaring flames at Taurin. "Too bad you couldn't recognize the truth when you heard it. Dacian would've." Eric focused his power and then placed a shield around himself. Now for the tougher part.

The flames wouldn't give him enough time to dissolve Taurin's shield around the house. Closing his eyes, he once again drew his immense power to him. Calling the elements had weakened him a little, but he still had enough power to finish the job.

Eric heard Taurin scream as the flames reached him. Pushing everything from his mind he focused on the living room wall. In his mind he visualized a giant fist punching a hole through it. He opened his eyes to the explosive sound of splintering wood and a collapsing wall. Without hesitating, he flung himself through the opening and into the violent storm beyond.

He was vaguely aware of Taurin staggering through the hole behind him just as the roof collapsed onto the spreading fire. The driving rain was putting out the flames even as Eric raced toward where his friends waited for him. Willing himself back to human form, Eric glanced behind him to where Taurin had fallen a short distance from the house. He must've managed to create a weak shield to protect himself in some small part from the flames. From the look of him, it hadn't done much protecting.

But Eric forgot about Taurin, the storm, and everything else in the world as Donna flung herself at him. He wrapped his arms around her and held her tightly as the wind howled and the rain soaked them. He kissed the top of her head, and she looked up at him, her eyes glistening. He wasn't sure whether the trails of water flowing down her face came from tears or the rain. He selfishly hoped they were tears.

"It's over now." He ran his hands up and down her back, sharing his heat through her rain-soaked dress. Finally he looked around. "Where's Conall?"

She blinked. "Didn't he come out with you?" Donna glanced around. "Come to think of it, where's Asima? She was here watching the house with the rest of us."

Holgarth joined them. "What happened in there, Eric?"

Eric raked his fingers through his hair as he tried to put everything together. "Asima appeared, surrounded Conall in a white light, and then they both disappeared. I assumed she just took him out here." He narrowed his gaze. "Conall had better be at the castle when we get back, or Asima is going to be missing a few of her nine lives."

Taking Donna's arm, he started to guide her toward the van. "I need to get back to the castle fast to make sure Conall's there. And you have a show to do."

"Oh, no." She glanced at her watch. "Ken will be going ballistic."

"You'll be there in time. Do you have a guest tonight?" He tried to focus on Donna's show, shutting out thoughts of his enemy who still lay near the house's burned-out shell. As a warrior, he'd learned to put the battlefield behind him once the fight was over, to not dwell on those he'd been forced to kill. Death and destruction had been part of his early life, and he'd remained sane because he'd found ways to cope with what he did. He made no excuses.

"Uh-huh. Amanda Maguire did the interior design for the castle, and Conleth Maguire painted it. They fell in love on the job, and since they live in Galveston, they agreed to stop by to give some juicy info about their experiences. Should be great."

Glancing back, Donna noted that the fire was out and the rain had lightened. "What're you going to do with . . ." She shifted her gaze to where Taurin had been lying. Gone. Donna looked at Brynn. "Where's Taurin?"

Brynn nodded toward the overgrown field next door. "I dragged him over there. The weeds will hide him in case anyone saw the fire and called it in. But I don't think we have to worry. The fire was only visible for a few minutes, and it would've been tough to see with all the rain." Without a backward glance, he and Holgarth headed for Brynn's car.

"Wait." Donna resisted Eric's attempt to pull her toward the van. "Is he still alive?"

Brynn flashed her a cold smile. His eyes were hard, and she didn't recognize the sensual seducer in this man. "*Alive* is a relative term when you're talking about night feeders. But yes, he's still alive."

She frowned. Everything she understood about the way people behaved came from her life experiences. In this situation someone would call the police and an ambulance. The police would arrest Taurin for attempted murder, and then the ambulance would take him to the hospital. She got the feeling, though, that she wasn't in Kansas anymore.

"What're you going to do with him?" She was good at asking questions when the answer was right in front of her.

"Nothing." Brynn's voice was flat and emotionless. "If he regains consciousness and can get himself inside before morning, his body will heal itself. If not"—he shrugged—"the sun will destroy him." Walking past Donna, he climbed into the car with Holgarth.

Donna watched until darkness swallowed their car, and

then she turned to Eric. "Taurin tried to kill you, and I can't forgive him for that. But . . ." She waved her hand in the air to emphasize her *but.*

Eric's expression was as hard as Brynn's as he continued to propel her toward the van. Once there, she reluctantly climbed in. This wasn't right, but she didn't know what to do. No police. It'd be too hard to explain the vampire, wizard, demon, immortal warrior, and shape-shifting cat thing. No ambulance. The hospital personnel would have a tough time finding a heartbeat, and she'd guess they wouldn't find Taurin's blood type in their blood bank.

Eric's anger was evident in every stiff line of his body as he sped back to the castle. He parked the van with twenty minutes to spare before midnight. She'd just have time to change into something dry. And she'd deal with Eric when she knew what she wanted to say.

He put his hand on her arm as she opened the van's door. "Brynn, Holgarth, and I were all born in a time when justice was harsh and final. Taurin understood what his fate would be if he tried to kill me or hurt anyone . . . important to me."

Important to me. From the way he looked at her and his tone of voice, she knew he was including her on his list of those he was willing to kill for. When she wasn't so befuddled, she'd have to think about the implications of that. "Okay, so I know a big bad Viking-slash-Highlander would think I was a soppy sentimentalist, but leaving someone injured in a field knowing the sun will fry them seems pretty cold. That's just me, of course." She sighed her frustration. That hadn't come out exactly the way she'd wanted it. "Look, I know he should be punished, but isn't there something a little less . . ."

"Barbaric?" Eric dropped his hand from her arm. "No." Without a backward glance, he walked into the castle.

Donna sighed. He was steamed, but too bad. When she had an opinion, she voiced it. She wasn't a gotta-feed-my-man's-ego kind of woman. *My man?* Whoa. That wasn't a place she wanted to visit right now. She followed Eric.

Before going up to her room for a quick change and blow-dry for her hair, she walked over to where Conall sat at the great hall's banquet table with everyone crowded around him.

"I don't know what happened. The last thing I remember is someone spraying something in my eyes that burned like hell. Next thing I know, I'm sitting here at the table. So who's going to explain this?" He glared at his friends.

Donna eased away from them and headed for her room. She was fooling herself if she thought she could ever belong to their inner group. Not that she'd want to. Conall would be perfectly okay with leaving Taurin in that field once he got the facts, because like the others, he belonged to a time when sudden and brutal death was the norm. She didn't know how to think like them. The sad part? This was only one example of how much separated her from Eric.

She was so busy worrying about Eric, Taurin, and why the hell it all mattered so much, that she almost bumped into Holgarth.

"Ah, just the manipulator of millions I wanted to talk to." Holgarth's smile was a little too pleasant.

Uh-oh. "I don't have time to talk, Holgarth. I have to change before my show."

"Your show. Exactly why I wanted to speak with you." He reached up to straighten his wizard's hat, which she assumed had slipped a millimeter off center. "I would like to be your guest tonight."

Donna had been eyeing his hat and remembering that during the wind and rain tonight it had stayed firmly planted in place. Maybe when he took it off at night, his head came with it.

Wait. What had Holgarth said? "You want to be a guest?"

"I hate repeating myself." His thin lips tightened in disapproval of anyone who didn't get what he said the first time. "I couldn't help but notice that you've only had one guest from the castle, and as fond as I am of Eric, he was a disaster. He had nothing to say. I, on the other hand, have much to say."

"I don't know. . . ."

"You came all the way from New York to broadcast from here, so it seems logical that your listeners would want to hear from someone actually connected to the castle." He offered her another thin-lipped smile, as though it pained him to move his mouth muscles into the appropriate position. "You wouldn't want to disappoint your listeners."

Relief washed over her. "But I do have guests connected to the castle. Amanda and Conleth Maguire are stopping by tonight, and they have some great stories to tell about when they were working here."

Something sly and triumphant moved in Holgarth's eyes. "Oh, I'm terribly sorry. I forgot to pass on their message. They won't be able to make it tonight. An unfortunate accident involving broken water pipes. They're busy stemming the rising tide while they wait for a plumber." He shrugged. "So I suppose you need another guest."

Donna narrowed her eyes. He may as well have hissed, "Gotcha." Because he was a sneaky snake, and she knew exactly who was responsible for those broken pipes. But she also knew her listeners would expect a guest. She sighed. "Okay, you're it. But you don't talk about Eric, Brynn, or Conall. And I assume you have the common sense to stay away from what happened tonight." She assumed no such thing and would be ready to cut him off the air at a moment's notice.

Holgarth's smile widened just a little. Donna could almost hear the creak of unused muscles. "My, we *have* become protective of Eric, haven't we?"

Donna felt like . . . like knocking his hat off. Holgarth brought out her inner brat. "*We* need to get our butts in motion so that *we* can be on time for the show."

Turning away, she headed for the elevator. All the way up to her floor, worries about Eric, Taurin, and Holgarth tumbled around in her head. Those thoughts fled, however, as she stepped off the elevator and froze. Her door was open and the lights were on. Donna should've felt fear, but all she felt was outrage. As if her whole world wasn't screwed up enough, some slimeball was in her room.

She blasted into the room propelled by righteous anger and the need to pound on someone until she felt better. There, who said she couldn't compete with the barbarian hordes downstairs? "Okay, dirtbag, what're you doing in my—"

Deimos straightened from studying Sweetie Pie and Jessica, his eyes wide with alarm. Which was so weird when you considered he could probably squash her with one finger. But she was mad and motivated.

"Who gave you the right to barge into my room? Does Sparkle know you're here?" She advanced on him, and he watched her warily.

"Uh, no. Uh, sometimes I work for the owner of this place when Sparkle doesn't need me." He edged toward the door, but Donna planted herself firmly in his path. "The owner told Holgarth that I should, uh, check on all the plants once a week. I checked all the plants in the castle except these."

"Right. So you just barge into my room without my permission?" Donna had to look up a long way to meet his gaze. Maybe she needed to calm down a little. He could probably pick her up with one hand and shake her like a castanet if he got really ticked. Besides, she had a show to do and a dying vampire to angst over. "What's your take on the plants?"

"A little droopy. I guess they need more stuff happening in the room." Red crept up his neck. "Umm, I don't want to get really graphic here, but I could tell you a few ways to cheat if you don't have time for all that"—he made a vague gesture toward the bed—"stuff. It won't fool the plants for long, but it'll, you know, help." He shrugged his massive shoulders.

Fascinated in spite of herself, Donna raised a questioning brow. "I'm all for fooling the plants. Let's hear it."

"Sparkle's been making sure I know all the ways to, umm, you know." He frowned. "I'd rather go to action-hero school. Anyway, she gave me CDs with sounds people make when they're having a really good time. And she made me watch videos showing people doing it in a lot of different ways. I could lend them to you, and you could play them for the plants." His expression brightened. "You could try talking dirty to them."

If Donna didn't spend so much time listening to the weird and wacky on her show, her mouth would be hanging open. "Deimos, why won't you say the word *sex*?"

The red crept up his face and washed over the top of his head. "It embarrasses me. I'm only four years old, dammit." After dropping that bombshell, he strode past Donna and out the door.

Donna stood for a moment trying to make sense of what had just happened. In a daze, she walked over and closed the door. Had Deimos actually said he was four years old? Was there a portal to hell beneath the castle attracting everything bizarre in the universe?

But she didn't have time to think about it right now. Any minute now Ken would be pounding on her door wanting to know if she'd forgotten she had a show to do. Slipping into a light swirly girly dress—may as well play into Eric's image of her as soft civilized fluff—she finished off by blow-drying her hair into submission. A little lipstick and mascara, and she was as good as she was going to get tonight.

She paused and took a deep breath. And what *was* she going to do about Taurin?

Before rushing from the room, she looked over at Sweetie Pie and Jessica. "Dream of hot guys with big cocks, long tongues, and magic fingers, girls." She'd have to practice her dirty talk, but that should keep them happy until she finished tonight's show.

"So, Holgarth, you're the castle's resident wizard. Tell us a little about yourself." Donna had decided that if Holgarth chose to reveal who he really was, she'd let him. As long as he left Eric, Brynn, and Conall out of his disclosure, he could rattle on all night.

He'd generate interest in the castle without implicating Eric in any way. She owed this much to the owner who'd allowed her to broadcast from his, her, or possibly its castle. Eric would be mad at her for putting Holgarth on the air, but then Eric was already mad and likely to get madder.

"I've been a wizard for seven hundred years, and rarely during those seven hundred years have I seen a nation so in need of experienced leadership." He offered his puzzled audience a withering stare meant to discourage any dissenting viewpoints.

Donna blinked. "Well, that's really interesting, but I don't—"

"Therefore I've decided to declare my candidacy for the office of President of the United States in 2008." He remained silent for a moment, allowing the horror to sink in.

Horror at least where Donna was concerned. She couldn't get the mental picture of a dour Holgarth staring at her naked self from Air Force One. Ick. "That's really admirable, Holgarth, but I think everyone would like to hear—"

"Please stop interrupting me." No one could make a person feel more like a ketchup stain on a white dress than Holgarth.

Donna held up her hand. "Sure. No problem"—*you bossy old fart.*

"I heard that thought." It didn't seem to have hurt his feelings, but then his feelings were probably made of tempered steel. "The first thing I'd do as president is disband the military. Why spend billions when I can dispose of our enemies during a commercial break before the eighth inning of a Phillies game?" He pulled his wand from beneath his robe. "This, my friends, is the only *true* weapon of mass destruction." He made a leisurely swipe through the air with it.

"Nothing happened." Ah-hah! Phony. Donna chalked one up for her side.

"Of course it did." He offered his audience another tight smile. Voters wanted charm and charisma, not a wizard who looked like his tightie whities were constricting certain vital organs. "Each of you has an extra ten dollars in your wallet." He looked faintly bored as everyone reached for their wallets and then oooed and aahhed over their ten-dollar bills. "Because I can save billions by simply waving my wand, those savings can be passed onto everyone in the form of lower taxes."

"You're buying voters?" Donna kept her voice to a whisper so her mike wouldn't pick it up. "That's despicable."

He raised one eyebrow. "Is there any other way to win an election?"

A half hour later Donna knew more than she ever wanted to know about Holgarth's brave new world. At least while Holgarth had been explaining his economic and health policies she'd had time to come to a decision about Taurin.

Once Donna opened the lines to callers, the night flew by. The show was almost over, and Donna thought she was home free, when the pod woman called. Great. Just freakin' great. Almost four hours of listening to Holgarth go on about the power of his wand—so elect the wand president, for crying out loud—and now she had to listen to this woman's tale of crazy sex with a creature of the night.

Repeat after me, I am a professional. "Hey, Linda. I'm glad you called in." Lying just got easier and easier. "What's been happening in your life?" Now would be a good time for a long station break. She glanced at Ken from the corner of her eyes. He grinned and shook his head. No help there.

"I have a horrible problem, and I thought maybe Holgarth could help me." Linda sounded close to tears.

"I'm quite capable of solving any problem, Linda. Remember that when you go to the polls in 2008." Holgarth was in complete politician mode. Any minute now he'd ask the audience if they had any babies he could kiss.

"I've fallen in love with one of the vampires who took me for a night of incredible sex. He feels the same way about me, but we have a problem. I want to become like him, but he belongs to a clan that can't turn humans." Sounds of soft sobbing. "I don't want him to have to watch me grow old and die. What should I do? And please don't tell me to give him up."

A problem? No kidding. Donna didn't think she wanted to hear this. Linda's human-falling-in-love-with-vampire scenario made her nervous. She was *not* in love with Eric, but she, well, *liked* him, and she had sort of *wondered* . . .

"Ah, a complicated but not impossible situation." Holgarth's voice was as close to warm as it would ever get, which meant it was still frosty around the edges.

Donna figured even an hour in the microwave wouldn't defrost him completely. That was just her opinion, of course.

"All vampires aren't the same, Linda. You must find a vampire belonging to a group that *can* change humans. I'm sure for a reasonable monetary reward you can convince one of them to share his blood with you. Do make sure you don't let him bite you, though, because once he's taken your blood you'll quite literally belong to him. This would not bode well for your future relationship with your beloved." Holgarth adjusted his hat again. Sheesh, he was as bad as Sparkle with her nails.

"But how do I get his blood? I can't bite him." Linda had stopped sobbing.

Holgarth looked like he was getting bored with Linda's inability to handle details. "You simply find someone with a bit of medical knowledge willing to draw some of the vampire's blood and transfer it to you."

"But-but what if the vampire doesn't have my blood type?"

Holgarth surrendered to his need to do some eye-rolling. He'd have to control that urge once he reached the presidential debates. Eye-rolling didn't play well in the polls.

"Once you have the vampire's blood, my dear Linda,

you will be a vampire, too. Blood type will be irrelevant." Holgarth looked as though the effort of dealing with nitwits had exhausted him.

"Thanks for your call, Linda, and it looks like we're out of time for tonight." She offered Holgarth a plastic smile. "And thank you for being a fascinating guest. Good luck in your presidential bid." Not. "And everyone join us again tomorrow for *Donna till Dawn* when we'll have Tom Carson with us to talk about parallel universes." Donedone-done! Thank. You. God.

Donna stood and moved away from the table. Holgarth joined her. "Do you really think you have a shot at becoming president?"

Holgarth glanced at his reflection in the bookstore window and once again shifted his hat. Jeez, did he have a slanted head, or what?

"I don't intend to run. Of course, if I did run, I'd win." His smile was almost sincere. "Because I'd cheat."

"I don't understand. What about what you told—"

Holgarth's sincere smile reverted to his usual superior smirk. "Did anyone ask about Eric, Brynn, Conall, Asima, or Lola tonight? In fact, did they ask any questions about the castle?"

Realization widened Donna's eyes. "You tried to distract them."

"Succeeded, Donna. I succeeded in distracting them." He shifted his attention from his own reflection to her. "I thought Linda's call was very thought provoking. And of course my answer was brilliant." He speared her with a steely stare. "Solutions are usually available if we search outside the box."

"I guess so." What the hell did that mean?

"I'm put in mind of something Napoleon said to me. I think his exact words were, 'The most dangerous moment comes with victory.' "

"Uh-huh. And that is important for me to know, why?" Donna kind of liked the old Holgarth—mean and sarcastic. This new Holgarth was weirding her out.

Holgarth shrugged. “Perhaps its meaning will become clearer in time.”

Donna thought about that. “Do you know something I don’t?” A horrible possibility struck her. “You can’t see the future, can you?”

“The future is always fluid. It can flow in many directions depending on our actions. It reminds me of a poem by Robert Frost.” He raised his gaze to the ceiling for inspiration.

Oh, cripes. He wasn’t going to quote poetry now, was he?

“In ‘The Road Not Taken,’ Frost says he took the road less traveled. For some of us, the less traveled road is the best. And once taken, we can never retrace our steps and choose another.” He turned and walked away.

Whoa, road-of-life symbolism. Was that deep, or what? Sounded a little ominous, though. Yeah, she definitely liked the old pompous and irritating Holgarth better. She scrubbed at the sudden rash of goose bumps on her arms. This new one was a little scary.

Donna glanced around. Brynn and Conall had looked in a few times during the show, but she hadn’t seen Eric at all. She tried to be glad about that. He’d be more steamed than he already was if he knew what she was planning.

Foregoing a meal in the restaurant, she went up to her room, changed into jeans and a T-shirt, grabbed her purse, and then left the castle. As she climbed into her car and drove back to the beach house, she prayed she was making the right decision. Everyone would be a lot safer if she turned around and went back to the castle. If she did, when she woke up tomorrow afternoon, Taurin would be gone. But she couldn’t. Her conscience was a nagging bitch, and she’d never have another peaceful moment if she didn’t do this.

Parking in front of the destroyed beach house, she got out of her car and paused to draw in a deep breath of courage. At least she’d had the foresight to stop at an all-night convenience store and buy a flashlight.

Tentatively she stepped into the high weeds and started walking. She shouldn't have worn sandals. There were probably dozens of snakes eyeing her bare toes with evil in their hearts. And she'd bet there were thousands of big creepy spiders hiding in the weeds waiting to fling themselves onto her unprotected person. She slapped at her bare arms. She was making thousands of mosquitoes happy tonight.

Mind to Donna. She was looking for a vampire. What were a few snakes, spiders, or mosquitoes on the creepy scale beside a vampire? Funny that she didn't think that way about Eric.

She was so busy thinking about snakes and spiders that she almost tripped over Taurin. That's because he wasn't where Brynn had left him. As she peered down at him, he tried to crawl another few inches.

Forgetting for a moment who he was and what he'd tried to do, she simply knelt down beside him. "Taurin, I'm going to try to help you."

With a pained grunt he rolled over onto his back and looked up at her. "Why?" His question was a hoarse croak.

Damndamndamn. He was still in vampire form. "Because I'm a stupid human with this pesky thing called a conscience. And things would be a whole lot easier if you changed back into human form." He was burned badly, and she didn't know how she'd get him into her car. Even if she drove the car into the field, he didn't look like he'd have the strength to climb in. And she certainly didn't have the strength to lift him.

"Can't. Don't have enough power to change." Every word he spoke seemed to be an effort. "Besides, I'm stronger in this form."

Donna slumped to a sitting position. Something hot and painful gathered in her chest. "What to do? How's this scenario? I call a cab on my cell phone. Cabbie gets here. I ask him to help my vampire friend into his cab. Cabbie runs screaming into the night. All right, let's assume we find a cabbie with an open mind who takes us to a hotel. I tell the bright and perky night clerk that I'd like to check my vampire friend in, and that said vampire will be staying until he gets back his strength. Does room service serve blood?" The hot and painful whatever was expanding. She could feel the pressure.

"Forget it. Won't work." He paused to gather strength. "Doesn't matter anyway. I failed Dacian."

Anger washed over Donna. "You are such a jerk. If Eric was the cold-blooded killer you think he is, he would've squashed you like a bug when you were lying on the lawn. He was willing to give you more of a chance than you would've given him. Did you even investigate the fire?"

Confusion and doubt touched Taurin's gaze for just a moment. "Didn't have to. I know—"

"You know nothing. You're living—or nonliving—proof that age doesn't bring wisdom." Whatever was in her chest was about to detonate.

"I—"

"Shut up. Just shut the hell up." She didn't know how to save Taurin. Eric was mad at her because he thought it was pretty much okay to leave your enemy in a field to die. Why? Because that's the way they did it in the old days, by gum.

Suddenly every weird, crazy, impossible thing that had happened this week rose up to smack her in the face. And the dam in her chest broke. Tears streamed down her face faster and faster. She sobbed great gulping sobs that shook her body. She cried for Taurin who would die, for her own inability to cope one more minute with anything, and for Eric. And because she didn't know why she was crying for Eric, she cried even harder.

Finally her sobs faded to dry rasping gulps. Wiping her eyes with the back of her hand, she gathered the ragged remains of her control around her. She wouldn't just sit here watching the sun come up, which was going to happen very soon. Scrambling to her feet, she ran to get her car. She'd do her best to drag Taurin into it.

* * *

Eric stood outside the castle. He knew where Donna had gone. She'd gone to save Taurin. But even as anger ripped through him, he admired her. She walked the walk.

He wouldn't go after her. He'd been right to leave Taurin in that field. She thought he was a savage, but she would've thought his response tonight was mild if she'd seen him as a Highlander. He would've taken Taurin's head back then. Even his civilized self probably would've taken Taurin's head if he'd had his sword with him. Lucky for Taurin that Eric couldn't conceal the sword when he wore a suit.

No, he wouldn't go after her. She couldn't do anything for Taurin anyway. By now he'd be barely alive and no danger to Donna. The vampire had been burned too badly to make it to safety on his own, and she wasn't strong enough to move him alone. She couldn't call for help because Taurin would still be in vampire form. He wouldn't have the strength to return to human form. The most she could do was to sit with him until the sun came up and then watch him die.

Eric frowned. It wasn't a good way to die. That bothered him. Maybe he should take his sword and give Taurin a clean death? Not a great idea. Donna wouldn't think death-by-sword was particularly merciful. She'd be on her way back to New York before he rose from sleep.

He glanced at the eastern sky where the first faint rays of morning were beginning to show. Damn. He had to know what was going on. So, yeah, he was going after her. Her ability to mess with his resolve bothered him. Focusing his energy, he prepared to do what he hadn't done since coming to Galveston. Moving into the deepest shadows, he stripped down, pictured what he'd become, and then became it. The great gray owl, the largest of its species, floated silently into the dark sky.

He landed as silently as he'd risen, unseen by the woman struggling in the overgrown field. Eric returned to human form, and as always it amazed him. There was no gradual change from bird to man, just the instant when one became the other.

He was naked, but he didn't intend to approach her. He'd just observe quietly from the shelter of the destroyed house to make sure she was okay. Uneasy, he watched her straining to lift Taurin into her car. Taurin was too far gone to give her any help at all. When he slipped from her hands, she grabbed him again to make another attempt. Eric could hear her labored breathing and sobs of frustration.

He wouldn't help. If he helped, he'd be admitting he was wrong and she was right. Worse yet, he'd become responsible for what happened to the vampire. And once Taurin regained his strength, he'd probably take another shot at Eric. All good reasons for not helping.

Loki's flame! Donna did this to him—made him resort to the old oaths, made him waver in his belief that he was right, made him *unsure* of himself. The last was her greatest sin, because he'd always been confident in what he did.

Eric couldn't watch this any longer. With a muttered curse, he strode toward her. He moved silently, and she didn't realize he was behind her until only a few feet separated them. Just before she turned, he touched her mind with the suggestion that he was dressed in jeans and a T-shirt.

She spun around and yelped in surprise. "Where'd you come from?" Hope and suspicion warred in her gaze.

He knew his smile didn't do a thing to help her decide whether he'd come to help her or kill Taurin. He was glad. It was his small revenge for her causing him so much . . . So much what? He didn't know. "I flew here."

Eric watched a puzzled crease form between her eyes.

"Never mind." He glanced at the lightening sky. "It's almost dawn. Get out of my way."

Wisely, she moved away from Taurin without arguing. Taurin was too weak to speak, so he had to make do with angry glares.

Eric grinned down at him. "Jeez, you look like hell. Too

bad you can't curse me out. In fact, you can't stop me from doing anything I damn well want." He let Taurin think about that for a moment.

Then he bent down, picked Taurin up, and deposited him none too gently on the backseat of Donna's car. He glanced at Donna and nodded toward the passenger seat. "Get in." Then he slid into the driver's seat.

Once Donna was in her seat with the door closed, he pulled out of the vacant lot and sped toward the castle in a race with the dawn. He didn't have time to dump Taurin off at a motel. Besides, Eric wanted him someplace where he could be watched. Glancing in the rearview mirror, he was relieved to see that Taurin had passed out. Relieved? He was absolutely *not* relieved that his enemy couldn't feel pain. Had he wandered so far from his Viking and Highlander roots? If so, it was Donna's fault.

She remained quiet, staring out the window for so long that he almost spoke to break the uneasy silence. "You did the right thing, Eric."

"Hmmph." She could interpret that any way she wanted.

"I didn't realize before tonight how really different our life viewpoints are." She leaned her head back against the seat and closed her eyes. "I guess part of the way I feel is shaped by the fact that I'm human. We have finite lives, pretty short as lives go. So I value any life. Every moment is precious." Her eyes popped open. "I'm not insulting you, but let's face it, you've lived for centuries, so you've seen a lot of people die. Maybe that makes you more casual toward death."

"That's a bunch of bull." Almost to the castle. Good thing, because he couldn't take much more without exploding. "Watching people die, whether it's one or a million, never makes death easier." She'd shoved his face in a truth he'd tried to ignore since he met her. If you let yourself care for a human, you'll eventually have to watch them die. Most of the older clansmen stayed away from human relationships, because losing loved ones never stopped hurting.

"So tell me why you chose to fly this time." She'd decided to back off on her discussion about how each of them saw death. Smart lady.

He parked the car near where he'd left his clothes. "In owl form, if I decided not to interfere, you'd never know I was there."

She got out of the car and watched as he walked over to his pile of clothes. "Okay, why're those clothes on the ground? You're already . . ." Her eyes widened. "Wait, you couldn't be dressed if you changed from an owl to human form. That means you must be—"

"Naked." Eric said the word with relish, and then he freed her mind to see him as he really was. Naked. It would make the end of a crummy night a little less crummy if she lost her cool. She didn't.

"You have a spectacular body, and under other circumstances I wouldn't mind doing some heavy-duty ogling, but right now we need to get you and Taurin inside the castle." She glanced at the sky. "Because in case you haven't noticed, daylight is officially here."

"You're no fun, talk-show lady. I was hoping for a little more reaction, maybe a bright red blush or an outraged shriek. It would've made up a little for the rest of the night." He turned his back to her and bent over to pick up his clothes.

She made a strangled sound behind him. "Wow, that is so . . . energizing. Hurry up and dress so we can get Taurin inside."

Eric pulled on his clothes. Then he picked up the unconscious Taurin from the backseat and carried him into the castle with Donna right beside him. He'd finally caught some good luck. No one was in the great hall. At this time of the morning only the cleaning staff would be working. He carried Taurin into the elevator and hit the button for Donna's floor.

She frowned. "You're putting him in the room across from me?"

He waited until the elevator doors opened before answering. "Uh-huh. Guests checked out yesterday. Once we have him settled, I'll call the desk to tell them the room's occupied until further notice."

Donna trailed him to the door. "You didn't stop to get a key. Don't—"

He focused on the door and it clicked open.

"Right. No key needed." She trailed him into the room and watched as he dropped Taurin onto the bed.

Eric turned to study her. "You might want to go to your room. I'm going to strip him before I leave." He walked over and pulled the drape closed to make sure no sunlight seeped into the room. "And before you accuse me of performing a kind act, I'm taking his clothes so it'll be harder for him to leave. He won't have the power to cloak his presence for a few days, and someone would notice a naked man walking through the castle."

She nodded. "What about his burns?"

"Blood would speed his recovery, but he doesn't get any blood from anyone in this castle. He'll sleep for a long time, and his body will heal itself while he sleeps." Eric turned away from her and started taking off Taurin's shirt. He heard the soft click of the door as she closed it behind her. He smiled.

"You're a real pain in the ass, but you served one good purpose tonight." Eric finished stripping Taurin and flung a sheet over him. "And when you wake up, we're going to have a long talk about your existence, or lack of it."

Eric gazed around the room before leaving. He didn't think Taurin had the power to shape-shift, but just in case, he put a shield across the narrow window. Then he strode from the room, closed the door, and placed a shield across it also. No one would get in or out until he was ready.

Now for the fun part. Stepping across the hall, he opened Donna's door and went inside.

She'd just changed into her nightshirt, and the look she sent him should've left a smoking hole in his chest. "And you're here why? Since I'm not in danger anymore, you can sleep in your own cozy bed today." She looked like she really thought he was going to leave.

"Sorry. You could still be in danger. I don't know when Taurin might wake up, and I have to be ready for him. I've already underestimated him once, and I won't do it again." He hoped he wore his guardian-warrior expression.

"He's still a danger? I thought he'd be down for at least a few days." She looked really worried.

And he felt really gleeful. "You never know with a vampire. He could fool us and be well enough to make trouble in a few hours." He'd told bigger lies, but none so personally satisfying.

Donna sighed and ran her fingers through her hair, giving her that sexy tousled look. "Fine. Go down and get something to sleep in." She reached for the remaining cookies. "I'm hungry." As she munched on the cookies, she eyed her box of chocolate-covered cherries.

He dropped onto the bed and pulled off his shirt. "I don't wear anything when I sleep. Too confining." Eric smiled as her gaze turned wary. "And don't even think about those cherries. I have plans for them."

14

Donna paused before leaving the room to look back at her bed where Eric still slept. She wanted to recapture her old confident and in-control attitude, but she was, well, conflicted.

One part of her, the part that felt a sisterhood with Sweetie Pie and Jessica, wanted to strip off her clothes, wake Eric, and put her chocolate-covered cherries to their rightful use—seduction.

Her other part, the one that wisely reminded her today was Friday and she'd be going back to New York tomorrow, suggested she not become more . . . attached to him than she already was.

With a sigh of regret for a lost opportunity, she chose to listen to her wiser self. Fine, so if she were honest, she'd admit it wasn't wisdom but hunger that drove her from her room. She was starving.

Luckily, Eric hadn't seen a need to shield the door since Taurin was tucked up safely in the room across the hall. He'd lied about his reason for spending the night in her bed, but she was just as much at fault. She'd figured he was lying, but she hadn't called him on it. Because she'd wanted him to stay with her.

She took a last peek at Eric before closing the door. He'd pulled the cover over himself, which was probably the only reason she was able to walk away from him. Eric's magnificent body would be too much for any woman to resist, especially one weakened by hunger.

Before going down to the restaurant, she walked across the hall to look at Taurin's door. She reached out tentatively. Yep, she could feel the energy field, or whatever it was, that Eric had put in place to keep Taurin in. *And me out.* Donna listened. Nothing. He must still be sleeping. If he woke before she left tomorrow, she wanted to talk to him. Talking was her business. Maybe she could convince Taurin to give up all this vengeance stuff. Right. Like that was going to happen. She'd have to come up with something substantial to make it worth his while. Donna wasn't quite sure what that would be.

But thoughts of Taurin slid from her mind as she headed down to the restaurant. Instead, she thought about leaving and how depressed it made her. Which proved she needed professional help. Because last night had really sucked.

She would've gotten around to admitting she wanted to stay because of Eric, but luckily the restaurant was almost empty so the waiter was able to take her order right away, distracting her from any scary self-revelations. Donna was busy rediscovering the joy of eating when Brynn sat down across from her.

"Thought I'd check to see how you felt today." He smiled at her.

Donna wasn't fooled this time. His smile might be able to bring a roomful of women to their knees, but she'd seen the man behind the smile last night. And that man had terrified her. "I'm okay." She wouldn't be okay if he found out she was responsible for bringing Taurin back to the castle.

"Son of a bitch." His soft murmur and angry glare aimed in her direction suggested he'd discovered something. About her. Something bad. Uh-oh.

Oops. He was a demon. Did demons read minds? From the way he was scowling at her, she'd guess the answer was yes. "Look, I couldn't leave him in that field to go *poof* with the first sunbeam. Yeah, I know you think I'm a marshmallow, but I'm a marshmallow with a conscience. Maybe you need to rediscover your inner marshmallow, if you ever had one." Hmm. *Brain to Donna. You're talking to a demon. Shut your mouth.*

"Damn." Translation—you're a stupid woman. "Who helped you with him? You couldn't do it by yourself."

She shrugged. "It's not important. And I'm not going to think a name, so you can get out of my head."

For the first time a gleam of amusement touched his intriguing eyes. "I could wait you out."

Donna smiled. "Not more than an hour."

He returned her smile. "I can stay more than an hour. I'll just offer my body, you'll turn me down, and we'll wait some more."

Her smile widened. "Maybe I'll accept your offer."

Brynn shook his head. "I don't think so. You're crazy about Eric." He glanced at his watch. "Gotta go. I don't know where you have Taurin stashed, but I'll find him without your help. Enjoy the rest of your meal."

Bemused, Donna watched him walk away. Crazy about Eric? Was she? She thought about that as she lifted a piece of steak toward her mouth.

"If you eat that whole steak and baked potato, they'll form a layer of fat on your hips that'll never ever go away. Fat hips are so not attractive to a virile vampire. And since I feel your rightness with Eric, I'll sacrifice my own lithe figure in the name of love. Throw down a piece of steak."

Donna paused with the steak halfway to her mouth and looked down at Asima. The cat sat beside Donna's chair, her expression saying clearly that since she'd asked, it was Donna's duty to fork over her meal.

Donna glanced around the restaurant. She'd chosen a table tucked into a dimly lit corner away from the few other diners because she wanted to be alone. Ha, fat chance. So far no one had noticed Asima. But then, Donna had a feeling Asima might have something to do with that. "Cats aren't allowed in restaurants. Major health code violation."

Asima did the equivalent of a cat shrug. "Should I care?"

Sighing, Donna dropped a piece of steak to her. "After the power you demonstrated last night, it seems to me you can get your meals anywhere you want. Why're you hitting on my steak?"

"Because I can." Asima waited expectantly for the next offering to drop her way. *"It's that delicious feeling I get when I've successfully manipulated someone. No offense, but you're easy."*

Donna narrowed her eyes and considered cutting off Asima's steak supply. "I got the feeling at the opera that Sparkle and you knew each other."

"Yes." She sat staring up at Donna until she got another piece of meat. *"She's a bitch."*

"And?" At the rate Donna was dragging info from Asima, the cat would have plenty of time to finish off her steak.

Asima looked thoughtful. Probably deciding how much to tell Donna. *"We met a long time ago. Things happened."*

"Uh-huh. How long ago? What things? And why'd she call you a gofer?" Resigned to the loss of her steak, Donna dropped another meaty bribe.

Asima delicately chewed the steak as she considered her answer. *"Oh, about two hundred years ago. She interfered in one of my assignments. I was molding this virginal young innocent into the perfect bride. Sparkle went behind my back, undermining everything I was doing. By the time the girl got to her marriage bed, she was a flaming tart."* Asima looked puzzled. *"I can't say that her husband minded—men are so clueless—but it was the principle of the thing."*

Two hundred years? "What about the gofer thing?" Donna had to put down her fork until her hands stopped shaking. She'd thought the portal to hell was underneath the castle. Wrong. It evidently extended as far as the Sweet Indulgence candy store.

Asima slid avaricious eyes toward the couple at another table. They'd ordered salmon. *"I'm the messenger of a goddess. I'm not at liberty to say her name, but trust me, she's a biggie."*

She stood, stretched, and then started to pad away. But she paused to glance back at Donna. *"Normally, I wouldn't have told you about Sparkle. All immortals, no matter how lacking in dignity, should be able to depend on their fellow immortals to guard their secrets from humans. But Sparkle distracted me from my opera. No one messes with my music."*

Even though Donna intended to confront Sparkle with lots of shouting and hand waving, she felt the need to defend her on one front. "Lacking in dignity?" She smiled at Asima. "So let me get this straight. Calling someone a slut queen is a dignified immortal put-down? Maybe it's just me, but it seems like Sparkle and you are alike in one major way. You both like to manipulate."

Asima offered Donna an irritated hiss before winding her way out of the restaurant followed by the puzzled stares of the other diners. She must've been too ticked off to care who saw her.

Donna finished off what remained of her meal and then tried to decide what to do. Choices. Walk over to Sweet Indulgence and kick some immortal butt? After all, Sparkle had let Donna think she was just an ordinary human who was obsessed with sexing up other people's lives. Shop? Go back to her room and watch Eric sleep? Watching Eric sleep won hands down. Amazing, since usually when shopping was in the mix, there was no contest.

But as she opened her door, Donna realized Eric was no longer sleeping. He was propped up against the headboard with his muscular arms folded over his broad bare chest. At least he'd kept the sheet draped across his hips. His dark scowl hinted that he hadn't been wakened gently.

Impervious to his scowl, Lola hovered at the foot of the bed, carefully laying out a row of . . . Donna moved closer so she could see.

"Come right in, dearie, and make yourself comfortable. Eric will need your expert advice on this." She glanced over her shoulder and beckoned to Donna. "Be honest. Which will look better on your man, boxers or briefs?"

No opinion came to mind as Donna stared blankly at the row of men's underwear lined up across the foot of the bed.

Lola smiled her sweet grandmotherly smile. "I understand. It's a difficult decision. But I can't make it for you. You're the one who'll be stripping these babies off your vampire's superbly muscled and breathtakingly sensual buttocks. So make sure you choose wisely."

Eric made a rude noise. "I tried throwing her out, but she just popped back in."

Lola ignored him. "Let's look at the possibilities. These red briefs would be perfect for him. Red, the color of passion. I love the symbolism. Briefs would hug his round firm cheeks while cupping his large and impressive sexual equipment."

"What do you know about his sexual equipment?" Her sudden surge of possessiveness shocked Donna.

Lola blinked at her. "I was simply assuming, dearie. Am I mistaken?"

"You don't have to answer that." For the first time humor curved Eric's lips. "It'll be our little secret."

The remembrance of exactly how well she knew the generous dimensions of his "equipment" made Donna shift her gaze to Sweetie Pie and Jessica. Their leaves were riveted to the discussion. Hothouse hussies.

Lola didn't seem to notice that Donna hadn't answered her question. "How about these white boxers with red lips all over them? Boxers are loose and comfortable. They give a man's cock and balls room to expand."

Donna made a strangled noise. Eric didn't make any noise at all.

"The red lips are a very sensual touch. Eric can walk

around all day with a reminder of your mouth on his body." Lola seemed pleased with her insight.

Since Eric didn't look like he was about to make a choice anytime soon, Donna would do it. Fast. Before Lola had time to go on to the next one. The one with the . . . No, Lola definitely couldn't get to that one. "Eric will take these first two."

Lola beamed. "One of each. Excellent choices. You'll enjoy the briefs. When your man is fully aroused, you can drive him wild by tracing the outline of his erection through the stretchy material with your tongue. Very erotic."

Eric's interest had picked up.

"Yes, well . . ." There were no words for this situation.

"But boxers have their advantages, too. When you're cuddled up on the couch with your man, and you feel the irresistible urge to arouse him instantly, you simply slip your hand—"

"Got it. I can fill in the blanks." What would get Lola out of the room? "You know, if you'd pack up your stuff and bop on out of here, I could get started on the arousing." If the possibility of Donna having sex with Eric didn't motivate Lola to leave, then she was out of ideas.

"Well, in that case, let me just disappear." Which she did. Instantly.

Donna took a deep breath. She never got used to that. "When I walked in, I could tell you were steamed. How did she wake you up?"

Eric's scowl returned. "I was already awake when she showed up, and I wasn't steamed at her."

Oh boy. Gee, Donna wondered who could've ticked him off. Since she was the only one sharing the room with him, it was a good guess the lucky person was—drumroll, please—her.

"I woke up thinking about chocolate-covered cherries and you." His scowl deepened. "The cherries were here. You weren't."

She wouldn't feel guilty. Wistful over what might have

been, perhaps, but not guilty. "Unlike you, I can't go for two weeks without eating. I went down to the restaurant." He needed to know about Brynn. "Brynn sat with me for a few minutes. He got into my mind while I was thinking about bringing Taurin back here. He doesn't know who helped me, though."

"He'll have a good idea." Flinging the sheet aside, Eric swung his feet to the floor. "Even when he finds where I've put Taurin, he won't be able to get through my shield." Eric decided he'd better talk to Brynn as soon as possible. Brynn wouldn't understand why Eric helped save Taurin. Hell, Eric wasn't sure he understood, either.

As he headed for the shower, he could feel Donna's gaze trailing down his back and over his bare buttocks. It felt good. So good that he decided to shuck all underwear wherever there was a chance he might get naked with her. Which was just about everywhere.

But not for long. It was Friday. Unless he thought of a way to keep her here, she'd be on a plane back to New York tomorrow. He didn't want her to leave. Standing under the warm spray, he tried to come up with a plan.

As he emerged from the bathroom, he could hear angry voices from the hall. The door was open, and he didn't have any trouble identifying Donna and Brynn's voice. Great. Now he'd have to deal with Brynn and then go into Taurin's room and deal with him. The fun never ended.

Ignoring the red briefs and lip-imprinted boxers, Eric dragged on his jeans, pulled a T-shirt over his head, and rushed into the hall before Donna and Brynn knocked each other out.

Brynn turned blazing eyes toward him. "If you don't have the balls to destroy Taurin, remove the shield and let me do it." He speared Donna with a withering glance. "I think I miss the old days when women had a lot less to say."

"Hah!" Her expression said no demon was going to make her back down. "I haven't had a chance to say squat because you won't shut your mouth long enough to listen."

Exasperated, she turned to Eric. "Explain to the demon of destruction here why we brought Taurin back."

Eric stared blankly at her. He'd forgotten. He'd known last night, but right now he couldn't think of one reason why his deadliest enemy was laying in a nice soft bed, in a nice secure room, in his castle. Go figure.

Donna threw up her hands. "Okay, *I'll* explain. We decided that being fried by the morning sun wasn't the best way to die. If we brought him here, maybe someone could talk some sense into his brain, whatever small part isn't stuffed full of plans for vengeance." She swept back strands of her hair that had fallen across her face during her vehement discussion with Brynn, and then directed a salvo at Eric. "Don't you guys have some kind of vampire prison?"

"Vampire prison?" Eric and Brynn spoke in unison.

Brynn shook his head and turned toward the stairs. "Eliminate Taurin, Eric, because if you don't, I will."

Eric watched Brynn until he was gone, and then turned back to Donna. "Sorry. No vampire prisons." He removed the shield in front of the door. "Stay out here while I go in. He'll sleep until tomorrow at least, but I want to check on things."

She nodded as he opened the door and then closed it behind him. Taurin was still deep in a healing sleep, but his burns were almost gone. Eric frowned. He couldn't postpone a decision on Taurin forever, but if he had to destroy the vampire, he hoped Donna was back in New York when it happened.

Thinking about Donna's imminent departure, Eric decided he wouldn't be in a mood to take any crap from Taurin tomorrow, even though the vampire would still be too weak to pose a physical threat. Taurin would need to feed to regain all of his strength. Assuming Donna left on schedule, he'd be feeling vicious enough to finish off Taurin if the vampire tried to attack him. For Taurin's sake, he'd better place a shield around the bed. That way the vampire couldn't move from his bed until Eric let him.

Eric had taken care of the shield and started toward the door when an idea hit him. Smiling, he opened the door, stepped into the hall, and after closing the door behind him, renewed the shield. Then he turned to Donna.

"After tonight you don't have another show until Monday. Why not stay here for the weekend?" Did he sound casual enough, or had some of his hunger seeped through?

"I don't know. My flight's already booked. And I wanted to visit with my family before going back to work Monday night."

Maybe it was wishful thinking on his part, but she didn't sound convinced she wanted to go. "Too bad. Taurin won't be awake until tomorrow at sunset. He might listen to you better than me. And if he doesn't listen to someone . . ." He shrugged, letting the unspoken threat to Taurin's existence hang between them.

"He'll die." She bit her bottom lip in indecision.

"You've had a hard week. If you stay, you can relax during the day and then come to the Vampire Ball at night." If his two enticements didn't work, he wasn't sure what he'd do. Amazing how important her staying had become.

"Vampire Ball?" She allowed him a small smile.

He guided her back into their room—when had "their" crept in—and only hoped she didn't hear the growl of his sexual hunger trying to claw its way out.

"Yeah. We have one every Saturday night. We go formal that night. Tuxes, a small band, and lots of atmosphere." Eric moved into her space, crowding her with his presence, his need. All the while knowing that the decision to stay would have to be hers. There'd be no compulsions, no mind manipulating, even though both were easy to use on humans who had no guards against them. But it was exactly for that reason he wouldn't use them. He wanted her to stay because it was her choice.

Leaning close, he touched the base of her neck with his lips, whispered against her skin. "Come to the Vampire Ball and dance the night away with creatures of the darkness. Although I wouldn't be surprised if one particular creature claimed you for his own." He felt a surge of triumph when she didn't shudder or put her hand over her neck.

"Let me think about it." She picked up her purse, and then met his gaze squarely. "I need to get away for a while. I'm going out to play the tourist and pick up some souvenirs for my family. Then maybe I'll go down to the beach for a few hours." She smiled up at him, but he could feel her tension. "I'll be back before my show."

"Sure, have fun." It wasn't often that he regretted the loss of the daylight, but now was one. He couldn't go shopping for souvenirs with her or lay on the beach soaking up the sun beside her. He couldn't smooth suntan lotion over those long beautiful legs and . . .

It suddenly hit him how much he wanted to go to the beach with her. It would have to be on a moonlit night, and he wouldn't be able to do the suntan thing, but he wanted it with an intensity that scared him. He'd need a lot more than a weekend to do all the things he wanted with Donna Nolan.

He watched her leave the room and then glanced at Sweetie Pie and Jessica. "Think we'll ever get a chance to use those cherries, ladies?"

Donna had spent her free hours in a frenzy of having "fun." Translation: trying to drive last night's horror and her conflicted feelings for Eric from her mind. She bought tacky souvenirs and lay around on the beach until it was almost completely dark. But somehow the whole thing lacked a certain degree of yippee and wow. What it lacked was a dark, dangerous, and gorgeous vampire by her side.

Narrowing her eyes, she decided she'd have some more "fun" without him. She wasn't like Trish. She didn't think that every man she was attracted to had to be her forever love. Sure she thought Eric Mackenzie was sexy as hell. Sure she intended to use those cherries before she left. But it didn't *mean* anything.

As she caught a quick shower before going out again, she also admitted that she'd decided to stay the weekend. Just to prove that it didn't mean anything.

She put on a pair of shorts and the skimpiest top she'd brought—maximum bare skin to catch any errant breezes—slipped into a pair of sandals, and left the room. Then she paused in the hallway trying to decide where to go in search of her elusive fun. The castle fantasies were beginning. She could sit in the gallery and watch. But then Eric would think she was watching him. Which she would be, so watching the fantasies was out.

"Sexy but tasteful shorts and top. Definitely not from the Sparkle Stardust line of crass clothing. And I love the sandals. So where're we going to have fun?" Asima rubbed her furry self against Donna's leg and looked up with excitement gleaming in her feline eyes. *"Take me with you. Please?"*

Donna sighed. She'd wished for someone to share her fun with, but she'd been thinking more along the lines of big and gorgeous, not small and furry. The old adage about being careful what you wished for was true. "Sure, tag along. I'm not sure where I want to go, though." She brightened. "When I was a kid, I wanted to be a pirate. Let's walk over to the pirate ship."

Asima didn't say anything until they were outside the castle. *"I think the best fantasies are the ones that aren't planned. What do you think? Oh, and would you pick me up, please?"*

Donna stopped to look down at the cat. "Would I what?

"Pick me up. The ground is still too hot for my paws." Asima stared up at Donna, obviously waiting to be picked up.

Did Donna believe that? No. She thought about arguing, but it didn't seem worth the effort. She bent down and lifted Asima's lazy little self into her arms. "Unplanned? Are you telling me I shouldn't go on the pirate fantasy?"

"It's your choice, but it'll never live up to your secret fantasy. Everything's pretty structured. Not much chance

to think creatively. And no one on that ship will live up to Eric. Believe me, I've checked."

"Uh-huh. And I just bet you have an exciting alternative." After her trip to the opera wearing a living neck wrap, Donna looked with suspicion on any of Asima's ideas.

"I always have alternative ideas. Look across the lake. Do you see that tangle of fake vines along the shore?"

Donna nodded.

"They keep an extra pirate ship anchored over there in a small inlet just in case the one they're using needs repairs. The vines hide it. It's dark back there, but the moon is full tonight. You'll be able to snoop around and imagine your own fantasy." She turned gleaming eyes toward Donna. *"Let's do it."*

Donna had some doubts about Asima's big plan. "Sounds like trespassing to me. What if I'm caught? And how exciting can walking around on a ship by yourself be?"

"Can we say cluck cluck?" Asima's eyes mocked her. *"You've lived for a week with vampires, demons, ghosts, and* moi. *So what's the big deal about climbing onto an old ship? Come on, Donna. It'll be fun."* Her gaze turned sly. *"I guarantee that anywhere you go with me will be exciting. Besides, if you're bored, all you do is get off and stand in line for the ship with the phony pirates."*

Fun was the magic word. She'd look the ship over and still have time to get in line for the fantasy featuring actors who wouldn't come close to the pirate who lived in her imagination. Asima had that much right. Besides, she'd had her fill of crowds today. It'd feel good to be alone for a while—if she could shut Asima up—to try and unravel her mixed feelings about Eric.

Donna started to put Asima down. They'd be walking on grass, and grass wasn't hot. Asima could trot her own little behind over to the ship.

"Hey, hey." Asima dug her claws into Donna's top and hung on. *"You can't put me down here. There're fire ant*

mounds in this grass. Do you know what a fire ant bite feels like?" She didn't wait for Donna to answer. *"If you did, you wouldn't even think of putting me down."*

Donna was such a pushover. She'd bet the park's groundskeepers went on fire ant search-and-destroy missions every day. But just in case, she'd hang on to Asima. "I notice it doesn't bother you that *I* might get bitten."

Asima wisely chose to leave that comment alone.

Donna soon realized the lake was bigger than it looked, but finally with lots of tripping and cursing she reached the other side. She fought her way through the fake vines and found the inlet with the pirate ship anchored in its middle. The ship wasn't as close to the shore as Donna would've liked.

"So I'm supposed to walk up that gangplank?" Duh, yes.

"Hey, would I take you someplace that wasn't safe? Put me down and I'll go across first."

"Is that a trick question? Because my gut says you're the queen of unsafe. Besides, I don't come from a seafaring family." She put Asima down and watched as the cat scampered up the gangplank onto the ship and then turned to wait for Donna. Oh, well, she'd come this far. Refusing to look down at the water, she joined Asima.

The pirate ship freed Donna's imagination. The darkness lit only by moonlight cast the ship into menacing shadows. Great atmosphere. She stared up at the tall mast, picturing sails billowing in the wind, and after poking around in the galley, she decided gourmet cooking was a nonhappening on this pirate ship. Running her fingers over the cannon, she could almost hear the shouts of "Avast, ye scurvy dogs!"

Asima padded ahead of her as Donna explored. The fake vines hid the rest of the park from her, and if she pretended hard enough, she could almost believe the darkened ship was authentic.

She lost track of time as she crept around exploring every nook and cranny, pretending she was a pirate captain whose ship was sliding silently through a black sea to attack some unsuspecting merchant ship—with luck an unsuspecting merchant ship filled with hotties she could take captive and use as she wished. She was obviously experiencing a hormonal-induced high.

She was in the captain's cabin, rooting around by pale moonlight, when she realized Asima was gone. Puzzled, she walked onto the deck to look around. She didn't find Asima, but she did discover that she was no longer a landlubber. Her bridge to terra firma was gone.

It didn't take long to connect the dots. No Asima. No gangplank. She didn't know what game Asima was playing, but she'd picked the wrong talk-show host to mess with. When she got off the ship . . . Hmm. How *was* she going to get off?

Donna glanced over the side of the ship. It was too far from the shore for her to jump. She could scream, but then she'd have to explain what she was doing on the ship. Nope, didn't want to do that. She hadn't brought her cell phone. Okay, she officially had a problem.

She was leaning over the railing trying to decide if it was worth jumping into the water, when she heard the soft laughter behind her.

Her heart leaped into her throat in a vain attempt to escape. Too bad, because it wasn't going anywhere without her. And *she* wasn't going anywhere because her lungs had stopped working. That was the only explanation for her inability to breathe. When they finally did start working again, she'd be sucking wind for a week.

Slowly she turned from the rail. If she'd spun quickly, she probably would've passed out on the deck. The damned moon chose that exact moment to slip behind a cloud, the sneaky bastard.

And in the suddenly stifling darkness, she saw the black shape of a man.

"Looking for a pirate captain, talk-show lady?"

15

"Eric?" Donna was in one-word mode as she tried to recover. She clasped the railing and concentrated on getting her heart pumping and her lungs doing their in-and-out thing again.

"For tonight I'm Eric the Evil, scourge of the sea, and captain of the pirate ship *Asima.*" He stalked closer.

"Asima?" There, she finally had her heart under control, but her breathing was still iffy.

"Uh-huh. She made me promise to name my ship after her in exchange for telling me where you were." He moved even closer.

That sneaky little witch. Asima had set her up. Donna opened her mouth to lash out at all feline flimflammers, but at that moment the moon emerged from behind the clouds.

Whoa, would you look at that. And "that" was definitely *not* the moon. Donna closed her mouth and slid her gaze the length of his remarkable body. Her very own pirate captain. The light breeze lifted his dark hair away from his face, exposing every hard line. Shadows lent his high cheekbones and firm jaw an exotic cast. His blue eyes seemed to gleam in the pale moonlight.

Eric had spoken last, so Donna supposed it was her turn. "I thought you had to work tonight. How'd you get away from the castle?"

"I didn't."

Who cared about his answer, because she was all caught up in his whole pirate persona—white shirt stretched across broad shoulders and open almost to his waist, exposing a wide vee of muscular chest, leather pants hugging narrow hips and strong thighs. Leather pants? Did pirates wear leather pants? Didn't matter. Leather pants were sexy. Calf-high boots completed the picture of a masterful pirate captain. Made her wet and wild just looking at him.

Surprising. Because in her youthful fantasies, *she* was always the captain, the masterful pirate queen of . . .

Wait. In her frenzy to visually devour every yummy inch of him, Donna thought she might've missed something important. "Umm, run that past me again. How'd you get away from the castle?"

"I didn't." He stopped a few feet from her. Leaning his hip against the railing, he crossed his arms over his spectacular chest.

"Okay. Got it. Sooo, you're not officially here?" Ah, another weirdfest supplied by her friendly Live the Freakiness theme park.

"No." His smile was slow, sensual, and brimming with enjoyment over her puzzlement. It assured her that even when he wasn't officially "here," he was more than enough to satisfy her.

"And neither am I." The deep sexy voice behind her—the one that was definitely Eric's deep sexy voice—spun her around.

The second Eric stood quietly with hands at his side watching her. He was dressed as she'd pictured the crew member on a pirate ship would look—bare feet, ragged pants that only reached to his calves, and shirtless. Something clenched low in her belly, promising that this would be a lot more fun than her childhood fantasies.

Donna swung her gaze back to Eric the pirate captain. Tentatively she reached out to touch him. Her hand swept right through him. "I don't know how you've done this—nope, don't tell me, don't want to know—but I can't see how a fantasy has a chance of being effective if neither of you have something a girl can hang on to. That's just me, of course. I'm sure you have a perfectly wonderful plan to make this a memorable experience." She glanced over the side of the boat and wondered how deep the water was.

His laughter mocked her foolish doubts. "Unfortunately, I only have one flesh-and-blood body, and at the moment it's occupied giving customers their money's worth in the castle." His voice softened, a sensual invitation to play. "But that doesn't mean I haven't been thinking about your pirate fantasy. Tonight, you'll have the pleasure of exploring both sides of your fantasy. You'll find that disciplining a defiant member of your crew can be erotically stimulating, and then you'll learn that being a pirate captain's helpless captive has its own rewards."

Well, poo. And here she'd left Lola's whip and bustier back in her room. "That sounds intriguing, but I guess I need a solid someone to make my fantasy real. No offense, but neither of you qualifies as solid. So why don't we put this off until another night?"

His smile faded as he moved closer. Instinctively she stepped back. Stupid. His body wasn't here. It was in the castle terrorizing the latest wide-eyed virgin-of-the-moment. He couldn't touch her.

"We can't put it off for another night, talk-show lady. We're running out of nights." His lips tipped up in a smile meant to tempt the barnacles right off ye olde pirate ship. "Of course, if you decide to stay for the weekend or maybe even an extra week, we could explore any fantasy you chose. And I'd make sure it was with full-body contact."

"Yes, well, I'm thinking about it." She'd already decided to stay the weekend, but a whole extra week? Did she dare? Sure she had vacation time coming, and she could call in a few favors from people who would sub for her. But did she *want* to? Yes. Would it be a wise move? No. Decisions, decisions. They used to be so easy for her only a week ago when the world was a satisfying black or white. Where had all the gray come from?

"You're thinking too much." Eric the pirate captain demanded her attention again. "Give yourself over to the fantasy, and see where your imagination takes you."

A week in the Castle of Dark Dreams had taught her to expect the unexpected, so she watched him warily.

And then his whisper surrounded her. "Turn to the disobedient seaman behind you. You've watched him every day, working in the sun, his body gleaming with sweat, and you've wanted him. Now you have him at your mercy. Imagine and enjoy."

Donna still didn't see how he could deliver the wow factor in her fantasy without his physical body, but she'd wanted her pirate fantasy for so long that she'd give it a try.

"Imagine, Donna." His whisper became part of her and made all things possible. "Your mind is more powerful than you think. It can take you anywhere you want to go. Imagine." The final word was merely a breath of promise.

Okay. Show time. Donna turned toward Eric the Disobedient, closed her eyes, and pictured the scene she wanted. A dark corner of her mind gleefully pointed out that a week ago she would've run long and hard from what Eric was suggesting. She was learning trust, and where trust existed could other bonding agents be far behind? She ignored the voice and opened her eyes.

The ship rocked in the swells of the open sea, and Donna grabbed the rail to keep her balance. Damn, where was her Dramamine when she needed it? Wrong, wrong. Pirate captains didn't get seasick, and they didn't need to hang on to things to keep their balance. Taking a deep breath, she dropped her hand from the railing and scowled at the member of her crew who'd dared defy her.

The wind whipped the sails, and dark clouds warned of

an approaching storm. The storm was nothing compared to the punishment she'd visit on his defiant body.

Her palms were damp with excitement and anticipation. She rubbed them against her thighs, taking in stride her pirate ensemble of white shirt unbuttoned and tied just below her full breasts—she didn't remember them being *that* full—and tight black pants tucked into high boots. She clutched a sword in one hand. Where'd *that* come from? Her clothes were so tight there wasn't a place to hide a butter knife, let alone a sword.

She knew her eyes glittered with evil intent as she glanced around the deck at the rest of her assembled crew. All women. She'd found that women, like the lionesses in a pride, were capable of hunting and destroying prey with more efficiency and less stupid chest-pounding than men. They weren't testosterone driven, and therefore didn't feel the need to prove their masculinity by taking chances that led to mistakes. Dead pirates didn't get to spend their booty. Dead pirates didn't get to shake their booty, either. Bummer.

But Donna, Bitch of the Brine, always took on one male crew member for sexual entertainment to ease the boredom of long sea voyages. Because men were so predictable. At some point during the voyage, they always felt the need to exercise their perceived male dominance. That was when Donna pounced and the fun began.

"Ladies, we have a seaman here who refused to obey a direct order from me. Therefore, I've called all of you together to witness his punishment."

Her crew whooped and hollered their glee at the announcement. Donna turned her attention back to Eric the Unfortunate. She blinked. He'd been stripped naked and now stood with his back to the mast and his hands tied above his head. He'd spread his legs to keep his balance on the rolling deck.

Donna didn't know who'd done the stripping and tying, but as fantasies went, this one was heating up. Eric's hard body was slick with sweat and every muscle was clearly delineated as he struggled to free himself.

Donna offered him her best diabolical laugh. "Accept your fate, my beautiful insolent animal." She trailed the tip of her whip—she'd lost her sword somewhere along the way—across each male nipple and watched them grow hard.

"Bitch!" His voice was harsh with anger and defiance.

"Thank you. That's the nicest thing anyone has said to me today." Oh, goody. She loved a man who had the guts to curse her. "But compliments won't change what I intend to do to you." She leaned closer, savoring the scent of angry male. "First I'll rub the butt of my whip between your legs. Back and forth, back and forth. Just to loosen you up." And in her mind she could see it happening—the end of her whip sliding between his strong thighs, the sway of his balls as her whip rubbed against them, the sensual writhing of his body as he tried to escape what she was doing.

"What the hell do you want?" His rasping question was rife with frustration.

"I want you hard and hungry for my crew. You look like a man who could keep a lot of women happy." She would slide the tip of her whip over his sex, teasing him with the possibilities for unspeakable pain or exquisite pleasure.

Donna's breathing quickened while she watched his cock grow hard as he imagined what she had planned for him. She felt the moist heat between her legs and knew she'd be at the head of the line to sample him.

"I'm going to invite my crew to touch you, sort of a preview of things to come." She reveled in his look of horror as he watched the ring of women closing in on him.

The women converged on him—sliding their hands over every inch of his bared body, kneading his butt cheeks and inner thighs, pinching his nipples, cupping his balls, clasping his huge erection, and then squeezing to hear his aroused moans.

She was feeling like doing some moaning herself. In a minute she'd clear her crew away from him and then drag his hot body off to her cabin where she could enjoy his punishment away from prying eyes.

Suddenly she felt a presence behind her. Before she could turn, she sensed a sword point at her back.

"Let me introduce myself. I'm Eric the Evil, and you were so involved with your crew member's punishment you didn't hear my men and me board your ship." His voice was dark and wicked, more evil than even her own. "My men will take your crew to my ship, the *Asima,* and then I'll amuse myself."

Uh-oh. That sounded ominous . . . but strangely arousing. She turned to face him as his men rounded up her crew and hustled them away. She had to look up a long way. Wow. Big, bad, and gorgeous. "*Asima*? Strange name for a pirate ship."

"I named it after a strange being." His grin was a slash of white against his tanned skin. "There're just the three of us here." He nodded toward the man tied to the mast. "He's your captive, and now you're *my* captive. What can we do with this scenario?"

"Nothing much comes to mind." She wondered if she could make her sword reappear by concentrating really hard.

"You disappoint me. Well, that's okay, because I have enough ideas for both of us." A rumble of thunder and a flash of lightning punctuated his threat.

Without warning, he flicked the point of his sword toward her shirt, and when she looked down it had fallen open, exposing her breasts. Double Ds? She didn't know who they belonged to, but somewhere a woman was waking up to find the boob fairy had left her two 32Cs.

Eric the Evil's interest was heating up as he slid his gaze from her breasts over the rest of her body. No surprise when she glanced down to find she was naked, like in not one stitch of pirate garb other than her shirt. She could now honestly brag that she'd met a man whose stare could melt the clothes right off a woman's body.

She probably looked pretty stupid standing there with just her shirt on, so she shrugged out of it. "Do your worst, villain, but the Bitch of the Brine will never beg." Fine, so maybe she'd beg a little.

He gripped his bottom lip between his teeth and studied her. Did he have any idea how sexy that was? Probably. After all, he was an arrogant, egotistical, and really hot bastard.

And then he smiled, a wicked tilt to his full lips. "Let me explain what I have planned for you." He took another step closer, and she took another one back.

She was almost backed against the naked body of Eric the Disobedient. In her mind she could feel the fevered heat of his body, the pressure of his bare flesh pressed to her back, and the prodding of his hard sex against her spine. As he writhed to free himself, or maybe to cop a better feel, his balls would slide across her bare behind. Just the thought of all that intimate contact weakened her knees. She didn't even notice when the first drops of rain began to fall.

Talk about a split personality . . . Eric's pirate-captain self watched as Donna gazed up at him, her eyes hot with growing sexual excitement. His physical body was definitely in the wrong place right now. If he were on the ship instead of waiting for his next paying customer, he could deliver on his erotic suggestions in a way that his talk-show lady would never forget. But he'd have to work with what he had.

"First I'll grab a fistful of that beautiful blond hair and pull your head back so I can take your mouth. Pirates aren't gentle, so it'll be a hard demanding kiss, the kiss of a conqueror." He could almost feel her soft lips and taste her sweet desire as his tongue plundered her mouth. "Then I'll kiss a path over your jaw and neck. And when I get to your throat, I'll let my mouth linger on the spot where your blood pounds hard with excitement." Her throat. His moan was deep, guttural, and agonized.

Her eyes gleamed with defiance and arousal. "I'll fight you. I'm not one of your sweet young virgins, afraid of the big bad pirate."

The rain fell harder, flowing over her body, leaving it wet and slick. And so hot. He knew if he could touch her, he'd probably singe his fingers.

"Go ahead, fight me. I like a woman with claws. But it won't change what I'll do to you." If the fates were kind, his next customer wouldn't come bounding into the dungeon and find him so hard that even his plaid couldn't hide the evidence. "I'll smooth my hands over your bare flesh while I put my mouth on your breast. Then I'll push your thighs apart so I can rub my finger over the spot that gives you so much pleasure. I'll tease your nipple with my tongue until it's so sensitive you want to scream. Finally I'll slide my finger into you, in and out, in and out, until you're riding my finger, wet and ready for me."

"You, you . . ." She seemed lost for words strong enough to describe what she felt, but her body had no trouble expressing itself.

Her breathing quickened. Throwing back her head, she closed her eyes to the pouring rain and then cupped her breasts while she rubbed her thumbs over her nipples.

Eric now knew the true meaning of torture. It was watching the woman you wanted standing naked in the rain stroking her gleaming breasts while you were stuck in a freakin' castle. He couldn't look at her breasts, her stomach, her open thighs, one more minute, or else he was going to tick Holgarth off by racing up the steps and abandoning the castle to a vampireless fantasy. And Holgarth hated to give customers their money back.

"Turn around and face your captive, woman." Relieved, he watched her turn away from him. Jeez, that was so much better. Now his other self could look at her breasts, stomach, and open thighs while his Eric the Evil persona got to admire that round perfect behind. "Look at the man you've threatened with torture." As torture went, it wasn't very impressive, but he wouldn't tell her that. "See how hard he is? He wants you as much as I do." Which was pretty much a no-brainer.

"I want you, I want him, I want both of you. At the same time." She sounded as though she'd just realized she was free to desire whatever she wished. "I want to untie him so he can go to his knees in front of me and slide his tongue deep inside me. I'll grab his hair to guide him deeper and deeper and . . . deeper." Each "deeper" came out more breathless than the last.

Eric the Evil scowled. Well, hell. He was jealous of himself.

Then she turned back to him. "And when I can't stand another moment, I'll drag you down onto the deck and—"

Time to reestablish the chain of command here. "Then I'll kneel between your rain-slicked thighs, put my hands beneath your bottom, and lift you so that I can bury myself inside you. I'll groan as all your heat and need clench around my cock."

"What will *he* be doing?" Donna sounded out of breath as she nodded toward her naked crew member, who, per her wish, was free of his bindings.

"Imagine." Eric watched as she nodded and then lowered herself to the ship's deck. He wanted to roar his frustration at not being able to follow her down, cover that warm beautiful body with his own, and share everything that he was—his passion, his hungers, his flesh-and-blood presence. "Close your eyes and imagine."

Once her eyes were closed, he whispered the ending of her fantasy. "I'll slide slowly into you, stretching and filling you. And then I'll ease out and plunge back in, harder, stronger. I'll listen to your whimpers of pleasure, enjoy the scent of aroused woman, and lean over to slide my tongue over your parted lips that taste of rain and desire."

"Yesss!" She spread her legs as she flung her arms above her head and arched her back, begging for more, so much more.

In the background Eric could hear sounds at the top of the stairs. The next customer was getting ready to venture down into the dungeon. No! Not yet. He wasn't finished. His body's howl of outrage didn't bode well for the unfortunate virgin or any other form of human bearding him in his lair.

Eric blocked out everything but Donna's pleasure. "The

man you've freed has secretly lusted after you and now sees his chance. He crouches over you, touching your body, flicking your nipples with his tongue."

She writhed on the deck, her naked body bathed in sweat. "I need to taste him. Now."

"As I plunge into you, deeper and deeper, you feel the spasms building that will wrack your body with the ultimate sensation. Your freed captive leans closer so that he can slide his tongue over your stomach as I drive you closer and closer to orgasm." Eric wasn't going to make it. He could hear footsteps slowly descending the stairs. His own sexual arousal had triggered his change to vampire, and he hoped he scared the crap out of whoever was interfering with Donna's fantasy. "You put your mouth on his sex, tasting his hunger, his excitement. While he moans his pleasure, you circle the head of his cock with your tongue and then slide your lips over him, moving lower and lower as you pleasure every inch of his heated flesh with your—"

"Oh. My. God." With a cry of joyous release, she shuddered in the throes of her orgasm.

The footsteps reached the bottom of the steps and stopped. Then he heard a squeal of fright from whoever was standing at the door of the dungeon.

And he had to leave Donna lying on the deck of that ship. No being there for her as she recovered. No calm explanations. *No sharing the pleasure.*

Damn it all to hell! Fury rolled over him in hot splashes of red and purple, buffeted him with the roar of an avalanche. And with all the sound and fury shaking him, he only had time for two coherent thoughts. In all of his eight centuries, leaving a woman had never triggered this much rage. And whoever had torn him away from Donna was going to get their money's worth of fright tonight.

He growled his anger and lifted his lips from his fangs in a deadly snarl. The twenty-something woman with a mop of red hair and wide green eyes screamed again and then slapped a hand over her mouth. Frozen in place, she stared at him in horror.

Hah! She hadn't seen anything yet. "You dare enter my lair, woman? 'Tis foolish you are. I'll sink my fangs into your neck and drink from you. Once I've taken your blood, you'll be mine forever. I'll come for you in the darkness of your bedroom, waking you from dreams of your mortal lover, and you'll go with me to hunt the living, for you will now be one of the undead." What a bunch of garbage, but it was scaring her. Hey, you enter a vampire's lair, you get what you deserve. Eric stalked toward her, but she was too terrified to move. He didn't care. They paid him to scare people. Well, tonight he was feeling the part.

As he loomed over her in the dimly lit dungeon, the woman finally found her voice and the power to move. With a wild shriek of terror, she tore out of the room and up the stairs. Two male grunts of pain hinted that she'd met Brynn and Conall on their way down to save her. She obviously felt she didn't need saving. Ah, another satisfied customer.

He had a few minutes before the next fantasy, and he was going to find Donna.

Donna lay on the deck while her breathing returned to normal and her body stopped shaking. Then she opened her eyes . . . and met the interested stare of Sparkle Stardust, who was leaning over her. "What're you doing here?"

"Saving you from this ship." Her gaze narrowed, and then she smiled her sly feline smile. "Well, well, sister. What fantasy did you get off on? Tell all." She sat down on the deck in her black silk top and pants.

"What fantasy? It was such a beautiful night that I thought I'd lay on the deck for a while and watch the stars, listen to the water—"

"Be fast-food takeout for all the mosquitoes in Galveston." Sparkle's expression said that Donna needed to practice her lying before taking her act on the road.

Sparkle was right. Donna itched all over. Wow, some fantasy. How could something be so intense it blocked out a mosquito attack by at least a million of the little bloodsuckers? Donna pushed herself to a sitting position, but she still fell quivery and not quite ready to try standing.

She glanced down. All clothes in place. Hadn't she been naked a few minutes ago? Yes. Maybe. Donna glanced up at the clear night sky. No rain. But she could still feel the cool wet slide of it over her heated body. Taking a deep breath, she tried to concentrate on Sparkle. "How'd you get on the ship?"

"I put the gangplank back up and walked on." She studied Donna. "I mean, here I am just taking a quiet walk around the lake and I hear this moaning. I thought someone was hurt." The sly smile was back. "Tell me about it."

A quiet walk around the lake? Donna didn't think so. She glanced pointedly at the nosebleed heels on Sparkle's sandals. "Love your walking shoes." Suddenly she remembered. Sparkle had some explaining to do. Like how she maintained her youthful glow when she was a senior citizen with a capital *S*. "You know, Asima and I were having a chat, and she mentioned that the two of you had a run-in with each other about, oh, two hundred years ago. I said, no way. Sparkle looks too good to be that old. So how often do you have to get a face-lift? Once every two months? Who's your plastic surgeon? He's good. Really good."

The corners of Sparkle's full pouty lips turned down. "I'm going to wrap Asima's long skinny tail around her neck and squeeze until her eyes pop out."

"Who are you? What are you?" Donna rubbed her eyes and then rotated her neck to ease some of her tension. "What is it about this place? Why're you all here?" She closed her eyes for a moment. She'd just had an incredible sexual experience she totally didn't understand. Her nipples still felt sensitive, and the relaxed satisfied feeling low in her stomach affirmed that yes, she'd had one hell of a fine orgasm.

And now Sparkle. "I figured you were a little too obsessed with sex, but other than that, I thought you were kind of normal." Donna threw her hands in the air. "What's normal? Right now vampires are normal. Demons, immortal warriors, and wizards are normal. A shape-shifting cat is normal." Horrified, she felt a tear slide down her cheek. "I'm the only one who's *not* normal around here."

Sparkle looked offended. "You thought I was *normal*? Here I'm trying to sex up your life, and you insult me right to my face." She took a deep breath before standing. "I'd stick around to explain the facts of life according to Sparkle Stardust, but I have some cat hunting to take care of. Eric's on his way, he can explain things to you."

Eric's on his way. No. Not yet. Not while her emotions were still tumbling over each other in an attempt to make sense of what she was feeling for him. Maybe she could get off the ship before he found her.

Donna followed behind Sparkle as she navigated the gangplank in her designer shoes without falling flat on her face. Glancing at her watch, Donna realized she didn't have time to work things out in her head, because she had a show to broadcast.

She had a guest tonight, so she wouldn't have to take calls for a few hours. Donna loved the wow factor she got from some of her callers, but this week had taken a little of the wonder out of it all. Because after what she'd experienced, nothing her callers told her could even make her lift an eyebrow. At least her show would take her mind off her pirate fantasy for a while.

As she made her way back toward the castle, Donna saw Eric striding toward her. No. She didn't want to face him until she had her emotions firmly under control again. Donna eyed the shrubbery next to the path. Would he think it strange if he found her hiding in the bushes? Would he believe that she was searching for her lost control?

Too late. Eric stopped in front of her, and she had to

look up a long way to meet his gaze. He was once again playing the part of a vampire Highlander. He played all his parts well, but she wasn't quite sure who the real Eric Mackenzie was.

"I'm sorry I left you alone, but a customer showed up." He reached out to slide his fingers along her jaw. "Are you okay?"

She nodded. Good thing he didn't try to pin down her exact degree of okay. "No problem." She thought about that. "And don't creep into my mind to see if I'm telling the truth."

His grin was a white flash of strong teeth in the darkness. "We have to talk after your show. You can order something from the restaurant and bring it back to your room to eat."

She nodded again. "Sparkle showed up after you left. Asima told me that she and Sparkle got into it about two hundred years ago. I confronted Sparkle. She said you'd explain."

Eric raked his fingers through his hair and muttered something beneath his breath. "Sure. I'll tell you what I know tonight."

Silence filled the space between them as they entered the great hall. She thought he'd let her go without saying anything else, but at the last minute he put his hand on her arm.

"Are you staying for the weekend?" He looked anxious.

Anxious was good. It made her feel all warm and fuzzy. "Yes."

"Great. How about hanging around for an extra week?" He didn't look too hopeful.

"Yes." She didn't know which of them was more surprised.

Leaning down, he kissed the side of her neck and was gone.

Stood to reason he'd kiss the side of her neck. Probably a kiss on the neck was more emotionally satisfying than the lips for a vampire. What did she know?

Taking a deep breath, she faced what she'd agreed to. She was staying an extra week in Castle Weird so that she could explore her emotional attachment to an eight hundred-year-old vampire.

Was she crazy, or what?

16

Win some, lose some. After the Earth shifted poles during her pirate-fantasy-induced orgasm, things slid downhill at warp speed.

Friday night, her last live broadcast from the Castle of Dark Dreams, and her guest was a bust. Brilliant guy, but his scientific explanation of why there had to be parallel universes was . . . well, beyond the understanding of any human mind. Therefore, he had to be an alien. That was the only explanation. But at least he could've had the decency to be an entertaining alien.

And when she went to open lines, she was besieged by calls from the pod women. They must've all saved themselves up for a night when she had lots of really serious stuff on her mind and didn't need tons of questions about sexy creatures of the night. Her guest wasn't much help. He said they all came from parallel universes. Ooookay. At least Sparkle wasn't sitting in the audience asking thought-provoking questions about sex and vampires.

Now Donna sat on her bed, all comfy in her nightshirt, finishing her chicken quesadillas. What was with women in the novels she read? Give them a few puny problems—significant other is a serial killer, deadly plague set loose on earth's population by aliens, Planet X poised to obliterate the world in twelve hours—and they lost their appetites. Not her. Give her something to worry about and she could eat her way through an entire Mexican restaurant's menu. She was worried now.

Eric lounged in one of the room's chairs, his long legs stretched out in front of him. He crossed his ankles and studied her. "I was hoping you'd try out one of those outfits you have in your closet. The one with the boots, mask, and whip looks like fun."

A quick glance, and a few people might mistake him for just another great-looking guy in jeans and a T-shirt. Very few. But Donna Nolan would never make that mistake. From the first moment she'd met Eric McNair—who was really Eric Mackenzie—she'd sensed his power, his overwhelming sexual temptation, and tried to tread warily around all that potent maleness. The score now stood at potent maleness 50, Donna's common sense 0. She was in danger of being swept.

Reluctantly Donna set her empty plate aside. If he weren't here, she'd lick the plate. "After my pirate fantasy, I sort of thought the virginal white nightie would be false advertising. And I'm too tired to do the Mistress Donna thing."

Eric simply nodded. She needed to say something about the fantasy, but nothing brilliant came to mind. Oh, well, she had to start somewhere. "So tell me about Sparkle. Who is she? *What* is she?" Donna would work up to her pirate fantasy.

"She's a cosmic troublemaker."

"Say what?" During her years on *Donna till Dawn,* listeners had paraded every possible supernatural being past her, but no one, absolutely *no one,* had ever mentioned cosmic troublemakers.

He shrugged. "Yeah, cosmic troublemaker is a new one for me, too. She says she's over a thousand years old, and I tend to believe her."

"You mean that woman selling chocolates and jelly beans, the one who worries about three hairs on her knee and a broken nail, *that* woman is a thousand years old?" Donna couldn't wrap her understanding around what it would be like to live even a couple of centuries. "Why is she here in Galveston—sun, sand, surf, ley lines intersecting beneath her candy store?" She flung her hands into the air. "Why are any of you here?"

"I'm here because I was hired to help run the castle. I was soaking up the moonlight on a small exotic island when Holgarth called. He explained the concept of the park and said the owner specifically wanted Brynn, Conall, and me to run the Castle of Dark Dreams because we were *more than men.* Why us in particular?" He shrugged. "After I stopped laughing, I started wondering who this mysterious owner was and how Holgarth had found me. By that time I was intrigued enough to take the job. My mission in life is to find out who owns the park. I've tried following tax trails and every other damned trail back to our mysterious owner, but so far no luck." He smiled his smoky, sexy smile. "Admit it. You're glad I'm here."

"Hmmph." Donna the Noncommittal.

"And Sparkle?" He shrugged. "I'm not too clear on what she does, but whatever it is, it has to do with sex. From what she told me, I got the idea that she was some kind of demented matchmaker."

"Matchmaker?" Scary concept. Donna still had dozens of things she wanted to know about Sparkle, but she'd take her questions directly to the sneaky source. Time to talk about her pirate fantasy.

"About what happened on the pirate ship. If I didn't experience it, I never would've believed that you could do what you did without once touching me." Donna fidgeted with the sleeve of her nightshirt. She never fidgeted. "I guess after eight hundred years you've had lots of practice." Fishingfishingfishing.

His smile was sleepy, as well it should be. Not only was

it almost dawn, but last night he'd given new meaning to the term *multitasking.*

"What I did was bring you to orgasm. Never avoid the word. An orgasm is one of the greatest pleasures any being can experience." His smile faded. "And last night was the first time I've ever tried to project my image over a distance." He met her gaze, challenging her. "I've never wanted to be with a woman as much as I wanted to be with you on that ship, even if I had to leave my physical body in the castle." His intense stare let her know the exact degree of wanting he was talking about. "So I tried it."

She must be glowing. She could probably rent herself out as a pink neon sign blinking HAPPY, HAPPY, HAPPY. Woohoo! *Uh, can we say overreaction?* "This was your first time? Maybe *you* should wear the white nightie."

He grinned. "Now it's my turn to dig. Could any other man you've known bring you satisfaction without touching you?" His smile was easy, but his eyes said dead serious.

"No." There were some answers that didn't need elaboration.

She watched satisfaction flare in his eyes before he looked away. "I'd like you to know a little more about me."

"Uh-huh. All ears here." She was as greedy for information about him as she was for those cherries still sitting on her night table.

"Eight hundred years of existence taught me a few lessons. While I was still human, I fought for my life first as a Viking and later as a Highlander. But I always knew my enemy. Now it's different. Living with one foot in the human world and the other in the nonhuman realm presents a whole new set of dangers. Humans who find out about me react the same way they would if a T. Rex showed up on their doorstep—kill it."

Donna thought of all her open-minded listeners, of herself. "Not all humans."

He didn't look convinced. "Well, most. And different entities don't usually have friendly relationships with each other. My friendship with Brynn and Conall is the exception rather than the norm."

Sure, she wanted to hear more about his world and the many entities she'd never known existed, but there was something else at the top of her to-know list, and its placement there scared her.

She leaned back against the headboard and tried for a casually interested—but not too interested—expression. "I guess in between all that fighting for your existence you've known lots of women." *Tell me everything. In detail. I'm taking names, dates, and other pertinent facts.*

She *wasn't* jealous, just curious. Trish was the jealous one in her family. Donna had spent her whole adult life reminding Trish that jealousy was petty and counterproductive. Nope, wasn't jealous.

Donna tried to ignore the nasty little voice in her mind—no doubt inherited from a bitchy ancestor—that pointed out how long ago most of Eric's women had lived. Most likely they all had bad hair and were in desperate need of an orthodontist. She was feeling smugly superior until the same nasty voice admitted that the women he had now probably went to trendy hairdressers with only one name and had perfect teeth thanks to childhood braces. Rats.

Eric shrugged. "Female vampires never attracted me. Too predatory. Hey, I like strong women, just not the kind that might rip out my throat if I forgot their birthdays." He smiled. "Come to think of it, human females might do the same thing."

"Guess you must be good with birthdays. You've lasted eight hundred years." Donna felt like screaming. He knew what she wanted to know.

His sensual lips tilted up. "But you want to know about the human women I've known." He paused.

It was a pause that warned, "You might not like what I'm going to tell you." She swallowed hard.

"I've enjoyed many human women."

She had mixed feelings about that. He liked human women. Good. He'd liked *many* human women. Bad.

He hesitated as though he wasn't sure he wanted to say anything else and then continued. "I've survived so many years because I never took chances with women or sex. Spending more than one night with a woman has always been dangerous. You get too comfortable in the relationship, do or say something to give yourself away, and the next thing you know you're fending off a wild woman with a wooden stake."

Donna tried to comprehend this level of distrust. "It can't be that bad."

"Live as a vampire for eight hundred years, then come back and we'll discuss how bad it can be." Eric watched her thoughtfully. "The few women who discovered what I was could never accept me. You're the first one who has. Oh, I don't mean sexually. You still haven't accepted that."

Donna lifted one brow. "And what was last night? Felt pretty sexual to me."

"I was in *human* form for your fantasy."

Right. "So you've spent eight centuries having one-night stands. I didn't know there were that many women in the world."

"It's kept me alive. Besides, I never cared enough to try to stretch it into a relationship." His expression said he knew he was revealing more than he should. "But that's for the best. I've seen what happened to other members of my clan who fell in love with humans. They watched their mates grow old and die. How many times can you lose the one you love before it destroys you?"

He met her gaze, and she understood. "I get it. You never take a chance so you never get hurt." Trish had accused her of the same thing, never taking a chance. "Can't you turn the woman you choose into a vampire?"

Eric glanced at Sweetie Pie and Jessica. Their leaves were all tipped toward him. Listening. This week must be the most fun they'd had since they were seedlings. "My clan doesn't have that power. Most marry within the clan and have children before they change. Afterward they stay mated for life. All vampire clans aren't the same, though.

The night feeders have the power to turn humans. That's one of the reasons they're so dangerous. They don't particularly care if the humans are willing."

He radiated tension as he glanced at his watch. "Guess I'd better be going. Looks like dawn has officially arrived." He stood.

Donna blinked. He was leaving? "Wait."

He paused to look at her.

"I mean, uh, I thought you were going to stay here and uh, protect me from Taurin and all." Wow, was she the golden-voiced queen of the airwaves or what?

"You don't need me to protect you from Taurin anymore. I put a shield around his bed to go with the one across his door." He yanked open the door with controlled violence. "Here's the thing, talk-show lady. Only one of us had an orgasm on that ship, and the one who didn't needs his sleep."

"Sure. I guess when you get up there in years, it's hard to maintain your sexual energy level. They have several reliable products on the market to help with that." Donna hoped her snotty attitude challenged his manhood enough to make him stay. The simple truth? She wanted him. *You want him sans fangs.* Yeah, that, too.

Eric kept his back to her. "If I stayed here now, we'd have sex. And because I'd want it so badly, I'd do it on your terms—strictly human form, no scary biting. But if you've been counting, and I know you have, you've noticed that we've gone beyond the one-night-stand limit."

She really really wanted to think of something funny to say so he'd understand that what was happening between them was nothing more than a one-night stand times three, or four, or . . . But this whole thing didn't *feel* funny.

"I've compromised with other women. I've held back the change during sex, and I've kept my teeth to myself. But I've found that I don't want sex between us to be a lie anymore. If you decide you want me enough to accept everything I am, let me know." He snared her with his heated gaze. "And I promise you that nothing you'll ever experience in your life will be more erotic." He quietly closed the door behind him.

Okay, huge life-altering decision closing fast in her rearview mirror. *Everything I am.* Love bites could be cool, but the whole concept of vampire fangs was so not a turn on. Eric had promised a sensual happening of colossal proportions. The bottom line. Did she believe him? Did she *trust* him? Donna didn't know. One thing she *did* know, she'd be lonely in bed. Sighing, she reached out to turn off her bedside lamp.

"Don't you dare turn off that light, dearie. We have some sexual strategy to work out before tonight's Vampire Ball." Lola shimmered into view, her sweet grandmotherly smile firmly in place.

"You are so lucky to have me as your adviser, Donna. Normally you'd pay a fortune for my level of expertise. It's like having your very own personal sensual trainer." Asima leaped onto the foot of the bed.

Lola and Asima spotted each other at the same time.

Lola plunked the basket of fruit she'd brought with her onto the bureau—*Random thought. How did a ghost tote around physical objects?*—and glared at Asima. "What're you doing here?"

Asima crouched on the bed and hissed at Lola. *"I'm going to make sure that Donna goes to the Vampire Ball tonight sexually armed and dangerous. Now that I'm here, you can leave."*

"Whoa, guys." Donna held up her hand. "How do you know I'm sticking around to go to the Vampire Ball? I'm supposed to fly back to New York in a few hours."

Lola pursed her lips at Sweetie Pie and Jessica. "I don't like to tattle, but the girls can never keep a secret."

"Count me in on that excuse." Asima yawned, exposing her sharp little teeth along with her boredom with having to explain herself.

"Those plants didn't tell you anything. Besides, I wasn't even in the castle when I told Eric I was staying. Don't either of you have anything better to do than spy on me?"

"No. At least nothing that's more fun." Lola looked militant about her right to spy.

"No. I mean, I will have something better to do soon, but right now I'm kind of at loose ends." Asima batted at a piece of fluff that dared to float into her airspace.

"Look, I appreciate your offer to help, but I can take care of the Vampire Ball and my sex life all by myself." Which wasn't completely true. She wasn't sure where she was going with Eric's need for her to love both of his forms, one of which included biting as part of its mating ritual. Love? She hadn't meant *love.* Exhaustion was messing with her mind.

"Well, dearie, I certainly don't want to hurt your feelings, but your progress with that beautiful vampire really sucks so far." She put her hand over her mouth and giggled. "Sucks. What a wonderfully descriptive modern word."

Asima's gaze slid between Donna and Lola. *"Exaggerating as usual, Lola."* She focused her attention on Donna. *"You've done a so-so job with Eric, but I'd like you to bring him to his knees tonight."*

Donna bit her lip, but she had to say it. "He can't dance on his knees."

Lola chuckled.

Asima narrowed her cat eyes. *"Do I look amused?"* Her expression said she'd continue trying to help Donna in spite of provocation. *"A man on his knees is in a prime position to do so many interesting things."*

Lola stopped chuckling and looked impressed.

Donna did some mental eye rolls. "Let's not play word games. I don't think there's one thing you can do to make the Vampire Ball more of a wow than it's going to be. Eric and I will work out our sexual destinies just fine without your help, Asima."

Lola smirked at Asima. "That means you can go away." She didn't look sweet and grandmotherly now.

Donna sighed. "That means you, too, Lola."

"Oh." Lola glanced down at her bowl of fruit and then picked up a large peach. "Males are so impressed with appearances. My girls at the Cock Crows at Dawn were the most beautiful in all of Texas. But natural beauty wasn't enough. There was lots of competition out there. So I taught my girls the subtle art of physical enhancement."

Asima snorted. *"Subtle? You?"*

Lola flicked her an irritated glance and forged onward. "Men flocked to my little bordello, and I made lots of money. Men aren't attracted to inner beauty, dearie. Not at first. They look at the pretty wrapping and figure they don't need to know what's inside."

Donna had always thought of herself as realistic where men were concerned—yeah, so Eric was the exception—but Lola's cynical attitude bothered her. "You can't generalize, Lola. All men aren't that way. Looks aren't everything."

"I hate to agree with Ms. Sensitivity, but men are shallow, Donna. If you don't believe me, go to the ball tonight with no makeup, hair pinned back in a bun, and wearing something long, straight, and brown." Asima widened her eyes. *"No. Don't listen to me. Don't even think about trying that."*

Lola didn't give Donna a chance to speak. "Let's look at this peach—perfectly round, a perfectly peachy color, and it looks perfectly ripe. Now suppose I had another peach—not perfectly round, not a perfectly peachy color, but perfectly ripe and sweet inside. Which would you buy, Donna?" She saved Donna the effort of answering. "You'd buy the one that looked perfect on the outside, because you wouldn't know how wonderful the other one was until you bit into it."

Bit into it. Donna winced. "Not fair. You can't compare people with peaches." Where was she going with this argument? She glanced at her clock. Nowhere. The only place she wanted to go was to sleep.

"If you agree to let me get you ready for the ball tonight, I'll leave so you can go to sleep." Asima played dirty.

Donna was tired and getting more ticked off by the minute. "Is there any way I can keep you out of my mind?"

Asima's expression was pure feline sneakiness. *"Work with me on the ball, and I'll show you how to shield your thoughts."*

Donna didn't have to think about it long. She was tired of everyone tramping through her brain. "Fine. You have fifteen minutes."

Asima turned a triumphant gaze on Lola. *"She wants me. Go back to your candy store and suck on some sour balls."*

"Candy store?" Donna widened her eyes as a horrible possibility grew. "Lola? Explain." But Lola obviously wasn't in an explaining mood, because her figure slowly faded away.

"Good. Now that we're alone, you can show me what you're going to wear—"

Asima got no further because the door was suddenly flung open as if by a giant invisible hand, and Sparkle strode into the room. She looked ready to breathe fire. Donna wouldn't be surprised if Sparkle had a dragon or two in her ancestry. Why not? Everything else was here.

Sparkle glared at Asima. "You are such a . . . cat. Sneaky, underhanded, and with a big mouth."

Asima blinked her big blue eyes at Sparkle. *"And that's bad, why?"*

"Shut up! Both of you!" Donna needed another plate of quesadillas. She scowled at Sparkle. "Explain yourself." She knew she had murder in her eyes, and she hoped Sparkle recognized it.

Sparkle shrugged, smoothed her hands over her black silk pants, and checked her purple nails for breakage. "Humans trust old women. I guess it's like a grandmother syndrome. And if the old woman ran a bordello, then humans would believe everything she said about sex, because she was, well, like their grandmother." She shrugged. "It's all perfectly logical."

"My grandmother knows squat about sex. And I can't believe you tricked me like that." Donna was furious, but she had to admit that Sparkle was good. It was weird, but something inside mourned the loss of Lola.

"You accepted Lola because you thought she was a ghost. It was easier to get my sexual message across that way." She didn't sound repentant. "Until Loose Lips over there blew my cover."

Asima looked unconcerned. *"I thought Donna knew. It never occurred to me that anyone would be fooled by that stupid disguise."*

Great. Now Asima was insulting her intelligence. "You've used five of your minutes, Asima. Ten left, and then you're out of here."

Asima slanted Sparkle a slitty-eyed warning, but Sparkle didn't budge. So she turned back to Donna. *"Let's see what you're going to wear to the ball."*

Donna glanced at the clock. Only nine more minutes. Sighing, she climbed out of bed and padded over to the closet. She pulled her red dress out and held it up. "This okay?"

Sparkle took it from her and looked at it from all angles. "No good. It needs to be shorter, tighter, and plunge a lot lower in the front and back."

Asima screwed her face up in what Donna assumed was a cat sneer. *"Why not have her just wear a red napkin. It needs to be longer and flowing with a smooth dip in front that teases but doesn't really reveal anything. Very classic."*

"Very boring. We want Eric crazy with lust for you, and lots of bare skin drives men to lust, even vampires." She wrinkled her nose at the dress. "And after I alter your dress, I'll get you some genuine slut shoes to go with it."

"Alter it? You?" Asima's eyes grew wider if possible. *"I think not. You'll make her look like one of those women in that Cock Crows at Dawn place you made up. I'll make sure it gets to someone who can make it elegant and unique."*

Without warning, Asima leaped at the dress Lola still

held and gripped the skirt with her teeth. *"Give it to me. This is my job."*

Sparkle's eyes were slits of fury. "Get your freakin' little teeth out of that dress. I'm the head honcho in charge of inciting horny men. I know what turns men on." She gave the dress a vicious yank, but Asima held on.

Donna squeaked her alarm. She assumed that superhuman strength was part of the immortal package, and that meant her dress could be in big . . . The sound of ripping material stalled her thoughts.

Sparkle still held the top part of Donna's favorite red dress. The bottom part was gripped in Asima's determined jaws. The two parts were no longer one. With a growl of semitriumph, Asima started to drag her half of the dress toward the door.

Donna got there first. "Uh-uh. You aren't going anywhere."

The expression on Donna's face must've given Asima pause, because she stopped.

Donna figured it was going to be hard to talk through clenched teeth, but she gave it a try. "Both of you destroyed my dress. Therefore, both of you will work together to make me a new dress for the ball."

Asima glared up at Donna, but never loosened her grip on the dress. *"Impossible. I have perfect taste, and she has no taste. We could never produce a dress together."*

"It won't happen, sister." Sparkle folded her half of the dress and then inspected her nails for damage. "It would be like . . . like a nun helping Michelangelo create his statue *David*. By the time the collaboration was finished, David would be wearing a tutu."

Donna was seeing red, and it wasn't the reflection off her ruined dress. "Listen up, kiddies. You. Will. Work. Together. On. My. New. Dress."

"Or?" Asima didn't look overly worried.

"Or I'll complain to Holgarth, and he'll ban your behinds from the castle. And if you do manage to slip past Holgarth, I'll never let you interfere in my sex life again. N-E-V-E-R."

Asima watched Donna warily as she backed out of the room dragging her half of the dress with her. Sparkle remained, seemingly unconcerned as she bent over to study Sweetie Pie and Jessica. "If you and Eric have sex somewhere besides this room after the ball, do me a favor and take the girls with you. I've never seen them looking this good. They've bonded with you and want to share your joy."

Donna felt suddenly drained. It'd been a long day and night, and now day again. She was about to crash. "Why is it so important to you that I look sexy for the ball? I mean, more than your normal obsession with all things sexy."

Sparkle straightened, slid her fingers across the remnant of Donna's silk dress, and then smiled—a scheming, manipulative, and secretive smile. Scary.

"You and Eric need to kick-start your relationship. Right now you're standing still. He wants you to accept his vampire nature. You're not sure about the biting thing. And yes, I've been sneaking around in your mind." She walked over and picked up the bag of chocolate-covered cherries. "I want you so sexed up at the ball that Eric doesn't care about anything but getting you into his bed, into your bed, or onto the banquet table in the great hall." She swung the bag of candy slowly in front of Donna's eyes. "I want you to use these after the ball. I want you so aroused that you don't give a damn if he bites you, licks you, or changes into his vampire form during sex. I want you to have the ultimate sexual experience, and then we'll take it from there."

Donna could only stare at Sparkle. "Why?"

"Because I'm all about sex. It's my destiny. I hook up people who're wrong for each other and make them right for each other. And in between the hooking up and the ultimate orgasm, all hell breaks loose. The all-hell-breaking-loose part is what I groove on. So when *you* win, *I* win." Sparkle leaned close to Donna and narrowed her amber eyes. "And if you ever repeat what I've just told you, I'll call your show every night and make your professional life a living hell."

Her smile turned genuine as she walked toward the door, her walk a sensual sway in her sexy sandals. "Now that we have that all settled, I'll be on my way. I'll hunt down Asima the anal retentive, and we'll come up with something for you to wear that'll give Eric an instant erection." She offered Donna a finger wave. "Later."

Donna staggered back to her bed and collapsed onto it. She just had enough strength to turn off the light. Then she stared into the darkened room with dawn creeping around the drawn drapes. When had her life taken a left turn into madness?

This was God's payback for all the times she inflicted her opinions on her defenseless family. She'd been wrong. Her parents shouldn't stay together just to make her happy. She'd been wrong. Her brother had a perfect right to still be in love with his wife even if they never set foot outside their house. It was their life to live. She'd been wrong. Trish had a right to fall in love with a man she'd known only two weeks.

Because heaven help her, there was a good chance that at the end of her two weeks at the Castle of Dark Dreams she might be in love with a vampire.

17

Eric's Saturday was a winner so far. It looked like he'd be able to slip into Taurin's room without Donna knowing he was there.

Sure, he'd kind of given her the impression he'd need her help with Taurin. But that was just to get her to stay for the weekend. He didn't really want her help. She'd muddy the waters with emotion.

Taurin and he would talk. If Taurin still wanted to kill him, they'd settle it like warriors. Taurin would probably want a gun, but the Mackenzie way was with swords.

Eric focused on removing the shield from Taurin's door, and then he pushed the door open. Taurin was waiting for him, burns healed and eyes blazing defiance. Eric decided to keep the shield around the bed for the moment.

"Looks like a few days of rest haven't done a thing for your common sense." Eric pulled up a chair beside the bed. "If you were smart, you'd pretend that you had a change of heart. Can't change what you don't have, though, can you?"

Taurin's smile was simply a baring of his teeth. "Would you believe me?"

Eric shrugged. "There's that, too."

"Get rid of this shield, Mackenzie, and we'll settle this for good." Taurin's expression turned contemptuous. "But that won't happen, will it? You're the same coward you were when you set that warehouse on fire and then ran away."

Eric narrowed his gaze. That did it. No one called a Mackenzie a coward. He had his fair share of the Mackenzie temper, and it wasn't a pretty thing to see. "Right. Let's settle it. I'll get you a sword."

Taurin's eyes widened. "Sword? You're kidding. Who fights with a sword anymore?"

Eric's smile was deadly. "I do."

"I want a gun."

"I'm sure you do." Eric stood. "Want to rethink who's the coward? A gun can kill long-distance. You can even run and hide before you shoot. No messy emotional confrontation with your opponent. But a sword forces you to stand toe-to-toe and look your enemy in the eye. I'll be back as soon as I get our swords."

"Gee, it's great to see how far you guys have come over the centuries. A few hundred years ago, you would've tried to hack each other to death. Now? You're still trying to hack each other to death. Ya gotta love it. The barbarian hordes are alive and well." Donna's sarcasm was coated with a thick layer of anger. "And thanks, Eric, for inviting me to talk with Taurin."

Eric didn't turn to look at Donna. "You know, this isn't your fight. Taurin wants to end it, so I'm giving him what he wants."

"That's what I like about you, Mackenzie. You always aim to please." She pulled another chair over beside his and sat down.

Eric finally met her gaze, and he put every bit of the cold fury he was feeling into his stare. "Don't criticize something you don't understand. Taurin and I are vampires, and we'll settle this in our own way."

Donna didn't look intimidated. "You know, you guys

need a mediator. Talking is my job, so I'll make a great mediator."

Resigned, Eric sat down again. "Sure, take your best shot. Convince the hardhead in the bed that I'm not guilty." She wouldn't be able to do it, but she couldn't accuse him of not letting her try.

Donna nodded, all business now. "I'll need the names of any vampires who were at the warehouse that night."

Eric didn't have to think about his answer. He'd gone over that night in his mind hundreds of times, trying to figure out what went wrong. "There were three others besides me—Hakon, Malcom, and Kyla."

"Kyla? A woman?"

He smiled grimly. "Female vampires don't sit home knitting fang warmers for their men."

Donna ignored his comment. "Taurin, did anyone come with Dacian that night?"

Taurin tried to look disinterested, but Eric noticed the slight tremor of his hands. "Gabriel was with my brother, but he stayed outside."

"Okay, guys, I need some phone numbers." She looked at both Eric and Taurin expectantly.

"You want to call them?" Eric wondered what Donna thought she'd find that he hadn't.

"Well, yeah." She sighed. "Look, I'm a radio talk-show host. I understand voices. I've spent years listening to tone and inflection. I'm good at recognizing the truth when I hear it."

Eric pushed his battle lust aside. He'd give logic a try. For now. "Couldn't hurt. But if you don't find anything new, will you let us settle things our own way?"

"Probably not." She looked at Taurin. "Do you know Gabriel's number?"

"Yeah, we've kept in touch." Taurin didn't meet Donna's gaze. "But he doesn't know I've spent all these years hunting Eric."

"How about you, Eric?" Her gaze was direct, her expression neutral.

Eric couldn't help it; he slipped into her mind, and was immediately buffeted by her rush of feelings—worry, uncertainty, and the need for his trust. Guilt prodded him, so he slid from her thoughts. "I'll get their phone numbers. The clan has a coded directory I can access online if I need a number."

Donna watched as he strode from the room, and then she turned back to Taurin. "Why do you want Eric to be the guilty one?"

"What do you mean?" His guarded expression told her he knew exactly what she meant.

"Oh, I don't know. Maybe it's because you never saw who set the fire, but out of all seven vampires who were there that night, you blame Eric." She shrugged. "Sounds like there's something personal going on to me."

She thought he'd deny it, so she was surprised when he nodded.

"Jealousy. Don't get me wrong, I still hold him responsible even if one of his friends actually set the fire. He was the oldest vampire in the group. He was in charge." Taurin's body radiated tension. "And Dacian trusted him. Dacian never stopped talking about Eric. It was Eric did this and Eric did that. I was just Dacian's kid brother who never did much of anything right. Being a younger brother sucks sometimes."

A smile touched his lips, once again reminding Donna that he was a beautiful man when his expression wasn't twisted with hate. "I'm still screwing up, but if Dacian were here, he'd slap me on the back, laugh, and tell me not to sweat it. He was that kind of guy." His smile disappeared. "But I *am* sweating it, and I'll keep trying until I get it right."

Donna shook her head. "If you know part of your problem with Eric is jealousy, why do you still hate him so much? And why're you telling me this now?"

"Have you ever hated, Donna?" He sounded casual, but his hard gaze said he was about as far away from casual as he could get.

"People? No. I've hated *things*—tests, cars with dead batteries, mushy bananas. But never a person. Not like you." She couldn't imagine what it would feel like to let hate for one person eat at her for hundreds of years.

Taurin's gaze turned distant, as though he was looking back over all those bitter years. "Hate's like a snowball. It starts out being about one thing, and then becomes about a lot of other things as it rolls along gathering speed and getting bigger and bigger."

"I still don't know why you're telling me this." If Eric knew a little of what was behind Taurin's hate, would it make a difference? She wanted to believe it would.

Taurin shrugged. "You saved my life and gave me another shot at Eric. I owe you."

"Jeez, you're such an immortal idiot." She wanted to reach through Eric's shield and shake Taurin until his teeth rattled. "Eric's the one who lifted you into the car. Eric's the one who carried you up to this room. Eric's the one who's kept Brynn from tearing your head off. *Eric* saved you."

Taurin raised a skeptical brow. "He saved me because you asked him to. A man in love does lots of stupid things." There was that fleeting smile again. "If you hadn't been around, I'd be history by now."

A man in love? Really? Nah. Donna couldn't think of one meaningful rejoinder. So it was a good thing that Eric chose that moment to return with his phone numbers.

"What now?" He stood beside her.

"I want you to call, explain what's going on, and then let me do the questioning. Asking questions is what I do." She watched as he moved around her to the night table and started punching in the first number. "Press the speaker button. Everyone needs to hear this."

"Sure." He waited while it rang. "Hey, Hakon. Eric. I have a favor to ask."

A half hour later, Donna had spoken to Hakon, Malcom, and Kyla. Donna sensed an emotion she couldn't identify when Kyla spoke of Dacian, but since it had no bearing on the mystery of who started the fire, she didn't pursue it.

All three said the same thing. They'd been stationed around the outside of the warehouse so they could warn Eric when Dacian showed up. No, they hadn't started any fire. Why would they when Eric was still inside? Yes, they'd let Eric know when Dacian and Gabriel arrived. And all they knew was that as the building exploded in flames, Eric and Taurin were the only ones who'd come out. And no, Eric would never kill by trapping an enemy in a burning building. Eric fought his enemies with his sword as all Mackenzies did.

Taurin listened with no comment, his expression unreadable.

Donna didn't hear anything that sounded like a lie in the three vampires' answers. She wondered if Taurin heard the truth in their voices, or if he'd even admit it if he did.

"Tell me Gabriel's number." She pressed the numbers that Taurin gave her, and then waited anxiously to hear the night feeder's voice. *Please, please answer.* Gabriel was her last chance to find something, anything, to diffuse Taurin's rage. She took a deep breath to calm herself. If this didn't work, she'd break a chair over Taurin's head before she'd let him hack at Eric with some dumb sword.

"Yes?" Nothing else, just the one word.

Whoa, he sounded seriously unfriendly. Donna bet that telemarketers never called *his* house at dinnertime. She had this mental picture of a Dracula figure in some dark alley bent over his victim and then cursing as his cell phone rang. Maybe she *did* interrupt dinner.

Drawing on all her experience in talking with people, she introduced herself and then told Gabriel the situation. She didn't try to minimize the danger Taurin was in if he didn't listen to reason. Then she waited.

"What the hell do you think you're doing, Taurin?" Gabriel's voice boomed over the speaker. "Dacian got you out of that warehouse so you could live, not destroy yourself trying to avenge him. You don't have the power to take down Eric Mackenzie."

"But he was responsible—"

"No, he wasn't." Gabriel hesitated for a moment as though he was trying to decide what to say. "Maybe it's time you heard the truth. Dacian made me promise never to tell you, but he didn't count on you trying to get yourself killed."

The room's sudden stillness was complete. Donna shivered. Both Eric and Taurin were locked into that utter quiet no human could ever achieve.

"Dacian set the fire. He was the most powerful night feeder in existence, and he could control fire. He told me to wait by the entrance to make sure you got out of the building." There was a long pause. "And Mackenzie, too. He never told me why he was doing it. I've spent two hundred years trying to figure out what was in his mind that night. There's only one possibility, because Dacian would never choose to die by fire. He wanted to disappear. I don't know why, but I've kept my mouth shut until now. He'd want me to tell you if it meant saving your life."

"Thanks, Gabriel." Donna could barely choke out the words. Numbly she listened to the click as Gabriel hung up. She didn't want to look at Eric or Taurin, but she couldn't hide from the jagged edges of emotion she felt in the room. Slowly she lifted her gaze.

Taurin's face was bleached white, his eyes wide and shocked as he stared at Eric. "He wanted everyone to think he was dead—even me. Why?"

Eric saw the exact moment the full impact of Dacian's deception hit Taurin like a punch in the gut. He clenched his hands into fists and stuck them under the covers, but Eric could still see them shaking.

"He didn't trust me enough to explain what he had planned." Taurin's bitter laugh was painful to hear. "So what else is new? He never trusted me to keep my mouth shut about anything."

For the first time Eric shared some of what Taurin was feeling. Dacian had been his friend. Then, without warning, he'd withdrawn that friendship and started killing members of Eric's clan. Dacian had never come after Eric personally, but he'd never tried to contact Eric to explain what ended their friendship, either. And yet, on that final day, he'd cared enough to make sure Eric got out of the building safely.

Eric felt like ripping something apart. Dacian had disappeared, taking with him any possibility of Eric ever learning what ended their friendship. "I don't think it was you, Taurin. At the end, Dacian didn't trust anyone." How could he put into words what he felt? "We were friends, and yet he walked away from our friendship without a word of explanation. He didn't trust our friendship enough to share whatever demons were driving him."

Donna filled the silence between the two men. "Don't put yourself down, Taurin. You kept the faith with your brother by trying to bring the person you believed killed him to justice. Now you've got to let it go and live for yourself."

"How?" Taurin stared at the ceiling, and Eric could see him battling to contain the emotion that would shame him. Too bad vampires couldn't cry. Taurin needed the release. "I don't know how to live for myself." Left unsaid was that maybe he didn't *want* to live for himself.

Taurin needed time for his sorrow to turn to anger at his brother. It would happen. It was already happening for Eric. Focusing, Eric removed the shield from around the bed. "You can start by working at the castle until you've paid me back in hard labor for the aggravation you've caused me."

What the hell was he saying? Taurin had tried to *kill* him. Brynn and Conall would tear a strip off him for this. But damn it, he couldn't handle the silent scream of Taurin's anguish. And beyond all other reasons was the friendship he'd once shared with Dacian. He'd do one last thing for that friendship and then call it even. He'd give Dacian's brother a chance at life.

"Do I still have to keep a shield across the door, Taurin?" Eric hadn't glanced at Donna yet to see how she was taking everything, but she'd been strangely quiet.

Taurin shook his head. "You'd really let me work here?" He seemed astounded that Eric would offer him a job.

As well he should. In fact, Eric was pretty astounded himself. It must be Donna's civilizing influence. His Viking and Highlander ancestors would be twirling in their graves if they were dead. They weren't, and if he was smart he'd never let them find out about this. "I'm not doing you as much of a favor as you think. Holgarth will be your boss. That qualifies as revenge." He stood and started to turn toward Donna but then paused. "You're strong enough to hunt now. One rule. Never near the castle."

Taurin nodded. "Sure."

Eric glanced at Donna. She looked like she wanted to say something. He shook his head as he guided her toward the door. They needed to leave Taurin alone to grieve for his brother, because in a way Dacian had died again in Taurin's heart today.

Once out in the hallway Eric turned to Donna. "I'd better go tell . . ." His words stalled as he saw the expression in her eyes. He wasn't quite sure what emotion shone in her gaze, but whatever it was, he knew it was good for him.

Without warning, she grabbed a handful of his hair and dragged his head down to hers. "You are a big, beautiful, wonderful man. I'm so proud of you for offering Taurin a job."

Eric barely had time to register her words before she covered his mouth with hers and traced his lips with the tip of her tongue. He opened his mouth beneath her lips and invited her in. She teased and tormented with her tongue, stroking and retreating, but finally giving in to her growing excitement by tangling her tongue with his.

Eric's desire surged along with the hunger he was finding it harder and harder to control, the one Donna couldn't accept yet. He fought the change even as he moved away from her.

"This thing between us . . ." That sounded weak. "This need I feel for you is pushing me to the edge. I've always been able to control the change even with a woman I wanted." He shook his head and smiled. "But you? You're something else, talk-show lady."

He saw his own arousal mirrored in her gaze, but then she glanced away. "I'll know when it's time. You will, too." She looked back at him and returned his smile. "But know one thing, vampire. You're my hero today."

Her compliment made him feel better than he had any right feeling, especially since now he had to go down and tell the others that he'd offered Taurin a job. "I'd better break the news to the bloodthirsty mob below. I guarantee there won't be cheers of joy all around."

"I'll go with you." She clasped his hand and pulled him onto the elevator. "We can track them to their den and lay the happy news on them. You can bully them with all your immortal-power stuff, and I'll talk them to death. We'll make a deadly duo."

He laughed. "They won't have a chance." Funny how she could make a confrontation he was dreading into something almost fun because they'd be doing it together. Every cautious gene passed down from his Viking and Highlander ancestors was vibrating a warning. He was enjoying her way too much.

Once they stepped from the elevator, they didn't have far to search for the others. They were standing in the hotel lobby outside the castle jewelry store.

Holgarth, dressed as usual in his blue robe and conical hat, looked suspicious. But then Eric suspected Holgarth came from his mother's womb suspicious. When the midwife slapped his bottom, he probably turned her into a toad before fixing his skeptical gaze on Mommy.

"I assume you've resolved your problems with Taurin." He cast Donna an assessing glance. "Although Donna looks much too cheerful for any blood to have been spilt. I hope you're aware that every day Taurin stays in that room the owner is losing money."

Brynn glowered. "Tell me you took care of him, Eric."

"I took care of him, but not the way you hoped. We got things straightened out." May as well get it over with so everyone could be mad all at once. "I offered him a job in the castle."

"Like hell, you did." Conall's cheerful reception of the news.

"Umm, Conall?" Donna's smile was sweet and really scary. "You're a great warrior." She widened her eyes to demonstrate how much she admired that in a man. "You defeated and killed your greatest enemy in battle. How did that make you feel?"

"Like a man." Conall wasn't dumb, and Eric could tell he sensed a trap.

"Personally, I haven't experienced the feeling. Of being a man, I mean. But I bet it doesn't get much better." Donna's smile widened right before she struck with the speed and deadliness of a cobra. "If you could go back to that moment when you struck your enemy down, would you do it again?"

Eric could see the memory of Morrigan's curse and all that came after flood Conall's eyes.

"Ummhmmph."

"I'll take that as a no." Donna's smile never wavered.

"My, my." Holgarth dipped his head to Donna. "I've always found that women have a certain facility with language and logic that most men lack. It makes up for so many other shortcomings."

"Sexist pig." She smiled while she said it.

Brynn entered the fray. "Let's get back to Taurin. He tried to kill you, Eric. How can you look past that?" He hadn't learned much from Conall.

Donna glanced at Eric. "Can I take that question?"

"Go for it." Eric had his fair share of male pride, but he wasn't stupid. Why argue with Brynn when he had a talk expert to do it for him?

"Brynn, remember the night you offered your body to me?" Donna's voice softened as Brynn looked away from her.

"Sure. But what's that have to do with Taurin?" Brynn looked uncomfortable with the topic, but he wasn't going to back down.

"What if I'd kneed you in the groin without giving you a chance to tell your story? How would you have felt?"

His brief smile eased a little of the tension. "Since you've never personally experienced being a man, words couldn't describe the pain." He held up his hand to indicate he wasn't finished. "I know that's not what you were asking. It doesn't matter how I would've felt, because the two situations aren't the same. I didn't try to kill you."

"I didn't know *what* you were going to do. You offered sex, you took off your shirt, you came toward me and scared the hell out of me. It would've been scream first, groin second. In that order. But I saw what was in your eyes, so I didn't do either. I saw that same look in Taurin's eyes, Brynn."

Without conscious thought, Eric felt a possessive growl forming. Yeah, like he possessed any part of Donna. He sat on the growl.

Brynn looked disgusted. "Point made. He can fill in wherever we need an extra body. But the first time he shows me any fang . . ."

"Off with his head." Donna sighed and turned to Eric. "Guess that was the best we could hope for."

Holgarth chuckled. Really chuckled. Eric could count on one hand the number of times he'd witnessed that phenomenon.

"You are a delightfully renewable source of entertainment, Donna." Holgarth rocked back and forth on his heels to emphasize how entertained he was. "Physically weak and ineffectual, you defeated two immortals by talking them into a corner. And because I feel a need to somehow celebrate your victory, I've decided to mentor Taurin. I'll teach him everything I know." He paused in his rocking. "That would truly be impossible, though, because I know so very much. But I'll do the best I can with him."

Eric gauged Donna's exact degree of outrage and

stepped in to save Holgarth. "Taurin couldn't learn from a better teacher."

"He'd be better off dead." Brynn's muttered contribution to the discussion.

"Poor Taurin." Donna sounded sincere.

"What's that old saying about whatever doesn't kill you makes you stronger? Taurin can see if it's true." Conall's input.

Holgarth merely sneered at their pitiful attempts to insult him. "Now I really must have a go at irritating the men setting up the great hall for the Vampire Ball. So many to annoy, so little time." He turned away.

As the others wandered away, Donna looked up at Eric. "Did you hear him? Physically weak and ineffectual? Maybe I should practice breaking bricks on his scrawny chest with my bare hands. Why hasn't someone murdered Holgarth?"

"I'm sure they've tried. Many times." He guided her into the jewelry store for a cooling off period. "To celebrate your triumph, I'm going to buy you something special."

"You don't have to do that. The rush I got is enough."

Eric grinned. No matter what she said, he recognized the avaricious little gleam in her eyes. Eight hundred years of experience with women had taught him that the sight and smell of jewelry triggered something primal in women from every age.

"I wouldn't mind having that jeweled dagger, though. Just flashy enough to please Sparkle, and classic enough to satisfy Asima. Oh, did I tell you that I want it so that I can slash Holgarth's pointy hat into shreds? It would be bonus points if his head was still in it."

Some were more primal than others. "Forget the dagger. Come over here." She followed him over to a showcase filled with smaller pieces. None of them had prices, because customers who bought these pieces didn't worry about the cost. He pointed at a necklace. "I want you to have that dragon." The first time he'd seen the dragon it had reminded him of his figurehead. He wanted to give her something that would connect her to his past. And he was almost ready to admit to himself why that was important.

He motioned the shop's owner over. "Gina, could we see the dragon?"

Donna accepted the small dragon, her eyes wide with awe. "Eric, it's beautiful."

Watching her face light with joy over the dragon, he wanted to tell her how beautiful she was in that moment. But he'd never been much for extravagant compliments. He spoke with his body. And his body had held its tongue for too long.

"It was created by an old Irish silversmith who lives in County Donegal. He never attaches his name to his work because he claims that the mythic creatures simply use his hands to free themselves from the silver. Legend says he can breathe the soul of the creatures he fashions into the metal. He used only a single diamond for the dragon's eye because it's a Viking dragon, born of snow and ice. No rubies or emeralds to warm it up." The dragon had fascinated Eric from the moment he noticed it and Gina showed him the card telling its story. He'd wanted to buy it, but had kept putting it off. Now he knew he'd been waiting for Donna to come along. It belonged to her.

She sighed as she traced the intricate details with the tip of her fingernail. "As much as I love this, Eric, I can't accept it. A piece of jewelry like this is a one-of-a-kind, and it probably costs as much as you earn in two months." Donna didn't try to hide her regret as she handed the dragon back to him.

He closed his fingers around the dragon and imagined its warmth after resting against the base of her throat. "You really need to get to know me better, talk-show lady. I've had eight hundred years to accumulate more wealth than I could spend in another eight hundred years. I live and work here because I enjoy it. I like being around Brynn, Conall, and"—he grimaced—"even Holgarth. And it isn't often I get such a kick out of buying something. So don't ruin my fun."

She laughed. "Since you put it that way . . ."

Eric tried to hand it back to her, but she stopped him. "The Vampire Ball starts at nine. I want you to come to my room then and put it around my neck yourself." She slid her fingers across his closed hand. "That okay with you?"

"Sure." The emotion shining in her eyes left him a little uncertain. Not a feeling he'd experienced too often in his long life. "Want to get something to eat at the restaurant?"

"Sorry, I can't." She glanced at her watch. "I'm only going to have time to get a sandwich and take it back to my room. I have a date with a dress to be delivered by my Fairy Godhags."

He watched her walk away. Fairy Godhags? Maybe there would come a time when the Castle of Dark Dreams was too weird even for him.

18

Donna did the tough stuff first. She called the powers that be in New York to tell them she was using a week of her vacation time. After assuring them she'd have warm bodies to take her place each night, she called said warm bodies to make sure they were available.

That finished, she thought about calling her family. She didn't. Fine, so she was a cowardly worm. They'd expect her to comment on their lives—she always did—but what advice could she offer when her own life was so . . . unique right now?

So she ate her sandwich, took a shower, caught up on her e-mail, and then watched TV for a while. Major concern. Would she have a dress to wear to the ball? Had Sparkle and Asima destroyed each other as they fought over material, hemlines, and necklines? She examined her nails for impending breakage. Sheesh, Sparkle was rubbing off on her.

When the knock finally came—they knocked, they actually *knocked*—she rushed to open the door. "It's about time. I . . ."

Her words stuck in her throat, so she swallowed them before she choked. Sparkle and Asima didn't even say hi as they rolled one of the hotel baggage carts into her room. Sparkle wore her barely there black dress and Asima had on her diamond collar. Their dress collaboration hung from the cart's crossbar. It was covered in plastic so she couldn't get a look. A variety of boxes filled the rest of the cart.

"Turn the TV off. We don't want any distractions." Sparkle started unloading the boxes onto the floor, bed, and bureau.

"Get your makeup mirror and sit here at the desk. We'll work on your face first." Asima leaped onto the desk.

Donna turned off the TV. "Don't I get a peek at—"

"No. And I speak for both of us." Sparkle carried a case over to the desk and opened it. The case was filled with makeup. "This will transform you into young, ethereal, and gorgeous." She seemed to realize how that sounded. "Not that you aren't already all of those things, but we'll just build on that fantastic beginning."

Donna had to admit, Sparkle lied with panache. "You guys sure are serious about this stuff. Jeez, you're not even smiling."

"We had to work together on your dress. Why would we be smiling?" Asima studied Donna before turning to Sparkle. *"She needs a light base to give her a delicate glow."*

"No. She's a strong woman. She needs a darker tone to give her an earthy sensual look." Sparkle rooted through the cosmetics.

"Eye shadow that'll make her eyes look all smoky and mysterious." Asima peered into the case.

"Wrong. Pale green eye shadow with glitter to give a hint of wicked woman." Sparkle looked for the green eye shadow.

"Brown mascara." Asima was looking a little pissed.

"Black mascara to make her eyes pop." Sparkle had a militant gleam in her eyes.

"Pale shiny lipstick. Her mouth should have a full wet look."

"A vivid red lip color that makes a powerful sensual statement."

Asima hissed at Sparkle. *"We need classic beauty that'll make Eric want to protect and cherish her."*

Sparkle gave an exaggerated sigh. "We want a hot sexy babe who'll make him want to drag her off to his bed."

"You want her to look slutty like you."

"Damn straight. You want to turn her into a prissy tight-ass."

As Sparkle and Asima's "discussion" disintegrated into virtual bitch-slapping, Donna calmly chose the makeup she wanted and put it on. "Okay, makeup's done. What's next?"

Blessed silence fell for the few moments it took for the combatants to stare at her.

"It'll do." Asima glanced away.

"Yeah." Sparkle transferred her attention to Donna's hair. "All tousled and sexy."

"Sleek and elegant."

Donna thought about her choices. "Sorry, Asima. I feel like tousled and sexy is me tonight."

Asima sulked. Sparkle looked triumphant while she helped Donna achieve the perfect tousled-and-sexy look.

For the next fifteen minutes Sparkle and Asima fought over nail color, panty color, and whether to wear or not wear a toe ring. Donna turned the TV on again.

"Shoes next." Sparkle opened several shoe boxes and then stepped back for Donna to look. "I'd recommend these black sandals. Black is always sexy." She picked up the sandals for Donna to examine.

Asima came out of her funk long enough to disagree. *"I think those metallic silver sandals with the ankle straps would fit your look for tonight."* She jumped from the desk so she could put a paw on her choice.

"I won't know for sure until I see the dress, but I tend to like Asima's choice." Donna thought the silver sandals would complement her silver dragon. She was a little wary of the four-inch heels, but they'd make her legs look terrific.

Now it was Asima's turn to glow. *"I think it's time we showed you your dress."*

Sparkle went over to the cart and pulled the plastic off. Donna was determined to wear whatever they'd come up with no matter how . . . "Oh, wow! It's gorgeous."

Long, sleeveless, red, and silky with a sensual cling. Asima.

A slit up to her thigh. Sparkle.

A top that plunged almost to her navel. Sparkle.

A diamond clasp beneath her breasts that would hold the material together so it didn't end up in a puddle of red at her feet. Asima.

The back plunged too, but since it stopped short of her behind, she didn't worry. Donna mentally crossed panties off her to wear list. Nothing was going to interrupt the smooth flow of her beautiful dress.

For the first time that night, Sparkle and Asima looked happy at the same time. Sparkle opened one more box. "We'll let you choose the jewelry you want. We won't say a word." She cast Asima a warning glance. "Will we?"

"My lips are zipped. Of course, since I'm not using my mouth to talk, I guess—"

"I'll wear these earrings." They were dangly and diamond. "I don't need anything else."

Sparkle frowned. "No necklace?"

"That's taken care of." She ignored their curious stares as she collected everything together and went into the bathroom to change.

When she came out, Sparkle widened her eyes and looked at Asima. Then they both stared at Donna.

"He'll be on his knees tonight." Sparkle's smile was genuine. "You go, girl."

"We did a wonderful job, Sparkle." Asima rubbed against Donna's ankle. *"You look beautiful, Donna. Classy, elegant, and we give you permission"*—there was a smile in her voice—*"to be a wildcat in Eric's bed."*

That last part came so far out of left field that even Sparkle blinked.

"Thanks for all of this." For the first time Donna stopped to think about where they'd gotten "all of this." "Umm, how much will everything set me back?"

Asima's eyes took on her sly feline expression. *"Oh, you don't owe us anything. We didn't pay for it, we . . . acquired it."*

Oh boy. Luckily, Donna didn't have time to think about what their "acquiring" involved, because someone knocked on the door. *Eric.*

Sparkle handed a silver beaded purse to Donna that she'd already loaded with key and essentials, and then she and Asima followed her to the door. When Donna flung it open, everyone gaped.

"Did I ever tell you that you bring the heat, vampire? Of course I did. In that tux, you're hot enough to melt all the chocolates in my store from right here." Sparkle slid her gaze the length of his body.

"They don't make men this way anymore." Asima stared up at him with admiration. Okay, so there was a little lust mixed in.

Donna bristled. Fine. She admitted it. She was possessive. She was jealous. And she had to get rid of her two sex consultants. "Thanks a bunch for helping me out, guys. See you later."

Eric didn't even watch them walk away. His gaze stayed fixed on Donna. "You're beautiful."

Donna never knew so many emotions could be packed into two words.

So are you. She wouldn't say the words because she'd sound like a continuation of Sparkle and Asima. But she hoped her eyes passed on the message that she thought he was the most spectacular man in the world.

Dressed in basic black and white, he was cool and elegant, but beneath it all ran the hot sensual current that made her want to peel all those clothes from his muscular body and perform erotic acts with him until dawn.

His eyes gleamed. "If we don't get going now, we might never make it to the ball." He reached into his pocket and pulled out the intricate silver necklace with her dragon on it. "Turn around."

Donna closed her eyes as he placed the necklace around her neck, and she tried to ignore the warm skim of his fingers against her skin. "Okay, I'm ready." But ready for what? Maybe by the end of the night she'd know.

It was almost midnight, and Donna understood why Cinderella had shucked that glass slipper. She'd danced most of the night with Eric, and her beautiful silver sandals were now officially instruments of torture. "I think I'm ready to sit out the rest of the night."

The great hall was packed with couples. But she was a cardinal in a flock of ravens. Donna supposed everyone thought vampires weren't the real deal unless they wore black. But that was okay, because as Eric had danced with her, he'd slid his fingers over the material in a way that told her how much he appreciated her dress . . . and what was beneath it.

Eric glanced around the hall. "I don't see any free tables."

Donna followed his gaze. Holgarth and his crew of minions had transformed the room. The long banquet table in front of the hearth was gone and in its place was a band. Intimate tables with lighted candles ringed the hall, and a bar had been set up in one corner. There was also a light buffet for anyone who wanted to eat.

But the people on the dance floor were what held her attention. Fake vampires abounded. Phony fangs were on full display. The only man who didn't look like the traditional vamp was the real one. And when some of her listeners introduced themselves and asked if she'd found any creatures of the night, she'd said no. Lying straight-faced was an art form.

"If you're tired, I could walk you to your room and then come back here." His pause was pregnant with all kinds of meaning. "Or we could go to my room."

There it was. The choice she knew was coming. Instinctively she understood if she turned him down now, he wouldn't ask again. After tonight the ball would be in her court.

But he wouldn't have to ask again, because she'd made her decision. It had been a gradual realization starting when she opened her door tonight to find him standing there, her vampire prince in a tux, desire for her gleaming in his blue eyes. And her decision was fully formed by ten o'clock as they sat out a few dances at one of the tables.

She'd asked him if he wanted to dance with someone else, because as the castle's resident vampire she knew he had obligations. He'd said no, that this would be her only Vampire Ball, and he wanted her to spend it with him. Brynn and Conall could pick up the slack for him tonight. And then he'd cast a speculative glance at the candle sitting in the middle of the table.

He'd been thinking about the chocolate-covered cherries. So was she. Donna had known if she didn't use them tonight, she'd probably eat them out of pure—or impure—sexual frustration.

Now she looked up at him. "I want to go to your room."

Eric nodded. "Wait here while I run up to your room for the cherries." He leaned toward her, his desire touching her without spoken words. It was in the huskiness of his voice, the scent of aroused male, and the raw need in his gaze. "Should I bring you anything else?"

She smiled, a smile she hoped showed him only her hunger for him and not any of the qualms she felt about vampire neck fetishes. "Bring Sweetie Pie and Jessica with you. They're sort of family now."

He nodded before striding toward the stairs. Once out of everyone's view, he used his preternatural speed to get him up the steps, into her room—who needed a key?—and out again with a plant in each hand along with the box of chocolate-covered cherries under one arm.

A little anxious, aren't you, bud? Yeah, he was. He

hadn't looked forward to something so much since . . . Since never. Eric went down the steps more slowly than he'd gone up. If this were just all about sex, then the next few hours wouldn't be too important. Great sex either happened or it didn't. But Eric had a lot more riding on his night with Donna than a sensational orgasm. Tonight, some important things had come together in his head, in his *heart.* Okay, he might not technically have a heart, but the emotion he felt when he was around Donna couldn't be any more real than if he *did* have that particular organ beating away in his chest.

He reentered the great hall and made his way to where she still stood. The way she looked up and smiled at him. The way her eyes showed how much she wanted him. And the way her body tensed with her lingering doubts—yes, he could still sense her fear—made him want to drop Sweetie Pie and Jessica on their collective bottoms. Then he'd show Donna how unnecessary her fear of his teeth really was. But Holgarth would turn his life into a living hell if he made love to her on one of the tables. *Made love.* Never in his eight hundred years of existence had he thought of the sex act as making love.

"I'm surprised you didn't haul my Dominatrix Donna outfit along with you." Her smile teased even as it stirred his sexual hunger.

His darker hunger, the one that would demand he include it in his sexual itinerary tonight, lurked beneath the surface of his awareness, but not for long. "We'll save that for later. Maybe some morning about five when no one's around we'll do some role playing in the dungeon." Now, *that* had made his dark hunger rumble its approval.

"Mmm. I can hardly wait. Do you have a candle?" She took one of the plants from him.

"Somewhere." He led her from the great hall and down to his room. She didn't say anything more until she stepped through his doorway. "I forgot how startling your dragon is. Does she have a name?"

Eric was busy setting the plants on the floor. "Hmm?

No, I never named . . . Did you say *her*?" He straightened. "The dragon's a he."

Donna shook her head and remained staring at the dragon as he set the box of chocolates on his night table. "I don't think so. I don't think you and a male dragon could've lasted together this long. All that raging testosterone." She moved closer to the figurehead. "How old is she? Really."

"Almost as old as me. Most of what I told you was the truth. I just didn't tell you the whole story. My brother, Var, carved the dragon for my longboat." He walked over to run his hand across the smooth wood. Eric didn't touch the dragon often, and doing so brought back some of the old memories. "Var never got his shot at becoming immortal. He was twenty-five when he was killed somewhere along the Scottish coast during a raid. The dragon is the only thing I've kept from that time."

He hadn't meant to put that sadness in her eyes. Time to lighten things up. "You've decided my dragon's female, so why don't *you* name her?" Eric moved to his bed and sat on the edge while he got rid of his shoes. He wasn't a formal kind of guy, and the sooner he got out of this tux the better.

Donna tilted her head to study the dragon. "I think you should name her Sparkle in honor of tonight. Our cosmic troublemaker's been a regular Energizer Bunny in her *subtle* attempts to shove us toward sexual bliss. She gave me the idea for the cherries, plus she and Asima worked on my dress and every other accessory I wore . . . except the silver dragon."

She placed her palm over the tiny dragon, and he swore he could feel the heat of her hand on his flesh. "The dragon belongs with you." *I belong with you.*

Silence hung between them for a moment. Then Donna took a deep breath and smiled at him. "I owe you an orgasm, vampire. The Nolans always pay their debts." Her gaze was sensual temptation. "And some debts are so much fun to repay."

Eric slipped out of his jacket, tossed it onto the chair next to his bed, and then pulled off his tie. He paused to watch her. "Come here, talk-show lady." No compulsions, no scooping her up and carrying her to his bed. She had to want this as much as he did—tough to imagine she could even come close—and she must be willing to accept him sexually in his vampire form. Freyja help him, he didn't know what he'd do if she walked out his door now.

"No." She lifted one foot at a time as she removed her sandals.

"No?" He was getting mixed signals here. She wouldn't come to him, but she was taking off her shoes.

She kicked her sandals aside and then smoothed her fingers over the silky shimmer of red temptation she'd worn all night. "I love this dress. It's easy access—no zippers, no buttons, nothing to get in the way of a woman who's anxious to give lots and lots of pleasure to that special someone." She removed the brooch that held her dress together in front. "And I'm sooo anxious, vampire." The dress slid smoothly from her body to pool in a crimson puddle at her feet. She stepped out of it.

Eric sucked in his nonexistent breath. She stood in only her silver dragon, the smooth unbroken flow of her beautiful body igniting a flash fire that threatened to roar out of control. Both of his hungers roared to life. He started to stand up.

"Whoa, tiger. Sit. I have entertainment planned." She glanced down at her body as though looking for something that was missing.

He could assure her that everything important was there. *More* than there.

"I had a super sexy bra and thong picked out to wear tonight. Very red. I was going to drive you crazy by peeling them off slowly and with lots of teasing. Sort of like peeling a firm, just-ripened banana." Her smile was sensual and rife with hidden meanings. "Oops. Wrong fruit." Her gaze dropped to where his erection was making an obvious bid for freedom. "Nope, I definitely can't be the banana." She shrugged, calling attention to the lift and thrust of her full breasts. Wasted effort, because his attention had been fully engaged since she dropped her dress.

"Guess you'll have to pretend I'm still wearing them." Her smile dared him to try.

"Sure. No problem." He gripped his lower lip between his teeth and concentrated on holding back the change.

"Last year I was looking for an interesting way to lose weight that didn't include eating celery sticks." She leaned forward and then reached behind her to release an imaginary bra. Her hair tumbled around her face, hiding her expression and focusing his interest on the invisible bra.

Her breasts would fill his palms perfectly. He had large hands, and it took a lot to fill them. Eric resisted the urge to rush over to her and test them for fit.

"Personally I feel that celery sticks have no redeeming value." She straightened and then stood for a moment contemplating the importance of celery sticks in the grand scheme of things. While she contemplated, she slowly rolled each of her nipples between her thumbs and forefingers until they were tight hard nubs.

Eric groaned. "You're killing me, woman."

"Goody." Her smile would've done credit to Donna the Dominatrix. She turned her back to him and slowly slid her imaginary thong off with lots of provocative wiggling. "So how do you feel about celery sticks?"

Who the hell cared? He was going up in flames without a ray of sunlight to be seen. "Celery sticks. I've never personally eaten one, but I understand the strings get stuck between your teeth. Vampires wouldn't be good candidates for diets that included celery sticks." He was growing hotter and harder by the second. If he still had lungs, he'd be gasping for air at the sight of her bare little ass, and as she turned to face him, her full luscious breasts.

"Anyway, I took this class that taught erotic exercise. We did pole dancing, that kind of stuff. It was fun, but I thought, yeah, like I'm really going to use these moves for a man." She pressed her back against the side of the figurehead and then slowly arched her back. The thrust of her breasts tempted, inviting his touch. "But guess what? I'm motivated. I finally found a man I want to impress." She turned her face toward him, her lips pouty and inviting, her eyes challenging him to watch and want.

"Didn't your mama ever tell you it isn't nice to tease a vampire?" His voice came out a husky rasp, but he was lucky he could talk at all.

"I haven't been 'nice' for a long time. Bad girls have more fun." She moved to the front of the dragon and reached up to touch its ferocious head. "Okay, I know. So I'm really only a bad girl in training, but I think you'll always bring out the bad in me. And that's good." With her arms still stretched above her head, she began to rotate her hips.

Eric ripped his shirt off and tossed it over his jacket, all without blinking in case he missed one of her man-killer moves. The growl forming deep in his throat was the beast stretching and coming to life. It had hopes for a mind-blowing night.

Turning her back to him again, she bent at the waist, spread her legs, smoothed her palms slowly, lingeringly up her inner thighs, and then touched herself. Mesmerized, Eric followed the almost hypnotic motion of her finger as she rubbed back and forth, back and forth, before finally sliding her finger into all that moist heat. He watched her bottom flex as her muscles clenched around her finger, and he imagined her flesh, hot and wet, tightening around his cock. He groaned.

When he finally decided he couldn't stand anymore, she leaned further over and grinned at him from between her legs. "Getting hot, Mackenzie? I sure am." She wiggled her behind at him.

"You have no idea." She had no idea how close he was to changing forms before he even got her as far as his bed. That would *not* be a good thing. "I'm getting close to the edge. Push at your own risk." He didn't know how she couldn't feel the heat shimmering off him in waves.

She straightened and turned to face him. Her face was flushed, and she was laughing. Strands of her hair fell across her face. "Oooh, you scare me."

"Good. Because I'm a scary guy." He was so hard and ready that it even hurt to smile.

She made a big production of reaching up to rake her fingers through her hair. "Want me to stop, hmm?" Then instead of dropping her hands, she slid her fingers down her neck and over her breasts. With a sensual sway, she moved to right in front of him, and then circled each of her nipples with the tip of her fingernail. "You're right. I think it'll feel a lot better if you do it."

"Wise decision." His voice had disintegrated to low and gravelly. "I've reached my personal tolerance level for sexy teasing by hot talk-show hosts." He stood so he could get rid of his pants. They joined the jacket and shirt. He didn't have anything else to take off.

"That is so not fair." She slipped to her knees in front of him. "I had it all planned. I was going to slide off your briefs—I'd hoped you'd wear the red ones so we'd be color coordinated—exposing all your sexual goodies slowly and deliciously. Now look. No briefs." She lifted her gaze to meet his. "Guess I go to plan B."

Eric stood staring down at her. Emotion flooded him. There were those in his clan who didn't feel emotion. He felt sorry for them.

And then she touched him.

Donna skimmed her fingers over his stomach and inner thighs. He spread his legs to give her better access, and she took full advantage. She cupped his balls in her palms and squeezed gently. He groaned. God, he wanted to tell her how good it felt when she touched him, but he'd regressed to a primitive state where he could only express his feelings in grunts and moans.

Sitting back on her heels, she lifted his balls and traced a line of fire with her tongue across them. Then she put her mouth over each one, teasing and tormenting them with her tongue. *Heat. Pressure.* How tight could he get before he exploded? Instinctively he thrust his hips forward. His enhanced senses kicked into high gear.

As she moved upward to his cock, he ran his fingers through her hair, each silky strand becoming part of the sexual experience. The scent of vanilla on her skin, probably from her shower, made the touch of her tongue on his flesh more intense. And he knew that for the rest of his existence, the scent of vanilla would trigger memories of her mouth on his body.

He wasn't going to last much longer. And as soon as he felt the change becoming inevitable, he'd take her into his bed.

She must've sensed his growing urgency, because she stopped tracing the length of his sex with her tongue and simply put her mouth over him. He gasped and welcomed the surge of red that always accompanied sexual excitement. As she tightened her lips around him and then began sliding her mouth up and down, up and down his cock, he gave an inarticulate cry and let the change take him.

Clasping her beneath her arms, he lifted her onto the bed. She clung to him while whispering all she wanted him to do to her. Consumed by her own arousal, she didn't seem to notice his eyes, his mouth, his *fangs.*

Eric kissed a path along her jaw and neck. And when he reached her breasts, he slid his tongue over each hard nub. Writhing against him, she reached between their bodies to clasp his erection.

"Now, Eric. Forget all the things I said I wanted you to do. You can do them later." To add emphasis to her demand, she nipped his shoulder.

Easing her onto her back, he knelt between her spread legs. She stared up at him with eyes glazed by sexual arousal. Her breaths came in hard pants that lifted her breasts still damp from his tongue. But he couldn't take her yet. She had to see him as he was.

"Look at me, Donna. Really look. And then tell me you still want me." He retreated within himself as her eyes cleared and she gazed at him.

"I want *you* in any form, Eric. This first time, with the neck and all, I'll be tense. But I trust you. I wouldn't be here if I didn't."

Eric closed his eyes against the wave of emotion. The red of sexual excitement remained, but now it was joined with deep purples shading slowly into all the colors of the spectrum. He'd never seen these colors during sex, but he knew what they meant. He hadn't needed the colors to tell him what he felt for Donna.

He opened his eyes. "I'll join my mind with yours, and we'll share what happens as one, feel as one." Forever *be* one, if he had any say in it. He smiled. "And the bite will only feel like a brief sting. Wouldn't be much of an erotic experience otherwise."

And as he looked down at her, he made a decision. Tonight she had to control what happened. "Mount me, talk-show lady. Ride me hard and put me up wet. No spurs needed." He grinned at her, and she rewarded him by visibly relaxing.

"I always wanted to be a cowgirl." She waited for him to lie on his back, and then she straddled his hips.

As need and desire took him, he joined his mind to hers. All the sexual hunger and intense pleasure he felt flowed through her also. She threw her head back and moaned. Slowly she lowered herself onto his erection. With him, she swam through the deep red of their building orgasm, heard the deep vibrations of lust, and tasted the rich and spicy blend of sensual joy.

With a wild cry she impaled herself on him. Then she began the rhythm that would lead to the ultimate physical sensation. Up and down, up and down. Each time harder, with tiny grunts as she tried to take more and more of him. He lifted his hips, knowing that if he drove deep enough, he'd touch her soul.

Sweat sheened her smooth body and moisture gathered between her full breasts. Bouncing breasts, one of life's great visuals. She whimpered each time she took him deep inside her, and her whimper found an answering chord within him.

The need to taste her life force rose on an unstoppable wave. She shared his mind, and he felt her shudder under the force of his hunger. His dark need was a living creature gnawing at him, scratching and clawing to have its way. His body shook with the powerful merging of both hungers. They were now one. He clasped her shoulders and pulled her down on top of him. Still driving into her, he pushed her hair away from her neck.

And then, for just a moment, he controlled the uncontrollable. He paused with his teeth an inch from her throat, giving Donna a chance to roll off him if she chose.

"Bite me, vampire. Give me the greatest freakin' orgasm of my whole life." Her murmur was hot against his skin.

He smoothed his tongue over her neck and then bit. The explosive pleasure rocked him as he felt the sexual connection no human could experience. But Donna was joined to his mind, so she felt what he felt.

She growled her excitement and raked his back with her nails as he drove into her at the same time he shared her essence. His orgasm was an avalanche of sensation obliterating all before it.

He released her as he climaxed, his shout a guttural cry of triumph. She straightened, grinding herself against him one last time while her orgasm took her. "Yesyesyessss!" No quiet happiness here. She was loud, joyous, and *his.*

For a while Donna didn't move, just breathed in deep shuddering breaths. Finally, she eased off him and lay beside him. He could feel her still shaking.

"I never knew I could experience anything like that. It was like my body couldn't hold everything I felt." Her voice was soft with wonder. "Thank you." Donna reached up to touch her neck where he'd bitten her. "It's healed." She didn't sound surprised. "Hey, I've read plenty of vampire romances. I knew you wouldn't leave the bite marks."

"Let's hear it for vampire romances." Now wasn't the time, but he had to tell her. "I've lived for eight hundred years and never felt what I felt with you."

She started to say something, but he laid his finger against her lips. "Hear me out, Donna. I love you. And no, it's not the incredible sex talking. For the first time in my life, I made *love* with a woman. Stay with me. Forever." He was doing this all wrong. It was too soon after what they'd just shared. She needed time to recover and think things out. But obviously his mouth was on autopilot tonight.

Her eyes were shadowed as she gazed at him. "Think about what you're saying, Eric. You wouldn't want to watch me die."

"No, but I want to watch you live." He smoothed a strand of hair away from her face. "It was easy for me to say I wasn't interested in a relationship with a woman, because I didn't know *you*."

She looked away. "I don't think I can do that to you."

Silence filled with everything he wanted from her and all she felt she couldn't give him bore down on him. "Stay with me until I rise."

She nodded and rolled onto her side, her back to him. He turned out the light, then drew her against him.

Eric lay awake long after Donna fell asleep. And as dawn approached, and he felt the natural rhythm of his own sleep pulling at him, he tried to push away the fact that she hadn't said she loved him.

And dammit, they still hadn't used the cherries.

19

New York was mad at her. Her boss had done the ranting and raving thing when she'd told him she was using two more weeks of her accumulated vacation time beyond what she'd already taken. Donna had agreed to do weekend broadcasts from the Castle of Dark Dreams for those two weeks to placate the powers that be.

And her family was ticked at her, too. They were mad because she wasn't telling them all. But she couldn't tell them all when she wasn't sure what all there was to tell. She'd know soon, though.

Eric Mackenzie had been part of her life for a month now, the chocolate-covered cherries still taunted her from their honored spot on her night table, and she'd finally made a major life decision.

Donna loved Eric. She'd used those extra weeks to examine her emotions from every angle. She definitely loved him. And because she loved him, she couldn't stand the thought of his suffering as he watched her grow old. Nope, she definitely couldn't die and leave him behind. Hey, she wanted a forever love in the true sense of the word.

Donna believed in fighting for what she wanted, and she wanted Eric Mackenzie. The solution? She couldn't grow old. There was only one way that could happen. And that's why she was sitting across from Taurin in his room.

"You want *what*?" Shock widened Taurin's eyes.

"Your blood." There were a few details she had to work out first. "How much would I need to turn me? Would there be a problem with blood type? Could I inject the blood directly into a vein? You don't have some silly rule about having to bite me first, do you? Because I think Eric would go ballistic if another vamp bit me. It's the whole she's-mine chest-thumping thing that men have going."

"I don't—"

"You owe me. If it weren't for me, you'd be searching vacant lots for your head." He wouldn't refuse her, would he?

"Will you let me get a word in here?" He raked his fingers through his dark hair. "Have you told Eric what you're planning? No way do I want him hunting me because you turned yourself using my blood."

Donna drew in a deep calming breath before answering him. "No, I haven't told him yet. And yes, I've done some deep thinking about the consequences of my lifestyle change. I won't use the blood without telling him. I promise you that."

Taurin nodded. "If you're sure this is what you want, then yeah, I'll offer my blood. Blood type doesn't matter, and no, I don't have to bite you. But in order for my blood to turn you, I have to will your change to vampire as you draw it. My intent does something to the blood. It's the whole mind-and-body connection. It doesn't matter how the blood gets into you, so don't worry about having to feed from my slit wrist." He smiled as she mouthed a silent "eww." "Eric will appreciate the irony of the whole thing. Once you have my blood, you'll be related to Dacian and me."

Donna frowned. "One thing, though. There's nothing to

the belief that the vampire who turns you owns you, is there? Eric would get a little cranky if someone hung a Sold sign around my neck. He'd probably start shining up his big old sword if it happened."

Taurin laughed. "Relax. My blood will turn you, but you'll still be your own woman." His smile faded as he studied her. "I hope Eric understands that you'll always think for yourself. Vampires are pretty controlling."

Donna smiled while her insides went tingly at the thought of Eric. Her love was still new and shiny, but she thought he'd always make her feel that way. "He understands." Very soon he'd get a sample of exactly how much thinking for herself she did.

"One last question." She thought she knew the answer to this, but she wanted to make sure. "The thought of drinking blood is an ick factor for me. Give me steak, potatoes, and apple pie every time."

"Nothing to worry about. Once you become vampire, you'll desire blood and the thought of solid food will make you queasy. And if the thought of feeding from humans bothers you, don't worry. It'll feel natural once you've changed. Feeding doesn't harm anyone so long as you choose healthy people and only take what you need. In fact, as you already know, feeding is a very erotic experience for the human. Afterward, you simply erase yourself from the person's memory. They wake up with a happy buzz." He reached over to put his hand on her arm. "I messed up my existence for a long time with my hate, but you have Eric and hundreds of years of love and life ahead of you. You won't regret the change. Anything else you want to know?"

"No. That's it." She'd spent days balancing the positives and negatives of what she intended to do. And every time the thought of spending many lifetimes with Eric carried the day.

"Okay, let me know when you have everything set up." He watched her walk toward the door.

Donna paused with her hand on the doorknob. She'd been so busy thinking about herself that she hadn't thought about Taurin. "Feeling any better about Dacian?"

His smile didn't reach his eyes. "I'm going to look for him. I won't get any closure until I know why he did it." Taurin glanced away from her. "But I won't have to do it alone. Kyla was one of the Mackenzies with Eric that day. You talked to her on the phone. She got my number from Eric and called me last week with an offer to help find Dacian if I decided to search. She didn't say anything, but I get the feeling there was something between them." He shrugged. "I didn't ask. Her reason doesn't matter as long as she helps me find him."

Hmm. Interesting. Donna wondered about Kyla and Dacian as she left. Once back in her room, she made plans for Eric and herself.

Her last night at the Castle of Dark Dreams, and Donna had never felt so jittery in her whole life. She'd asked Eric to come to her room as soon as he finished with his last fantasy. Everything was set. Donna had hired a nurse to teach her what she needed to know. She was ready.

He didn't knock. Her door swung open, and he strode into her room. Eric always oozed confident male, but there'd been a lot less oozing going on over the last few weeks. He hadn't nagged her, but he'd watched her with those amazing blue eyes that gave nothing away, but told her everything. He didn't want her to see his emotions, didn't want her to accuse him of trying to influence her decision.

Eric glanced around. "Not packed?" He frowned as he noticed for the first time that the room was lit only by candlelight. His gaze wandered to the box of chocolate-covered cherries open beside her bed and then returned to her. He didn't comment on the small insulated box resting beside the chocolate box.

His gaze stripped her soul bare. "Hmm. Bustier, boots, whip? Nice outfit. Looking for some last-minute fantasy fulfillment?" He nodded toward the chocolates. "I was wondering if we'd ever get to those."

If she didn't sense the agony beneath his seeming indifference, she'd sock him right in his big fat arrogant male . . . whatever. "We have important things to talk about, vampire."

Something flickered in his eyes. "And?"

"Get naked first. Oh, and do it fast. As Sparkle would say, 'You bring the heat.' I don't want the chocolate-covered cherries to melt before we're ready.

A smile tugged at the corners of his woman-pleasing mouth. "Anyone ever call you on that attitude of yours?"

"Get naked and we'll discuss my attitude over melted chocolate." Sitting on the edge of the bed, she tossed the whip, took off her boots and bustier, and stripped off the fishnet stockings. "We can do the Dominatrix Donna thing afterward—if you have the strength." She laid down on the black silk sheets she'd bought—sure, they were a little slippery, but they looked and felt cool. And cool was good if Eric and she generated the fire she hoped for. "Come to me." Her voice was a sultry growl. Hey, she could get off on playing the seductive vampire. Arching her back, she watched his gaze follow the thrust of her breasts and felt his interest as a slide of shimmering energy touching her nipples.

Eric's smile widened, but his eyes were blue heat as he rid himself of his clothes and joined her on the bed. She started to reach for a chocolate, but he put his hand over hers. "Me first."

Her breathing quickened and her heart pounded—maybe the last time she'd experience those sensations. No, her human reactions were too much a part of her now, and even if there were no panting and pounding going on, she'd feel them.

Reaching into the box, Eric chose a chocolate and placed

it carefully in her navel. Then he picked up the candle from the night table and slowly passed it over her stomach.

Donna clicked her inner camera, recording forever the muscular flow of his bared body turned golden in the candle's glow. The flickering flame cast shadows across the familiar lines of his face, hiding his expression. Maybe that was best.

The heat reached deep into her, touching the fear that he'd reject her, melting the fear away and giving her courage. Melting was going on elsewhere as well. She felt the chocolate warming and turning liquid as the candle's flame heated her body.

And then, with a strangled groan, he put the candle down and leaned over her. The slide of his tongue reaching into her and scooping the rich chocolate into his mouth was so erotic it brought tears to her eyes. *Don't cry.* She had to be strong now.

He licked the last drop of chocolate from her and then closed his lips over the fruit. Taking her into his arms, he offered her the cherry.

Savoring the taste of chocolate, cherry, and aroused male on his lips, Donna closed her teeth over the cherry. He watched her eat it, his mouth a breath away from her lips, his eyes suddenly filled with all he felt for her.

Then before he could move away, she gently tugged on his deliciously sensual bottom lip and slid her tongue across it, leaving it temptingly damp and chocolate-free.

He said nothing as he shifted to kneel between her parted thighs. She opened to him, feeling the heavy coil of hot anticipation low in her stomach. Her body clenched around the mental image of his hard length pushing into her, spreading her, filling her.

Eric put his hands beneath her bottom, lifted her to meet his thrust, and then paused with the thick head of his cock pressed against her flesh as the change took him. He stared directly into her eyes, challenging her to once again recognize what he was, what he would always be.

She met his gaze directly, and when the change was complete, Donna slid her attention down to his impressive erection. "Come in from the cold, vampire."

With an inarticulate sound, he pushed into her. His thrusts were hard, desperate, and as he plunged into her again and again, he opened his thoughts to her.

She arched her body, trying to take more of him, tears mixing with her shattering orgasm. She could never walk away from his love and the fear of losing her she'd seen in his mind.

Donna closed her eyes, quieted her breathing, and spoke to him. "I don't want to spend my pitifully few human years with you." Even with her eyes still closed, she felt his shudder. He thought she was rejecting his love. She hurried on. "I want to spend centuries and centuries with you." She opened her eyes.

"I love you, Eric Mackenzie, and tonight I *will* become vampire."

His reaction was a hiss of denial as he swung his feet to the floor and sat up. "No. I won't—"

"I'm the mistress of my own destiny—jeez, I sound like I'm reciting an epic poem—and the choice is mine." She moved to sit beside him.

"I can't give you—"

"Children? When the time is right, we'll love a child that no one else wants. A child doesn't have to come from my body for me to love it."

"Your family will—"

"Still love and accept me. No matter how they feel about my life choice, they'll always love me. Of course, Trish will be wildly jealous that I fell in love in *less* than two weeks."

"You love your job and—"

"I've already talked to them. I'll only be working Saturday and Sunday nights from now on. And I'll be broadcasting from here. My boss has already confirmed it with the castle's owner and the Houston affiliate."

"I can't ask you to—"

"You're not asking, Eric. I'm telling you. I love you. You're stuck with me. And that's that."

His smile was shaky. "I can't cry, talk-show lady, but consider what you see in my eyes tears."

And what she saw was a love to cherish throughout their immortal lives.

She opened the insulated box and took out the syringe with Taurin's blood in it. "This is Taurin's blood."

He stiffened.

"This is his wedding gift to us, Eric. Put aside pride and accept it. Because of what he's giving us, we'll be together forever." Her smile was getting a little watery. "Just think, you'll spend centuries with a stubborn wife, but hey, I like to dress up in bustiers and high-heeled boots. And I wield a mean whip."

She handed him the syringe and the cord he needed to tie off her arm above her elbow. "This is my gift to you. I've spent my whole life trying to control everything in my life. This time I want *you* to be in control. I want you to be the one who turns me. Do it. Now."

Eric leaned over to brush his lips across her mouth, telling her without words what her gift meant to him. "You won't manifest all of your vampire characteristics immediately. It'll take about a week before you're completely turned. Tonight all you'll notice is the increased clarity of your senses."

He said nothing as he prepared her, but as he began to inject her with Taurin's blood, he met her gaze. "I'll love you for the rest of my life, whether it be two minutes or two thousand years."

While Taurin's blood flowed into her, she pushed back all of her new life's uncertainties, and remembered Napoleon's quote: "The most dangerous moment comes with victory."

Then it was done, and as she felt the first surge of her enhanced senses, she turned to the vampire she loved. "I'm ready to play Dominatrix Donna now. Afterward, we'll wake everyone up to pass on the happy news. I get to wake up Holgarth." She savored the thought of all the nights to come stretching into the far distant future. "Tomorrow night we'll finish off the cherries."

Beside the bed, Sweetie Pie and Jessica put out new shoots in celebration.

And outside her door, Sparkle and Asima high-fived.

Turn the page for a special preview of
Nina Bangs's novel

Wicked Pleasure

Now available from Berkley Sensation!

As she drew nearer to the doors closed against the damp and chill, Kim noticed a corner protected from the spotlight's glare. Within the shadows lurked a darker shape, massive with no identifiable form. And for the moment it took her to catch her breath, fear rippled through her. Strange emotions, dark shadows—this place was messing with her mind.

Kim glanced around. Castle and surrounding area lit by bright spotlights, people still walking around even in the drizzle. Fear? What was that about? Hello? She was a demon destroyer. Black blobs skulking in the shadows didn't scare someone who hunted demons. She wasn't even afraid of a big butt-ugly minion of the Supreme Scumbag. Okay, maybe she was a little afraid. Very little.

Throwing whatever stood in the shadows a casual and totally fearless smile—she was still practicing her totally fearless smile in front of her mirror—Kim reached for the door.

"Do you really want to go inside? You're not dressed to kill." The voice was light, female, and amused.

Startled, Kim almost dropped Fo.

The scary blob separated, revealing the shapes of two people, a man and woman. The woman stepped out of the shadows. Short blond hair, a pixie face, and large dark eyes. She looked perky. Kim winced at the description. Ms. Perky's long black sleeveless dress was slit up the side, plunged low in front, and was set off by the sparkle of diamonds at throat and ears. Silver sandals with four-inch heels helped with the height thing, but Kim figured that she'd barely break five feet two in her bare feet. Wasn't she freezing to death out here without a coat?

"Dressed to kill?" Kim glanced down. "Well, no, I guess not. Can't I go in wearing jeans?" Why didn't the man step out of the shadows?

The woman's laughter was friendly, her smile contagious. Kim smiled back. Sheesh, how embarrassing. Lucky her family wasn't here. Kim could see the black-bordered blurb in the family newsletter: Kimberly Vaughn, formerly known as a tiger in the demon-destroying world, has been disowned by her family for the crime of being afraid of her own and other people's shadows. The Council of Demon Destroyers has reduced her to the rank of scared-rabbit.

Fine, so even on her most ferocious day, Kim would never describe herself as a "tiger of the demon-destroying world." That title would go to her sister, Lynsay.

"No one will stop you." The woman inventoried Kim's outfit. "But you're still not dressed to *kill*."

"Kill?" Kim didn't get it.

The shadow man hadn't moved, didn't seem to even breathe. *He* certainly wasn't filled with friendly perkiness. In fact, something about his complete stillness made her shiver. She pulled her jacket more tightly around her.

"Only vampires pass through these doors on a Saturday night." The woman's smile widened. "The Castle of Dark Dreams holds a Vampire Ball every Saturday night. Everyone does the basic black clothes and fake fangs thing. Oh, and I'm Liz. I've been staying here for a few weeks. Really neat place." Liz's expectant pause meant Kim would have to reciprocate with name and trivial info.

"Kim Vaughn, and I'm an architect." She got an adrenaline rush just saying that out loud. "The owner hired me to plan a few additions to the castle. So we'll probably run into each other again."

"I'll only be here for two more days, but I'll look for you." She slid her tongue across her lower lip. Liz sounded really eager, and her smile was really friendly, but Kim decided that something about Liz and Shadow Man was really creeping her out. Probably just a byproduct of the last few minutes' weirdness and her scared-rabbit syndrome.

Fo's paranoia must be catching. "Guess I'll go in and take a peek at the great hall." Kim reached for the door again.

"*Psst,* Kimmie."

Damn, Kim had forgotten she was still holding Fo.

"Uh, she's a demon."

Kim glared at Fo.

"I'm whispering. She can't hear me." Fo looked aggrieved that Kim didn't appreciate her attempt to be discreet.

Kim cast Liz a cautious glance. Yep, Liz had heard Fo. "It's just my cell phone. My brother did some creative programming. He has a warped sense of humor." She hoped her smile said amused embarrassment.

Kim never found out what Liz thought of her brother's warped sense of humor because at that moment the man stepped from the shadows.

Oh. My. God. Kim felt frozen in place, not able to close her mouth or blink as she got her first look at him. At the same moment, the emotions struck again with enough force to almost bring her to her knees.

"Umm, Kimmie? Did you hear me? I said she's a D-E-M-O—"

Kim flipped Fo shut and crammed her back into her pocket, all without taking her gaze from the man. She couldn't reason away what she'd just felt. Even as she stared at him, she could feel her ordinariness trickling away, and she hated him for that. *Because the emotions were coming from him.* She knew it, felt it on a primitive level.

He narrowed his gaze on her, *through* her, to the confused person inside. She tried to rub away a slight pressure between her eyes. Great. A sinus headache would complete the night.

"So your cell phone thinks Liz is a demon?" His voice was a husky murmur that would be right at home on a foggy London street at midnight, quietly menacing with a promise that danger could be deliciously tempting.

Kim forced herself to blink before her eyeballs dried out. "It thinks *everyone's* a demon." True. "My brother programmed it to accuse people of being demons as a joke." Not true.

"The laws of probability would suggest that it might be right sometimes." His soft laughter shivered along all of her nerve endings. "If demons existed."

He leaned closer to her, but she couldn't move, couldn't *breathe*. Thankfully, the scary emotions had disappeared. She didn't question why.

But holy cow, would you look at him. Six feet plus of broad-shouldered hard-muscled body. Fine, so she couldn't testify to any bare-body specifics because he was wearing a black tux and what looked like a black silk shirt. But only a hard-muscled body would do justice to that *face*.

Kim drew in a deep breath before she turned as purple as Fo's eyes. "Sure. *If* demons existed. They don't, so the message is a big ha-ha."

Right now demons weren't on her personal radar screen. Where did great looking cross the line into spectacular? This guy not only had leaped across the spectacular line but was closing in fast on unbelievable. *No one* looked this good. If he were a building, he'd be the Chrysler Building in New York City, one of her personal choices for most magnificent building in the world.

Liz moved up to put a proprietary hand on his arm. "We need to get going, Brynn."

The man, Brynn, deliberately glanced at his watch. "Not yet." He didn't look at Liz, and his words were shards of chipped ice. Didn't sound too lover-like to Kim. In fact, he moved away from Liz's grasp and closer to Kim.

While Brynn was eyeing the time, Kim was ogling him. Hey, scenery this good came along once in a millennium. She couldn't tell much about his hair other than it was at least shoulder-length, because he'd pulled it away from his face and secured it with a leather tie. In the uncertain mixture of light and shadow she wasn't sure about its color. Maybe rain-darkened blond.

He shifted his attention back to Kim. "You don't believe in demons, but let's say they existed, in theory of course. And just for the hell of it, let's say your cell phone could really identify them. Would your cell phone also be able to destroy them?"

There was a dark eagerness to his question that would've normally registered on her really weird scale, but she was still too wrapped up in the glory of his face.

"Yeah, I guess so." His *face*. If you just listed each feature—firm jaw, full lower lip, wide-spaced eyes—you might dismiss him as merely another example of yummy maleness in a world loaded with delish guys.

This man had all the intangibles, though. Every woman who ever looked at him would recognize his sensual, dangerous, and primal call. Kim didn't know many women who wouldn't answer. He was simply perfect. And since Kim never trusted perfect in an imperfect world, she was instantly suspicious.

Uh-huh. Time for a teeny tiny bit of self-honesty here. If Mr. Sinfully Sexy crooked his perfect finger, she'd probably leap on him, knock him down right here in front of the castle, rip his clothes from his body, and have her wicked way with him. Kim took a deep calming breath. Yeah, she'd still be suspicious, but who said she couldn't have a good time while she waited for him to do something dastardly, hmm?

"Come on, Brynn. I'm cold and it'll be time in," Liz leaned over to glance at his watch. "five minutes."

She sounded whiny, and the malicious enjoyment Kim got from the thought surprised her. And what exactly would happen in five minutes?

"You may as well go back inside, Liz, because I want to talk to Kim for a few minutes about her cell phone. In fact, I guess I've officially been with *Kim* for the last four minutes. So all bets are off. Enjoy the rest of your night." More shocking than Brynn's terse dismissal of Liz, was Liz's response.

"You'll pay for this next time." She didn't look perky anymore, just royally pissed off. "I'm starved." Liz speared him with her gaze, and Kim couldn't remember ever seeing such open sexual hunger on any woman's face. She cast Kim a speculative glance before turning and striding away from the castle, anger in every click of her heels.

Away from the castle? Didn't they have food inside? Maybe she didn't want food. Kim figured Liz had a pretty healthy appetite for Brynn's body. *Say something.* "Uh, this is probably none of my business, but I think I missed something."

He lifted his face to the light breeze that had suddenly kicked up and closed his eyes. "Liz and I play a game each night. She lost this time." He opened his eyes and then stepped closer.

For the first time she got a good look at his eyes in the full light . . . and forgot to breathe. The Big Bang theory became real for Kim in that moment, because looking into Brynn's eyes opened up a whole new personal universe for her.

She was surprised he couldn't hear the kaboom kaboom of her heartbeat. Kim controlled the need to flatten her hand over the organ in question so it wouldn't leap from her chest. Chasing your heart down the street would be so not cool.

There were a thousand stories in his eyes, and they were all sexual. Color? Old whiskey held up to candlelight so that the rich gold shone through—potent, ageless, and . . . Warm should be the next word on her list. It wasn't. Every emotion she'd felt just a few minutes ago shone in those eyes. Cold. So cold. She exhaled sharply and shivered.

Forcing her gaze away from those eyes, she tried to concentrate on what he was saying.

"You saved me from a night of mindless sex." He didn't smile when he said it.

Mindless sex? The men she'd known would salivate like Pavlov's pooch at the mention of mindless sex. She didn't understand him, and she certainly didn't understand his emotions that had sort of wandered off course and found her. "Gotcha. Well, I guess I'll take a peek into the great hall. Are you coming in, too?"

"No." His gaze drifted beyond her into the night. "I think I'll walk for a while. There's a certain pleasure in aloneness. Don't you feel it? The quiet. The *peace*." His voice was smoke, sex, and warm secret places.

She would've believed his voice if she hadn't looked into his eyes first. Warm wasn't part of his agenda. Kim finally managed to move. She stepped back. Standing too close to those waves of pheromones couldn't be good for her sensual well-being. "You're right. I wouldn't mind being alone more." She couldn't help it if she sounded a little wistful. She was supposed to keep Fo with her all the time, and the detector didn't have an off button. So essentially Kim was never alone.

She had a feeling that *his* "alone" meant something else. Could a man ever get too much female adoration? The thought was revolutionary. But Kim could almost imagine what would happen inside the castle if all the women knew he was outside by himself. There'd be a bloody catfight, dozens of women scratching and clawing at each other. The winner would eventually drag her battered body out here to claim her prize. Kim frowned. Something touched her that felt uncomfortably close to envy.

"Would you mind if I took a quick look at your cell

phone before you go inside?" He'd shifted closer again, invading her space, bringing with him the scent of wicked joys and dark fantasies.

"Oh, sure." She reached for her real cell phone in her other pocket and prayed he hadn't seen which pocket held Fo.

"I don't think so." He covered her hand with his larger one, and she swore she felt the heat from his touch all the way to her backbone. "I think *this* is your talkative little phone." He dipped his fingers into her other pocket and pulled out Fo.

Damn. Kim snatched Fo from his fingers, flipped the detector open so he could see, and hoped for a miracle. One in which the screen remained blank and Fo remained silent.

It wasn't her night for miracles. Fo's huge purple eyes blinked open, and she stared at Brynn. Only the slight widening of Fo's eyes gave warning, but Kim knew what was coming and was helpless to stop it. Now Kim knew how the Wicked Witch of the East had felt just before Dorothy's house flattened her.

"Woohoo! DemondemonDEMON!" Fo's small metal case pulsed with excitement. "Big beeeautiful DEMON. Can we keep him for a while before we destroy him? Huh, can we?"

Kim closed her eyes and wished for an out-of-body experience. Preferably one that would take her at least a mile from this man. "I'm already visualizing the duct tape over your mouth, Fo." Kim's hissed threat didn't seem to slow down Fo's happy vibrating.

All right, she'd have to open her eyes sometime. He'd either be surprised or amused. Those were the usual responses to one of Fo's outbursts. Except for the president's secret service. It took a lot to surprise or amuse them. Fo had barely escaped with her nano-parts intact.

Drawing in a deep breath of courage, Kim opened her eyes. Then blinked. He was fascinated. Really fascinated. He carefully removed Fo from her nerveless fingers.

"It's a joke. It's only a cell phone. My brother programmed her, umm, it, to say that. It didn't mean what it said. I mean, she's, uh, it's not real, so it didn't know . . ." *Shut up.* Kim closed her mouth and waited for his response to that bit of hysteria.

He narrowed his eyes as he studied Fo. Fo studied him right back. "What happens if I press this button?" He indicated the red destroy button.

"Not much. A little noise, a little light. Pretty harmless." Unless you're a demon. "The whole thing's a gag. I've been trying to tell you that."

She reached for Fo and then watched in horror as his finger hovered over the red button. The demon-destroying beam would get him right in the face. It wouldn't kill a human, but it would blind him for about a half hour. She didn't need to start her new job with him clutching his face and accusing her of trying to kill him.

Kim ripped Fo from his fingers. "It was great meeting you, but it's chilly standing out here." She clicked Fo shut and put the detector back into her pocket.

She refused to meet his gaze, but Kim sensed his amusement . . . and something more, something darker.

"When you're ready to go in, just press that button and someone will greet you." He pointed to a button beside the doors. "Welcome to the Castle of Dark Dreams, Kim." Then he turned and strode away.

Bemused, she watched him until he disappeared in the darkness, and then she reached for the doorbell.

"Would you like a brochure, dearie?" The voice behind her said old and wizened.

Kim gave a startled squeak and leaped away from the door. Okay, so with everything that had happened tonight she had a right to be jumpy. She turned to meet the sharp gaze of a walking stereotype.

The woman looked old. Very old. Her white hair was short with waves that marched across her head in perfect order. Small wire-framed glasses perched on the end of her nose. A round face, faded blue eyes, a small mouth, and many many wrinkles completed the picture of everybody's grandmother.

Trouble was, Kim's grandmother didn't look like this. Grandma was slim, trim, and stylish with great hair. She'd threatened to give all her money to cat charities unless her family promised to make sure when they laid her out that no gray roots showed and that she had fresh highlights. Grandma wasn't going to knock on the pearly gates looking like a night hag.

Kim glanced down at the brochure the woman held out to her. The grandma image continued. White cardigan, baggy flowered dress that showed the tops of knee-highs when the wind caught the edges of her skirt, and black chunky shoes.

Kim took the brochure because she didn't want to insult the woman. "Thanks."

The woman smiled at Kim. It was a prim smile. "I'm Miss Abby. Taught first grade for thirty-five years here in Galveston. Kids'll either kill you or make you stronger. I got stronger. When I retired, I started my own business. Ye Olde Victorian Wedding Chapel. I'll marry you in style."

What to say? "Umm, I don't think—"

"That's the trouble today, youngsters don't think. Keep the brochure. You never know when you might meet the perfect young man and want to hitch up with him in a hurry. In my day, young ladies didn't just up and marry someone fast unless they were in a family way. But times change." Her expression said not for the better.

Family way? Who said things like that nowadays? "I guarantee I won't be needing a wedding chapel." Not unless Mr. Ordinary popped out of the castle wall.

The woman waved at her. "Keep the brochure. Pass it on if you can't use it." She walked past Kim. "I have to leave a pile of them in the lobby. Get a lot of business from the castle."

Strange. Miss Abby's walk was a lot more chipper than the rest of her. But a faint squeaking distracted Kim from Miss Abby's walk. Birds? Not at night. "Do you hear a squeaking noise?"

Miss Abby glanced back at Kim. "That's my girdle,

dearie. Every lady should wear one." Her gaze said no girdle, no lady. She didn't give the button a second glance as she pulled the door open and disappeared inside.

Kim was on Miss Abby's slut list, but somehow she couldn't drum up the energy to care. She'd take a look at the great hall and then spend the rest of her night trying to reason away Brynn's very scary emotions that had scraped off on her.

Finally, she noticed the whispering coming from her pocket.

"She's a demon, Kimmie. I've been trying to tell you, but you weren't paying attention." Pregnant pause. "Some day a demon is going to get you, and you'll be dead, dead, dead. And I'll make sure they put 'I told you so. Love, Fo,' on your tombstone."

Kim sighed. "What a sweetheart." She pushed the button.